QUANTUM CANNIBALS

by

NATHAN ELBERG

Stories From The Milky Way, book 1

"Though people differ in color and creed, they all love, quarrel, protect their children, etc., exactly as we do. The message is clear: we should love them because they are like us. But that statement has its questioning brother: what if they aren't like us?"

Edmund Carpenter, <u>Oh, What a Blow that Phantom Gave me</u>.

PREFACE:

Although the peoples and cultures depicted in this novel are fictional, the cultural practices are real. They represent beliefs and behaviors from around the world, which have been shuffled and recombined. Even if a particular people seems familiar it should not be taken as representative. It should be especially noted that the fictional Tunniq of this novel are *not* the Inuit of the Canadian Arctic. They occupy the same type of geography, and as a consequence much of their food, clothes and dwellings are similar.

The bizarre naming practice is adapted from an article about the Asmat of New Guinea, published in American Anthropologist, v. 61 no. 6, 1959. The Asmat of today have given up headhunting, and are suffering greatly under Indonesian occupation. Muslim Indonesian immigrants have not been shy about forcibly displacing the now-Catholic natives. Harassment and extra-judicial killings by security forces are common. To learn more, visit www.freewestpapua.org.

The taming of a blizzard described in the novel has been adapted from the 1932 book *Intellectual Culture of the Copper Eskimo*, by Knud Rasmussen.

The Trail of Tears was an actual historical event, a part of the forcible removal of the Cherokee Indians from their lands in 1838.

The tower scene, as well as the flying snake are adapted from the Zohar, the Book of Splendor, attributed to the second century sage Simon bar Yochai. Its motifs are scattered through this novel.

The Bronze Age mantra of 'balanced opposition' is derived from Dr.
Philip Salzman's excellent account of tribal culture, *Culture and Conflict
in the Middle East*.

ACKNOWLEDGEMENTS:

I've discussed the novel's scientific material with and had it reviewed by a number of scientists, including Drs. Laura Segall, and Hoshea Allen. I am responsible for any scientific absurdities herein, not them.

It's easy to get lost among the mysteries of the Sefirot. Thanks to Dr. Ira Robinson explaining how to "...return to the place."

A special thank you goes out to Esti Mayer for allowing me to use her wonderful artwork on my website, and on the cover of the first edition. My father used Esti's mother's artwork as the cover for a book of his, so we are following family tradition.

Thank you to my editor, Peter Gelfan, of The Editorial Department, and to Jane Ryder of Ryder Author Resources (and President of the Quantum Cannibals Fan Club) for their encouragement and assistance.

Thank you to my children and friends who read the manuscript, providing suggestions and encouragement. My wife said I should write a book, and I always do what she tells me, sometimes. Thanks, Sandra.

Nathan Elberg, Montreal, Canada
December 2017, July 2020

TABLE OF CONTENTS

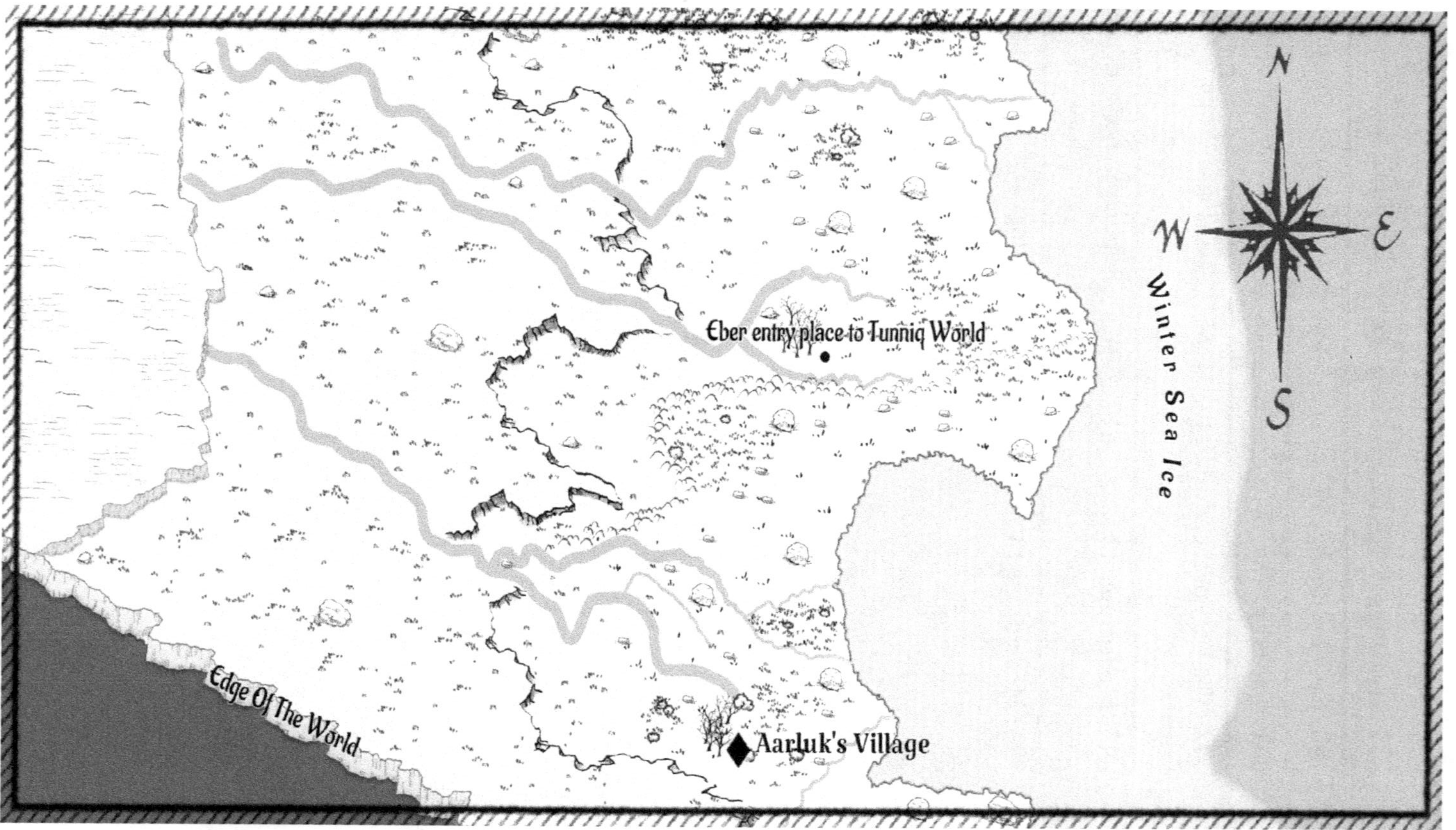

Eber entry place to Tunniq World
Winter Sea Ice
Edge Of The World
Aarluk's Village
Home of the Tunniq

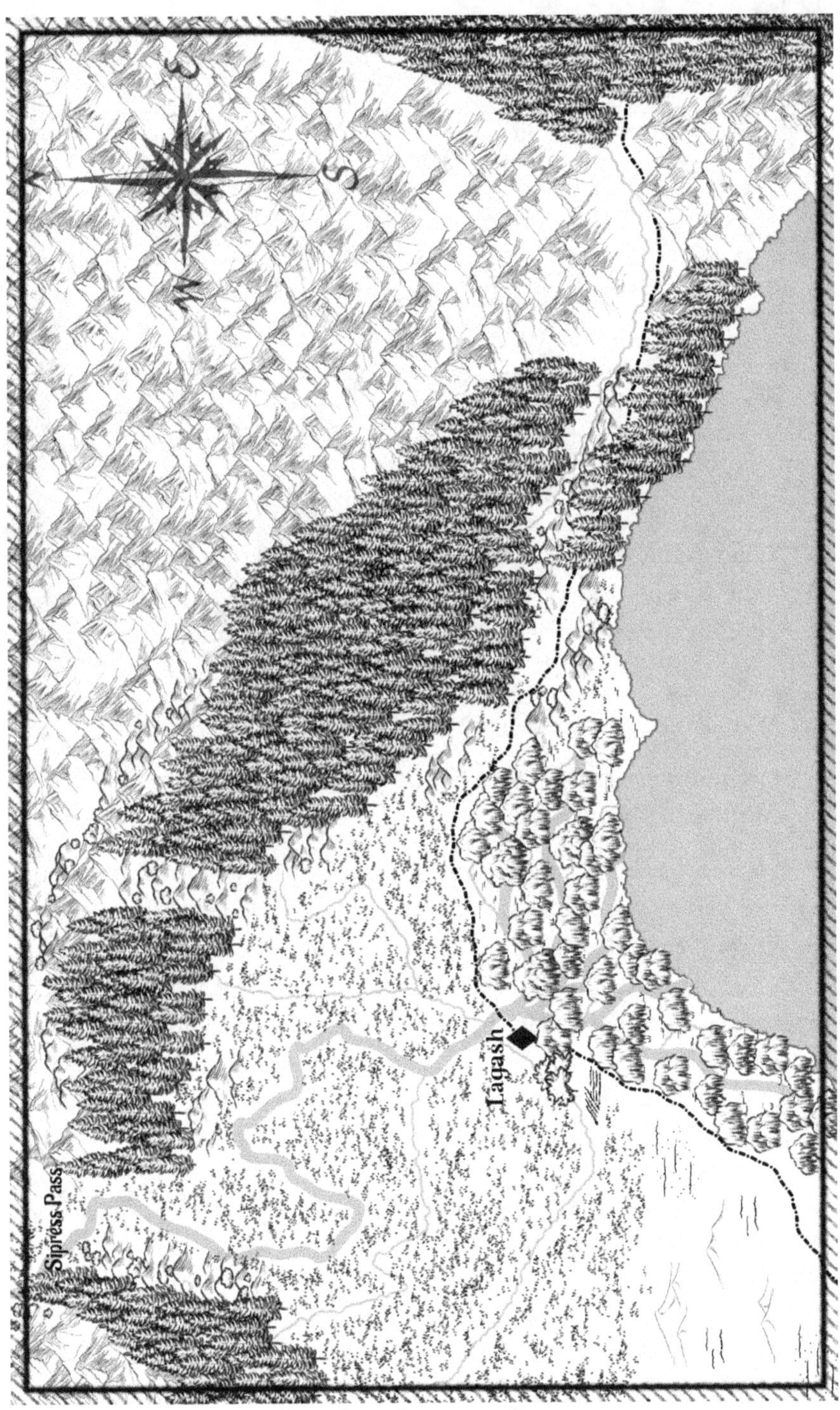

Lagash and surroundings

THE EDGE OF THE WORLD 1

Falun didn't want his wife to kill him; it would be too embarrassing. She was beyond furious, which by itself wasn't unusual. "If you don't get a name for our son," Puah said, "I'll call him Falun, and he'll get the life that has that name now."

"You don't scare me, you miserable woman."

Her sons from her previous husband were strong enough to back up her threat. Falun was terrified.

He had figured her anger would eventually pass, and then they would get back to their normal lives. But while the moon waxed and waned, and the snow covering the bleak tundra turned to mush, Puah's ire and Falun's terror continued to grow. He had hoped that her voice would eventually wear out from all her screaming, or that one of the neighbors would kill her to quiet her down. But she drank enough walrus fat to keep her throat working, and the neighbors were intimidated by her threats, even though they were aimed at her husband.

The worst of it was that she was right. Two sons were already dead, and that was too many. He had to find a life; he had to find a name for their youngest.

He had tried. He had organized raiding parties, traveled to the closest villages, but everybody there was kin. You couldn't take the name of someone who had taken a name from your brother. Falun's alternative to being killed was simple: he had to travel far, and attack someone who wasn't related. The small clusters of cramped animal-hide and snow houses that made up encampments were widely scattered, some being several days' travel by dog sled from their closest neighbors. Some were a lot further than that. But everyone knew what made a good place to live, so travelers and raiders knew where to find each other.

To journey to an encampment far enough that most of the people wouldn't be family meant getting a lot of supplies for the trip. It meant lavish gifts for the hunters traveling with him. Falun had spent weeks in preparation.

Better that then face Puah and her sons. One of them, Miriaq, was going along on the raiding party, which meant that Falun couldn't abandon his quest and quietly live somewhere else. Falun's younger brother was also going, as well as Aarluk, a huge woman. Aarluk was distantly related, having the same curly brown hair and blue eyes as Falun. Her parents had originally thought she was male and named her accordingly, but when she became a shaman and Traveled between Spheres, she changed into a woman. It was a sign of fearsome power. Ijiq, Aarluk's husband, spent a lot of time at other encampments, probably because his wife was too ugly, and he wanted better-looking women. Now he would be able to enjoy himself for a while at home.

The late summer days were unusually warm. The sky never darkened, and in many places the snow cover had melted completely. They were traveling overland across the rocky scree, the barren plains dotted with occasional outcrops of moss and lichen. Here and there small fields of grasses flourished, punctuated by dwarf shrubs. Rivulets meandered across the landscape, few deep enough to reach your knees if you stepped in them. The salmon ran in schools of ten to twenty, and if your timing was right, you just had to reach into the icy water to pull out food for a week.

The caribou didn't run in herds in these parts; the vegetation wasn't thick enough to support them. Occasional elk could be spotted, but it took a fast runner and strong arm to spear any of them. At least here below the escarpment, the land was flat enough that any marauding bears could be spotted from afar.

They traveled northeast, perpendicular to the Edge of the World, past which there was no existence. Falun had once dared his sister to stick her arm through the green mist of the Edge. When she pulled it back with a scream, the skin had been burned right off, as if she had held it over a fire pit. Within a day her flesh had rotted and fallen off, and by the following day she was dead. Falun had a good laugh at her foolishness.

It was after the first sleep, when they were eating some salmon they had just caught, that the dogs became nervous. The raiders all went for their weapons.

Miriaq spoke first. "It's not a bear."

Falun glanced at the flat horizon and grinned. "Success already! Hide!"

"We've been spotted."

Strangely, whoever it was in the distance was running directly towards the raiding party, arms waving.

The raiders saw that there were two of them approaching, a man and a woman wearing strange garments. They looked thin and emaciated, which would make them less useful. Still, the man would get Puah off his back and provide a name for his child. The woman... The raiders grinned at one another.

The two strangers were also smiling, despite their apparent hunger, despite the hunting party they were coming right at.

The man stuck out his hand. His yellow hair suited his pale skin. He was tall, thin, and weak looking. "We are so grateful to see you. We haven't eaten in days. You must help—"

Falun swiftly swung the butt of his spear and brought it across the man's face. Blood started pouring from his nose and mouth. The girl screamed. Another swing of the spear went across the man's knees, and as he buckled Falun struck him hard on the back, dropping him to the ground.

Aarluk grabbed the girl and ripped off her clothes, sticking some in her mouth as she dragged her off to the side. The rest of the raiders averted their eyes, disgusted by the idea of a woman being with a woman. They set into the thin man lying at their feet, kicking him in the head, in the gut, between the legs. Miriaq grabbed his arm and twisted till the bone popped loose from the shoulder. The man's eyes were still open, but he was too shocked, and had no strength to scream. Falun bent down, and grabbing his hair, lifted the man's face towards his.

"What's your name?"

The man tried to speak but was having a hard time getting words to his lips. Falun punched his broken nose. "What's your name?"

"Simon," came the whispered answer.

Falun kicked Simon's forehead, as the raiders broke out in wide grins, slapping him on the back, congratulating him.

"That was too easy. My wife will be disappointed to hear that I had such a simple time of it. But at least people will stop complaining about all the noise she makes yelling at me."

Everyone laughed.

Aarluk walked over and eyed Simon, passed out on the ground. "Stop giggling like little girls. There's a naked woman waiting, while you make stupid jokes. I'm going to Travel between Spheres to give Simon strength. We can't have him die on his own after all our effort."

Aarluk pulled a small drum and some powdered lichen from her pack. She mixed a few small rocks with the powder, and threw it all at Simon's motionless body. Sitting on the ground, she drummed a simple beat while the others busied themselves with the woman.

Falun finally interrupted Aarluk's trance. "He's still sleeping. Did you do all your Traveling in the girl, so that now you have no strength left to give him?"

Aarluk ignored the insult. "I can't get him to enter the pathways between Spheres."

"Maybe you should try it the way you and your husband enter each other."

Aarluk laughed. "We're going to have to carry him. Can the girl still walk?"

"If we beat her enough, I'm sure she'll find the strength."

Haran, Falun's brother, approached: "Simon said they haven't eaten in days. Let's feed them before we start back."

Falun picked up the fish he had been eating when the dogs first alerted them. He took a mouthful, chewed it carefully, and then leaning over Simon, spat into his mouth. Haran poured in a few drops of water. Aarluk put some fish on her finger and held it over the girl's mouth, forcing her to put her lips around the finger to get food. Simon coughed, choking briefly on the mush in his mouth, and then lapsed back to silence as he swallowed it.

They repeated the procedure over and over, until both of the strangers had consumed enough to give them some strength without tying their empty stomachs in knots.

Haran lightly brushed his fingers over the girl's cheek. "What are you going to do with her, Falun? I don't think Puah wants a daughter."

"Maybe we can bring her to Tuli. He's got a son who's almost ready to get a name."

"What are you talking about? She's a girl! Couldn't you tell?" Haran snickered.

"I know, I know." Falun ran his fingers along her exposed, trembling thigh. "But it's getting harder and harder to find a name for a son. Maybe this girl can be a man."

"Why are you insulting me?" Aarluk hissed. He stood swiftly and grabbed Falun by the front of his parka. "Only the strongest Sphere-Travelers are able to change from man to woman, or woman to man. Are you saying she's as strong as me?" Aarluk swept her arm over the shivering body. "Do you think she's so powerful?"

Aarluk let go of Falun and bent over the girl. "Can we take your name?"

She didn't respond.

Aarluk grabbed her face. "Answer me: where's your strength? Are you a Sphere Traveler?"

A groan came from her throat.

Aarluk released her and glared at Falun.

He lowered his gaze. "You're right, Aarluk. She's not very strong." Falun used his boot to turn her over, and grinned. "If we can't use her name, we'll use her other parts. I'll keep—"

"No. I claim her." Aarluk placed his boot on the girl's back. "I have no children. It's easy to name a daughter, if she doesn't already have one."

Falun opened his mouth to speak, looked at Aarluk, and then stopped.

The big Sphere Traveler bent over the trembling, terrified girl. "What's your name?" she asked.

The girl just whimpered.

"I'll name her when we get home if she's forgotten who she is."

Falun pulled out a horn trumpet, and triumphantly blew nine staccato notes. The shrill noise was the sound of life weeping.

2 THE EDGE OF THE WORLD 2

A table. Osnat recognized the object. It was a table, with a white tablecloth. Delicately carved ebony-wood dishes, silver utensils, burgundy cloth napkins were arranged neatly in front of two high-backed white leather chairs. They faced slightly towards each other, and the front of the inside armrests were tied together with a white leather lace, topped with an ornate bow.

There were sounds. Singing, cries of joy, merriment. Laughter.

A whisper: "Osnat."

She could barely hear it above the sounds of music and dancing.

"Osnat, my darling."

"Simon?" She looked up at his soft smile, at the tracks of tears on his cheeks.

"You're alive. I thought they were going to kill us both when we first came upon them."

The table, the dishes, the music of her dream faded. The happiness of her wedding was replaced by the joy of her husband being alive and near her. The pain of her husband's injuries battled for attention with her joy.

"I'm all right, Simon."

"What have they done to you, Osnat?" he whispered, his battered lips barely moving.

"Aarluk took me into her home. When a man propositioned me, she punched him in the face. She's fed and clothed me, hovering like an eagle over her nest. She's very protective. She brought me here, saying I had to watch you."

"I don't know if they realize you're my wife, Osnat. They may think you're my daughter. Maybe that's why that ugly whale is looking after you. The less they know, the better."

"Simon, what about you?" She lifted the animal hide covering him, revealing the bruises and welts covering his body, the waste he was forced to lie in. His dislocated arm was free, but his other limbs were strapped to the ground.

"They want me alive for now. They spit chewed food into my mouth from time to time."

"That's disgusting."

"It hurts too much for me to chew. I'm part of some bizarre ritual, Osnat, and I'm afraid to imagine what it is. You have to escape before they brutalize you. Better to die running than be part of whatever this is. Promise me you'll get away."

"I can't leave you. Don't you remember what we said to each other, our wedding vows? 'I have bound myself to you forever; I have bound myself to you with righteousness and mercy, I have bound myself to you with faithfulness...' Simon, my chair is always tied to yours."

"There is no righteousness in this place; no mercy. Osnat, you must live. I won't. My jaw, my ribs are broken; I can't eat on my own. You bound yourself to me with faithfulness. You told me you think you're pregnant. Your faithfulness should be to our child." Simon touched her hand. "You're stronger than these savages. Use your strength. Our baby must live."

"In a world like this?"

"You will teach him righteousness, mercy, and faithfulness. One day our family will return to a human world. These creatures may look like us, but they're animals."

Looking around, Osnat found some scraps of hide. "I'll clean you up a bit. Tell me if I'm hurting you."

Simon nodded and closed his eyes. His faraway look changed to a grimace as she worked; he tried to hide how her act of affection was hurting him.

The tears Simon refused to let out poured from Osnat's eyes instead. She couldn't protect his life or heal his wounds; at least she could give him back some of his dignity. He was so battered, it was impossible to touch him without causing him anguish.

Simon lay on his back, eyes loosely closed, light breath coming from his lips. She watched him sleep, hoping his dreams were more pleasant than the nightmare of life. They had gone searching for food, for life. Thousands of people, everyone from their community was waiting for their return, to say that there was some way of survival here. Simon and Osnat had been elated when they saw the distant people, thinking that they found help, found humanity in this barren place. They had run to them, waving their arms to make sure the others didn't turn away.

Better the thousands should starve than meet this fate. Maybe the other scouts would find something.

Falun and Aarluk pulled aside the tent flap and entered.

Sniffing, Falun said "Ah, you've cleaned him up. Now we don't have to."

Osnat felt a flash of hope. If they had intended to clean him up themselves, maybe their behavior would change. Maybe they'd act like people instead of predatory animals.

"Bind her," Aarluk directed, pointing at Osnat. "She may try to protect her father."

The flash of hope turned to darkness.

"What are you going to do to him?" Osnat asked.

Falun unceremoniously picked up one of the scraps of hide Osnat had used to clean her husband, shoved it in her mouth, and tied it in place. He lashed her hands together behind her back and forced her onto her side, facing the tent wall. He bent her legs behind her, and bound them with the cord holding her wrists.

"No, she should see, so she'll be able to recognize Simon." Aarluk turned to Osnat with a smile. "Don't worry; I've done this many times."

Falun repositioned her, and shoved her face to the side, so she was looking directly at Simon. He stretched her arms painfully backwards.

"Gently," Aarluk said. "If you hurt her, I'll make you suffer."

Osnat could see the slightest trace of a smile on her husband's face as he looked towards her. They had hauled him upright, his back leaning on a tent post. She had never felt so terrified, even when Aarluk and the others were having their way with her.

Falun also smiled. He picked up a spear and held the stone tip against the base of Simon's throat. Osnat could see it pressing harder and harder. She tried to scream, but couldn't, with the feces-covered gag in her mouth. Simon's eyes grew wide, as death pushed into his neck.

The ragged point slipped through the skin with barely a sound. Falun left the spear in place as blood pulsed into a bowl he held in one hand; with the other hand he picked up a stone knife. He cut into the throat and around the neck, then removed the head from the body, putting it into a skin sack.

Aarluk nodded in approval. She handed Falun a heavier, saw-tooth stone knife. "Cut through the sides of the trunk from the anus to the armpit, and from there by the collar bone to the throat."

Osnat tried to will herself to pass out. The sound of the stone sawing through Simon was beyond revolting. She turned her head away as best she could.

"Now chop through the ribs."

Osnat turned back. She was on fire now. She wanted to see everything they did to her husband. She wanted to fuel her rage, to inflame her lust for vengeance. She vowed death to these sub-human creatures, or to die trying. She would turn her heart to ice until then.

Falun put his hands under the sides of Simon's chest, pulled it off, and carefully placed it to the side, bones down like a bowl.

"Now the limbs."

Falun inserted his knife into the sockets, prying the joints loose, and then cut through the flesh. The arms and legs were stacked neatly together. Aarluk reached into Simon's chest cavity and pulled out the heart. She grabbed the entrails in a bundle, and yanked them from the backbone with a vigorous jerk. She deposited these in the upturned chest cavity. Osnat felt her world going dark, with a feeling of relief that she'd soon join her husband on his journey.

***

Osnat carefully squinted open her eyes. The smell of blood, of death, seemed to have dissipated. She was facing upwards and was no longer bound. Breathing deeply, she pondered the nightmare. Every recent turn that life had taken descended further into disaster, each situation desperately worse than the previous. Each time there was a breath of hope, it was followed by being thrown deeper into another abyss. Slowly, hoping she was waking from a terrifying dream, she turned her head towards the sound of rapid breathing coming from the side.

The face was that of a boy, the start of whiskers on his chin. He was grinning, looking at her. She turned further. His chest was bare. No, not just his chest, he was naked. Aroused. A wave of revulsion swept through her.

She squinted, and saw that his hands were tied behind his back, sitting upright against the tent post that her husband had been butchered on. She was safe from him for now.

She squinted at the round thing in his lap. It was hard to see in the poor light, with her hair hanging over her eyes. And something in her mind definitely wanted to keep her from seeing.

Aarluk bundled into the tent, her eyes sweeping everything. The floor was bare, except for Osnat and the boy. Aarluk caught sight of the boy's excited state, lifted the round object off his lap, and kicked him hard in the groin. He would have collapsed if not for being tied to the post. She put Simon's head back on the boy's thighs and started screaming at him.

"What kind of pervert are you? She's going to be your daughter! You don't want to have sex with your daughter!" Aarluk gave him another kick, this time in the ribs, and the boy moaned in pain.

"You're just becoming a man, just getting a name, and you show that you don't deserve it. Maybe you should get what your father's other offspring got. I'll tell Falun to stop the feast. How do you think she'll feel about her father being wasted?" Aarluk asked, pointing at Osnat.

Osnat stared at Simon's head resting on the boy's naked legs. He was groaning and sweating now, having lost his excitement. *Feed your fire*, she told herself.

Aarluk turned a motherly smile to Osnat. "He's not your father till after the feast is complete and everything eaten. Are you hungry?" Aarluk winked at her.

She was more miserable, more repulsed, than hungry. She shook her head. Like a grenade exploding in her heart she realized what the feast was, and fainted again.

3 THE EDGE OF THE WORLD 3

"Not like that, you fool!" Aarluk pointed at her daughter's arm. "You want to temper the bone, not turn it to ashes."

Osnat lifted the bone spear a little higher over the flame. The fire wasn't large, little more than two pieces of driftwood, glowing red. Too hot, and the ice would melt around the smoke holes, eventually collapsing the cramped hut made of layers of snow, ice and skins. It had taken Osnat a long time to get used to the smoky air in the shelter. Her eyes had teared continuously, and she would cough until the fire went out.

The hut was barely tall enough to stand in at the center. The walls sloped roughly down to the ground, which in turn was covered with thick piles of sleeping hides. In the far end were the remains of some dead animal, probably seal. Tunniq meals often consisted of chips of raw meat hacked with a stone axe off a frozen carcass. A stone pot lay next to it. A few small lamps burned animal fat, providing meager, yet sufficient light.

"That's better. Keep turning it, so no part gets hotter than the rest. It's not that hard to make a proper weapon."

"I'm trying, but my arm is getting tired." Osnat was more accustomed to holding test tubes, rather than weapons over a flame. The bones she usually handled were for soup.

"If a bear ambushes you in a tent, would you rather have a well-rested arm or a good spear? If a man wants to stick something between your thighs would you rather let him do it, or have something to stick into his heart?"

Her "mother" was counseling her on killing people? "What would happen if I put a spear into the heart of someone trying to rape me?"

Aarluk laughed. "You would have to gather the blood from the wound and prepare the meat for the feast. You would have a full belly, and gain people's respect. Men would fight to be your husband, and I would be complimented for teaching you well."

Osnat nodded silently. It was four months since she had been captured, and her husband dismembered. Three months since she ran out of tears. The sun had stopped showing itself since the last new moon, the passing of the days now marked only by a periodic glow on the distant horizon, not discernible through the ice window of her home. The aurora spread itself across the sky on some evenings, a beautiful, dancing curtain of light. Osnat was mesmerized the first time she saw it, trying to read messages in the shifting patterns. It was the same joyous anticipation she had felt when she and Simon spotted the people in the distance on that horrible day. By the fourth or fifth time the aurora appeared, she considered it like an advertising poster on the side of the road: pleasing to the senses, but meaningless. At least the Northern Lights didn't lead her into another abyss of greater horrors. Aarluk explained that the dancing curtain was made up of the dead who couldn't accept their passing, trying to escape back into this world.

The stars and moonlight were the main illumination in the sky now. Yet the Tunniq traveled, hunted, built homes, laughed, fought and lived as if the days were bright. Aarluk explained that it would be one more cycle of the moon before the sun touched the sky again.

Osnat pondered the thousands of people that she had left behind. They must all be dead now; frozen, if they hadn't first starved, eaten if they'd run into the likes of the people she was with. Even if any were alive, it was unlikely that they could rescue her.

From what? Aarluk provided her with food, shelter, and warmth; bearskin clothes and sealskin boots. She taught her to rub fish oil on her exposed skin to protect it from the wind. Before the sun had disappeared, she had painted soot around Osnat's eyes, to cut the glare from the endless fields of snow. Now she was teaching Osnat to hunt, fish, make weapons and other implements.

Osnat was alive because she had been captured by cannibals. The irony would have brought a smile to her face, but she thought of all the other dead, waiting in vain for Simon's and her help. Perhaps some of the other scouting parties had been more successful and encountered a less brutal way to remain alive. What had happened to her brother, her cousins, her world? She had to find out. She had to fulfill her promise to Simon; she had to fulfill her oath to herself.

Osnat backed away from the flame, extending her arm further to keep the bone weapon in position. "Where does all this firewood come from? I haven't seen any trees here."

"Trees?"

"Wood comes from trees. They start out as tender saplings, soft as lichen. As they grow trees become hard and thick. Men cut the trees down and use them for fire, for furniture, for houses. We just have to make sure that we don't cut down more than are growing."

"You let these trees grow, and then kill them when you need them?" Aarluk was intrigued.

"They're plants, like shrubs or grass. If they don't grow here, then I don't understand how you have wood."

"This land is not a place of growth. It's a place of death. Nothing grows here."

"Children grow."

"When you come into this world, you're pulled in by your fingernails. If the one who bore you is skilled, you may live to be old enough to have children of your own. If you were born with the parts of a man and the one who sired you finds you a name, you may live long enough to take a wife."

"What if your father doesn't find you a name?"

"All the dead help keep the living alive: the dead trees, the dead people..."

"In my home, eating people is the most horrible thing you can do."

"This place is your home," Aarluk snapped. "I'm your mother, even though you didn't come out from between my thighs. You were dead without me."

"In my former home—" Osnat said contritely.

"Your former home is beyond the Edge of the World. Nothing exists on the other side."

Osnat sighed. "Does getting a name always mean killing someone?"

Aarluk grinned. "I haven't heard of someone having his head lifted from his neck and continuing to live. Maybe one day it will happen. There used to be more people to take names from. While everybody tries to avoid a raiding party, once the child takes a name, he takes on the family the name came from. They visit each other; exchange gifts, and act with proper respect. But as the number of people grows less, as villages disappear, we take names from people who are closer and closer. Soon there will be no one left to raid.

"Without a name, a person does not exist. Falun lost two children because he couldn't get them one. Puah would have given Falun's name to Simon if he hadn't found you and your father. Falun's your grandfather, and it would be nice if you occasionally gave him a smile."

Osnat let out a long breath. She had gotten used to Aarluk's presence, being with her most of the day and night. But every time Falun's name was brought up, every time she saw his face, she saw him cutting into her husband's flesh, heard the saw cutting through bones, and smelled Simon's blood pouring from him.

"I don't think so, Aarluk."

"And you could call me 'mother.' We won't talk about it further, but live; live right, and you'll have your vengeance."

"What do you mean?"

"We won't talk about it further, daughter."

Osnat silently pondered the mathematics of Tunniq names. The number of boys who could become old enough to have children was restricted by the number of men close enough to kill for their names. This meant the population couldn't grow. And the fact that they were having trouble finding victims for their headhunting meant that their population was shrinking. What did that imply for Osnat, and the people she left behind? These people had homes, were warm, and well fed. Would they be well fed if they didn't feed on each other? Could her people survive in this land without becoming like the Tunniq? Could she?

What did Aarluk mean by "vengeance" on Falun? The only proper way to avenge her husband would be to do to Falun what Falun had done to him. And to kill everyone else in the raiding party, as well as the gloating brat now called "Simon."

What if her baby has the parts of a man? Would Osnat want to get him a name in the usual way? She put that thought aside. She would not stay with these creatures long enough for her son to need to acquire a name from someone else. When it was time, Osnat would choose one. Simon, no doubt, if a boy. If any of her people would still be alive, she'd find them. If not, she and her child would live on their own. Die on their own, no doubt.

That wouldn't be fulfilling her promises.

Before avenging the death of her spouse, before leaving this village of cannibals, Osnat had to learn how to survive in this terrible land. How to find food and water, make clothes and build shelter. How to butcher animals, prepare their hides, make weapons from their bones. She understood how much she needed Aarluk. And Aarluk seemed to understand how much Osnat needed retribution.

"Can we talk about the wood? Where does it come from?"

"We find fields of wood where a stream emerges from a valley. Maybe they were once the trees you describe. I'll show you a field next time I take you hunting."

"Is there enough wood?"

"We're more concerned about keeping a piece of charcoal alive to light the next fire than we are about finding wood."

The fusion lighter hidden in her pack could be very useful if it still worked. It had taken a lot of persuasion, a lot of yelling to be allowed to take it with her, but it was worth it. And after her, the police allowed anyone who wanted to bring their lighter.

When Osnat had first been brought to the encampment where she now lived, the massive, ancient stone cliffs behind it looked like the walls of doom. The craggy escarpment stretching into the distance was probably what made life in this land possible. It provided shelter from the wind; its erosion created river valleys once garbed with wood. In some places, the rocks were yellow or blue, glowing eerily in the darkness. Osnat assumed it was a radioactive ore. Someday, she didn't know how, she might use her lighter on them. It was a comforting thought.

***

Osnat stood poised over the seal's breathing hole. The wind was raging, her back and her arms were groaning from immobility. But she refused to move. She sensed time passing by the shifting faint echo of sunlight at the edge of the distant horizon, and estimated that she had been standing here, spear in her hand, for about half a day. Aarluk was sitting far off to the side, chewing on fish. She had told Osnat not to waste her time hunting seals when food was plentiful and her belly was growing, but Osnat insisted on learning the skill. As a devoted mother, Aarluk couldn't refuse her.

Osnat's feet were warm in the caribou skin sack she used to keep any noise from getting through the ice and warning her prey. The little down-and-sinew indicator she had threaded into the breathing hole looked frozen in place, but Osnat couldn't move or ask Aarluk to check it, without scaring off any seals that might be approaching. The wind was picking up from the east. The sounds and the damp smell in the air indicated a storm coming; soon Aarluk would come over and haul her back to the camp. Osnat heard a faint sound, like a child splashing in the bath; the little feather indicator moved ever so slightly to the side. She slashed furiously down with the harpoon, aiming for the fat animal swimming just below the breathing hole.

Unfortunately, an arm on a pregnant body standing rigid for so long cannot suddenly spring into action and function as hoped. Osnat's harpoon crashed into the ice about a hands-breadth from the breathing hole, its point and barb splintering. She jabbed again for the hole with the remnants of the harpoon head, but by now the seal was long gone. Osnat's knees fell to the ice. She shut her eyes tightly, trying unsuccessfully to keep the tears back. She looked over at Aarluk. Her eyes were wet too, but from laughter. Osnat's missing the breathing hole after all that time waiting was the funniest thing to Aarluk. Osnat stayed on her knees, watching her approach. Aarluk put a comforting arm around her.

"You're going to be a great hunter, my daughter."

"I'm sure I'll kill a lot of ice if I continue like this."

"That's why we call it ice hunting." Aarluk cracked up again. "Come on; let's go. The storm is hitting."

They started back towards the camp, their sides to the wind and snow. It seemed to Osnat that they were in the middle of a cloud; it was hard to see anything more than an arm's length away. Although there was no sun, the sky had dissolved into a pounding whiteness. Aarluk plodded on and Osnat followed, wishing she had pushed harder to bring the dogs. Aarluk had insisted that they were going seal hunting for the sake of Osnat's training, and depending on dogs would only hamper that.

"Where are you taking us?" Aarluk suddenly asked.

"I'm following you." Aarluk knew Osnat had no idea where they were. Why did she have to mock Osnat's lack of a sense of direction in this miserable place?

Aarluk angrily grabbed her cheeks in a powerful hand. "Why should I allow you to follow me? I sat outside in a brewing blizzard, watching you try to catch a seal. I didn't want to, but you insisted. I accommodate you. I answer your questions, I teach you how to live, I give you food, shelter and clothing, and yet your eyes are filled with hatred for me. Why should I take care of you? So that one day you'll know enough to kill me? I don't understand you, daughter, but I do know one thing: you're dangerous. I'm leaving. Find your own way back to the camp. If you don't, all the better for me."

Aarluk shoved Osnat to the ground and stalked off. She didn't take two steps before vanishing into the whiteness.

Horror was the first thing that flew into Osnat's head. She stared wildly at the direction Aarluk disappeared into, her feet frozen as if stuck in blocks of ice.

Don't panic, she told herself. *You've been in worse situations before... No, that's a lie.* But panicking would not keep her alive, and Osnat had made some vows to her dead husband, to her not-yet born child. She wasn't ready to abandon them yet. She had two alternatives. Firstly, she could go looking for the camp in this storm. She was sure to get lost and die. Secondly, she could stay put, be buried under the snow, freeze and die.

Neither course of action was very promising. She stared into the wind, the snow driving into her skin, despair driving into her heart.

What if she had a nice cozy shelter, where she could turn on the heat and have a satisfying meal? She had a snow knife with her, a small sac of oil for protecting her skin, and she had been lugging the pack with Aarluk's fish. Osnat tested the snow, probing, feeling. It wasn't the best for building, but it would have to do. She dug down, carving out blocks. She started building up a wall, a row at a time, parallel to the wind. She made a narrow hollow, long and high enough for her to put the pack down, and for her to sit. She began another wall of snow blocks on her other side. The pieces weren't well shaped, they didn't fit together properly, but she shaved them with the snow knife, and blowing snow soon filled in the gaps. She angled the blocks so that the walls leaned together, coming to a ridge along the center.

Osnat was starting to feel good about her ability to survive when half the ridge collapsed. Now she had to dig deeper into harder snow, which broke apart more easily as she tried to carve it. The storm was blowing into her shelter. Her eyes were stinging, her heart was pounding, and her spirit breaking. She sat down, closed her eyes, and wondered if the only way out of this place was to leave this world. She had heard that the last stage of freezing to death was actually a warm and pleasant sensation. Maybe it was time to try. She opened her eyes and looked around at her gravesite.

Osnat had won awards and a large salary for her creative research. She had been considered one of the top scientists in her field before she was denounced and sent on the Trail of Tears. Would she die now, helpless, abandoned even by cannibals in this horrible wasteland? Or could she use her creative skills here to keep herself alive?

She set back to work on her shelter, using the broken harpoon and the snow knife to keep the ridge from falling. Instead of building a roof coming to a point, she eventually succeeded in making a dome. Snow pounded on the sides and drifted in through the edges. She took out her flask of fish oil, and poured some into the little cup she had with her. She pulled a few hairs off her fur parka, twisting them together into a little rope, which she set in the cup as a wick. She dug out her lighter and stared at it. After a few moments, when the wick had a chance to absorb the oil, she flicked the lighter and touched the small flame to it. She held her improvised lamp up near the top, careful not to let it get wet or blown out.

Its warmth soon put a sheen on the inside of the snow, and the cracks filled up, the roof hardened.

Too afraid to congratulate herself yet, she gingerly put the lamp down, pulled off her mitts, and dug a fish out of the pack. Not long ago, she would have grilled something like this, using delicate herbs and spices. Now she was happy to eat it raw and frozen, carefully avoiding the bones. Hunger was indeed the best seasoning.

Storms like this could last for days. Then again, with the winter darkness unbroken, with the pounding whiteness she could only measure the passing of time by her hunger. The lighter had been the only technological implement anyone had been allowed to bring. She looked at her wrist, where her watch used to be. If she didn't get too cold, she could probably outlast the storm in this little hut, but then what? Contemplating the question made her want to walk out into the storm, into oblivion. Was there something useful she could do to distract herself?

Osnat's lab had been the first to commercialize quantum biology. With photosynthesis as the basis, they had developed applications that had revolutionized the treatment of severe trauma victims. Not, she considered, revolutionary enough to help people whose heads had been removed with stone knives. Her last project, interrupted in mid-stream, was the development of a wheat plant that continuously produced new grains without the need for growing a stalk from seed. If that had been achieved, Osnat's royalty income would have been sufficient that she'd have been able to devote the rest of her working life to the biology, taxonomy and habitat of the human spirit, an arcane subject that was her secret interest.

Some said that the spirit was separate from the body and was all that mattered. That bothered Osnat. If a person was divisible, then maybe they would be willing to sacrifice their body for the sake of their spirit. Or sacrifice other people's bodies: kill for the sake of spiritual elevation. Like the need for spiritual harmony that was used to justify the Trail of Tears.

Osnat turned her mind to her work before her apprenticeship as a hunter. She liked to write her formulas down when working, as they became exceedingly complex at times. The snow walls of her shelter were not a good surface for her calculations, especially with the sheen from the lamp. Could her habit of long complex formulas be broken? Could they be put into simpler equations, which logically followed each other? She'd eventually find something, maybe some animal skins to write them on.

She had enough fish left to get a good start on the task. She remembered most of the core elements of her research. Leaning her back on a block of snow, fish skin and bones at her feet, the wind screaming over her shelter, her fish oil and fur lamp the only light, Osnat put her thoughts to the Uncertainty Principle, Entanglement, and the other spooky features of quantum science. Now her fate was uncertain, her life entangled with savages whose decisions meant life, death or worse for her. It was as if she had fallen victim to a cosmic trickster, a quantum demon who had taken everything meaningful to her, turned it inside out, and beat her savagely with it.

Self-pity, although reasonable, was not what she wanted to dwell on until the storm would blow itself out. Her equations, her formulae, her experiments drew her back to another world, one that Aarluk had described as "non-existence." She could comfort herself that yes, it existed in her mind, but what did that mean? And the events that brought her here from that world proved that indeed it was an illusion, it never did exist; at least not in the form she thought it had.

It was hard to reach any breakthroughs in a snow hut in the middle of nowhere, in the heart of a blizzard. Still, Osnat was able to review the essential principles of quantum biology, and simplify a few elements of the electron transport chain. The tiny flicker of her oil lamp kept her eyes open, and helped her concentrate on her work. The roar of the wind, the constant patter of snow driven against her hut kept her ears open, adding to the hypnotic mood. Could the spirit be one side of the wave/particle paradox? How could it be mapped without changing it? Perhaps it was a quantum phenomenon whose probability function had been collapsed into physical reality by being observed. If so, what form of consciousness was the observer? Three heaps of fish bones and skin lay in the snow, marking her progress.

In the back of her mind, Osnat noted a slight change in the rhythm of the wind's roar. There was the regular rise and fall, with occasional higher pitched gusts. But now there was a counter-rhythm, a kind of low-pitched repetitious sound; on, then paused, then on again, then a different pause, on again but louder. Sometimes the sound of two storms would meet, fight with each other, and combine with horrible fury. Osnat sighed, exasperated. She shook her head and gave a start, recognizing the sound from an earlier hunt. The counter rhythm was not another storm, but something exponentially more dangerous. Polar bears were the only animals that stalked and hunted human beings for food. It must have smelled the fish, and would be delighted to find a much larger meal: her.

She reached into her pack for the broken seal harpoon. Using it on a Polar Bear would be like cutting a thick, grilled steak with a toothpick... utterly useless. Osnat roared back at the bear from inside her hut, putting all her aggression, all her anger into her voice, trying to keep her terror from seeping in. How do you fight such a raging beast? Bluff it if possible. Stab a sensitive spot: an eyeball, or the throat. The throat would be pretty thick-skinned, and her puny seal harpoon would likely snap apart. The eyes were good, if she could get them both quickly, and then out-maneuver the blind beast. Osnat had once heard you could stun a tiger by biting it hard on the nose. Were Polar Bear noses as sensitive? Probably not. Tiger noses were soft and moist. Such an organ would freeze and fall off in this climate.

There was no way to appease the Bear. All it was interested in was her life. She crouched down, prepared to spring to battle. And she prayed that she be spared. In the merit of any good that she'd ever done in her life, in the merit of her ancestors, please send salvation.

The animal's growls were now a low rumble. She could sense it circling her little shelter, sniffing at its prey. She turned to follow, backing off the little she could from wherever it was, her small, fractured spear clutched in her mitts.

Half the shelter collapsed under massive white and red forelegs that smashed through the top, a roar of rage coming from the animal's throat. Bright, fresh blood soaked the snow as Osnat's broken harpoon headed towards the beast's right eye. It barely acknowledged the attack.

It didn't make sense. There were copious amounts of blood all over the bear before her spear even touched it. It must be hers, but then she should be in pain, she should feel weak.

Aarluk scowled at Osnat through the smashed remains of her snow hut. "I'm glad to see you were ready to protect my fish. I wouldn't want some stupid bear to steal them, after all the effort I put into catching them. Come on, let's go."

Osnat stared at the huge rent in the bear's throat, and then threw her arms around Aarluk. All the terror, all the anger poured out of her heart, poured in liquid form from her eyes. After a few minutes she was finally able to speak. "Thank you for coming back for me."

Aarluk gently disengaged her arms. "Never mind that; I didn't leave. I just stayed back so you could learn to find your way. We'll cut up the bear, and then go. I'll follow you, so I can keep an eye on what's left of my fish in your back-pack."

Osnat blanched. Not again. "I don't know where to go; I can't find the way under normal conditions. I certainly can't find it in a storm like this."

"Bah! Without ever having been taught, you built yourself a snow hut. You lit a lamp without having a flame. You were facing certain death from the bear, yet you prepared to fight. You knew how to move back, so that when it came through the walls it wouldn't strike you. You're one of us now, maybe stronger. You're Tunniq. Stop whining; stop thinking. Shut your eyes if it helps. Let's go."

Osnat looked at the person who had raped her when they first met. Now the overwhelming feeling she had for Aarluk was - well, she didn't know what it was. There was no word, no concept that encompassed gratitude, deep affection, revulsion and terror. It wasn't love, it wasn't hatred, nor was it somewhere between those feelings. But it was absolutely what she felt.

"Yes, mother."

THE EDGE OF THE WORLD 4

Aarluk deftly set to work butchering the Polar Bear. She made a careful incision down the belly, and with Osnat's help separated the skin and fur, a virtually intact warm winter coat. She quickly rolled it up, tying it in a bundle with a strap of braided intestine.

"We have to hurry before it freezes, and we can't do anything with it." Aarluk stripped the muscle off the bones, which Osnat then cut into pieces that weren't too heavy to carry. As they butchered, Aarluk cut off little chunks, which she chewed on; Osnat declined the invitation to do likewise. "We'll take what we can, let the storm bury the rest, and then we'll come back for it," Aarluk said.

Aarluk was big for a woman. Aarluk was big for a man. She tied most of the bear meat together and hoisted it easily over her shoulders. The wind was packing the snow, but with all the weight, she sank to her shins with every step. Osnat carried the bear hide and a lesser amount of meat. They put the rest in the excavation that Osnat had made for her temporary shelter.

"How will we find it?"

"The same way you'll find our way back to the camp."

Osnat was back in the same situation as when Aarluk had first abandoned her in this storm. She had to find her way back to the camp without any visual clues. How? Osnat started to panic, her knees trembling.

Aarluk laughed. "Do you want to build another bear trap, with you as the lure?"

Osnat looked at her blankly. She wanted to do as Aarluk told her, but had no idea...

"Tell me, Osnat: when you throw a ball, do you first measure and calculate? Or do you just throw?"

"Um, I throw..." Osnat played defense on her lacrosse team, so she didn't do much throwing. More blocking, and when she wouldn't get caught, tripping.

"I suggest we leave now. If you agree, then bridle your mouth from speaking and your heart from thinking, and if your heart runs, return to the place."

Osnat squeezed her eyes closed at the strange directive. She could not figure out which way to head. Into the wind? Away? Across? There was no sun; there was no moon, no stars by which to orient herself. She wasn't going to lose herself to panic. Taking a breath, she threw back the hood of her parka, exposing her cheeks to the storm. Her eyes still closed, she turned slowly in a circle, stopping with her back to Aarluk. She opened her eyes, replaced her hood, and set off, her mind a blank whiteness, a reflection of the snow. Aarluk followed, a small smile on her lips.

Osnat didn't know how long she had been walking when she realized she no longer heard the crunching of Aarluk's boots behind her. She looked around: no sign of Aarluk, and her own footprints were covered over just a few feet from where she stood. To her own surprise, she didn't panic, or even fret. She simply stood with a sense of detachment, and waited.

When Aarluk finally caught up with Osnat, she smiled. "You've learned important things today: how to trust your senses, and how to find your way. You also learned patience, waiting at the seal's breathing-hole, waiting in your little shelter in the storm, and waiting here for me. I can trust your judgment. Let's continue."

They hadn't walked more than a few minutes when Aarluk turned to Osnat. "My back is tired from carrying all this meat. Let Ijiq bring it into the camp and store it safely." She cupped her hands around her mouth and yelled "Ijiq!"

Osnat was shocked to see him appear out of the blowing snow. Ijiq smiled at Osnat, hugged his wife, and started praising her skills as a hunter. A small crowd gathered, curious about what Osnat and Aarluk had with them. A half dozen yelping dogs ran over to the meat lying in the snow, but kicks quickly drove them back. Falun, Haran and Simon were among the onlookers, peering and poking at the meat and hides Aarluk and Osnat had deposited on the ground. They heaped compliments on Aarluk; polar bears were not easy prey.

"Your praise should not be for me. I struck the blow, but it was my daughter who was responsible for the kill. She set a trap, baited the bear, and waited calmly for its arrival. Any of you who eats this meat, you're eating her gift. Anything you do against her is taking food out of my mouth, is taking happiness from my belly."

Why was Aarluk warning them off? Osnat's constant sense of fear in this small settlement had only recently faded. Did she have to remain ready to jump at shadows? Was everyone an attacker waiting for an opportunity? She looked around at the faces of her community, hoods raised against the wind and snow. When her baby came, whose head would she lift off to get it a name?

Osnat gazed past the people to the camp, the homes behind them. She couldn't see anything because of the storm that had been raging for who knows how long. She couldn't see anything above her, or behind her, for that matter. The sun, even daylight, was a distant memory. Warmth, to be able to wander about without layers of dead animal skins was a strange idea to her now. In this bleak land, in these hard conditions, was it any surprise that these were hard people? Osnat had developed her morality in a land of soft furniture, running water and climate-controlled homes.

In Aarluk's view, Osnat was now Tunniq. Osnat's chest heaved with restrained weeping, not so much for what she had lost, but for what she was becoming. She looked over at Puah and Aarluk, who were having a heated exchange. Maybe one of them would kill each other right now. That was just the kind of thing that happened here. Maybe someone would find a reason to kill her. Or maybe it was time for her to kill someone, to establish her authority.

"Why did you run away for so long? Are you afraid of the storm?" Puah said. "That it will defeat you? How are we supposed to go hunting in these conditions, with the sky's tantrum?"

"My daughter, a newborn hunter, managed okay. Do you need some food from a newborn?"

"I don't know how you caught that bear, but I'm sure it isn't your daughter who's feeding you. Maybe it's because you're charming the animals that the rest of us are going hungry."

Puah grabbed for Aarluk's throat, but Aarluk seized her arms, forcing her to the ground. Miriaq came running, but halted as Aarluk hissed a warning.

"I must be a pretty powerful Sphere Traveler to be able to charm animals, or maybe you're all just lousy hunters. In any case, my daughter is even more powerful than me: she can bring fire. Osnat and I are going to eat and rest now. Then I will attack and crush the storm. Puah, you bring the storm, since this is your challenge. After it's dead, my daughter will take back her father's name, and burn down your tent, with you inside."

Puah spat on the ground. "If you fail to stop the storm Simon and Falun will rip the baby out of Osnat's belly, and give her their own. She will then belong to us, and we'll see whose tent gets burned down." She turned and glared at Osnat, who glared right back.

Osnat addressed Puah, eyeball to eyeball. "Your life is over. You threatened my baby, who never was a threat to you. I will soon collect your name and bury it under the snow where I relieve myself. I will take back Simon's name, and then burn down your tent with you inside, just as my mother has promised."

Inside, Osnat trembled. Out of nowhere, and for absolutely nothing, an aura of death had overtaken the camp. One moment there was celebration of a successful hunt; the next, war was hovering. This was like the Games League she participated in on the other side of existence, only much deadlier. Unless there was some way to stand down, people were going to die soon. And unless she was one of the killers, she was going to be one of the killed.

"Now what?" Osnat sat on the fur-covered bench in their hide-and-snow home. Ijiq had lit some oil lamps, and together with the wood fire it was bright, almost cheerful inside. Smoke rose, spread around and drifted out the vent hole. At one end of the bench a bowl was filled with fish eyes, like a bowl of candy. Strips of animal flesh hung from a sinew rope running along one side. On the other side was a collection of femurs from different creatures, waiting to be made into weapons or tools. Elk bones, dog bones, human bones... Ijiq assured her that the previous Simon's bones weren't in the pile.

Aarluk cut some chunks of meat and tossed them into a bowl of water over the fire. "We'll have a hot meal, and some sleep. After that, I'll kill the storm. Then we'll kill Falun, Puah and Simon. Now rest. You've been working hard. You need your strength." She reached for a skin bag, and grabbed a handful of dried berries, which she threw into the pot.

"I worry about you, daughter. There are things you should be eating raw that you need to live, but they disgust you too much. These berries will help a bit, but you need to learn to swallow fresh food without gagging."

"I'm worried about me, too. I'm worried about killing. You say we'll kill them, they say they'll kill us, they threaten my baby, and that boy Simon wants nothing in life but to have sex with me."

Ijiq looked up from the side where he had just finished relieving himself. "Of course Simon wants to have sex with you. Everyone in the camp who isn't forbidden to you is going to have sex with you. Aarluk adopted you only after she tried you out."

"Don't you know? Everyone is forbidden to me." Osnat was astounded by how calmly she could discuss it.

"You wouldn't be carrying a baby if everyone was forbidden to you. It wouldn't take."

"The baby is from before, from the one who isn't forbidden to me."

Ijiq and Aarluk shared a look of astonishment.

"And who would that be?" Ijiq calmly asked.

This was a problem. Osnat had promised Simon, the real Simon, not to reveal that he was her husband. It was an important secret to hold on to.

"I can't reveal that. It isn't anyone here."

Aarluk sighed. She walked over to Ijiq and put a hand on his shoulder. "Osnat, how did you make fire in the shelter where you trapped the bear?"

"I'm sorry mother, I cannot reveal that either."

"How is everyone forbidden to you?"

"I forbid it."

"You forbid it? Everyone in this camp wants to go between your legs, and you forbid it? Are you such a powerful Sphere Traveler? Why didn't you forbid it when I first met you?"

Aarluk wrapped her arms around her husband, hugging him tightly. "Maybe she won't take vengeance on you," she whispered into his ear. Releasing her hold on Ijiq, she turned to Osnat. "Are you going to kill us, too?"

Osnat smelled fear inside the little home. It overpowered even the scent of the smoky fire. Aarluk and Ijiq were her best protection; she would be dead long ago if not for the food, shelter, and training that she got from them. If Aarluk hadn't adopted her, all that would be left of Osnat would be in tent corners where people relieved themselves. She had to keep them as allies, but hold them somewhat on edge. Her mother could turn once again into her rapist, or instruct someone how to cut her up for a feast. They were looking at her with trepidation.

"There are enough threats between Falun, Puah and us. Let's not worry about each other. Aarluk, you said before that we should rest. Let's eat, rest, and then do what we have to. Ijiq, since you weren't out hunting with us, could you make sure no one attacks us while we sleep?"

"Ah, don't worry about that," Aarluk said. "They need me to kill the storm. After that, killing people will begin in earnest. I'm glad I don't have to worry about my daughter killing me. Tunniq don't kill their parents. You are Tunniq, aren't you?"

"What else is there? The other side of the Edge of the World doesn't exist if no one's aware of it, and I stopped looking a long time ago." Osnat expected a slap, or at least annoyance in response to her evasive reply.

A puzzled look came over Ijiq. "And if nobody is looking at the moon, does it exist?"

It was Osnat's turn to be surprised. She did not expect this kind of question. "No, it doesn't."

Ijiq shut his eyes as he digested Osnat's words. A thin smile started to take shape. He swept down on Osnat, squeezing her in his arms, pressing his cheek to hers with happiness. Aarluk joined in the hug.

They stood like that for a few minutes, Osnat's feet suspended in the air, her body squeezed between two huge people. She didn't understand what was going on, she didn't comprehend what it was she understood that was so important. Did they understand the concept of the moon as a quantum object, existing as a probability wave? Did their savage minds have an instinctive appreciation of advanced physics? What Osnat understood least of all was that she felt affection from Aarluk and Ijiq, and to them.

"We should let her breathe," Aarluk finally said, and they both released her.

"You should let me eat."

"It's not cooked the way you like. The meat's still raw on the inside."

"Thank you, mother, for being careful of my tastes. But since I'm Tunniq, I eat like a Tunniq." She dipped the ladle into the broth, and put it to her lips, carefully chewing the chunks of barely cooked meat. "One more question. Why is the Edge of the World so dangerous?"

Ijiq put down his bowl of broth and looked into Osnat's eyes. He spoke quietly but firmly. "It's made from the trapped souls of Sheyds."

"What!" Osnat's new-gained respect for their insight was quickly being challenged.

"The Source of Blessing wove the souls of Sheyds into a curtain, the Edge of the World. They're trapped there for five thousand years. We don't know when that time began, and so we don't know when those Sheyds will be free."

"Sheyds?" Osnat was too astounded.

"They're like shadows; there, but not really. They chase away animals, they make thick ice thin, they twist people's insides.

"I don't understand." She wanted to say *don't be ridiculous*, but that would have stopped the discussion.

"None of us truly understand, except an old man in another village, who says he's seen them. Let's not talk of it more," Aarluk said.

"But—"

"I want to rest now. I need my strength to kill the storm. You should rest also."

Aarluk lay down on the hide she was kneeling on. Ijiq stretched out beside her and pulled a cover over them. They fell instantly asleep.

***

A gentle hand on her shoulder shook Osnat out of the garden she had been dreaming about. "Come, Puah has the storm ready."

Lifting the skin blankets, she raised her head slowly off the sleeping platform and shivered. The storm was blowing harder; she felt the walls of their shelter trembling as the wind rose and ebbed. A stream of snow came through edges of the hides that covered the snow walls. The wood fire had been allowed to burn out, and the only light was from the flickering, uncertain flames of a couple of oil lamps. Through the ice window there was a dark, foreboding whiteness. Osnat could hear the snow hammering onto the pane.

"Why don't we just wait for the storm to pass? That way, nobody will have to carry out any of their threats to kill each other."

Aarluk grimaced. "Did you leave your brains behind in your dreams? Didn't you hear Falun and Puah? They've challenged me, saying that I'm too weak to subdue the storm. They haven't gone hunting in days, and the village is almost out of food. With the bear you trapped and the fish, we have more food than everyone else put together. If I don't kill the storm, they will attack us, to take ours. I'm afraid of what they will do to you."

"But you offered to give them food."

"I'd be happy to, though not enough to fill their bellies; better that they're weak from hunger. Puah opened her mouth without thinking, and now she has the obligation to provide everything, so I can kill the storm."

"What does she have to provide?"

"She had to build the Dance House and supply food for the festival. It's the last she has, and it's all going to be eaten. And Puah has to provide the baby."

Osnat was afraid to ask. The baby? Were they going to kill and eat a baby? But there was only one that she knew of in the camp, and it was a girl with a name; she couldn't be killed just like that. Could she? A baby boy had been born recently, but his father didn't want the responsibility, so the tiny thing had been placed under the snow.

"Listen carefully, Osnat." Ijiq squatted in front of her, putting his hands gently on her shoulders. "It's dangerous to kill a storm. If the baby gets angry, it could crush us with its foot. You mustn't do anything to upset it."

She stared at him blankly.

"One of our people attacked a family of giants and killed the parents. Their baby decided to avenge them by flying into the sky and turning his crying into bad weather. Other beings tied a bib around his face, keeping his cries and tears from reaching us. But sometimes it slips, the storms reach through and a Sphere Traveler must go to it, to make sure the bib is tied back in place."

"Why do you call it "killing" the storm?"

Aarluk helped Ijiq up. "It's like the baby is having a tantrum. Sometimes the crying takes on a life of its own. In such a case, tying the bib doesn't help. That's what happens in a very bad storm, or when it's been going on too long. Then the only way is to kill the storm. Often, it fights back."

"Are you going to get killed?"

"Several times, but that's normal."

"What!"

Aarluk shrugged.

"Is there no easier way? How about getting the baby to stop crying?"

"Everybody's been working on that. We offer it food; we explain that we aren't the ones who killed its parents. Sometimes that works, but this storm has clearly come alive."

Tucking his sleeves into his sealskin mitts, Ijiq eyed her grimly. "The Dance House is right against the cliff wall. It's a distance to walk. Hold on to us, because you cannot see your hand in front of your face outside, and the wind gusts will knock you over. If you get separated from us, you're finished."

Ijiq handed each of them a snow knife. With it, they could at least carve out a temporary shelter. He went first, crawling through the entranceway. He had Osnat hold on to his foot as he exited, and Aarluk held on to hers.

Osnat had never seen the weather so bad, the snow so thick. There was no light in the sky, no lamps showing through tents. The darkness was a pounding, dismal white that blocked all vision, which hurt her eyes.

They locked arms as they walked slowly together, inching their way towards the Dance House at the cliff face. Aarluk wasn't carrying her drum, nor had she changed into her Sphere Traveling costume. Maybe the weather was too fierce for her to carry it. Maybe she was afraid the costume would get ruined in the storm.

Gusts of wind from across the plain almost blew them off their feet. Aarluk and Ijiq held on to Osnat as if she was a feather that could be blown away and lost forever. They progressed between the gusts, stopping when the wind lashed out at them. Osnat marveled at the fury of the baby crying over the loss of its parents. Could she avenge the death of her husband as this baby avenged its loss? *Spare me*, she cried silently to the storm. *My family was also murdered by these people.*

The baby screamed in response, a blast of wind that knocked the three of them off their feet. Scrambling not to be separated, Osnat managed to get hold of Aarluk's leg, clinging as they waited on the ground for a let-up. Ijiq crawled in front of her, put his face almost in hers, his back to the wind, and smiled. "Don't face the baby. It considers that as arrogance, which infuriates it more. Always show your back, and it won't sting as much."

Osnat nodded and started to roll over. She felt Aarluk press up against her back, and was grateful. They lay there silently, the snow starting to build up around them.

"Let's go some more." Holding each other's arms, they stumbled a few more paces, bodies bent against the storm, before the wind knocked them over again. This time Ijiq and Aarluk lined up beside each other, backs to the wind, sheltering Osnat from the worst of it.

The gale kept up its assault, knocking them over once more, keeping them bowed to its strength. This short trip to the cliff face was more exhausting than her seal hunt had been.

At last they spied the faint illumination of oil lamps through an ice window, as they reached the Dance House. Nervous dogs filled the long crawl-way entrance. This was an exceptional storm, that the dogs would be allowed in.

The Dance House had hide-covered snow benches all around its sides. Rough wood posts and crosspieces supported its roof. Children ran around, playing games, happy to be somewhat relieved of the confinement the storm had imposed. Their laughter and the general feeling of merriment was a counterpoint to the storm baby wailing outside that had brought them all together here. Boys barely old enough to walk wrestled with each other, girls almost old enough to give birth wrestled with older boys. A short girl laughed as she tried to grab a small, dead puppy that some taller children were tossing one to another. Women sat with their hoods down, combing the knots in each other's hair with ivory implements. Falun and Puah were arm-wrestling. It appeared the money, if there had been such a thing, was on Falun, but his wife was managing to hold her own. A naked baby relieved itself on the trampled snow beside them, much to the adoration of her mother watching nearby. Osnat told herself to watch where she put her feet, as she tried to decide if the little girl was disgusting or lovable.

Osnat pulled off her hood and stood to a side, catching her breath. Miriaq was hacking away at a frozen seal carcass, happily giving out small chunks of meat to everyone. He yelled at Simon to get up, to give her room to sit. He jammed a piece of meat in Osnat's face. "Breath on it to warm the surface, or it might stick to your tongue."

Osnat marveled at the scene. Facing a relentless storm that only worsened as it progressed, facing starvation, with an uncertain hope of surviving, they had a festival. They didn't succumb to bleakness. Rather, they celebrated life's joys, its challenges and its vagaries.

A burst of laughter, as Falun finally pinned Puah's hand against the snow. Smiling malevolently, he picked up the baby's turds beside him, and with great ceremony dropped them in his wife's outstretched, immobilized hand. That gave her a burst of energy, and with a gleeful yell, she wrenched her arm free. Falun rose quickly, and started running around the festival house, Puah cursing and laughing as she looked for a clear shot to throw his gift back at him. Everyone chuckled and darted out of the way, encouraging her revenge while not wanting to be in the way of the toss. Falun bolted to a side and grabbed his younger brother Haran's hand. Pulling him out in front of him, he yelled at his wife, "throw!" She heaved the turds, which, frozen by now, bounced off the long strips of decorative white hide hanging down the chest of Haran's parka.

A large, flat drum hung loosely from one Haran's hands. Something about him made Osnat's skin crawl. Her eyes darted to Aarluk, wondering why Haran was dressed to Travel between Spheres, when it was Aarluk who was supposed to kill the storm. Aarluk smiled cheerfully at her, continuing to gnaw on a chunk of frozen meat.

Whispers and hisses settled the children down on the floor, the adults on the snow and hide benches around the walls. Haran walked over and squatted in front of Osnat, resting his hands on her knees.

"I have a few helpers; my dead father, and a blue stone that I found, which looks like a head and neck. I tied long caribou hairs to it, and so made it into a Sphere Traveler; it Travels alongside me. But I'm weak, and my helpers don't always come when I want."

All the women except for Aarluk were clustered around the two of them. They all began encouraging him, "No, you can do it... Your helpers will surely come."

Haran shook his head. "It's difficult to make hidden forces do your bidding."

The more the women encouraged him, the more he proclaimed his weakness. Every time he spoke, he seemed more and more detached from the people around him. The crowd grew denser as the men joined in the encouragement. Haran's eyes became wild, his breathing uneven. His arms twitched. He stood up slowly and turned, staring one at a time into the face of every person in the Dance House. He looked into Osnat's eyes, putting his hands on her face.

"Who are you," Haran whispered, a sound of bewilderment in his voice. Haran straightened himself, his eyes jumping around the room, his arms twitching spastically as if they had their own minds. "Who are you," he screamed at no one in particular.

Osnat sensed that Haran was afraid. Of what? Her?

"Your own people," came the response from a few.

Haran was oblivious to answers. He stared again at Osnat. "Who are you?"

"She is one of us."

Staring into nothingness, he nodded in trepidation. Haran turned away and gazed wildly around the room. "I cannot, I cannot." His head hung low, his eyes half closed; he slouched as if he had no bones to hold his body up. He shuffled slowly back and forth, and a gurgling sound came from his throat. His eyes bulged; his body twitched and shook as if he was being electrocuted.

A smoky odor filled the air of the Dance House, as something otherworldly took control of Haran. He spasmed and yelled, rolling on the floor and springing upright. He stared blankly, then turned sharply and stared at nothing again as tears started to roll down his cheeks.

"What do you see?" people demanded.

Haran shouted the names of people who had died, some recently, some long ago. Some of the onlookers cried at the names of their lost relatives. Others shouted for their deceased relatives to save them from the storm. Osnat blanched at hearing Eber names. She too shouted desperately for their help, too astonished to feel ridiculous for doing so.

Haran shouted at the air in front of him. "Why are you evil? Leave us!"

"Who is it?"

"Two people who went east. They died and want to harm us."

A sinister feeling spread over the people in the Dance House. The two were alive and among them, before heading out on a short trip a few days ago. Now they had turned into evil, the very kind of malevolence at the root of the storm.

A noise at the entranceway caused everyone to gasp, afraid. But it was just two more people, the sickly Tuli and his wife. They crawled in, their eyes and mouths full of snow.

This was the third day of the storm. Except in Aarluk's home, there was no meat for tomorrow; nothing to eat, nothing to keep them warm. It was a blizzard, it was a gale, but now the menace seemed to be alive. The storm-baby cried, the women wept, the men muttered to themselves.

With a shout, Haran suddenly dashed over to Aarluk and grabbed her by the throat. He lifted the big woman from the bench, brutally flinging her back and forth. They both screamed, but Haran's grip tightened, and Aarluk was soon silent, her head lolling limply, her eyes closing. Haran continued to yell at her, dragging her around, when a hiss came from Aarluk's lips, and her eyes opened wildly. They staggered together around the room, falling to the side, getting up, crashing into people, almost knocking over the oil lamps or running into children. Haran continued to yell as he dragged Aarluk around.

Finally he released her, and she fell to the ground. Haran immediately grabbed the back of Aarluk's neck in his teeth, shaking her like a dog that has gotten the better of its prey. A thick, deathly silence filled the Dance House.

Haran then began rubbing her back, her head, her neck. For a few moments Aarluk remained still, but then moaned and slowly got to her knees. He encouraged her up, smiling, pulling at her arm.

As soon as Aarluk got to her feet, the whole thing started again. Haran grabbed her throat, dragging her around, subduing her, subduing the storm, until once again Aarluk lay prone on the floor. Three times she was dragged about and choked. But after the third time Aarluk came back to life, it was Haran who collapsed. Aarluk rose slowly from the floor after releasing Haran's neck. She lifted up the storm, disguised as one of the growling dogs from the crawl-way, and passed a knife down its belly. She commanded the Dance House with the wildness in her eyes and the horrible reddish-blue sheen that had come over her face through the ill-usage she had just been subjected to. All understood that this was a person whom death had just touched, and they involuntarily stepped back when Aarluk put her foot on Haran's chest.

She cried out, her voice trembling with emotion. "The sky is full of naked men and women rushing along, raising gales and blizzards. Do you hear the noise? It swishes like the wings of a great eagle. It is the flight of naked people! The weather spirit is blowing the storm out. The helpless storm-baby shakes the lungs of the air with his weeping. Do you hear it? And look! Among the naked crowds of fleeing ones, there is a single woman whom the wind has made full of holes. Her body is like a sieve, and the air whistles through the holes.

"Do you hear her? She is the mightiest of the Sphere Travelers. But my helpers will stop her. I see him her coming calmly towards me, confident of victory. Do you hear?"

Osnat had been gradually drawn into the visions. She saw the great eagle; she saw the naked people. She saw the woman whom the wind had made full of holes. She screamed as she recognized the woman; it was her. Osnat felt the air whistling through her body, ripping at her insides. She didn't feel calm, or confident of victory. How could she, a powerful scientist, have become part of the storm afflicting her people?

Nobody heeded her scream, her terror. Of course. She was one of the naked ones Aarluk was subduing.

"Do you see the Travelers, the storm, sweeping over us with the swish of the great eagle's wings?"

At these words Haran rose from the floor, and the two Sphere Travelers sang hoarsely together:

"I raise my eyes to the mountains;

Where will my help come from?

To the Source of Blessing in my distress I cried, and He answered me.

From the deep I called you;

Hear my voice, may your ears listen to my pleas.

We yearn for you, among those looking for the light of dawn,

Looking for the light of dawn."

When they had finished their hymn, all the other people joined in, an entreating, wailing chorus of distressed people. They had no food to give their children the next day. They prayed for calm so that they could hunt; they prayed for life.

And suddenly it seemed as if nature became alive. The storm was visible, a chariot speeding across the sky amidst a throng of naked beings. The crowd of fleeing dead ones came sweeping behind through the billows of the blizzard, and all visions and sounds centered in the wing-beats of the great eagles with their sharp, bent bills. Osnat too, was fleeing; naked, full of holes, imagining that she was alive.

The visions, the sounds, the fleeing dead ones passed through the Dance House, leaving the two Sphere Travelers on the floor, their arms on each other's shoulders. They sat down on a bench, pulling themselves back, sending away the visions, the trances. The other people slowly filed out of the Dance House, through the narrow tunnel entrance. The wind still raged; the snow still beat down upon anyone and anything that dared venture outside. Nonetheless people seemed satisfied, confident that the weather had been taken care of.

Osnat was in a daze, not a trance. She touched her body, once again solid. She had never experienced anything like this, never heard or read of anything like this. Ijiq slowly guided her back home, a smile on his face and an iron grip on her arms. Osnat swore to herself that she would never allow her baby, or any of her descendants to believe in foolishness such as killing a dog, or any of this, to appease a storm.

5 MODERN AGE 1

Saima had to run. As the wind drove each frozen drop into his skin, the sting reminded him that his feet were hurting less than before. This was bad. Frozen flesh, dead flesh brings no pain. Earlier, when his hands and feet were throbbing, he could barely focus enough to look ahead through the darkness to know where he was running. With the pain easing, he could now concentrate on the way towards shelter. He tried not to think about his toes turning white with frost, eventually black with rot. He ran on, jumping over the deeper puddles, trying not to lose his footing on the ice that met his soles.

Saima knew the way home; he had traveled this route before. But the scattered light twisting on the icy raindrops warped the landscape, moving landmarks from where he expected to find them. Looking back over his shoulder had distracted him. It was not a time to be far from shelter. Not a time to be worrying about something behind him.

His father Jako had died many years ago in weather like this. The tempest had carried on for days; they had run out of meat, out of oil for the lamp. His mother's breasts had dried out from hunger; his baby sister only stopped wailing when she ran out of strength. His father and uncle had gone to the seals' breathing holes. After a day of standing patiently in the raging sleet, Jako had said he was tired, and lay down in the shelter of a snowdrift. His brother begged him to get up, but Jako spoke blissfully about how warm and comfortable he was feeling. There was no point in both of them dying, so the brother left him. On the way back home Saima's uncle tried another breathing hole and caught a fat seal. Enough meat to feed the families for a few days, enough fat to light their small homes.

Freezing to death was a well-followed tradition amongst the Eber people. Food was often hard to come by, warmth was rare, storms were frequent. Sometimes it was just bad luck. You'd be out on the edge of the sea ice, and it would crack. The piece you were on would become a raft, and you would float out to sea to die.

Freezing wasn't always fatal. His oldest son had lost fingers to frostbite while hunting at the foot of the craggy escarpment near their village. Saima had promised him that on this journey, he would find them a warmer place to live, away from the eerie, glowing rocks.

What was the death rate in their land? High. Nothing of course like right after the Trail of Tears, when the Ebers were moved to their new home. They had learned much since then.

Where the hell was he now? Nothing looked familiar, nothing smelled right. Had Saima's daydreaming led him further off course? Now he was feeling silly. No one in his family got lost. His people always had a sense of where they were. On land they could read the wind, the sun, the stars, or even the clouds. On water they could sense the direction from the slap of the waves against their flimsy boats. Here the wind swirled from all directions. The few bits of light broke against the icy water that attacked and coated everything around him. It wasn't a landscape Saima could feel in his bones. It was alien, alive, twisting and threatening.

Not only did his family never get lost; they didn't panic, either. He might have done the first, but there was no point doing the second. He took a deep breath, shut his eyes, and listened intently to the screaming gusts of sleet. Realizing that it wasn't just the wind that was howling, he resumed running. A huge, shivering, black, waterlogged dog cried into the storm, eyeing him suspiciously from a distance. A fellow despondent traveler. Saima frowned, whistled and beckoned to the miserable creature, lost and cold. Hobbling over, it was soon nuzzling forlornly again his legs as Saima held his hand out for it to sniff. He winced as he spotted the white bone jutting through its leg. Winning its trust, Saima ruffled the fur on its head, making calming sounds. He squatted, and whispered soothingly to the dog's face, apologizing and thanking it for coming to him. Saima rose and rubbed the pitiful animal's neck. His knife blade sliced swiftly through its windpipe, and the dog crumbled to the ground. Turning it over, Saima quickly split its belly open. He removed his mitts and stuck his hands inside, luxuriating in the soft heat of the now-dead flesh.

Saima shut his eyes, and tried to match the feel of the icy rain with how it felt before he went off course. The storm roared around him, as if his life was a big joke, and the wind was tired of hearing it.

There were three ways to deal with a storm. One was simply to endure it. The second was to choke the life out of it. The last was to appease it. Saima wasn't equipped to choke it, so appeasement was his best choice.

"Calm your tears, child," he addressed the storm assaulting him. "Quiet your breaths, child," he spoke to the wind. "Your family is gone, but not by my hand. I have brought you food." He swept his hand over the carcass lying at his feet. Everyone knew that appeasing a storm was frowned upon; it only encouraged more bad weather. Saima wasn't particularly hungry, but he cut off a piece of muscle. If he was eating the carcass, the dog hadn't died just to appease the storm child. The morsel would also keep him warmer for the rest of his trek home; presuming of course that he would find his way back.

The tempest eased a bit, pondering Saima's offering. He knew he didn't have long till the wind and sleet would be at it again with a vengeance. He closed his eyes, shut out the sounds, and felt for home. A feeling of familiarity crept in, and he began to untangle the twisting of his senses by the storm's rage. He took off again, the warmth in his stomach making him forget the silence of the nerves in his feet.

Would tonight make a good tale? Would his children listen in awe to the story of his adventure? Would they tell their offspring about Saima's strength facing the storm? His family had a cycle of stories of adventures of the ancestors, how they persevered, lived, starved, killed, were slaughtered. The stories said that after the Trail of Tears it was Saima, his ancient namesake, who was first captured by the Tunniq. His brutal death led to the expeditions, and their extermination. If his great, great, whatever grandfather had not been captured and eaten the Ebers would have never gained the implements and knowledge they extracted from the Tunniq. Tools and weapons, and the ability to use them, which kept them alive in succeeding generations.

The river was just ahead. Shelter wasn't too far beyond. He could climb down the glossy rocks along the shore in front of him, hopefully not slipping on the ice and cracking his skull. The safer way across was off to the west. Saima looked around, and quickly calculated the time it would take him to get there, and how long it would take to get back where he wanted to be. He ignored the risk factor of falling through weak ice and drowning: if that happened, there was no conclusion to his equation. It was akin to dividing by zero. He dismissed the safer route.

The rocky riverbank looked impassible. Saima stepped on the upslope sides of the boulders, treating each one as a dangerous trap.

At the shoreline, Saima surveyed his route across. He saw an opening in the ice off to the side, and paw prints leading from it. Tracks that looked like impossibly large bird feet, probably something distorted by the sleet, circled the opening.

He set off using the hole as a baseline, trying to sense the fast parts of the river, where the ice would be the thinnest. He ignored the groaning and cracking sounds that answered every footstep. At one point he noticed that the ice was so clear, he could see little wavelets beating on its underside. As he shuffled across, he spotted tracks leading towards the area of transparent ice, but then veering away. He followed them with his eyes, and saw that someone's footprints ended abruptly at the hole he had avoided. A set of dog tracks had been with the humans' but had split off.

Saima understood what had happened. A man had started crossing the river with his dog. He veered away from the clear ice, thinking it too dangerous. The dog, with better senses, didn't follow the new route. The man stopped to beckon to it, to protect it from the apparent danger of the clear ice but the river couldn't support his stationary weight. The dog continued on its way, breaking its leg before finding Saima and its own demise. Though he had no doubt before of the correctness of killing the dog, to him it was confirmation that everything was in place. The dog was supposed to have died with its master. Saima had fixed this.

The ice was too thin on the far bank of the river. His boots quickly filled with icy liquid as he plunged towards solid ground, and he was grateful for the warmth from having just eaten. The scramble up the far shore was harder than the way down, as now he was fighting against slick, highly polished gravity. He used some twisted remains of bushes at the top to pull himself to level ground, sat down on a stone, and emptied the frigid water from his boots. The wind and ice ripped at his naked, wet feet, but he didn't feel it; they were already frozen.

It took some time to get his boots back on, as he had to manipulate his unresponsive toes with his hands, which were also starting to re-freeze. He tested his gait, and once satisfied, took off at a slow lope up the rise that fronted this shore of the river. He knew this was the final, deciding sprint. The alternative outcomes were warmth and life, or a cold death. He felt the latter snag his ankles. He had to distract himself so it wouldn't pull him down, but he had no strength left to force his mind clear. Saima picked a simple exercise that he had used for years. *Two, three, five, seven....* Not working. The simple prime numbers were no match for the ice, the wind, the frozen feet, and the exhaustion. He tried a higher number: *five hundred nine, five hundred twenty-one...* He reached the top of the rise, and was now moving on instinct alone. *Two thousand, two hundred three; two thousand, two hundred seven...* Nothing existed but his goal, and the numbers he recited to himself. The low, slush-covered dwellings that he passed were dark and silent.

He reached the door. Three thousand, six hundred and thirty-seven. He stopped, looked behind him, and composed his thoughts. He had come here to find how to take back what had been stolen from his people many generations ago. He couldn't let himself get thrown off course by a storm, by a dog, by anything. He spoke into the little baffle at the side of the doorway: "Saima. Open." A blue light came from the security scanner, reading his violet eyes and finding a match. The electronic door silently slid aside and Saima stepped down through the entrance.

6 MODERN AGE 2

Footsteps running towards him greeted Saima as he folded to the floor in the hallway.

"Saima, what happened? I've been worried sick. Why didn't you contact me?"

He took a deep breath of warm air. "The wagons were grounded, so I walked. Ran, actually."

Alex put his arm around Saima, helping him stand. "From where? It's been hours."

"I was at the Old Post Club. There was someone I had to see."

"That's practically across town! Saima, I'm your host, I take care of you. Linda would be very upset if anything happened to you. You should have used your communicator; I would have come to get you."

"How? I didn't see any wagons. The whole city is dark. Besides which, if you're so concerned, you'd be trying warm me up now, instead of lecturing."

Saima didn't mention the fight that had made him start running, or the strange person who attacked him. Though the man looked feeble, he had been getting the better of Saima. When Saima had pulled his knife, the man gaped at the jeweled blue handle; Saima snatched the opportunity to run. If he had concentrated on the way ahead rather than looking over his shoulder, he wouldn't have gotten lost. Hopefully, the kid behind the counter at the Old Post didn't follow through on his offer to call the Police; that terrified Saima more than his attacker.

The man must have been drugged. What else could have given his skin that strange pallor? "I've waited five thousand years to pay you back for everything you did to me," he had said in a raspy voice. Saima had been lured to the Old Post by a message: "I've known your family for a long time, and would like to meet you." It was signed "Mekelat," or something like that.

"Of course the city is dark," Alex said. "Most windows don't let light escape, so it doesn't disturb the wildlife. You didn't see anyone else outside because Jackson had the Collective Council call a storm curfew. Since you're a northern savage, we wouldn't expect you to know about such things." He gently touched Saima's face. "You're right though; I shouldn't be lecturing you."

Jackson, Saima wondered to himself. *Who ...?*

Alex pressed a button on his collar. He stared into space, before nodding. "Linda says you should take a shower to warm yourself up. Then we'll get you into some dry clothes and feed you."

Alex bent down to remove Saima's boots, pulled off his socks, and frowned. "Your toes are white!"

"Let's see if any turn black," Saima said.

Alex made a face, not understanding the significance of frostbite.

"Does this hurt?" He jabbed Saima's feet with his finger. Getting no response, he gently massaged the soles. "Do you feel this?"

"Not at all."

Alex began unbuttoning Saima's clothes. "You're all wet."

"Can't I go to the shower before getting undressed?"

"The air in the house is warmer than your clothes. Besides which, I don't want you dripping all over the floor. Linda would be upset." He placed Saima's clothes in a bin next to the closet.

They took the elevator down. Saima felt quite uncomfortable with Alex's eyes on him.

"Someone's in the shower already; the water's running. Can I have a blanket while I wait?"

"It's okay, go in. I'll get undressed and follow you."

"I can shower by myself."

"It's large enough for a few people at a time. No one has to be uncomfortable."

Saima stepped into the steamy room and jumped right back out.

"Alex, your wife's in there!"

"Of course she is. She's concerned about you."

"Alex, she's naked."

Alex continued to undress and responded calmly "No one takes a shower with clothes on. Get in."

Saima stepped in, and stood under the steaming, streaming water. Linda wore only a silver wire necklace, from which hung a large turquoise. Her body was glistening. She approached him and knelt at his feet, pushing her long black hair from her face. She smiled quietly, poured some lotion onto her hands, and began gently massaging. She worked her way upwards.

Saima had felt more comfortable by the river, with his boots full of ice water. "This isn't right. Please don't do—."

She stood up and pressed herself to him, running her fingers through his matted brown hair. He shivered from the warm touch as she wrapped him in her arms. Alex pressed against his back, wrapping his arms around both of them.

Saima's whole body suddenly tensed. He screamed, and then crumbled sideways to the floor, holding his feet, writhing in pain. Alex stared in astonishment.

Linda kneeled, and touched Saima's thigh. "What happened? What's wrong?"

Saima rocked back and forth on the shower floor, his eyes shut tight. Linda reached over for her robe, and once covered began stroking Saima's hair, this time touching him as if comforting a child rather than seducing a man. Saima turned his thoughts inward, and was grateful. The dog came to him earlier at just the right time, and now the pain of thawing feet had hit him just when he needed to be knocked down. Alex stood back, surprised and disappointed.

"Go get dressed," Linda told her husband, before turning back to Saima. "What hurts so much?"

"Towel," he groaned.

She handed him one. He covered himself as best he could and slowly rolled over onto his side, a grimace on his face.

"You need me," he moaned.

"You're a handsome man. We'd enjoy each other."

She was indeed an attractive woman, and, as much as it repelled him, being squeezed together with her had been a sweet sensation.

"That's not what I meant. I'm didn't come here for sex. It's not right."

"I know exactly what you meant." She traced her fingers playfully along his chest. "Alex and I need you to fix things. Right now, I'm having longings that are making me ache. I need you to fix them."

Saima tried to argue but couldn't come up with the words he needed. Linda crouched over him, water dripping from her breasts onto his face. "Lie still," she finally said. She bent down and put her lips to his thawing, throbbing toes.

He opened his eyes to the sound of approaching footsteps. The water was still running, the shower full of steam. Linda lay on her side next to him, her head nuzzled on his chest. Saima examined his fingers; saw that his skin was wrinkled like a dried berry. He wiggled his toes, immensely relieved that they were all pink. Alex, fully dressed, turned off the water and padded over to the two of them. He gave his wife a shake.

"The generator is making that strange noise again. What do we do?" He gazed at Saima's nakedness. "Would you like to spend time with me?"

Linda locked her eyes on Alex: "That's not what we need him for now." Turning to Saima, she said "You want to fix things that are breaking down? Deal with the noise from the generator."

He couldn't argue; Alex and Linda had brought him south to be their handyman. "What's a generator? What's it supposed to sound like?"

"Alex, take him there."

"Can I have some clothes first?"

As they walked, Saima tried to find out more what a generator is, how it works, what the strange noise meant. Anything he learned might be useful; might help him formulate a plan. As Saima dressed in the closet, pressing for more information, he realized that Alex knew about as much as he did. There was this machine that was important to his hosts, and he was supposed to fix it. All Alex could say was that the house was "dead" without it.

What gave a house life? Amongst the Ebers, it was people: laughing, working, crying... Life was defined by the energy of the living. Were Linda and Alex so dependent on this generator that its failure would keep them from being alive? It wasn't his hosts that were "dead" without it; rather, it was the house that needed the generator. He looked at the light coming from the walls, at the warm air blowing in, and began to comprehend what a generator is.

Alex opened the door to the utility room. "Hear it?"

Saima flinched as he recognized the sound. *How...?* He composed himself, and turned to Alex: "I'm going into that room without any equipment, without any weapons. I must have my mind pure. You have to make up for what your wife did. I need your vow not to touch me, not to offer yourself to me in any way for at least a month. I still may not survive in the utility room, being unclean and unable to defend myself. But I'll try anyways, because I'm grateful to you and Linda for taking me in. Give me your vow, and then wait outside the door. Don't come in, because then your life might be in danger also. If the sound isn't fixed by tomorrow, then you'll know I didn't make it. Guard this door with your life."

Alex hesitated. "Is it so dangerous? How will us not having sex—"

Saima folded his arms and tried to look grim. "If you're willing to risk your own life fixing the problem, I'll wait outside the room. If you want me to deal with it..."

Alex looked at his feet. "I promise. Please, be careful."

Saima went in, voice-sealed the door, and released the grimace from his face. Linda was a leading archaeologist, Alex a celebrated poet. How could they be so foolish? Saima didn't like taking advantage of Alex's naiveté, but had quickly realized this was his best chance for stopping his sexual advances. Diverting Linda's advances would be more difficult. She was married, but at least the right gender. She was quite talented in the shower; he didn't entirely want to succeed in diverting her.

But for now, he was glad to be alone as he lay down on the carpet, daydreaming of his village. After some time, his thoughts turned to home, to the flag that fluttered noisily in the wind over the Dance House by the escarpment. It was where they kept the ancient grain parchments, filled with arcane formulas, written by the woman who was said to have destroyed the Tunniq.

Saima sat up, read some instructions and warnings pasted around the utility room, and looked for the 'off' switch for the fan. Once the blades stopped turning, he pulled out the paper that was stuck noisily behind the safety grill. He put it in his pocket and resumed his daydreaming. He was in no hurry to rejoin Alex and Linda.

With the cooling fan off the system soon shut down, and the house was plunged into darkness, into "death." Saima quickly fell into a light sleep. When he felt the room getting cold, he knew enough time had passed without power. He felt his way to the fan switch, turned it on, and closed his eyes again. He heard the click of the reset, felt the system start up, and dreamed of Linda, wondering how his civilized hosts could be so dependent, so ignorant of their technology.

To the people of this place, the Ebers, or "northern savages" as they called his people, were brutes with a natural ability to fix things. A lot had been breaking down recently, including the Edge of the World, the barrier that had kept the Ebers locked up north. Now that it was possible to pass through some small openings, a few had been flown out. To Alex and Linda and those like them, they were importing repairmen. The Ebers viewed their mission differently. They were scouts, looking to recover what had been taken from them on the Trail of Tears. They would do whatever it took to accomplish that, even if it meant laying waste to their hosts' society.

Saima dreamed of his wife. She was racing towards the base of the cliff near their village, her fierce gray eyes peering quickly under each huge boulder that was angled enough to provide shelter underneath. Her long legs carried her over the rough terrain, the caribou skin pants protecting her from the sharp edges she clambered over. Her matted long black hair flying behind her, her fiery mood resembled a storm looking for a place to strike.

Many years ago, a piece of the escarpment had broken off, crashing to the bottom. The craggy, broken remains of the cliff looked like a face, a scowling old man, threatening harm. The storming runner, the sullen face, the angry bear threatening them, gave Saima a feeling of impending disaster.

Orpah was the deadliest person with a spear that Saima knew. But he still didn't like what she was doing: putting herself in danger to protect her son and her husband. As Orpah ran towards the largest of the cliff remains, the white bear turned from the two humans it had been eying hungrily. Orpah yelled at it, "I'm going to kill your cub if you threaten mine."

She wasn't concerned with any danger to herself, just the threat posed to her child and husband. Saima watched with fear and admiration as she flew around boulders, skimmed over fields of broken stone. She was searching for the hungry bear's den. The big creature was starting to realize that, and turned away from its human prey, its instinct for its cub overpowering its hunger. The bear started trotting towards Orpah, occasionally casting its eyes back to its intended meal, as if warning Saima and his son to stay put. Its growl sounded like a roar of pain, but it was pain offered, not felt.

Orpah picked her spot: the top of a rock-fall right against the cliff, where the bear would have to clamber up to reach her. Saima didn't like her choice, literally putting her back against the wall. The bear was racing toward her, and Saima could hear the cub answering its mother's call. The ferocious beast started climbing through the field of boulders, its agility alarming Saima. Orpah calmly crouched and aimed.

The sullen face on the cliff struck first, as the old man's visage suddenly collapsed, tumbling and thundering to the ground.

Orpah looked up as she heard the crack of old man's angry features separating from the mountain. The bear, focused only on eliminating the threat to its cub, leapt at her. Saima's scream was vanquished by the pounding of the rocks down onto the bear, down onto his wife. Clutching his son's hand, he watched the rocks pour onto her. More and more, they thundered, burying her for all time. Saima felt as if the world was collapsing onto her remains.

The pounding wouldn't let up. He rolled over on the carpet, hearing his muffled name through the door. His eyes were wet. He wanted to keep them closed, to hang on to his connection to her. The moment of re-living Orpah's death in a dream was a moment with her. The pain of it was greater passion, greater fulfillment than coupling with Linda could ever be.

He knew he'd see Orpah again. It was a dream that didn't let go. The actual rock collapse had been quicker, but Alex had prolonged it with the sound of his beating at the door.

Saima took off his shoes and flexed his toes. They felt a little numb, but he'd expected worse. He pulled off his socks and inspected his feet: a few small patches of white skin, but no major discoloration.

The pounding on the door continued. Saima expected that keeping his vow, Alex wouldn't say anything that the door could misinterpret as an instruction to open.

"Alex, can you hear me?"

"Yes, Saima. You fixed the noise." Alex knocked some more. "Come out now."

Saima was tired. His long, cold run in the sleet and wind had burned up a lot of his energy. Although he let Linda do most of the work in the shower, their coupling took the balance of his strength.

"I'm almost done. I've got to make sure the noise doesn't come back."

Saima was also hungry; a nice bowl of steaming oatmeal, fresh roasted trout, and hot tea was what he wanted. But he was also patient. You had to be to survive on his side of the Edge of the World. You couldn't get a seal by pulling one out of a breathing-hole like you could get cereal from a pantry. Saima sat down quietly on the floor, closed the pounding on the door from his mind and began to drift. He pictured Orpah again, crouching at the base of the cliff, taking aim at Linda while Alex cried for her to protect him. The spear flew into Linda's breast.

Linda hissed at Saima: "Am I so ugly? Is sex with me so unpleasant that you now think of killing me? We try to make you comfortable, we feed you; we want to keep you happy. Is that why you dream of a spear through my breast?" She opened her mouth, and tiny birds flew out, brightly colored birds with long thin bills. They swarmed over Saima, hovering in the air around him, flying backwards and forward, stabbing at his heart with their beaks.

Saima snapped himself awake. He heard Alex yelling at him. Enough, he decided. "Saima. Open."

The voice recognition was flawless, as the door slid open to his whisper.

Alex grinned. "I'm glad you cured the noise so quickly. The police are here to speak to you about last night." Alex said the words as if there was no hidden portent, no threat in their meaning.

Did that kid at the Old Post call the police after all? Saima's palms started to sweat. His mind raced, probing memories, digging into his thoughts. He didn't know what "police" meant. The word was part of the Eber stories that you weren't supposed to think about. It was an alarm signal, a cue to be very afraid.

"About last night? Why?"

"They're interviewing everyone in the area about our neighbor's dog. Saima, it's good you made it back last night. It was dangerous out there."

"Don't you think I know that?"

"It's not just the storm. The dog was found lying in the snow, her leg broken, belly slit open, looking like someone had cut off part of her insides. What kind of animal would be so vicious towards a poor dog?"

"Was the dog running around on its own?"

"John, my neighbor's son always takes her out."

"So, what did John say?"

"He's not back yet."

"Aren't the police looking into that?" Saima was heartsick; they cared more about the dog than the missing people. "What do police look like? What do they do?"

"They're ordinary people. They wear green uniforms. Some have guns, swords, or other weapons. They're generally friendly. They're all trained psychologists. When there are problems, when someone's out of control or something bad is happening, the police come to deal with it. Linda uses them often at the university."

"So, when your generator made an out-of-control noise, you could have called police instead of me? Or if someone wants to have sex with you, and you're not interested, police stop them?"

"The police maintain our customs, not our machines. If someone is violating customs the police bring things back to harmony. If the generator was so loud that it disturbed the neighbors, they could complain to the police that it violated their tranquility. If someone was refusing to have sex, the police would deal with it."

"How?"

"They would get the person to follow the appropriate customs."

Was a shower with your host's wife customary? "What else?"

"Let's say some people are living in a community and the majority of people decide they don't want them. The police would make them leave. Let's say someone brutally killed a dog. The police would try to find out who did it, and why."

Saima's hackles rose. "And when they found out...?"

"They would use psychology to restore harmony in the person, so that he wouldn't do such things anymore."

Saima let go of the breath he didn't realize he was holding. His life was not contingent on this interview. He would use it to learn why 'police' were such a source of terror to his people.

"I'm hungry. I'd like something to eat first."

"I'll bring some crackers and cheese into the common room. She's waiting for you there. Want a tea?"

Saima nodded. The police sounded harmless, but he would have to keep his guard up.

7 MODERN AGE 3

"**I**'m Lieutenant Detective Tammy Finer. I'm investigating the death of Bella, the dog. Do you agree to talk to me?"

She was standing at the arched entry to Alex and Linda's common room. A large blaze crackled in the fireplace set into the wall, sending wisps of scented smoke into the room. Four low leather couches sat opposite each other in the center of the room, small tables guarding their armrests.

The curved walls were lined with shelves: some with worm-eaten books, some with shards of broken pottery, and others with fragments of leather or parchment.

Finer gazed blankly at the fire as she recited her script. She was medium height, with shoulder-length brown hair, deep blue eyes with long eyelashes, and an odd dagger-shaped mole on her left wrist. She carried a packsack, a collection of odd devices around her waist, and a sword over her shoulder. She wore an olive-green jacket with brass buttons over a tight, garish red sweater. Her knee-length skirt was crisply pleated.

Saima picked up a cracker and a little ball of cheese. "I've never met police before. Can you explain this to me? What's a detective?"

Finer's look of boredom vanished. "So it's true. You're really a northern savage." She took a breath, composing herself. "A Detective is a person who finds answers to problems by looking for clues and asking questions. I'm Class L, a Lieutenant, which means I'm trusted to make sure everything is done according to the Codes, without a Recorder present to monitor my behavior. The police operate by a strict set of rules. Do you agree to talk to me, Saima? I would like for you and me to be friends."

"No."

Linda practically jumped out of her chair, gesturing with her pipe. "Saima! Don't refuse! The Detective is a—"

"I appreciate your assistance, Professor, but I will handle this," the Lieutenant said.

"Isn't your Recorder supposed to be asking these questions?" Linda said. "You could be making Saima uncomfortable just by talking to him, and you won't have a transcript."

"It would be better, but he never showed up. I can't wait, because I'm supposed to meet my Captain in a couple of hours. I'm authorized to work without him; I'm not going to waste our time."

Saima sipped his tea. "Why can't I say 'no?' If the Lieutenant asked, that means I have a choice." He turned to Detective Finer. "What happens if I say 'no'?"

Finer clasped her hands in front of her. "I asked, because I want you to be comfortable. If you don't cooperate, you'll be sent back to the northlands, and I'll find some other way to get answers."

"If I get sent back to the northlands, what happens to Alex and Linda?"

"They won't be allowed to have a northern savage."

Saima felt Detective Finer's eyes drilling into his head. He stepped back and fidgeted with the fragments of pottery on the shelves. These people said they wanted him to be comfortable but walled him in with their bizarre rules. Saima had been hunted before. He knew not to let all escape routes get cut off, even if it meant giving some ground.

"I'll answer your questions."

She smiled, and sat at the end of a couch, patting the place next to her, and motioning to Saima.

"What's your name?"

Saima frowned. "Saima."

"What's your full name, including family name?"

"Saima, son of Jako, Leopard clan. Olive Tree clan from my father."

Linda's eyebrows went up in surprise, before her eyes squeezed closed in concentration.

Finer forced a smile. "There are no leopards or olive trees in the northlands. Are you sure you're not from the bear or lichen clan?"

"I know who I am. Do your interrogation rules allow you to mock me? That makes me very uncomfortable."

Finer's embarrassment almost matched the red of her sweater. "Sorry. I was trying to make a joke. I'm not very good at jt."

"We won't report the offensive joke, Detective. Just don't take away our savage." Linda grinned. "He's terrific in the shower. My husband is waiting for a turn with him."

Saima's embarrassment almost matched Finer's sweater. " Lieutenant, I know my ways are strange to you. I'll try to explain things as best I can."

"Thank you." She touched his shoulder. "Saima, where were you last night? Did you see anything unusual?"

"I was at the Old Post Club, responding to a message."

"What time did you go? When did you come back?"

"I left here for the Old Post after lunch."

"Can you be more precise?"

"The wagons weren't operating when I came back."

Alex chimed in. "The northern savages don't measure time like we do. They come from a land where the sun can disappear for months. You won't get a more precise answer."

"I'm going to take a copy of your door records, Alex," Finer said.

She turned back to Saima. "How did you get back from there?"

"I ran."

"You what?"

"Ran."

Detective Finer seemed to be having trouble digesting this. "Did you see anything unusual while running?"

"There was a dead black dog on the ground."

"Bella," the others whispered.

"I also saw human footprints and a set of dog tracks leading to a hole in the river. The dog had made it to the other side, but not the person."

Linda grabbed Alex's arm. "You have to write a poem for poor Bella." She put her head on his shoulder and sniffled. Detective Finer dabbed at her eyes with a tissue.

Saima had just told them of the death of a human, but these people were weeping for a dog.

Detective Finer composed herself. "Did you see any other animals?"

"No."

"Okay. Please wait while I get my equipment from the wagon."

Saima's hackles rose. "Equipment?"

"For Sphere Traveling. I have to communicate with Bella."

This was too bizarre. You don't Travel between Spheres to consult dead animals.

He calmed himself as Finer re-entered the room carrying a large canvas bag. She was wearing a long, grey cloth coat, and a tasseled leather headband. She sat on the floor with her back to the fire, and carefully emptied the bag beside her.

She looked carefully around the room, meeting everyone's eyes. "You must not disturb my Traveling. Don't interrupt the song the datura sings for me." Her gaze stopped at Alex. "You will assist. Please."

Finer drank the contents of a small glass vial, stood up, and slipped off her coat. She was naked except for a gray breechcloth and the headband. Why did she have to be naked? Saima watched her pick up a drum, somewhat surprised that it was made of metal, with a plastic skin. How could she go anywhere with that? A real drum for Traveling between Spheres is made from the wood of the cosmic tree that rises between them. When beating it, you climb its branches. If she wanted to reach Bella, Finer should be using an inverted tree, with its roots in the air, its branches in the ground. Either way, the drum should have been wood and animal skin; not something manufactured. Plastic had no life-story to tell, no matter how pleasant the sound. Tales of the Tunniq Sphere Travelers described drums covered with human skin. No drugs were needed with such powerful instruments.

The lights dimmed as Finer chanted and beat a simple rhythm. Saima couldn't make out the words as she closed her eyes and began to move about the room, seemingly in a deep trance. Her tongue darted through her lips, her hips swayed, her head tossed to and fro as she writhed. Saima was also being pulled into a trance, but not of Traveling. Finer was beautiful; slender and lithe, with pert breasts and muscular legs. Her shoulder-length brown hair swayed, as if the curtain between Spheres was taunting; dancing and inviting travelers to pass through.

The beat held fast as she stuck out her tongue, jerked her head backwards, and suddenly strutted across the room, growling like a leopard. She stopped in front of Saima, her head rolling slowly from side to side. Her eyes faced his but were seeing some place beyond. Her chant was an unintelligible, guttural moan. The fireplace flared and hissed.

She dropped to her knees and lifted up her arms. Alex silently strode over and wrapped her Sphere Traveling coat around her, pulling her hands through the sleeves. She rose and stepped into the chamois trousers he placed in front of her. He wrapped a headdress on her, consisting of five leather bands. Each was tapered on one end, the other end rounded, like a snake; glass beads simulated eyes. Little plastic bones hung on Finer's high, cream-colored moccasins.

She stood upright in front of Saima. Her eyes rolled loosely in their sockets, like small rafts on a storm-tossed sea. Her lips were still chanting, but without any sound. Saima gazed at her coat. A metal deer skeleton was affixed over each breast. A single square hole, the entrance to the pathways between Spheres, was over her belly. Little boats, rafts, bows and arrows, the moon, the sun, and some stars lay in a fractal pattern around it.

She dropped to her hands and knees and started gasping rapidly. A kind of mewing, beseeching noise came from her throat. Saima saw more snakes on her back; leather strips half a span wide, five spans long.

Saima was impressed by the Sphere-Traveling costume. It was clearly the work of an expert. He wasn't impressed by the person wearing it, clearly a dilettante.

She lifted her head, and Alex tied an apron to her front, attaching it around her neck and waist. A thick line went about two thirds of the way down the center of the apron, and then branched downward into thinner lines. This was dangerous. The inverted tree confirmed she was traveling to the Abode of Confinement, below the Spheres, where people acted as animals. A large brass mirror swung loosely from the apron. On one side of it was the image of snakes and wolves. The other side was highly polished, and Finer sank deeper into her trance when she looked at it.

The drumming resumed; the chanting found a voice again. Finer alternated between crawling around on all fours, writhing seductively in front of Saima, and jerking her limbs as if she was the puppet of a drunken puppeteer. The snakes hissed and danced, their black, glossy tongues darting in and out.

Finer suddenly tripped. She fell, crashing into the wall, knocking down parchments and shards of pottery from the shelves. She tried to right herself, but tumbled backwards, a silent scream on her face, her hand furiously striking the drum.

Saima bolted upright and yelled urgently at Alex. "Come on!"

It was clear Alex had no idea what was going on.

Saima tossed the drum to the side and lifted her arms. "Come on" he yelled again, more urgently. These people clearly had no understanding of Sphere Traveling, of its dangers. That could be useful.

"We're not supposed to touch her," Linda said. "Why are you so concerned? I can also dance naked, if you'd like."

"Alex! Grab her feet."

The two of them lifted her off the shards she had been rolling on. The leather coat had protected her.

"Get these things off of her."

"She said not to disturb—"

"Do what I tell you! Didn't you see her trip and fall? That's not part of her Traveling. She's not where she wants to be."

Alex nodded, and pulled off her moccasins and trousers. Saima removed the apron, coat, and headdress, carefully keeping his arms away from the snakes. Alex reached for her breechcloth.

"Leave that," Saima hissed. "Linda, take Alex's place." Alex opened his mouth, but Saima cut him off. "None of you understand what's going on; your talk could doom Detective Finer. You must obey me without a word if you want her to survive." They nodded silently.

Linda adjusted the breechcloth while Saima averted his eyes. They dressed her in her regular skirt and sweater, leaving the jacket with brass buttons for later. Finer lay on her back, rocking her head, her moans occasionally punctuated by screams in some bizarre tongue. She hissed and spat, but nothing came from her mouth. Her eyes were smoky; her hair smelled burnt.

Saima took one of her hands in his. "Everybody leave."

Linda looked at the floor, at all the things from the shelves. "Don't touch—" she began to whisper.

"Leave silently."

Alex sat in his place, staring. Saima stared back, and then looked down at Finer lying on her back, panting urgently. With a circular motion, he rubbed the air above her belly, over the entrance to the pathways between Spheres. He slowly lifted his eyes, giving Alex an icy glare.

Alex couldn't know the degree of threat in that motion, but decided it was time to leave. Saima also had no idea of what threat there was in it, but was glad he had taken it the right way. Saima didn't like misleading his hosts, but at the moment he was more concerned with the Detective's survival. Holding Finer's hand, Saima closed her eyes with his other hand, leaned against the wall, and let himself go.

8 MODERN AGE 4

Traveling between Spheres was usually done with a proper drum, with proper clothes and preparation. Never in haste. But Finer was in the Abode of Confinement because of Saima, and she was in trouble. It was said in that place formless entities took on substance, able to inflict all kinds of harm. Time and space were different there, and Finer might have already undergone an eternity of who knows what kind of suffering.

"Lights off, fire down," he barked, and the room went dark. He bent his face over Finer, whose breath was coming in fast, short gasps. Pinching her nostrils closed, he put his lips to hers and breathed slowly, in and out, in and out... Her breathing eased, came more evenly. She was drenched in sweat. He kept his lips next to hers, and softly asked the Source of Blessing to protect him. The dim lights from the fire danced against the walls, casting eerie shadows as they dissolved. Saima shut his eyes and put his fingers over her mouth. He pressed lightly as his hands, then his arms, and then the rest of him slipped into Finer, into her trance. He was startled to find he was an ant held snugly between her teeth. She was a blue serpent flying around the ceiling of Alex's common room. Down, he urged her, descend towards the world. She shot painfully towards the floor, passing through something; he didn't know what. The sound of the crackling fireplace faded, giving way to shouts of irredeemable fury.

Saima was startled to recognize the place. He was inside a flickering, dancing magnetic curtain: the aurora, the Northern Lights.

Finer lay on a pallet of emptiness. A teenage boy was kicking her in the face and ribs, screaming furiously. "You don't care about people, just the damn dog. My life was worthless to you."

John, who fell through the ice. He looked at Saima, sneering. "She disgusts you too."

"Let her go."

"You were more concerned about my life than she was. You mourned for me at the river. For that I'll let you leave."

"Not without her."

"Why do you care? You think she's a foolish dilettante."

Saima frowned. John was right.

"The minds of people who don't belong here are transparent to those who do. I know what you think of Detective Finer. Including what you think of her naked." John laughed. "Maybe that's why you want her back."

Saima couldn't argue about that either. "She's a living person. As misguided as her quest is, she doesn't belong here. Think of how you valued life before you lost yours. You died because you wanted to save a dog. Your beliefs were the same as Finer's."

John stared as the taste of warm dog flesh flickered through Saima's thoughts. "Those beliefs were right in the Abode of Life, not here."

He resumed kicking and spitting at Finer. She moaned, trying feebly to protect herself. A hazy, unformed plan came to Saima's mind. Shutting out his thoughts, he concentrated on the senses he usually lived by. But there was no wind here; there was no sense of heat or cold. The light was diffuse; there was no point from which one could establish position. The only smell was his own sweat. Everything he used for judgment was missing. But he could grasp, almost touch emotions: Finer's terror and John's rage. There was another vague feeling, diffuse and undefined, yet as real as anything could be in this strange place: loneliness.

"Tammy, it's Saima. I'm here to take you back."

To his surprise, the feeling intensified. He flinched as understanding crashed into him. It wasn't Finer's loneliness; it was John's. He felt abandoned by the world he had recently left, by people more concerned about a dog. Finer embodied that abandonment. Could Saima allay his misery?

He tensed, as he sensed someone behind him. A short, muscular man with a small, flat face, and slightly slanted eyes beckoned him.

"My apprentice left a weapon for you in Linda's common room. Use it," he whispered.

Saima looked back at John, whose face was ashen, his body trembling at the sight of this person.

The short man smiled. "You better save her. She traveled five thousand years to save you."

"What?"

"Go ahead. Stalling might have cost your life."

Saima reached his left hand back into the Abode of Life, into Linda's common room, and picked up a broken, blood-stained potshard from the floor. Screaming, he swung it savagely at John, stabbing him hard in the chest before he could react. Blood pumped out of his ragged wound like water from a faucet, as his other-worldly body dissolved. Saima had forced John to complete his journey to the Abode of the Dead. The aurora would be dimmer today.

Detective Finer lay on her back, her eyes barely open. Her skin was clammy, her breathing slow and weak.

Saima threw himself protectively over her, stroking her hair and whispering urgently for her to return with him to the Abode of Life. He put his lips back to hers, to fill her lungs with air, to fill her heart with a desire to claw her way back. A different feeling of desire was clawing its way into his own heart. He pushed it aside; it wasn't appropriate.

Saima had no idea how long the datura would keep her uprooted. He had to abandon time to pull her out of the Abode of Confinement. He had to be a chain around her ankles, dragging her towards the world.

Reaching for her abandoned Traveling costume, he took his knife and slashed off the sleeves. He put his legs through the widened armholes and put the coat and apron upside down over himself, thereby turning the tree the right way. Careful not to slice into any of the snakes, he cut the headdress into pieces and tossed the scraps in the fire.

Saima lay back down over Finer, stroking her hair, looking deep beyond her eyes.

He pictured the shard of clay he had used to send John to the Abode of the Dead. He had only caught a momentary glimpse as it had arced into his vision and then into John's chest. Yet he could see every detail with utter clarity. Patterns, parts of words were dug in the clay by a sharp instrument. Saima saw the stone point engraving lines; etching its message to... he didn't know whom. But he knew the message was personal, and that confused him.

The shard faded from Saima's mind. He was still on top of Finer, his lips hovering over hers, his eyes gazing into her depths. He saw her stirring and resumed breathing into her. She struggled briefly and took a deep breath on her own. She wrapped her arms around Saima and hugged him with what little strength she had. She planted a kiss on his cheek, and then gestured for him to roll off her.

"Thank you, my friend," she whispered.

The common room was around them, its floor under them. They lay beside each other next to the fireplace, its painted flame frozen in motion. Their heads touched one wall of the large room, their feet the other. Saima took her hands and held them one at a time in the flame, warming them. He rubbed fire into her cheeks, restoring their color. She reached an arm up and touched the ceiling.

"Help me, Saima. I thought we were back in the Abode of Life, but it's not supposed to be like this."

"We're feeling the effects of your drug."

"How can... Where are we?"

"We're in the Abode of Life, but not in its measurements. None of the dimensions of existence will mean anything till the medicine leaves your body."

"I'm scared."

"Look at the clock over the fire-place."

"It's broken."

"No. You don't see the hands moving because it's part of time, which doesn't apply here. When the hands move again, we're back in ordinary existence. Now open your mouth as wide as you can."

Finer looked at him quizzically, but obeyed. Saima took a pencil from a table, and stuck the blunt end down her throat as far back as he could go without hurting her. He moved it around, while pressing his other hand against her belly. Tears came to her eyes; she tried weakly to move away from him. She sniffled, and then retched, her stomach emptying out. The hand that had been on her stomach went to her hair, soothing her, calming her while she vomited and wept. The datura had to let go.

Saima stood up and took off the vomit-covered Sphere Traveling costume. He threw the chamois coat and apron with the entrance to the pathways, the tree, and snakes into the fire. The frozen flames roared and sparked, hungry for this dark meal. The stench of burning plastic, the rank smell of burning leather seeped across the room. Saima took some tissues, put them into her hand, and moved it to her face. Finer panted as Saima put his arm around her shoulders. The silence was opaque except for the ticking of the clock, the crackle of the flames.

The hands of the clock moved forward. Finer grabbed her temples, her stomach; she reached for her groin, burrowed her face in the floor. She gasped, her eyes open wide; she screamed, her eyes scrunched closed. It was as if every kick from John came back to her, separate, but at once. She whimpered, grabbing at Saima for help. He held her in his arms, stroking her hair, whispering soothing words.

The coat was ashes; the hands of the clock had traveled far before Finer managed to lift her head from his shoulder. She looked at his eyes with wonder.

"I've never met anyone like you."

"Your first northern savage."

"It's more than that, Saima." She stood up and pulled off her now filthy sweater.

Saima averted his eyes and passed Finer her jacket. "That's what friends are for."

"Saima, I feel horrible for how I treated you. I feel horrible for how I ignored John. He was going to punish me for eternity."

"You're back and he's dead. He can't do anything in this world. Do something to relieve his loneliness."

"What can I do?"

"I don't know. Make him the focus of your investigation. Try to find his body."

Finer sighed. "I suppose I can investigate the person as part of the dog inquiry, without getting Committee approval."

"I'll help."

"Thanks. You know more about what happened than anyone else." She walked over to the fireplace, warming her hands. "Is there something I can help you with?"

That was something Saima hoped to hear.

Linda's voice came through the intercom. "You did it, Saima. We're coming in."

"No! It's still too dangerous!"

Finer gave him a worried look and grabbed his shoulders. "Still?"

"Until we deal with your Sphere Traveling, you're in danger of getting yourself and others into a great deal of trouble. It's clear you had little idea of what you were doing."

"I've never had this happen before. Usually I take datura, dance around a while, have fantastic visions, and then fall asleep. When I wake up I feel refreshed and creative, and use my imagination to better understand whatever problem I'm investigating."

Saima walked over to the shards of clay lying on the floor. He picked some up, looking at them, turning them, sniffing, gently biting some. He placed them carefully back on the shelves. Finer joined him, looking at the shards, the shelves, at Saima.

"How did you design your Sphere-Traveling costume?"

"I bought it."

"Where? Do you understand what they sold you?"

"I got it at the Shaman Shop. They have beautiful costumes from all the top designers. Mine was a genuine Shirokogoroff, copied from an ancient costume in the University Museum. It wasn't the prettiest, but it's supposed to be the most effective."

"And what happened today never happened before?"

"No. Can you explain it to me?"

"I understand Sphere Traveling. The costume means something only in the presence of someone who understands it. You clearly don't."

Finer looked at the smoldering remains of her previously treasured costume. "Destroy my drum. It's also dangerous."

"Your drum's a toy."

Detective Finer gazed at him, seemingly lost in thought, searching... "You are truly my teacher..." She inclined her body gently towards him, her long brown hair tumbling all around.

This was embarrassing. Was she doing that on purpose? Saima wished she had a sweater or something under the jacket, as he stared at the cleavage in front of his eyes. "Please," he begged. "Don't."

Finer straightened herself and smiled. "Will you teach me about Traveling between Spheres? I want to send my spirit flying."

"There is no separate spirit. There is just the person." He turned back to the shards on the shelves, but Finer was at the front of his mind: naked, writhing, hissing. He tried to focus his thoughts on the pieces of clay. They looked like fragments of shattered bowls, covered with inscriptions that were at once unreadable, but familiar.

"Will you take me as an apprentice?"

"Will you keep your clothes on when you're with me?"

"You don't like the way I look? Did you like Linda better? Many people enjoy her talents." Finer wore a smile and pretend pout. "That's why they love to visit her and Alex. But you wouldn't have known about that." She picked up her weapons, strapping the short sword over her shoulder. She buttoned her jacket all the way.

"I've never had an apprentice, Detective. Why do you think I can teach you?"

"Listen to me, Saima. You didn't come from the northlands in order to have sex with the Erbils."

"Who?"

"Alex and Linda Erbil. I'm guessing that you didn't come for the sake of being their repairman either. You came here to accomplish something.

Tell me what it is; maybe I can help you. We'll work together till you're sent back home."

Saima moved away from the shelf and began to pace. His mind raced as he stood in front of the fireplace, watching the flames repeat their programmed leaps. He had no idea how he was going to recover what had been stolen from his people; he wasn't even sure what it was. Finer was dangerous, but with the danger, came power. Or did he want her help because of how she looked naked?

"If you're my apprentice, then you'll have to come home with me. You better think about it. Talk it over with your family. You said your Captain is supposed to be here now. Isn't he? Talk to him about it."

"I don't need to talk it over with anyone... I'm Police." Finer smiled. "Just Wendy, my team captain; she'll want to rip my heart out if I tell her I'm leaving. She's not here, and it's not her decision anyways." Finer stood by the shelves, running her finger lightly over the fragments. "You still haven't told me why you're here, Saima."

"I want to recover something that was stolen a long time ago."

"Perfect! I'm a Detective. We'll look for clues together." She had a broad smile on her face. "You'll help me with the dog."

"And John?"

"Him too."

Saima walked over to the door, wondering if she took her detective work as seriously as her Sphere Traveling. "We better let the others back in." He looked for a handle, but there was none. He stared in frustration, and then remembered. "Saima, open." The pneumatic valve hissed softly as the door slid to the side. He watched it, wondering if by trusting the police he had just destroyed his mission.

"Think about my proposal," Tammy said as she walked through the doorway.

Linda surveyed the damage to her collection. "Saima, how did you do that?"

"Do what?"

"I don't know... all those strange—"

Saima sighed, and tried to compose a simple explanation. He looked at the consternation painted on her face. "Later. I need to rest."

9 EARLY BRONZE AGE 1

Tanayt Asenath was not supposed to do housework. According to the marriage contract her father had insisted upon, Jacob could not ask his wife to do things like clean their home, cook meals, or wash clothes. Her father felt, and Jacob agreed, that she was too great a scholar to devote her energy to such mundane activities.

She inspected the long beige skirt, pleased that the stains from this morning's lesson were gone. Jacob had not asked her to hang the laundry on the roof, as she was now doing. He was dead, and the laundry needed to be done. Although her children were old enough to take care of these chores themselves, Asenath enjoyed doing ordinary things.

The Ebers looked to her as their leader because of her vast wisdom. Other people treated her deferentially because she was the head of the Ebers, or Clay People as some called them. People also treated her deferentially because she was stunningly beautiful. Tall, her full figure and long limbs gave Asenath a commanding presence. Both men and women were afraid to look past the long lashes into her violet eyes. Such beauty, people reasoned, could only be a result of divine favor. Her straight black hair was always covered by a kerchief and was said to possess mystical powers.

Asenath accepted her beauty, her wisdom as a gift. The former, she ignored; the latter, she nurtured and fed. She didn't feel arrogant about either. "Tanayt" wasn't a name, but a title her people had bestowed on her. It was reserved only for the greatest sages, for the most able of leaders, and hadn't been given to anyone in hundreds of years. Certainly not to a woman.

Her father had been the community's leader. After he died while fleeing an assassin, Asenath's husband took his place. Jacob in turn was killed by a mysterious disease a couple of years later, after having spent a few days among the mosquito-infested marshes. Asenath had already been teaching in the Academy and was a trusted advisor to the community judges. Ordinary people, both Eber and non-Eber, came to her for advice, for counsel, for support. When Jacob passed away, it wasn't even a question as to who the next leader, the next head of the Academy would be. It wasn't a matter of nobility, of descent. Asenath was appointed by the love of the people.

The Ebers were tradesmen and merchants. They were also problem-solvers for the other inhabitants of the land: the Madai in the towns, and especially for the Marsh dwellers. These people were plagued by Sheyds, quasi-human sprites and troublemakers. The story behind them is that they were in the midst of being fashioned when the Source of Blessing hung the yellow moon in the sky, marking the end of the creation process. The Sheyds were there, but not fully. Resentful, they took vengeance by wreaking havoc on the lives of completely formed, fully sentient humans. Many Sheyds held the hope of taking over and retroactively changing things, so that they would be the solid ones. It was a battle that began moments after the dawn of man. The Ebers had devised a way to trap the Sheyds using specially inscribed clay bowls, giving the humans a decided edge. Sheyd trapping was a distraction, but they couldn't refuse the pleas of people desperate for protection from hidden causes of trouble.

Asenath's house was small: typical two-story wattle and daub. Its exterior was the rust color of the local clay. Corner posts supported a wood roof frame, with thick, square crossbeams that extended out past the walls. Many people decorated the protruding roof beams of their houses with carvings, or hung beads and ribbons from them. Asenath's roof beams were plain. There were no beads or ribbons; there were no carved hands on them. So why was there a hand on one? As she watched, a large, muscular arm covered with coarse hair swung onto the roof beam. A leg followed. A face and torso she didn't know stood at the end of the beam, leering. The man balanced on one leg and scratched his groin.

"Your husband didn't let you be a woman; didn't even let you do the laundry like a woman is supposed to. I'm a real man, and I'm going to make you feel like a real woman."

"In the merit of the righteous, protect me. In the merit of wisdom, protect me." Asenath's whispers were inaudible to her visitor.

"Turn around for your own sake. Go away, and we will forget this happened." She addressed him calmly. "I don't allow you near me."

"I didn't ask for your permission."

"Are you married? Do you live near here? You don't look familiar." She smiled.

"I just moved to Lagash with my family. We're building our home on the eastern road. I heard about your body. I see the stories are true. Now it's time for a closer look." He took a step forward but stopped suddenly, as if he had walked into an invisible wall. Teetering from encountering something unexpected, he tried to steady himself. His foot slipped. Flailing, he just managed to grab the end of the beam with one hand as he fell to the side.

Asenath walked over to the fence surrounding her roof and peered in his eyes. He leered at her again, his neatly combed hair and clean-shaven cheeks contrasting with the ugliness of his plans. He tried to lift his leg back over the beam. He couldn't. He swung his other arm, to try to get a better hold with both hands. He couldn't. He gripped the beam as hard as he could with one hand, digging his fingernails into the wood. Asenath noted the makeshift ladder he had used to climb up, that he was desperately swinging his feet towards but was unable to reach. He was hanging over her garden, where beans were held up by closely spaced wooden stakes. If he fell, he might end up like a sieve.

"Don't worry, I won't let you fall." Asenath smiled at him. He swung his arm wildly, trying to get a better hold of the beam. He remained suspended by his one hand.

Asenath turned back to her laundry. She smiled at her children's clothes as she clipped them to the rope; there was great satisfaction in simple activities.

There were just a few socks and towels left in the last basket when the man gave up on freeing himself. "Help me, please. I didn't mean what I said. I was only trying to get your attention."

Asenath took a dishtowel from the basket. She had to give a lesson in the Academy in the evening, and she wanted the clothes to be dry enough to take down and fold before then. She clipped the towel next to the shirts.

"Please, have pity; don't leave me here like this." There was an edge of panic to his voice. "I heard you are a wise and merciful woman. Please be merciful to me. I wasn't going to hurt you."

Asenath walked back over and glanced at him. Some neighbors had come out and were looking to see what the commotion was about.

"Please, let me down. Undo your magic."

"It's not magic."

"Asenath, are you all right?" her next-door friend called from atop her own roof. "I'll send my daughter to the Academy, to let your children know what's going on."

She didn't want her children to be upset by this, but she also didn't want to keep them in the dark about something they were entitled to know about. "The situation's under control. Thank you."

Now the invader started to scream. "Mercy, help me!"

More people gathered.

"Look into my eyes, and tell me why you climbed up to my roof."

He was sobbing. "I just moved to this town. I heard that you are the most beautiful woman alive, that looking at you was like looking at the source of all beauty. I realized that I had to have you. Please, be kind."

Asenath spoke loudly, as much to the gathering crowd as to the man dangling by one hand from her roof beam. "A person who is kind when it is time to be cruel will end up being cruel when it's time to be kind."

"When will you let me go?"

"Why do you presume I will ever let you go?"

"Ja'ix will never let go of you, your children, or your children's children. I curse you with my death," the man screamed as he removed his hand from the beam. A gasp rose from the gathering crowd as the man remained suspended in the air, strapped in place by invisible bonds. Sweat poured from his brow as his hands and feet jerked around, trying to find a hold. He twisted and turned, he kicked and he cried. He could do everything except move from where he hung.

The crowd below grew, as Asenath returned to the clothesline. She hung up the garment in her hand, and turned to the sound of a pair of feet coming up the stairs. Her friend from the next roof approached her.

"I'm afraid. What if Chief Taiku comes, and brings soldiers? They might decide to kill all of us just to amuse themselves. What if one of the Sphere Travelers comes to free him? Asenath," she whispered urgently, "what if every thief or brigand were to suffer such a fate? A quarter of the town would be in the air."

"I'll deal with the Chief when he comes. If more thieves and brigands were to suffer this kind of fate, maybe they wouldn't make up a quarter of the town. And several Sphere Travelers are on their way now, bringing spirit rope-cutters," she said without a trace of mockery. "One of them is actually climbing the stairs now."

In fact, three people were coming up the stairs: Aua, a short, muscular and powerful shaman with a small, flat face, and slightly slanted eyes. Strangers from afar who mocked his appearance quickly learned to retract their words.

Most Sphere Travelers could get to only one other Sphere from the Abode of Life. Asenath suspected that Aua could reach more, perhaps the Sphere of Splendor, maybe even Strength. There were thirty-two mysteries, thirty-two pathways amongst the Spheres, and getting lost among them could be much worse than deadly. Wisdom and Understanding were near the top, and between them lay Knowledge.

Aua had his two frail-looking apprentices, Aleku and Geordi with him. Asenath was careful not to look in their direction until they had time to prepare. After a minute she turned to them, their faces on the floor in respect. The Traveler addressed her: "Teacher..."

"Please get up," Asenath said. She was embarrassed every time they did this, but they would be humiliated if she refused to acknowledge their bowing and scraping before her. "I am not the One to whom you should bow. I am not the Source of Blessing."

They got up slowly, holding their hands sideways in front of their faces, a sign of submission, of respect. The two apprentices kept their eyes downcast, looking only at Asenath's feet. Aua slowly lifted his eyes to hers.

She smiled warmly. "You are here to free this man, who tried to steal my honor." She gestured towards the side of the roof.

"Only if you will it. The man's daughter suspected that he had gotten himself in trouble once again, and prevailed upon me for assistance."

"I do not will that he be free, but I won't interfere in your attempt to release him. Do as you wish."

The three visitors fell on their faces again till Asenath finished descending the stairs. They began their drumming and chanting immediately. It was loud; it was annoying, as was their prancing on the roof above her. The moans from her attacker had already faded to background noise, and she now had to move the shaman's performance away from her senses. Asenath pulled some manuscripts from a shelf, some tobacco from a jar, lit her pipe and began to read. All the sounds, the vibrations paled into nothingness as her mind dove into the texts, danced with the words and letters. Her heart flew as insights took to the air, soaring like a flock of swans rising as one from a marsh.

Students at the Academy had been shocked that morning when Asenath instructed them to carve flat oak staffs, about four spans long, and a hand's breadth wide. They were to be a gift for the Chief in appreciation for his protection, she explained. The students nodded, understanding it to mean protection from the Chief himself. Handing out carving blades and long, straight planks, she told them to consider the assignment a meditation on wood and death. Their previous exercises had all been about knowledge, about ideas.

The whole person is capable of touching the Source of Blessing, Asenath explained; not just some intangible spirit. Human existence can be sanctified through study, honest business dealings, or weapon-making. She warned the students that any staff that wasn't properly carved would result in its maker being expelled from the Academy and the community.

This was all strange enough, but they loved and respected Asenath. She then proceeded to add consternation to their feelings. Standing outside the Academy entrance, she took a carved staff like she had told them to make, but with obsidian blades embedded along the edges. With a couple of sudden overhead swings, she beheaded a donkey that was tethered there. The beast's splattered blood was a large part of the reason for the laundry she was hanging to dry.

The lesson tonight was to be the value of life, and its cost. She read, she pondered, she meditated... Her students were counting on her for insight, and she in turn wanted to give them the life hiding in the texts, waiting to be released.

She became aware of the shadows in front of her. She lifted her head in acknowledgement, and gave her visitors time to prepare themselves.

"Is he leaving with you?" This time, to make a point, she didn't tell them to get off the floor. Asenath knew that all the conjuring the three of them had tried wasn't enough to undo the invisible bonds by which she had tied the man to her roof beam.

"No, Teacher, he remains as you left him. Chief Taiku is coming, with some of his soldiers. Word is that he's furious."

"Be blessed, and be wise, my friend," she said. It would be rude to Aua to acknowledge his apprentices. "I am pleased to see you and will be pleased if you leave in health."

They scrambled off the floor and left.

Asenath understood the warning about the Chief. She also understood the reason behind Taiku's rumored rage.

He had been her best friend when they were both children. They played together, ran together, got into mischief together. She always won their foot races, he always sped past her on their math contests, calculating solutions to complex problems they made up together. When one had troubles, it was to the other that he or she turned.

It had been in the meadows west of town. They had both recently reached childbearing age, though neither was thinking of marriage. That would have meant breaking up their friendship; the Ebers and Madai married within their own people. Asenath had arranged to meet some girlfriends to pick raspberries, but the others never showed. When she didn't pass his window on her way home at the expected time in the late afternoon, Taiku quietly went searching for her. He found her lying on a flat stone at the far edge of the meadow, her clothes torn, her body bruised, her lips cracked and bleeding. The way she held her legs tightly together as she sobbed told him what had happened.

"Who?"

Asenath whispered the name of an older acquaintance of Taiku, a member of a related clan.

"Leave him to me." Taiku took water from his drinking flask, and washed her as well as he could, without further hurting her body or honor. They were about the same height, so Taiku put his shirt over her, and knotted the remains of her clothes together, giving her a modicum of modesty.

"Can you walk?"

She nodded weakly.

They walked together, Taiku supporting her; at times carrying her in his arms. As they approached town he let her modestly walk on her own, though he was ready to jump to her aid if she appeared to stumble. A crowd, seeing her clothes, her bruises and black eye, gathered around as a silent escort.

Asenath's mother saw them approaching, and with a wail ran to meet them. She took the weight of her daughter and brought her inside to a couch. She began to minister to her as Asenath's father came running in, alerted to the news.

"Who did this?" he asked Taiku.

Taiku repeated the name. "You leave him to me," he said, holding back tears. "It's my duty to protect— to avenge her."

"How did you know where to find her?"

"She's my closest friend."

The next day, the rapist's carcass was discovered on the rock where Taiku had found Asenath. He had been castrated, his mouth stuffed with the remains of his manhood, his hands and feet bound with twine.

Asenath went outside to wait for the Chief. They gazed at each other as he approached, no expression crossing their lips, a cloud of dust behind him and his soldiers.

"Chief Taiku." She bowed her head as he dismounted, lifting her hands in front of her face.

Four of his soldiers formed an ominous semi-circle around her. Taiku stood at the apex opposite her, his brother Vlad next to him. "My Teacher," the Chief said, nodding at her.

She walked up to him, eyes humbly downcast. She stopped an arm's length away, lifted her head, and stared challengingly into his face. As he met her look she grinned, and then suddenly sprinted away, racing down the narrow road. Taiku laughed and took off after her. His soldiers started to follow, but he waved them back. It didn't take him long to catch her.

"You're losing your racing legs."

She smiled at him. "It's not appropriate for you to discuss my legs."

"Sorry, let's talk about something else." He paused, giving her a wink. "Cube root, six thousand."

They both stood silently in the middle of the roadway, the perplexed soldiers and others watching from a distance. The sun hovered above the treetops in the distance, the long shadows creating a sense of mystery. Buzzing flies marked the rotting carcass of a hawk lying in the grass just to the side of the road. Taiku silently ground his boot heel in the dirt. Asenath stood stone still, the breeze afraid to move even a wisp of her hair.

"Eighteen point two," she yelled triumphantly. Modesty said they were too old to hug, but that didn't stop them from feeling the glow of the invisible bonds that joined them. They walked slowly back towards her house, ignoring the puzzled onlookers.

"What did you teach your students this morning?"

"The value of life. The cost of life. Kindness through cruelty." She had a faraway look, as her mind drifted back to her texts. "I assigned the students a meditation on wood and death."

"And?"

"Simon's designed a macana, a weapon good for slashing and chopping at enemies. That's the meditation. I've got the Academy students making them. Will you have the obsidian blades I asked for? The students don't know what they're making; I don't want them to panic."

"Maybe they should. The rumors are true. Ja'ix is headed to Lagash." Taiku reached into a pouch attached to his belt, and pulled out something small, wrapped in a cloth. He held his palm in front of Asenath as he uncovered a little hand, severed at the wrist. The person it came from couldn't have been more than seven or eight years old.

"A refugee gave this to me. It's his daughter's. One of Ja'ix's soldiers, a man named Omer, accused her of stealing something. This was her punishment."

"How did such cruelty come into the world?" Asenath whispered. She walked to the side and leaned on a tree, putting a hand over her eyes. She took a few deep breaths, straightened, and turned back to Taiku. "No. You must not panic; you can't let people who do such things intimidate you," she said, a fierce edge in her voice. She took the cloth Vlad offered her and wiped her eyes.

"You must return their cruelty to them, multiplied. Don't be afraid of being like them. You're not, no matter how vicious you have to get to stop them." She pointed at Abner. "If you capture any of their soldiers, impale them and leave them to die at the side of the road. If that even slows them down, it's worthwhile. And even if it doesn't, you won't be wrong to have tried."

"What if we have to kill children to defend ourselves?" another soldier asked.

Asenath's chest heaved as she took another deep breath. Her damp eyes were her only reply.

Taiku looked back towards her house. "Will you let your attacker go?"

"Had he come to steal my possessions I would have done nothing to him. But he came to steal my honor. You know I can't let that go."

"Release him, and leave him to me. I've told you: I'll protect you forever."

Asenath paused and considered his proposal. "As you will, it shall be done, Chief Taiku. But please first bind him with ropes, so he doesn't ruin my beans."

Taiku bowed towards her. "As you will, it shall be done, my Teacher."

He shouted instructions at his men. The hapless attacker was soon standing before them on the road, his hands bound behind his back. Taiku held the bone handle of his long, bronze knife out to Asenath. "Return his cruelty to him, multiplied."

Asenath frowned and turned her head. "That's your prerogative, my Chief."

"You want cruelty? Ja'ix will peel you like an over-ripe fruit." The attacker spat onto Taiku's face.

Without another word, the Chief grabbed the man's hair, dug the point of his knife into his throat, and sliced his head off. He had his men sit the corpse against a tree, and place the head on its lap.

"Bury him without a grave marker. Throw his head in the river so his name will be forgotten." Taiku marched off without a backward glance at Asenath, the onlookers, or the corpse.

10 EARLY BRONZE AGE 2

The long, grassy meadows on the western side of the Klee-Dekel River seemed alive. Undulating hills made it appear as if the meadows were breathing; rising and falling like the chest of a giant. The tall grasses were interrupted by sprinklings of raspberry bushes, the occasional cluster of fruit-trees. A few creeks lined by bulrushes ran through the meadows. Rabbits, gophers and gazelles gathered at the scattered ponds, under the watchful eyes of foxes and cheetahs. Small birds trilled as they cleaned the air of insects. Red-winged falcons, their wingspans as long as the height of a man, circled under the clouds perusing the buffet spread out below.

At this season, the Elam shepherds were in the foothills rather than the high mountain pastures. As their herds ate their way through the plains, they would move their camps towards the Klee-Dekel, eventually getting close enough to spend a few weeks fishing before heading back to their mountains.

A hummingbird hovered over a man lying flat on his back, picking at the flesh of his exposed heart with its elongated beak. The man and the bird were depicted on a square leather talisman, its chiseled lines highlighted with charcoal. They were portrayed from above, below, and the sides all in one drawing. A sheep-gut thong suspended the engraving halfway down the muscled chest of the man wearing the leather engraving. Under the grizzly talisman, hammered metal plates were attached to a suede shirt. A knife with a blue, jeweled handle hung from a cloth belt holding up leather pants. Blue paint covered his face, matching the deep color of the man's eyes. A metal forehead plate over a leather helmet ridged with dark blue bird feathers completed the uniform. Until he removed the talisman, he was Huitzil, the hummingbird Master of War rather than Vlad, the Chief's brother. Three of the men with him wore similar armor, but without the talisman or paint; they were themselves.

The remains of a small deer raised a tall column of smoke from the smoldering coals of their fire. The soldiers hadn't taken the long trail into the hills for the sake of a meal. The deer, the smoke, was to help the Elam find them. They waited silently, listening to the people gathering on the other side of the slope.

Huitzil stood and walked towards the crest. He was pleased to see so many stern-looking men rise up to meet him on the other side. Some carried spears, some sticks. A few had bows in their hands and quivers on their backs. Many were unarmed, not having considered the possibility that the visitors were hostile.

The Elam had clans, similar to the Madai. Unlike the Madai, their clan leaders still made the important decisions. None of them were here though. They were at their encampments, nursing their babies, looking after the houses, cooking... Although the Clan Mothers didn't like to over-rule actions or decisions their men sometimes had to make on the spot, they had the authority to do so. The men in turn avoided making decisions that were likely to be overturned.

Huitzil wasn't going to put any of them on the spot. He was, however, going to deliver an important message.

He took a few steps towards them. The Elam flinched, and gave a collective start as he approached, putting their hands protectively over their hearts. Huitzil ran his eyes along the line of men, meeting their glares with his own.

"We're having a War Dance in five days."

Except for the pounding of hummingbird wings, silence hung in the still air. After a moment, Zeresh, the only woman among them, stepped forward. "Why are you telling us this? Are we supposed to attack you now, so you can jump on us and eat our hearts? Why are you declaring war on us?"

"We're not. We want you to Dance beside us." Vlad took the leather talisman off from his chest. "We need you to join us in the battle. You know the stories the refugees tell; they've passed by your homes. A river of destruction is coming towards us."

The woman who had spoken out jabbed her spear in the air at an invisible foe. "We won't let anyone take our homes."

Vlad walked over to her, deliberately standing in reach of the spear. "Listen to the refugees' descriptions of the invaders. Act according to their words, not your dreams of strength. My brother could easily level your encampments, take your animals and women if he was inclined to. He's not. The invaders are. They have destroyed towns much stronger than Lagash. Join our Dance, and Huitzil will eat their hearts."

Looking at each other for confirmation, the Elam dropped their weapons, and raised their hands in front of their faces, palms to the side.

"We will all come," Zeresh said.

"Will you fight alongside the Madai? Will you listen to the Chief? Or have your own wars?"

She shook her spear. "We're not stupid Marsh people, always fighting each other. Don't insult us."

Vlad nodded. He turned and started walking towards the other soldiers. This was good. If Zeresh made a commitment, none of the Elam were likely to challenge it.

The shepherds watched as Vlad and his escorts rode off. Their children were going to have to take over caring for the animals for a while. All the Elam had to be advised of this news. All had to prepare for war.

***

Balthan anxiously paddled his thin boat in the early dawn. The only sounds were the trilling of birds, the grunt of frogs, the chirp of insects. The Yellow Moon was a huge bright disk sliding towards the horizon. On most days, it rose later and disappeared more quickly than the small red moon, which came up before the day dissolved into darkness, and hung in the sky to greet the morning sun. The red moon, according to the stories, was a sky traveler that had been captured by the planet, and was trying desperately to flee. One day its mate would come to free it from the confines of its endless orbit, executing a cruel vengeance upon the captor.

Balthan knew these marshes; every bend in the streams, every island and islet. In the deeper waters the tall, dark reeds stood higher than a man. Green and thin, they made you feel you were in the center of a small, closed world.

Normally, Balthan would stop to gather wild grains that grew along the streams and islets. Normally he would stop to gather the berries that his children considered a special treat. He smiled as he reached his hands into the water and lifted out a beautiful oil-fish as it glided by, a gift for Asenath. For her, he would stop.

She was leader of the Ebers, who lived at the edge of Lagash. They were slow-tempered and quick-witted, able to see the motion, the flow of things, whether it was the logic of an argument or the movement of the winds. They could fix almost anything, because when they looked at a break, they saw it becoming broken, and so understood how to bring it back to a state of repair.

Most important to Balthan and his people was that the Ebers could trap Sheyds. They weren't known as the Fix People, though they fixed things. They weren't known as the Quick-Witted people. They were known as the "Clay People" because of the traps they made; engraved upside-down clay bowls.

The Sheyds had killed his cousin Qimiq's son, making it look like Balthan was responsible; Balthan was now fleeing his vengeful cousin as much as the Sheyds. He needed to reach the Clay People before either overtook him. A large iridescent, blue-green dragonfly hovered annoyingly over his skiff as he pictured Asenath's gentle face. He addressed Asenath as 'Protector;' she preferred he call her 'friend.'

He frowned as the image of her dark hair and violet eyes dissolved into a cascade of thick blond hair, green eyes, and flawless silver skin. A voluptuous Sheyd kneeled in front of him in his little skiff. She wore a thin cotton blouse and skirt, which clung tightly to every detail of her perfectly sculpted anatomy.

"My father doesn't like you, but I think you're cute. I've never been with a human." She put her arms around his neck, pressing her chest to his.

Balthan panicked. What did that mean? All his senses evaporated as her lips touched his, as her tongue entered his mouth, slid down his throat and then withdrew. He felt a hand on his pants, another pushing him down onto the soft pallet of sweet petals his skiff had become. His clothes fell apart as she climbed on to him. His breath disappeared; it belonged to her now.

"You taste good," she said, as she washed her green blood off his groin. "You're my first."

Balthan breath returned; he floated in a sea of ecstasy. It had never been like this. Not with his wife, not with his brother's wife, not with anyone. He took her hand. "Will you marry me?"

"You don't even know who I am."

"What's your name?"

"Lillian. Sheyds can't marry humans."

"Marry me, Lillian. We'll be together for eternity."

She wagged a finger at him. "If we married, you would become a little like a Sheyd, insubstantial. I would become a little like you, formed."

"You're perfectly formed."

She gazed into the distance, thinking aloud. "If my body was more human, no one could trap me. If you were a little insubstantial, you wouldn't die. Not while we were married."

"Please..."

"I have to talk to my father. I've never been raped before."

"What! I didn't rape you."

Her hand dissolved under his. Balthan flinched as he looked around. The dragonfly paused momentarily, as if examining him. The oil-fish he had just taken from the water smelled of rot; Balthan tossed it over the side. He looked at his clothes; exactly as they had been. He sweated in the cool air. What, if anything, had just happened?

The Yellow Moon had disappeared, and the Red Moon was waiting anxiously for the sun. The water under Balthan's skiff was getting shallower, and occasionally it scraped the muddy bottom. The reeds were getting thicker, taller; the Clay People weren't far. Balthan stood up, stepped onto the rocky shore, and bent down to pull up his canoe. The tall reeds rustled, and he lifted his head to find himself staring through the thick, dark air into Qimiq's scowling face. Around him, standing in their boats were other men of his clan, dressed for battle, their hair adorned with falcon feathers. They were all armed, with metal-tipped spears, clubs, and knives. This was no illusion.

His only chance was to attack, and he looked to see who he could disarm first.

"Cousin of mine, we come as kin."

Qimiq's words disarmed Balthan. "You're dressed for war."

"We'll deal with my son another time. Yesterday some Far Marsh people came. They stole two of our buffalo and cut an ear off the ones they didn't take. They destroyed reed islands and drowned chickens. We must have revenge."

"How do you know it wasn't Sheyds?"

"Balthan, you blame everything on Sheyds. The Clay People love you; they live off your fear. We knew you would come to see them, so we just waited here." Qimiq put his knife in its scabbard. "Unless Sheyds look and talk like Far Marsh people, it wasn't Sheyds."

Balthan considered the group of scowling men surrounding him, and the certain death if he attacked. Why would Qimiq invent a more serious battle if his purpose was to avenge his son? He could have easily killed Balthan. Was this something to do with the invaders the Dry-landers were worried about? "What's your intention?"

"Revenge. Will you join us?"

"Is there a choice? Me against my brother. My brother and I against my cousin. My cousin and I against my far cousin. The Low Marsh against the Far Marsh people. The Marsh people against the Dry-landers. The Marsh people and Dry-landers against the Elam. Our horizon against the far side of the horizon. Our world against the next. Our God against all Gods."

By now the sun was in the sky, burning off the drifting haze. A small green Fire Snake splashed playfully in the water not far from the men, occasionally darting its black, glossy tongue at Balthan and Qimiq. Blue Fire snakes were extremely poisonous; red, harmless. A green snake could be either.

A sudden clap of air, a black streak exploded with a shriek: a falcon smashed into the water, and then rushed away, the small snake flailing in its talons. Straight up the raptor went, carrying everyone's startled gaze. It paused, a flutter in front of the sun. The snake separated from its captor, and streaked downwards, exploding on a boulder. Little bits of bone and flesh scattered, a few splattering two of Qimiq's men.

Blanching, Qimiq turned to them: "Good-bye, my brothers. You lived well, and brought honor."

The men opened their mouths to answer, but paralysis was already setting in. They gasped, and collapsed straight and rigid into the water. The falcon fell, too, spiraling with its wings frozen in mid-flap. It thumped into the reeds, disappearing as quickly as it had appeared.

Their vengeance hadn't started, and already death was thrown into their midst.

11 EARLY BRONZE AGE 3

There was no blood, human or donkey, in this load of laundry; just a few tablecloths from the Academy. Donations to the school from communities west of Lagash had dried up, so Asenath stopped hiring people to do the washing. She tried to clear her mind of brooding thoughts as to why the donations ceased.

The excitement about the man who had climbed onto her roof had also dried up, although the tale became more dramatic with each re-telling. Most people had moved on to other matters. Asenath certainly had. She had spent a day in the hills with her cousin, discussing what they would do when Ja'ix attacked. Much of her time was spent grading exams, and the macanas the students were making.

Simon came up the stairs. "Mother, let me finish hanging the laundry. I told you I would do it when I came home."

"Doing simple things clears my mind. Laundry can be a meditation."

"Then I want to meditate now" he said. "Dinah is waiting outside with a Far Marsh man. I wouldn't ordinarily let him bother you, but he has a disturbing story."

Asenath sighed, handed her son a couple of clips, and went down the stairs. Her daughter stood next to a thin, unkempt man, with a look of terror in his eyes.

The man seemed both cowed and pleased by the aura of mystery and power that surrounded Asenath. She listened carefully to his story, and told him she would travel with him early the next morning. She sent her daughter to borrow four horses, so she could leave at first light. She pulled her cobalt-blue high-collared dress out from the bottom of a deep chest of clothes. Judging from his story it was probably too late for that symbol of authority.

That evening she had trouble concentrating as she gave the lessons at the Academy, distracted by the gathering clouds. Not rain clouds; something darker, more foreboding. They seemed to be gaining momentum.

***

Asenath went to the next hut in the little village. The open doors on either end were not enough to rid the place of the smell of decay, the aura of death.

Each home was the same. Many of the people were lying sick, unable to move a limb. Many had died, their frozen lungs unable to draw a breath. The large Guest House was usually filled with chattering people, food, and life. It was empty now, its fire-pit cold. Barrels of grain waited for the miller, baskets of cucumbers shriveled in the heat. This was the second Far Marsh village Asenath had visited this morning, and both were wrapped in death.

The sun seemed to struggle to climb up into the sky over the hamlet, not wanting to brighten the carnage below. The reeds waved gently as if in a light breeze, while the mosquitoes hovered, waiting for their next meal to show itself.

Asenath gently closed the latticework door behind her, and walked silently down towards the narrow, rocky beach. She turned to the three Academy students with her. "We don't need to inspect every hut. They'll all be like the ones we've seen. What happened here isn't just the work of Sheyds. They had human help."

One of the students spoke up. "If the Tanayt pleases, the reeds in the distance are moving, but there is no wind, and the waters are still."

Asenath considered this, and frowned in concentration. Digging with the side of her foot, she found a round, flat rock. She picked it up, pulled her arm back, and pitched the stone towards one of the nearby islands. She listened intently for the splash, and watched the movement of the nearby reeds. A cold feeling ran through her as she flexed her fingers and looked around at her students. "We're caught in the middle of a ruthless attack, and the assailants won't consider us innocent bystanders. Prepare your hearts."

Asenath and her students had known that riding into villages filled with inexplicable death was a dangerous undertaking. There was a thick line however between taking risks and facing imminent death.

"Does the Tanayt feel we should run?"

"There's no time. It's already upon us. Focus your will; focus whatever merit you have on avoiding their weapons."

***

Balthan was very displeased. It had taken a long time to prepare enough Fire-Snake venom and gather enough berries to go around. They had to buy berries from the Dry-landers, trading reed mats, grains, and even buffalo. They might have to go hungry for a while, but if they eliminated their Far Marsh rivals, they would gain control of a desirable area. The gifts of candied berries they had distributed to the Far Marsh people were eagerly accepted and shared.

They had divided their warriors into five groups, one for each of the Far Marsh villages. They anticipated that there wouldn't be much resistance, as almost everybody would be dead, dying, or too busy tending the sick to defend themselves. Balthan and Qimiq forgot that when they first planned this battle it was supposed to be a simple vengeful raid, stealing and maiming a few animals. When the Low Marsh people discovered how easily they could create Fire Snake poison berries, the antagonism took on a life of its own.

The four people standing on the shore didn't seem to have detected Balthan and his fighters. They gazed over the waters and the reeds, exchanging few words. It was hard to make them out because the sun was behind them, but they were tall, and their clothes didn't have the cut of Far Marsh dress. One of them might have been a woman, but it was hard to tell.

Balthan moved his skiff quietly to where his other warriors were crouching. There were eight of them, which meant two for each of the people on the shore. Using gestures, he assigned them their targets. They drew their bows, and nocked arrows. This was the first actual fighting that they were doing, and they were tense. It was preferable to kill before your enemy realized he was under attack.

The woman was smart. She threw a rock far into the water, studying the movement in the reeds when he and his fighters flinched. Balthan didn't like the thought of who she probably was.

He had a knot in his gut as he nodded to the others to begin firing. Something wasn't right. To his dismay, the people on the shore didn't seem surprised as their arrows started to fly. More to his chagrin, they had no trouble ducking them. The arrows flew in, the targets moved a little to the side, and the arrows fell to the ground. The one that might be a woman didn't even move. The arrows heading towards her simply dropped out of the air before they got close.

They would quickly run out of arrows if this kept up. Balthan signaled a new strategy. They were to fire simultaneously at one target at a time, spreading their shots so that ducking one would put the people in the path of another. They weren't skilled archers, but with eight arrows flying at one target, the warriors should be able to strike blood.

The first man went down. Balthan immediately directed fire at the next. The woman yelled at the remaining two men to run. As they turned to flee, she threw herself in the path of the oncoming arrows, lost her footing, and fell. As before, the arrows dropped to the ground in front of her. Before she could get up, Balthan directed another volley at the next man, away from her protection. He too, went down.

The hunters, having the clear advantage, quickly moved their skiffs towards the shore. There was no point concealing themselves anymore. A short spear took down the third man as the woman climbed to her feet. The knot in Balthan's stomach twisted and wrenched when he saw the recognition in her eyes.

As she stared at him, Balthan looked around, and recognized the three students he and his men had killed. They were the ones who several months earlier had placed traps when Sheyds were plaguing his house. He hadn't understood at that time that the Clay People were really working for his enemies, the Far Marsh people. Undoubtedly Asenath had sent the Sheyds, which was why her students were able to deal with them so easily.

"Balthan, you've been trapped by Sheyds."

Her face wasn't so gentle now; she looked like she was in pain. Every time in the past that Balthan had gone to her he was the weak one asking for help. He had never thought of it that way before, but it was humiliating. Let her beg now, let her offer him gifts. The Clay People didn't belong here anyways.

"Balthan, listen to me. This isn't the kind of person you are. You've been trapped. You shouldn't have been able to poison the Far Marsh people so easily. Make the Sheyds let go of you."

Again Asenath was humiliating him. "Do you think I'm stupid?" he shouted. "We're smarter than you; we're smarter than the Far Marsh people. No one but us could make Fire-Snake candy. The Far Marsh clans attacked and stole our animals. You probably told them how to do it."

"No, Balthan, we told the Far Marsh people no such thing. When they came to us and said the Low Marsh people had attacked them and destroyed their grains, we told them they were mistaken, that Balthan and his families would do no such thing. They decided to forget the matter. They refused to let the Sheyds snare them. You stepped into the trap. You know the Far Marsh clans don't rely on animals the way you do. Why would they attack yours?"

"If we stepped into a trap, then how come three of your students are dead and we're all standing?"

"Look around, Balthan."

He glanced to his side and saw three of his warriors lying prone on the beach, wisps of smoke rising from their bodies.

"Balthan, free yourself from the Sheyds."

"I'm not trapped by a Sheyd. You're the one who's trapped. I'll free you from breath." At his signal two of his men loosed arrows at her. Both the men and the arrows fell to the ground before they reached her, the life gone out of weapon and human alike. Behind, two men who had used the argument to cover their movement responded to Balthan's next signal and shot at her back. The arrows struck home, and Asenath fell forward, her face hitting a rock. Circles of blood bloomed on the back of her dress, and on the sand around her mouth.

A Golden Mangrove snake slithered out from underneath the rock where she had fallen. The way it bore itself out of the bloody sand, hissing and staring at Balthan, it seemed as if it had come out of her mouth.

The three remaining Low Marsh people looked warily at each other as a group of ravens started circling in the sky above them. Maybe the snake was telling him Asenath was right; he had been trapped by Sheyds. If so, he'd given them what they wanted, but Balthan sensed that it only made them hungrier.

***

Taiku was disturbed when he heard about the horses Asenath had borrowed. He sent Ner, one of his soldiers, to the Academy to find out why. Simon told Ner about the deaths of the Far Marsh people, and how his mother had left early in the morning to see how she could help. It was clear to Ner that Simon wasn't happy about his mother's undertaking.

The gallop to the nearest Far Marsh village took a couple of hours. Taiku inspected the huts, the corpses, the footprints showing where Asenath had walked. Four horses grazing peacefully under a tree meant that she had continued by boat. It took him another few hours to ride overland to the next village, deep in the marshes.

The trail approaching it was narrow and soft; more an accumulation of damp mush than solid ground. Taiku's throat tightened as he saw large black birds resting on a tree, looking content.

The Guest House was the same as in the other village. He went inside, bending over bodies, looking for signs of life.

A soldier held out a basket full of berries. Taiku shook his head. "I can't eat."

The soldier shrugged and put the basket down.

Taiku stared at it. These berries weren't abundant in the marshes. "Bring some back to Lagash and feed them to a dog. Don't touch them."

Abner grasped Taiku's arm. "Come."

Thin columns of smoke rose from the beach. Taiku broke into a run when he saw they were coming from corpses. He recognized Asenath's hair, her kerchief, her body lying prone on the rough beach, circles of blood on her back. Her students lay nearby. Taiku's heart stopped beating as it disintegrated into jagged shards, as his thoughts dissolved into trails of damp mush.

He couldn't. Asenath's and his closeness was not for others to know, and his breaking apart now would expose it. Taiku stitched his heart, stitched his mind precariously together.

There were Marsh corpses as well. Usually when a person is killed, you can tell how it happened. Most of these corpses had no visible wounds. Smoke rose from the smoldering bodies as they gradually turned to ash.

Abner pulled the arrows from the bodies of Asenath and her students. He showed them to Taiku. "Low Marsh."

Taiku nodded. A couple of abandoned skiffs were at the shore. The attackers were at home in these marshes, knowing all the streams, islands and pathways. He wouldn't be able to catch them.

"I want them all dead. Every man who is old enough to have done this."

"Are the men responsible? Maybe they were pushed into it by Sheyds."

"Sheyds don't poison whole villages. Sheyds don't force people to shoot arrows."

Taiku knelt beside Asenath, running his fingers through her now-matted hair. A painful, tingling sensation ran through his fingertips. Remembering that she would not consider his touching her hair appropriate, he straightened her kerchief instead, covering as much as he could. Rage and misery boiled inside him.

"I want all their men rounded up and brought to the Meeting House. Since they're such experts with poison, making it for us will be their only livelihood now. Anything you want in the Low Marsh villages is yours to take. Burn the Low Marsh homes. We have to control these savages, and the best way is to extend our rule over them." He pointed to the homes. "Begin by removing the still living from the dwellings. Put all the corpses in one or two huts and burn them. We'll send healers to see if they can help anyone still breathing. Find something to cover the students' bodies. When you're done here, bring them to the Academy. I'm taking Asenath home." He lifted her gently, draping her stiffening body over the horse, in front of the saddle. He softly kissed her fingers, and then gently bound her to the pommel.

***

Asenath had remained in the Academy's library long after the evening class, reading through an old manuscript about the journey of the dead. It was something rarely looked at, as it was considered speculation. Could anyone have actually visited the Abode of the Dead, and returned to describe it?

She was taking that journey now. The pain from the arrows, from striking her face on a rock had ended quickly. That could only mean her life had ended just as suddenly. The manuscript spoke of an intermediate place after death, a strange and potentially dangerous space that had to be passed.

"Welcome, Tanayt."

A tall man with a warm smile stood before her; someone she'd never seen, but familiar nonetheless.

"An old donkey driver's been pestering us with riddles. Perhaps you can assist us with them?"

"Riddles...? I've just been killed. I'm sorry, I can't think about riddles now. How can I help my people when I'm dead?"

The man shook his head. "You will have to determine that yourself."

"Can I go back?"

"Do you deserve it?"

Asenath had asked the question rhetorically. This man though, responded as if it was possible.

"Who are you? Can you send me back?"

"Simon. Do you deserve it?"

Asenath gasped in fear. Her son? No, it didn't look at all like him. "In the merit of all my studies; in the merit of all the people I have helped, please send me back."

"I have to consult other Taanas. Would you like to work on a riddle in the meantime?"

"No. I'll wait."

Simon lifted his hands sideways in front of his face and left.

Asenath tried to figure out Simon and his questions. Was it actually possible to return? And why riddles?

She felt a breath over her. That made no sense. Such sensations should have been left behind. She looked around and was horrified. What she heard was a thousand times worse.

"Well, look who's here. It's the chief trapper. How nice of you to die, and so release all your victims."

Several dozen silver-skinned creatures, resembling people but with disproportionate features and bird-like feet crowded around her, leering. All were naked; the men were aroused.

"We had no bodies in the Abode of Life with which to fight back, but here we're as solid as you. You denied us our pleasures in your world, holding us under those damned clay bowls. You're going to make up for the misery you caused us. You are going to give us pleasure of the flesh. I'm going to make you suffer for all those bowls with the name Mekelat on them. And my friends will do the same for the bowls with their names."

One Sheyd grabbed her arm. A voluptuous, blond female Sheyd pulled off Asenath's clothes, pausing to dig sharp fingernails into her breasts.

"My daughter likes your dress. Ask nicely and maybe she'll give it back one day." Mekelat roared at his joke.

The girl smiled a wicked smile. "I should be able to find a good husband, wearing something like this." She faded, clutching her trophy.

They bound Asenath's wrists, and then fought each other for turns; pushing, shoving, laughing as they raped her. This wasn't what Asenath had anticipated from the old manuscript. But she would endure it until she was ready to move on.

Perhaps this was a required rectification of her past deeds. Arrogance was not a character trait of the righteous. Was it one of hers? She guessed that Simon's answer about going back was "no."

There was no sun crossing the sky, no moon to mark the movement of time. The whiteness all around was broken only by the Sheyds, fighting, shoving, raping... It went on and on, one after another, beyond count. Sheyds never tired.

As if reading her thoughts, the creature on top of her grabbed her hair, pulling her face towards his. His putrid breath filled her nose; his broken, yellow-green teeth were practically biting her lips. "You held me forever under that bowl, and now I'm going to be forever on top of you. Time is something for the Abode of Life; it has no meaning here. There is no end to our raping you. In your way of thinking, this is for an eternity. The only change you'll notice maybe is that we get more inventive in what we do."

Was it possible for a dead person to pass out? According to the old manuscript, she existed now only as consciousness. To lose that would be to wink out of existence. Whatever it was, she lost sensation, she lost feeling; she had only a vague awareness of the repulsive creatures on her, the creatures who tortured people simply for their own amusement. And for having stopped them from doing so, she was now being tortured for eternity. Perhaps this was a challenge: escape, defeat them... How, with her arms bound, a Sheyd constantly coupling with her?

"Wake up! We have a new treat for you to enjoy!" The one on top gave her face a hard slap. All the Sheyds roared with laughter. She heard a retching sound, and lifted her head enough to see Mekelat poised over her nakedness, his finger stuck down his throat.

An avalanche of thoughts and emotions crashed into her mind. Strangely, the feelings were not of revulsion, but of anger, fear, and desperation. The Sheyd's weight was suddenly off her, and she heard his raspy voice screaming. Roars of rage mixed with yelps, and cries for mercy. She looked up to see Aua frowning at her. He was in his Traveling costume, snakes writhing, eagles dancing on his arms and chest. Around him were soldiers; Taiku's soldiers, slashing with clay knives at the Sheyds. Green blood gushed from collapsing silver bodies, like water bladders that had suddenly sprung a leak.

The soldiers and Sheyds were beside her, above her, beneath her. Battles seemed to be fought through her. Abner, one of the soldiers immediately to her right stabbed a Sheyd five fights away without extending his arm. A Sheyd kept Asenath between it and the soldier attacking it. The knife went straight into the Sheyd's neck, without touching her.

At first Asenath had reconciled herself to the rape, that there was no way out. Her rescue came when she began to think of fighting back.

Aua untied her wrists, handed her a robe from a pouch in his apron and knelt, his face to the floor. The soldiers followed suit. The Sheyds were already all on the floor, inert deflated bags of silver skin.

"Teacher: it's my desire to serve you."

"I am not the One to whom you should bow. I am not the Source of Blessing. Please rise."

She stood watching the prostrate soldiers and powerful Sphere Traveler slowly lift themselves up.

"Taiku got a strange sensation in his hand that didn't go away after he touched your hair. He considered it a sign that you were in trouble. We decided to invade the Abode of the Dead," Aua said.

"I'm happy that you did. I am in your debt forever."

"You paid everything in advance while you were alive, my Teacher. The eternal debt is to you."

Taiku stood in front of her, his arms, his chest covered with the green gore of dead Sheyds. Asenath grinned at him. "Even when I'm dead, you provide what I need." Like a flash of lightening out of a cloudless sky, she suddenly understood the blast of thoughts that had slammed into her mind when Aua and the soldiers had arrived. She stumbled at their impact.

Taiku grimaced. "I'm going to make some changes, things I should have done beforehand. I'm going to take control. I'll make sure the Ebers are protected, and your children are provided for."

"Taiku, I know what you did. I understand everything."

He blanched. Fear lit his eyes, and his legs trembled. "What do you understand? What do you know?"

"When I arrived from the Abode of Life, the Sheyds could read my thoughts. They knew my worst fears, and mocked them. When you, Aua and your men arrived here, all your thoughts exploded into my head. I've sorted them out. I know how the events that brought me here started."

"You know my thoughts? You know what I'm thinking now?" Taiku whispered in terror.

"Yes." Asenath looked at him, then suddenly stepped back, her eyes wide with shock. "What happened the first time as well... the raspberries."

They both stood, Taiku mortified.

"Taiku, you are—"

The last words were spoken to nothingness. Except for Aua, as suddenly as the invaders from the Abode of Life had arrived, they disappeared.

"The shock of what you said broke my trance's hold," Aua said.

"Aua, I don't think Taiku heard my last words. Please make sure he knows he's my friend forever."

"A voyage like this has never been done. I don't know if I'll be able to."

"I hope you will find it in you to remain my friend, Sphere Traveler. You have taught me much by coming to my aid. Aua, this place of nothingness is fading. One of us is leaving now... I am pleased to see you here, and I will be pleased if you leave in health."

12 EARLY BRONZE AGE 4

Taiku lay on the dirt floor of the Chief's Meeting House. He couldn't get up while tears were dripping from his eyes. He wasn't crying just for the loss of his beloved friend Asenath. Now that she knew he was to blame for her death and more, Taiku couldn't avoid accepting responsibility for what he had done; more so for what he was going to do. What he had to do.

Ja'ix was coming. There was no doubt now. At first the occasional family on the run had stopped in Lagash; now more refugees were arriving every day. They told of bands of men charging into a village. Archers with their longbows would target a baby playing in the mud or a farmer at his crops. Children were killed or taken hostage. Some villagers were skinned alive; others had their tongues and fingernails torn out, or horseshoes nailed to their feet. Once all resistance had been eliminated, the invaders stole crops and animals. When they returned a bit of the food they had taken, they expected appreciation for their generosity.

Nobody could stand against them. Their horses were huge and fast, and the men carried extremely long swords. When Ja'ix's gangs attacked, their youngest hostages were always on the front lines. Defenders would feel uncomfortable killing children who looked fresh off their mothers' breasts, and Ja'ix used the hesitation to his advantage.

He said he was an envoy, fighting to spread the message of the "Master of Spirits." Man had a base animal soul and a divine spirit, he explained. Those who didn't accept Jaix's message clearly lacked the divine spirit that elevated them over animals, and so they were to be treated as beasts. From his bloodthirsty reputation, from the numbers he was said to have massacred, it was clear Ja'ix believed there were many animals in human form. 'Priests' would remain at every village he over-ran to enforce obedience, or "harmony" as they described it. The priests never hesitated to kill anyone who questioned their edicts, and that, together with fear of the soldiers returning, kept the villages in line.

He had started far to the east, many years of travel away. At first a small band of nomadic cutthroats, his men had been able to pacify large territories over time. The younger hostages eventually became imbued with the ruthless character of their zealous captors, and were no longer hostages, but hostage-takers.

Ja'ix's armies passed over lands like a glacier, slow but inexorable. They traveled in a broad swath, uprooting, destroying whatever existed previously, planting obedience in the ruins. From this crop, they harvested more brutal fighters.

The refugees told of an Eber community that had lived near Ja'ix's home village. When they refused to join in his cause, he slaughtered all the men, ordered his soldiers to rape the wives and daughters, and then took them as slaves.

One of the regions Ja'ix conquered possessed advanced skills in metallurgy. Daggers, knives, all metal instruments had to be short if they were to be strong and sharp. The glacier picked up speed once Ja'ix got hold of the skills necessary to make swords long enough to stab a man while sitting up on a horse.

According to the stories, there were more men in Ja'ix's armies than there were people in Lagash, even when combined with the population of the nearby mountains. If you added in the Marsh people maybe the numbers were equal, but no one really knew. Taiku's intention was to bring everybody together, under his control. United they stood a chance of resisting.

Now he had the results of his first efforts, as he lay on the ground, weeping silently for the deaths he had brought about.

But self-pity was not an indulgence he could afford. He wiped his eyes on his sleeve and stood. "Where's Aua?" He needed the Sphere Traveler.

There was a collective sigh of relief. "The last anybody saw, he was standing before Asenath. Now there's no sign of him," Vlad said.

Taiku turned to Ner. "Bring me one of his apprentices." Ner inclined his head and ran off.

He turned to the rest of the men in the courtyard. "We did well rescuing the Tanayt from Sheyds. We must get ready, to prevail in the coming battles. Me against my brother. The Madai against the Elam. The Madai and Elam against the Marsh People. All the people of Lagash; Madai Elam, Marsh and Eber against the far side of the horizon. Both sides of the horizon against Ja'ix."

***

Many years earlier, Taiku's grandfather Muuad had fenced off a small quarry that was the only source of obsidian within a month's travel. Few people cared, because the stone was used mainly for trinkets. It took years of trial and error till Muuad perfected the technique for shaping it into razor-sharp knife-blades, spear tips and arrowheads.

With its increased value and his control of the supply, Muuad prospered. He appointed his son Asahel as Chief, though his only authority to do so was his ferocious disposition and enormous wealth.

Gentle and mild-mannered, Asahel was the opposite of his father. He resigned when the clan leaders objected loudly to his plan to control spring flooding. Muuad named the young Taiku as Chief.

One of Taiku's first acts when he became Chief was to order his engineer Zeruiah to build a gated spillway to control the river's spring flooding. The resultant fertile fields greatly increased crop production, which was then heavily taxed. Hardly anyone complained when Taiku subsequently claimed ownership of the town's grain storehouses, because until his engineering works few people had extra grain to store. The clan leaders remained silent, despite the infringement of their authority.

Those who did protest were advised that their homes and farms were needed by the community. In compensation, Taiku gave them new homes among the extensive tar seeps scattered around Lagash. It may have been the tar; it may have been something else, but many of the relocated people became sick after moving: nausea, headaches, unexplained bleeding... Some people lost all the hair on their body before they died. Others, who didn't get sick right away developed strange lumps under their skin. After a short time, people who interfered with Taiku's plans realized that their best course of action was to flee Lagash.

It didn't take long for the prosperity brought to the community by Taiku's projects to erase any remaining objections, and the Madai clan leaders acknowledged that the Chief was now in charge of Lagash, not them.

The town was set in the valley of the Klee-Dekel River, which meandered along woodlands and fertile plains from the mountains in the north. The town had grown at the delta, where small islands and then marshes forced any large boats coming down-river to a halt. Lagash became a natural trading center for merchants coming along the coastal roads.

More and more of the Madai livelihood came from dealing with merchants and traders. Lumber, minerals, fertilizer, and furs all made their way south through Lagash to go east and west. Woven fabrics, refined metals, and grains went north.

A growing number of traders following the coastal roads used Lagash as a stopping point. While most of them were respectful of the town and its inhabitants, others helped themselves to whatever they wanted. Sometimes it was fruits or grains, sometimes a goat. Once in a while women were abducted. Many people suspected that the children that occasionally disappeared were also taken by traders, but there was no way of knowing for sure.

When he was Chief, Asahel hadn't interfered with the travelers, advising people to politely stay out of their way. This meant a few families had to abandon their orchards and fields on the main road. The travelers often slept in such areas, which they picked clean of any produce. They chopped down fruit trees for firewood, littering the ground with their waste. When one of them broke his foot in a hole left by a previous traveler, he and his burly companions stomped up to Asahel's home and demanded compensation. This left a strong impression on the young Taiku.

When he took over as Chief, Taiku abandoned his father's polite approach, posting guards on the road to greet travelers and collect tolls. Many travelers responded by waiting until dark, and then slipping through. Taiku built heavy gates to close the roads at night; within a few days, these were hacked to pieces and burned.

Frustrated, Taiku had the western gate rebuilt. The next night, as travelers hacked at the posts and ropes that held up the gates, Taiku's soldiers rose up from the dark, hacking and burning the trespassers. Their charred remains were left at the edge of the road, a warning to others. The gate remained intact afterwards.

On the eastern side of town, the road ran across the islands that dotted the river; small wooden bridges spanned the rapids between them. Taiku asked Zeruiah to erect a moveable bridge, which he could close at will. The engineer was tall and thin; strong winds often sent her grabbing for support. Her mobile bridge was so well designed though, that she could move it in and out of position in mere minutes.

Everyone felt more secure, grateful for the Chief's violent inclinations. Lagash prospered.

It had been at the bridge on the east side of town that Taiku's toll-collectors first heard of Ja'ix and his hordes. Wayfarers with no trade goods were a cause of suspicion, but when a woman showed the guards her child's hand, amputated at the wrist, Taiku's men believed the horrific stories.

These refugees lived hand to mouth, eating whatever they could scrounge; stealing when there was nothing to scavenge. They were destitute and hungry. Their desperation created a smoldering rage in their stomachs to get back at those who had destroyed their lives.

Taiku set up a shelter for them at his family's obsidian quarry. He put the men to work and gave the women little garden plots. Armed soldiers were posted around their compound, which gave the refugees what they needed most: a sense of shelter from harm. They were grateful for the meager food and roof over their heads. They were grateful to see that there was life ahead for them.

The stronger men hacked the obsidian from the ground. The weaker ones were taught to shape the stones into tools, whether blades, spear-points or axes. Taiku's soldiers encouraged them to talk about what had happened. The refugees spoke about Ja'ix's brutality, about their lost families, arduous escapes. Taiku didn't want the embers of their rage to cool down. As a man sharpened a spear point, a soldier would banter about striking it into his tormentor's heart. As a refugee shaped a knife blade, a soldier would discuss the best technique for slitting throats. The obsidian was carved into dreams of vengeance.

When Taiku visited the refugee camp, he was greeted by declarations of gratitude and loyalty. A few volunteers headed back towards their homelands, to spread word of the welcome they got from Taiku. The refugees themselves built more barracks, to house the anticipated deluge.

Not everybody was pleased about the new residents.

"For all we know, some of the refugees may be Sheyds in disguise. With Asenath gone, who will trap them if they are?" Jared, a senior soldier, asked Taiku.

"Asenath wasn't the only Sheyd-trapper."

"What if some are actually Ja'ix's agents?

"Good question. We'll keep our ears to the refugees. I'm putting you in charge of them."

"What about the Elam?" another soldier asked. "They've attacked us before."

Many years earlier, before the Ebers had come to the region, the Marsh people used to run to the Elam with their Sheyd problems. The Elam considered it an affront to their honor that the Clay People were considered more powerful in that respect. In a daring raid, they snuck into Lagash, captured a few Eber girls, and burned a few houses. They knew that a more aggressive raid would threaten the Madai, and bring retaliation. They calculated correctly that a limited attack, hurting only the Ebers would bring no response. Many years later, the captives returned to the Eber community, husbands and children in tow. Some people claimed that Asenath's family was descended from such a captive and her Elam husband.

Taiku sighed to himself. How could he fight Ja'ix if his soldiers were too eager to fight their neighbors? He glared at the man, not deigning to respond.

Ner returned into that silence, to bring word from Aua's apprentices.

"Aleku is Traveling between Spheres, looking for Aua. He'll come when he finishes; he has a vision to bring you."

Some Sphere Travelers experienced what was not yet present in the world. Usually it was visual, sometimes aural, sometimes just an indescribable sensation of movement. Few of them gave clear guidance for appropriate action. Rather, their visions left you with a sense of foreboding, of a coming apocalypse. None of the other Sphere Travelers were anywhere near as lucid as Aua. Taiku desperately wanted him back.

From the long-ago moment he had left her castrated rapist tied up on a rock, Taiku had been terrified that Asenath would find out that he had told an older acquaintance she was going raspberry picking. The man had bragged that he could conquer any woman. In a moment of youthful arrogance, Taiku had challenged him to try to seduce Asenath, certain that he would fail. Now that Asenath knew that Taiku had caused her rape and her death, he desperately needed Aua to tell him that Asenath didn't hate him.

***

Aleku sat across from Taiku, the flames from the fireplace a golden glow on both men's faces. Vlad knelt quietly on the ground, off to the side. A few insects flitted and buzzed, but otherwise the silence was palpable. It wasn't the walls that kept out the sounds of chirping birds, the soft chatter of soldiers outside. Rather, it was the intensity of the three men in the room.

Aleku spoke his vision:

"The heavens collided, making a deep abyss with ten columns of white fire and smoke, and below them a red sphere; they could not be measured either according to their depth or according to their height. Behind this abyss, I saw a place where there were neither the firmament of heaven above, nor the firmly fastened ground below, nor water beneath, nor any birds; it was a place waste and dreadful. I saw seven stars, like huge burning mountains. I was told "Each star is seven swarms of Sheyds. This is a prison for the stars, those that transgress the command of the Source of Blessing at the very beginning of their rising. Therefore, the Source of Blessing becomes angry at the swarms and weaves them into a curtain for five thousand years, until the time when their sin is completed."

Taiku frowned. Stars, Sheyds, five thousand years? White fire? As expected, Aleku's vision was presented to him as if through a smoky glass. There was a truth behind it, but it was difficult to grab hold of.

"What can I do?"

"The Source of Harmony must be destroyed if redemption is to happen."

The Source of Harmony? Was that the same as the Source of Blessing? If not, then harmony wasn't a blessing. A competing power?

"I don't understand."

"Nor I. The solutions to ten mysteries will be revealed by Source of Blessing at their allotted times."

"I need answers now."

Aleku took a shayd-trapping bowl and smashed it against the table. He picked up a jagged shard, and scratched Taiku's forearm, soaking the edge in blood. "In five thousand years your blood will be a weapon. It will aid your friend."

The scratch didn't help. The answer didn't help either. "And Aua?" Taiku hoped he could at least get a clear answer to this.

"Aua has not died, but isn't tied to what manifests now."

Taiku insisted quietly: "I need him."

"Asenath needs him. Aua's protecting her from cannibals."

13 THE EDGE OF THE WORLD 5

Osnat knew she'd had a good sleep; her joints were creaking from having been still so long. Her stomach growled with hunger. Her throat was parched from the smoke that told her a nice wood fire was burning. It also meant a nice meal was being cooked. She rolled over and opened her eyes, looking at the ice window off to the side. It was darker outside than it had been in many days.

"Ah, she's finally awake. Now tell her." There was tension in Ijiq's voice.

Osnat lifted her head to see Haran sandwiched between Aarluk and Ijiq, his eyes downcast. He was sweating, despite the coolness of the air. Aarluk and Ijiq looked grim.

"Aua came to see me when I Traveled yesterday to kill the storm. He warned me."

"Aua?" Osnat had never heard the name.

"A powerful Sphere Traveler. He said he had dwelled with you in the Abode of Life and fought for you in the place between Spheres. He says you are his master and teacher, that he's been your guardian across thousands of years."

Osnat stared.

"Continue," Ijiq ordered.

"Aua said that I must not allow anything to bring you harm or his Chief will destroy me in this world, and he will destroy me in all other Spheres. The only way for me to protect myself is to protect you." Haran's face was ashen. "I will obey."

Osnat smelled danger. How could Aua, whoever or whatever he is, cause such alarm? "You know how powerful I am. What harm could you do me?"

"Simon is your husband."

Osnat blanched. Aarluk slowly rose to her feet, staring at her daughter.

Ijiq was in a rage. "How can you say that?"

His eyes barely lifted to Osnat's. "When I touched your face yesterday and asked who you are, you answered."

"It's true, then." Aarluk sat back down, stunned. "This changes everything."

Osnat stood up, waving an angry finger at Aarluk's face. "It changes nothing. The only difference is that you now know the identity of one of my helpers. Haran has learned how powerful he is, and you know how powerful I am."

"How powerful are you?" Aarluk's eyes narrowed as she stood right back up.

It was all or nothing now. Things were falling apart too fast. "I can bring the mountain-side down on this village." Or maybe on herself.

Aarluk laughed nervously. Ijiq stared.

"I promise that when it's time, I will bring the escarpment down on this village. And you will keep your promise that we'll kill Falun, Puah and the false Simon."

If Haran appeared terrified before, it had been perfect serenity compared to how he looked now. Osnat reached up and grabbed the front of his parka. "Speaking of this to anyone will cause me harm. You know the consequences of that. Follow my instructions exactly or you will suffer excruciating misery for the rest of your life, and way beyond that."

As she threatened Haran, Osnat realized she was talking herself into a trap. The most exaggerated threats were taken seriously. If she didn't follow through, she would lose all credibility. With that, she'd lose her ability to protect herself. She had to stop the escalation, but terror was getting the better of her, spewing threats from her mouth.

"Come outside. I want to check our meat cache, to make sure the storm didn't blow it over." She addressed herself to no one in particular, concerned that Ijiq might take this as an affront to his skill at stashing the meat. If no one followed her outside, she stood a reasonable chance of getting lost in the blizzard before taking ten steps from the door. But unless she found a way to step back from her barrage of threats, she was certain to be lost forever.

Osnat stepped outside to a dazzling, starry sky. Overhead the aurora danced in cheerful celebration, the storm baby finally having ceased its tantrum. A light breeze blew a pleasant coolness over her skin, cleansing the sooty feeling from her face. The clear sky cleaned the soot from her mind. A deep breath, and her thoughts were no longer racing haphazardly. It was true: Aarluk, with Haran's help, had indeed killed the storm.

A grunt made her continue forward. Aarluk, Ijiq and Haran followed her out. She walked around the hut, seeing, as she expected, the skins covering the meat firmly in place. Osnat walked among the huts, grinning at the few people outside. It felt so good to see a calm sky. The hint of light on the distant horizon spoke of a coming end to the long, long winter night. Osnat had no illusions that the approaching sun was a sign that her life would change for the better. That was going to take action on her part, such as carrying out all the asinine threats she had made. Where and how would she live after she buried the village under the mountain? Was the radioactive ore sufficient? She was a biologist, not a fusion technician.

Osnat was the only one smiling. It occurred to her that her family was the only one in the village with a decent supply of food. Maybe she could get away with feeding everyone instead of killing them. It might be safer.

"Aarluk, how long will it be till people can get enough food for themselves?"

"If the hunting is good, within a day or two. Many of them are weak from hunger though, which will make it harder."

"I want to hold a feast for everyone. With the polar bear meat, we can give people the strength to go hunting, so they can feed themselves."

"It's easier to kill people who are weak. Why do you want to give them strength to fight back?"

"If we feed them, they'll be grateful. Then they wouldn't want to kill us, and we wouldn't have to kill them." Osnat's logic was impeccable. With the break in the tension, there'd be an opportunity to cool down all the anger, deflate the threats.

Ijiq turned to Haran, grabbing his coat, pulling him close. "If you repeat a word of what you just heard to anyone," he hissed, "Aua is going to cut off your ears and boil them along with your tongue." He turned and whispered to Osnat. "There's not enough wind to mask everything we say. Don't talk. We'll take a walk towards the cliff, and there you can explain to me why you want to kill yourself and us."

Osnat started to reply, but Aarluk's glare closed her lips. She trudged silently with her retinue towards the escarpment. Muffled voices drifted from shelters as the wind-packed snow crunched under their boots. The occasional dog whined, but for the most part they lay quiet, grateful, it seemed, for the let-up in the weather.

They stood in the moon-shadow of the ragged cliff. From a distance it was a massive wall, with small valleys punched through intermittently. Up close, it was marbled with fissures, overhangs, and veins of yellow, blue and rust. Some straight, some like a wind-tangled spider web. In many places the veins were luminous, having an eerie glow. If a human had painted this landscape, it would have been by a surreal, twisted mind.

They stood beside the empty Dance House. Ijiq put his arm around Osnat, drawing her close. Aarluk and Haran stood to the side, discretely turned away.

"If we feed the other people, they'll be stronger when we fight them. I don't know what you mean when you say they'll be grateful to us if we give them meat. But whatever you think, it wouldn't stop them from trying to kill us. People admire your strength for baiting the bear. If they eat from it, their admiration will be stronger. But they won't love you for it; they won't feel they have to leave you alone."

"They're not stupid," Osnat argued. "Food is hard to get. Sometimes people starve. Why would they kill someone who brings them food?"

Ijiq shrugged. "One day, you feed them. The next, you might feed on them. What happens one day says nothing about what happens the next."

"But there are patterns in life, probabilities. One event leads to another. If every time I go hunting I caught a seal, and every time Puah went hunting, she caught nothing, who would you go to for food?"

"That's a silly question. You're my wife's daughter, and you or Aarluk are going to kill Puah pretty soon."

Osnat shook her head in frustration. "Okay, let's say neither of us was related to you. Who would you go to for food? The one who always, or the one who rarely caught a seal?"

"I'd go to whoever had food," Ijiq said, sounding slightly annoyed.

Osnat clutched her hand over her eyes and screamed silently. The idea of statistical probability was meaningless here. Every event, every day, such as they were in this place with no winter sun, was discrete, separate, and alone.

One more try.

"Let's say you were away, and you came back to the village hungry. Who would you go to for food? The one who usually caught food or the one who rarely caught food?"

"I'd go to my wife, of course. She would know who had food. But it would be a shameful thing to go begging for something to eat."

Another last try.

"Who would a woman prefer to marry? A successful hunter or a man who has a lot of trouble?"

"Women like men who make them happy when they lie together. They like a man who can get names for their sons. But what's that have to do with giving everyone food? A hunter who always catches seals when he goes to the breathing holes may get stuck on a broken piece of ice and float away to die. We can never know what is going to happen tomorrow. Today certainly doesn't tell us. Did you know last winter that you would be Aarluk's daughter? That Simon would be another person?

"But there are some things we do know," he said, touching his fingers softly to her cheek. "Strength is respected. Other people's fear keeps you out of their cooking pot. If you want to feed your bear meat to people, I can't stop you. But if you think you're feeding them to have their friendship or loyalty, Aarluk will soon have to look for another daughter."

Osnat had no response. Not only did the Tunniq not have a concept of probability; they didn't recognize linearity. They were vicious, but they weren't stupid. All those ways of thinking that Osnat considered part of being human were not part of the Tunniq, who were definitely the same species as her. Maybe she was the one who lacked understanding. She stared at Ijiq, who gazed calmly back at her. She remembered the first moment when she realized that the people they found were not going to help them. It was a moment of terror, of anger and bewilderment. This was a similar moment. She was terrified because the line connecting the events of her life had just been erased. It was all chaos. Osnat was furious at losing that sense of order, the only thing at times that kept her mind from falling apart. And if there was no orderliness in life, if there was no pattern, how could she know what to do next? How could she know anything?

She continued to stare at Ijiq. Bewilderment flooded her thoughts and overflowed through her eyes. The tears froze on her skin as they rolled down her cheeks. She made no attempt to wipe her face or slow the waters. The flood in her mind would have to recede before there was any point to that.

"Come into the Dance House and pull yourself together." Ijiq shepherded her inside and sat her on a bench. He found a glowing ember in the remains of the earlier fires, and ignited a couple of oil lamps, casting a dim glow around her. "Take your time. We'll stand outside and make sure no one disturbs you. When you're ready, let us know."

Osnat nodded silently, her eyes cast downward. After everything, after surrendering all that had made up her past life, after being separated from her family, seeing her husband butchered and eaten, having her life threatened, and still maintaining her sanity, was it now slipping away because she was told not to feed the cannibals who wanted to kill her? Or was this proof that she had actually lost her mind a long time ago, and only now realized it was missing? She lay down on her side along the narrow bench, her arm as a pillow beneath her head.

Osnat had made a promise to her husband, to her unborn baby. How could she keep it if her mind was gone? She had to search for it. "Where is your strength?" Aarluk had asked after raping her. She had to find it.

On the floor was the dead puppy the children had been playfully tossing about. Haran's drum lay on the bench across from her. The remnants of the earlier festiveness now gave the place a sense of gloom. Or maybe it was just her, feeling abandoned by the universe. Aarluk and Ijiq cared for her, but it was an affection she trusted only by necessity. She would never understand how Aarluk could change so quickly from enemy to protector, "mother," as she considered herself. Osnat turned her thoughts to her previous family, which according to the Tunniq, was outside the realm of existence. The tears flowed as Osnat pictured herself at her wedding, her parents proudly escorting her down the aisle. She remembered her father's joyful blessing when she asked his permission to marry. Her brother Shelah introducing her to his friend, Simon. Being appointed head of her research lab, graduating university. Now she was a young girl, camping with her family in the mountain wilderness. They had come to watch the salmon swim up through the rapids to spawn. "Where is paradise?" her father asked playfully as she inhaled the cedar-soaked air. Happily following Shelah across the creek by jumping from rock to rock. Being stranded when she was afraid to make the last leap back to shore; her brother running off laughing, leaving her marooned. Staring at the fish throwing themselves through the water, banging against rocks, determined to get home regardless of the obstacles. Feeling the cold, wet spray on the back of her neck. Waiting for her brother to come back and help her, waiting and listening to the strange sounds from the rapids, from the wind beating its way through the tall forest, growing more tearful by the moment.

"Mama!" she wailed.

Aarluk quietly came into the Dance House, seating herself on the floor off to the side. She picked up the drum, started humming and softly beating a rhythm, dum-da-da-dum-da, dum-da-da-dum-da...

One of the oil lamps burned out, leaving only a soft flow of light around Osnat. Osnat's eyes closed, her thoughts slowed. Her feelings drifted to the quiet beat of the drum.

More memories: of strange places, unfamiliar places, but her memories. A place between the Abode of Life and the other Spheres; a place of many dimensions. How could that be? A muscular man with a gruesome leather engraving over his chest. A Sphere Traveler named Aua, telling her he would always serve her. Revelation, understanding, she didn't know of what. Green blood all around, monstrous men on top of her, pawing at her, suddenly gone. Sand was in her mouth, fingers running through her hair to comfort her. A horrible pain in her jaw, as if she had been smashed in the face. She cried out in her heart as she felt piercing pains in her back. Warmth. Sun. Endless marshes, small farms and villages. Lecturing in the Academy, trapping Sheyds. Aua bowing to her, his face on the floor, reverently calling her his teacher. Tying up an attacker with invisible ropes. Hanging laundry. Having children. Getting married…

The memories poured like water, but they weren't from a life she recognized. Attacks, butchers, war… A verdant new home, new friends. Someone who lived somewhere warm, someone who was loved, who protected others, someone who was killed. Someone who was killed by the people she protected.

A long trip across the desert. Strange lives, strange creatures, strange places… The memories swirled through her too fast, too confusing to grasp. Millennium swept upon millennium, the world trembling as a second moon blasted into the northern sky, either an ominous warning, or a promise of blessing.

A brook, pouring from a Rock made of pure light. Its waters pleasant and soothing. Osnat listened to the water gurgling and bubbling. A gentle breeze rustled lightly; the air smelled clean and whole. Birds chirped; even little frogs sang sweet hymns. All were praising the Source of the water: the Rock, the Light…

Her tears ceased their flow. Osnat's bewilderment coalesced into a formless understanding that could not be put into words. She didn't try to unravel it, to figure out how she fathomed such things. She squeezed it tightly to her heart and felt comforted. She bent down, cupped her hands together, and drank the sweet pureness, the wisdom of the brook.

A mother has no tolerance for anything that threatens her child, but will put up with anything to keep it happy and safe. Aarluk waited patiently, kept drumming, kept humming as she watched her daughter lie quietly on the bench, as she watched her daughter's heart dance across outlandish places, strange events, bizarre people and creatures. She felt the touch of the pains, the warmth, the profound understanding. Aarluk realized that with Osnat she had joined with something much deeper, more powerful than anything she had ever experienced. Something from outside existence, which meant there was something more than the existence Aarluk recognized. The safest thing to do would be to remove her head from her body as she lay on the bench. But Aarluk did not become a great Sphere Traveler through being afraid, walking away from risks. Few Sphere Travelers had ever been powerful enough to switch from being a woman to a man or man to a woman. Even though Aarluk still had the parts of a man and the remains of a beard, she was still known to all as a woman, as wife to Ijiq, and now as mother to this thin, frail girl, who had promised to bring down a mountain and destroy her world.

The wild journeying had quieted. Osnat was at peace. She had been in another Sphere long enough; too long, and a person wouldn't want to come back. Aarluk knelt beside Osnat, stroking her hair under the hood of her parka. Running her hand up Osnat's spine, massaging her neck with powerful fingers she whispered for her daughter to come back to the Abode of Life. "Together," she added, "we'll send our enemies to the Abode of the Dead."

Osnat heard her mother's whispers, felt her hands on her back and neck. It was nice to be mothered, even by Aarluk. It was too comfortable to open her eyes yet.

There was the day Osnat had been appointed director of a major research laboratory. There was the day that she had been rounded up by the police along with all the other Ebers in her city and forced through a wormhole device that dumped her in this cruel place, across the northern radiation belts. There was also the day that her husband was butchered and eaten. Ijiq was right. One day did not predict or lead to the next. There was nothing in the calmness of this day, nothing in the starry sky that hinted of the violence that Osnat was going to unleash on these people, on this world.

"Yes, mother."

Aarluk jumped. She hadn't been expecting an answer. Osnat squeezed her hand and smiled. She propped her chin up on her hand.

"How far is it to the place where we first met?"

"If the weather holds out, we could be there in a few days. We can't cut across the sea ice; it's too rough."

"Can we pass the place we cached the bear meat?"

"If we have to."

"When can we leave?"

"After you bring down the mountain, as you promised."

"I'm not going to bring down the mountain in order to kill, Aarluk. I'm doing it so my child and my family can have a better life."

Aarluk lifted an eyebrow. "Your family?"

"My baby, my mother, her husband. Haran will help us. But there are some things I have to know first; there are some things I have to prepare. It's not a simple thing to do. Even you aren't strong enough to bring it down with your arms."

"How will going to the place we first met help bring down the mountain?"

"We're going further than that."

***

Osnat was sitting in their tent, bone needle in her hand, patching a seam in one of the bed coverings. The twisted-gut thread was surprisingly supple. Osnat wondered how it would smell in spring. How would anything of this place smell in warm weather? Burying your waste inside under the snow, hanging week-old meat and un-cured skins was one thing in the cold, another when it thawed. Osnat had long forgotten about such extravagances as washing.

"We'll leave as soon as everything is packed," Ijiq announced as he crawled in. "I've told people we're going to look for elk. We'll go west along the escarpment till the valley, and then cut across. I'm going to get hold of a long sled for our trip. Pack everything up, and after I return we'll take down the house."

Osnat carefully placed the needle and thread into a case and put the blanket down. If they were setting off on a long journey, it was better to change into less scratchy clothes. Bear-fur was best for extended traveling. She pulled off the caribou pants, relieved herself in a clear spot on the floor, pulled on the bear pants, and her boots over them. She grabbed the bottom of her coat and reached upwards, turning it inside-out over her head. She heard a sound at the tent entrance, and was surprised that Ijiq, or maybe it was Aarluk, was back so soon. Squeezing her head through the neck opening as she pulled the coat off, she turned towards the entranceway, wondering if she was supposed to have finished packing already. Her jaw dropped to see Simon grinning at her.

"You knew your husband was coming. I'm glad you're getting ready." Simon lifted off his parka, and then dropped his skin pants. Underneath he was wearing the remains of her Simon's pants: ragged, torn, but definitely her Simon's. They gaped at each other, both bare-chested. Osnat noticed a familiar bulge in the pocket.

"Let's get our pants off and get this done quickly. You owe your husband."

Osnat whispered: "In the merit of my dead husband, in the merit of all the righteous people brought to this land to die, protect me." She stood still, her arms crossed over her chest, and gave Simon a faint smile. "For your own sake, walk away and leave immediately. You don't want to approach me."

Simon leered, and took a step forward. He tried to take another one but couldn't. "What's going on?" he fumed. He tried to retreat, but couldn't move backwards either.

"Don't make a sound," Osnat instructed. "Clasp your hands behind your head." She walked up and stood right in front of him. There was excitement in his groin but terror in his eyes as Osnat reached into a pocket in the front of the pants. He felt her fingers, but she didn't grab what he expected. Her fingers closed around something in the pants, and she withdrew her hand.

"Again," Simon demanded.

"Take off those pants. You're not fit for them."

Simon obeyed, and stood completely naked, his arousal overwhelming any other feeling.

Osnat stood an arm's length in front of him. "If you are my Simon, you should be able take me now. Are you?"

Simon didn't move more than a finger-length; his arms were stitched to the side of his chest, his feet to the ground. His eyes bulged, he sweated. He was ready to burst.

Osnat walked slowly around him. She poked him in the chest, on the shoulder, on the back. She lightly lifted his eyelid as he tried to wiggle his head away. She moved her hand towards where he wanted her to touch him, but stopped short. He desperately tried to move closer, to make contact, but just left himself panting.

"As I thought. You are not my husband. Since you are not related to me, it's not appropriate for me to be like this in your presence." She quickly dressed in her bearskin traveling clothes and turned back to the task that Ijiq had given her.

Simon was red, he was shaking. He managed to grab himself momentarily, but without touching him, Osnat pulled his hand away. He was desperate. As she walked around him, gathering up blankets and supplies, fear started to overpower his desire.

"What have you done to me? When will you let me go?"

"I told you to leave. You decided to step forward. You did it to yourself."

"How do I get myself out?"

"You give back the name you stole."

Osnat had rarely seen anyone lose consciousness. Once in the lab her assistant had passed out watching Osnat remove the brain from a live dog. It was an important experiment, and she didn't tease her assistant for collapsing on the floor. Osnat had seen people sweat; she'd seen people terrified before the Trail of Tears, but rarely actually faint. She'd certainly never seen someone faint, yet remain upright. The invisible bonds that kept Simon from moving or from touching himself kept him vertical, though all the tension was clearly gone from his muscles. He stood like a marionette, whose puppeteer had gone for coffee. Soon, Osnat hoped, she would learn to tug the strings, to direct events in the way she wanted.

Ijiq returned with a fine sled, having convinced an uncle that it would benefit him more if Ijiq had it. A couple of dogs came with it, adding to Ijiq's team. "Your belly is growing, I want you to ride comfortably," he told Osnat.

She had already brought most of their things outside through the door. They heaved the last skins off, and Ijiq walked through the snow wall, collapsing it. The resulting loud moan startled him, as he stared at a shivering, naked Simon, now covered with snow. Ijiq looked from Osnat to Simon and back, completely astounded.

Simon moaned again, teeth chattering, eyes welling with tears. His skin was covered in chill bumps, but he just stood there, not getting dressed, not even brushing the snow off himself. A crowd quickly gathered to stare. In response, Simon lifted frightened eyes to Osnat.

Falun came up with a broad smile on his face. "You finally got into her. I'm proud of you, son. This is the first step, as we put that family in its place, which at the end, will be in our stomachs." He put his arm around Simon. "Don't stand around like an idiot now. The first sex is good for everyone, but it's time to get dressed. You're not going to get any more women by freezing your parts off."

Ijiq stared at Osnat. "Did you...?"

"Not what Falun thinks I did."

"What did you do, Osnat?"

Simon was shivering, shaking, and turning white from the cold. Falun slapped him hard in the face. "Come on now. That's enough of this nonsense." He grabbed Simon's arm and pulled. It wouldn't move.

Falun wrapped his broad arm around Simon's shoulder, and gave him a push, nowhere. The tears were streaming from Simon's eyes. By now, the entire village had gathered around Falun, Simon, Osnat and Ijiq. Falun motioned to Haran to help him as he reached for Simon's feet. Haran hesitated, but with a brief nod, Osnat told him to go ahead. Haran put his arms around Simon's chest as Falun knelt in front of him, grabbing the back of his ankles. With a grunt, Falun tried to lift them, but they didn't budge.

"He must be frozen to the ground! We have to dig the snow underneath him."

Osnat walked up and knelt at Simon's side. She took hold of one foot and lifted it a hands-breadth in the air. Simon was now suspended on one leg, swaying slightly as Osnat walked back to Ijiq. With a menacing look, she pointed at the naked, shivering boy. "Know that he lives only as long as I allow it. He stole my Simon's name, and doesn't deserve to have it. When I find a way to give back the name to the one it belongs to, I will do so." She circled her arm around, pointing at the stunned villagers. "Know that you all live only as long as I allow it. Do nothing to anger me, and I will allow you to live a little longer. Do anything to me, and you will suffer. Talk to each other about how to hurt me and you will suffer. Everything you say is heard in another Sphere. My friends there will report your evil words to me, and I will be angry. If you doubt my words, ask the boy whether I am to be taken lightly." She put Simon's foot back on the ground.

"We're leaving the village for a while. We'll be back." Osnat made a show of peering at all the faces in the crowd. "Haran is coming with us as a hostage, to make sure his family behaves. Simon is going to freeze to death soon if you don't keep him warm. I won't stop you from doing that."

A humble Falun approached slowly, his palms open, his arms out to the side. "Will you let him go?"

"He threatened my life, my honor, my baby. Should I let him go so he can carry out his threats?"

"I won't hurt you or your baby. I don't know what you mean by "honor." Please let me go," Simon pleaded.

"It means you'll stop demanding to have sex with me."

"Yes," he hoarsely said. "Can I go?"

"I'll decide later." She looked at Puah. "Your son will freeze to death by then if you don't cover him."

She hissed back "I can't move him!"

"If you spend your energy being angry with me rather than keeping your son alive, that's your choice." Osnat walked over to the last items in the remains of their tent, carrying them to the sled. Ijiq pulled down the bear meat cache and loaded it on. The crowd made way for Aarluk. She fastened the dog's harnesses to the front of the sled; the lead dog in the center of the team, the others fanned out alongside it. An orderly arrangement would be meaningless.

14 THE EDGE OF THE WORLD 6

The faint, far-off glow of the spring sun on the horizon showed occasionally at their backs as the four travelers rode over the wind-scoured surface. The snow was firm, packed down by the many days of fierce winds. Its surface formed series of shallow, undulating ridges. The moonlight, the starlight glistened lightly off the cold surface, a taunting reminder of ocean sands sparkling under a warm sun.

It was Osnat's turn to ride on the sled, as it was most of the time. She only got off occasionally to keep herself warm, to keep her limbs from getting stiff. The constant strutting of the aurora in front of her was spellbinding. The crunch of Aarluk, Ijiq, and Haran's boots trotting on the snow played a hypnotic rhythm, as Osnat's memories drifted to places beyond existence: beaches, forests, cities…

Her mind drifted between her old work, and the task she had ahead of her. Many people had praised the former, saying it would save countless lives; make the world a better place. The task she faced now would transform her life; probably end it. If she was successful, she would end the lives of others by destroying their world. Would the Osnat of a year ago recognize this woman riding on a sled, bundled in furs, getting ready to slaughter an entire village?

Osnat had declared herself Tunniq. If that was true, killing was not something that had to be justified any more than going for a walk. It also meant the brat Simon was her husband.

He was a child, really. Just past puberty, barely escaping the death sentence of namelessness. The murder of her husband wasn't personal; it was a way to hold on to his own life. Could she judge this Simon for how his people take names? As a Tunniq, he did nothing wrong.

Osnat's stomach turned at what she had just said to herself. Just because a group of people believe in something, that doesn't make it legitimate, whether it be cannibalism, theft of names, or banishing an entire people to a cruel and barren wasteland.

And if she was indeed Tunniq, then the question of right or wrong was as relevant to her as calculus was to a polar bear.

They had turned north, and passed through the wooded valley they had told their fellow villagers was their destination. The landscape was mostly flat and windswept, with occasional gouges, ridges and valleys. Sometimes Osnat would get out of the sled so it could climb more easily over rough terrain.

The dogs were suddenly yelping. Aarluk, Ijiq and Haran looked at each other, and the sled veered abruptly off towards the esker that they had been riding parallel to. Osnat had been walking, lost in her daydreams, and ran to catch up. The faint glow of the sun was behind the ridge, so it was impossible to see what was in its shadow. The animals' monotonous course had been broken by an indiscernible source of excitement. Nobody pulled out any weapons, which told Osnat that whatever they were heading to was neither food nor foe.

It looked from afar like a little field of tree stumps, maybe twenty or more, all clustered together along the side of the ridge, with one larger stump overlooking them. The dogs were frantic with excitement.

The long whip cracked in front of the lead dog, bringing the sled to a halt. Aarluk stared, and then fell to her knees. Haran and Ijiq clutched each other's arms, trembling. Twenty small torsos were planted waist-deep in the snow, their small faces eroded by what must have been months of ice, wind and snow. A couple of the children had their arms frozen tightly around the legs of an adult, whose hands were on the backs of their heads, trying to comfort them. None of them had any coats, mitts, or hats. Some of the arms were in short sleeves, as if they had been ripped out of a summer day and tossed into this place.

Osnat's legs buckled. She stared at the little girl in front of her. Nothing was left of her frozen eyes. Her brown curly hair came to her shoulders. A headband wrapped around her forehead kept it out of her eye sockets, kept it from blowing off of her crinkly, freeze-dried scalp. Her blouse was a deep blue; it had a little button on the collar with concentric rings on it. Osnat took off her mitts, reached over and touched the button.

"Nancy," the button announced in a soft child's voice. A tracking device, it seemed, for the adult to monitor her charges.

Aarluk dug frantically in the sled.

"What are you looking for?"

"My drum. These children are still trapped. We have to release them!"

"Leave your drum. It will be of no use. I can take care of this."

"Trapped in such desolation, having suffered such a cruel death. They will be vengeful. We must free them, and flee."

"I know what these are. Leave your drum and stand back."

Aarluk looked at her, puzzled.

"Now," Osnat pressed. She had to do this before the horror overwhelmed her.

Osnat handed Aarluk her mitts, and gently pried the button loose from the little girl's collar. She put it in a small leather pouch, and then made her way, one by one, to each of the children, listening to their names, collecting their buttons. She reflected that their clothes should have been completely in tatters, judging by the erosion of their faces.

Finally, Osnat stood face to face with the adult. The features were so decayed she couldn't tell if it was a man or woman. Osnat tried to imagine the horror, the responsibility of shepherding so many small children, trying to comfort them in face of a certain and pitiless death. How could this be? Children were supposed to be with their families. Who was this person? Who were the children who died with her?

The button on the adult's collar was slightly oblong, larger than the children's. Osnat had lied to Aarluk. She didn't know the buttons that spoke. Certainly, the technology to make them was part of her world, but the scientific community had fiercely resisted any technology like tracking devices that could impinge upon people's privacy. Most scientists resisted, that is. And most of the resistors had been sent across the radiation belts to this place.

"Move the sled away," Osnat commanded.

"What are you going to do?" Haran and the others were getting nervous.

"Just move back. Hold on to the traces." In her heart, Osnat thanked her husband for modifying his lighter to generate an intense heat field, rather than the little flame needed to light a pipe full of tobacco. In her heart, she apologized for teasing him about it. "Pipes are for women," Simon had laughed back at her. Nonetheless, he had taken his lighter with him when they set out on the Trail of Tears. Osnat had forgotten all about it till she saw the bulge in the pocket of the pants the false Simon had foolishly put on.

She stood in front of Nancy, turned and stretched her right arm towards the feeble, distant glow of the sun. Her left fist pointed towards the child, Simon's lighter barely protruding between her fingers. "Come to me, sun," she called dramatically towards the sky. The ice started melting around the stump of the body, boiling off in hissing clouds of steam.

The corpse dissolved in the blast of heat, hair igniting in a quick flash of foul-smelling flame. Within a few minutes, all that was left was a pool of water mixed with ashes, a blouse and a skirt. Osnat waited for the clothes to cool, picked them up and walked over to Aarluk.

"Keep all the clothes together."

Aarluk took the garments, holding them as if she was touching fire. She yelled at Haran, who carefully stored them on the sled.

Osnat repeated the process on all of the children, respectfully cremating them, and gathering up the remaining garments.

When there was only the frozen adult with the two clinging children left standing, Haran stopped her. "We should speak to them; find out who they are, and how they came to be here."

Osnat nodded in agreement. She walked over to the adult. "Please forgive the delay. We wish to hear you first." She addressed the two attached children as well. After a brief discussion the three Tunniq quickly set to building a snow house over the frozen people, with enough room for the living to enter. Haran and Aarluk both had their drums. They motioned for Osnat to come inside with them, while Ijiq stood watch.

Haran lit a small oil lamp, casting a pale, yellow glow. There were no costumes, no elaborate dances, no throttling of one another. Simple drumming, focusing their thoughts on the three people in front of them. Aarluk and Haran had their eyes closed, while Osnat stared.

Who were they? They couldn't be part of the Trail of Tears, unless there was an unannounced change of policy, and they were separating children from their families. But then why were they all wearing those buttons and uniforms? And what material were those uniforms made of? They remained unaffected by her lighter, by what must have been months of exposure to conditions that could erode skin and flesh.

The Collective Council had decided recently that in the interest of fairness and harmony, science, technology and innovation were part of the public domain. The protests by many scientists, mostly Eber, against this decision had probably played a large part in her ending up here. According to the Council, any new invention, any new useful idea belonged to everyone, so that the whole world could benefit. If there was a new fabric that was already being distributed, Osnat would have known about it, unless it was part of some clandestine project. Rumors said the Collective Councils had their secrets. Such secrets meant that these could indeed be Eber children.

Osnat's mind was racing as she tried to puzzle this out. She berated herself for not understanding, for somehow missing the factor that would make it all fit together. She glanced around at Aarluk and Haran, both deep in trances.

She flinched. Why was she was speculating about a question the three people in front of her could answer? Osnat slowed her breathing, relaxed her eyes so that she was looking as much at nothing as at the three. With difficulty, she cleared her mind of questions, of speculation, of theories. Using the wisdom of the brook, she reached out to the people in front of her.

Fear was the first thing she felt. It was a small trace that grew into a deluge, quickly cascading into a terrifying roar. Overwhelming fear, then hunger. Impatience and a musty smell. Trapped, no way out. General Failure. Crowds.

Images came, too. Traveling in a sealed, opaque vehicle that wasn't supposed to be opaque. A huge building. Equipment, stored food, hunger, murder... Open doors, too high to reach. Corridors, machines...

Her own terrified scream brought Osnat completely out of the trance. She found herself sobbing on the ground, her face against the snow. She lay there, too hurt to move.

Haran and Aarluk came out of their trances to find Osnat on her knees, her arms tightly wrapped around the frozen bodies. Aarluk stroked her hair softly, "We know, we know..."

They knew the pain. These children had been marooned inside a huge building along with thousands of other people, when their vehicles failed. Unable to escape, they lived on food that had been stored there. When it ran out people panicked. A group exploring the building found strange devices, each with an arched gateway; a series of hoops, actually. Everyone who went through them disappeared, presumably to the other side of the sealed exits. To the other side of the Edge of the World, actually.

Haran and Aarluk didn't know all of it, though. Osnat had screamed when she saw the terrible devices, the portals that had brought Osnat here, along with the rest of the Ebers. When she had gone through one, all the devices were in small, hastily constructed buildings. The portals which these children had passed through were in an immense facility, large enough to house a small city. It had to be from another time, a later era. A time when people wore button-size trackers on their collars. When their clothes were indestructible. When they completely trusted technology, and when that technology was not always worthy of that faith.

If the children and the Ebers both started in different eras but ended up together, that meant at least one of them had traveled across time as well as space. From what she had seen, all the Ebers had ended up more or less in the same place, arriving at more or less the same time regardless of where they started from. There had been portals in different cities, and they were tied to the same destination. Now she knew there were portals in different times, and they were connected to the same point in time as well. How far apart were they? Decades? Centuries?

Osnat doubted that the Collective Councils that exiled them had known where these devices deposited their cargo, any better than the schoolchildren had. They just knew that they sent the Ebers irretrievably far away. With a start, Osnat realized something else: the three they had just communicated with described huge crowds in the building, many thousands of people. Where were they?

Haran flattened the shelter he had just built, and Osnat respectfully cremated the last of the children and their guardian.

"We won't find any more of them alive near the esker," Haran said. He finished tying the drums and sack of clothes onto the sled. "The ridge may look like some kind of protection, but it isn't." He snapped the whip, and the dogs started forward.

Osnat looked at the embankment. The westerly storms, the winds, the snow had blown over the elevated 'highway' and curled back in. While the slope they had just climbed was steep, the other side of the esker's ridge was barely discernible, a gradual descent. Under it stood countless corpses. She watched as the dogs sniffed an erratic course along the surface, tracing countless scents; the countless frozen people.

They traveled to the northeast. Osnat felt uneasy about all the ones she left un-cremated. Her duty though, was to the living. She was grateful when she climbed back on the sled, sore from walking and trotting without a break.

Her gratitude for sitting didn't last long. They had descended from the esker when it had narrowed and turned east. The terrain here was rougher, and the sled pitched precariously from one side to the other. They were close again to the escarpment. The swaying, sparkling fabric of the aurora highlighted the cliff's many scars and bruises, crags where the edge seemed to have been smashed away. The majestic dance of the curtain of light in the sky seemed to mock the cliff's wounds, mock the pain and tragedies of the world below it.

Osnat was getting carried away by her imagination. It was probably her fear of confrontation that was making her see wounds in the rock. Not confrontation with other people or hungry animals; rather, it was her hopes that she was afraid of facing. When she and Simon had initially gone to find help, they left thousands of people behind. From the moment they set out, she had looked forward to returning. Even as her mother was raping her, as her husband's blood was pouring into a bowl, as she fought off a Polar Bear, she held on to a shred, a feeble spark of hope that some of the people for whom she had gone to find food and shelter had survived.

Soon she would confront those dreams, and know whether that small spark would blaze hot, or like her heart, turn to ice.

"We'll camp here," Ijiq's voice brought her out of her daydreams as the sled dragged to a halt. It didn't take them long to put up a cozy snow house, big enough for the four of them.

Aarluk spread some skins on the floor, while Osnat thawed some meat over a small lamp. Ijiq fed the hungry dogs and brought the rest of the food inside. Osnat reminisced about the Polar Bear smelling the fish in her makeshift shelter during the storm. She hoped that there was nothing outside that was strong enough to break through a wall of solid snow.

The four of them ate quickly. Within moments, they were asleep.

Aarluk, Ijiq and Osnat awoke with a start at the sound of Haran yelling in his sleep. Osnat reached over to wake him, but Aarluk grabbed her arm.

Osnat was too agitated by her sudden waking to be able to go back to sleep. She was also agitated by anticipation. Today she'd know. Outside, the dogs barked; a sign that she should get up.

Osnat moved the snow-block out of the entranceway and crawled through. The sun was higher in the sky than it had been for many months. She gazed eastward as it struggled to rise over the horizon. She pulled her hood back, to feel the light on her skin. Osnat walked around the side of the hut, and found the dogs all looking nervously at something in the distance.

"Come outside, now!" she barked to the others, watching the far-away dark dots grow larger.

Within moments the four Tunniq were standing outside, all of them clutching weapons. Two figures approached, waving their arms, running and stumbling, picking themselves up and running some more. As they got closer, Osnat could see that they were emaciated and gaunt, big eyes gazing out from above hollow cheekbones. They were wearing odd garments, layers upon layers of thin cloth. Rags of faded colors wrapped around their hands served as mitts; around their feet, as boots. Osnat pulled her hood back up and tightened her hand on the wooden club. She glared a warning at each of Aarluk, Ijiq and Haran, and took a step forward.

Ijiq moved over to the excited dogs and yelled something at them; they immediately sat down. Light gusts of wind picked up loose flakes of snow and sprinkled them over the four people standing and waiting.

The taller of the two runners stumbled again as they got near, falling on his face. When he couldn't pick himself up quickly his partner went back to help him. She clearly was having difficulty too, and looked pleadingly at the people who stood gazing at them. The man crawled forward a few paces, and finally hauled himself to his feet. They approached nervously, their eyes darting around, unsure what would happen to them next.

"We are so grateful to see you. We haven't eaten in days. You must help—"

"What are your names?" Osnat demanded, an icy look in her eyes, her club swinging loosely in her hand.

The two looked at her, dumbfounded.

"You had better answer," Ijiq growled. The man looked around, taking in the dogs, the hut, and the people. He licked his lips, shuffled his feet... The woman with him started shivering, whimpering. Haran walked over, slapped them both, pointed to Osnat, and then stepped back. Osnat in turn dropped her club on the ground, extended her left arm to the sun, and pointed threateningly at the two with her right fist. Aarluk, Ijiq's and Haran's eyes opened wide in surprise and fear. They had seen what that posture meant.

The two strangers stared at Osnat, stared at the fear in the eyes of her companions. The air shimmered in front of them. They stood agape, still, as a small pool of melted snow formed at their feet. Another gust of wind blew sparkling flakes of snow around, which settled on the four Tunniq, but melted as the wind approached the strangers. The woman stopped shivering. They were frozen, but now from confusion.

Osnat put her arms down. "I am the key to your life. I am food, I am shelter, I am warmth. Give your oath to obey me without question, and you shall have all of these." She paused, waiting for a response. The strangers stared at her, as if she was a ghostly apparition.

"I told you to answer her!" Ijiq gripped the hilt of his stone knife.

"We will... obey" the woman whispered. The man continued to stare, repeating the words only when she elbowed him.

"What are your names?" Osnat glared.

"Eric."

"Norma."

Osnat closed her eyes, rocking slowly on the balls of her feet, concentrating... "Eric, you are alone. Norma, you are Leopard Clan. Go inside, my companions will feed you."

Osnat smiled to herself at the confusion on Eric and Norma's faces. How long would it take them to understand? Aarluk approached her.

"Aren't they your family? Why did you frighten them? If you plan to kill them, let's do it now."

Osnat was surprised. "Mother, you and Ijiq are my family. I know from her name that Norma is related. I don't want to kill any of them, but I don't want to have to fight them. Better to get their obedience right at the start. Now that Norma has taken an oath, I can rely on her. Her people take their oaths seriously. Eric, I don't know. Please, can you get some of the children's clothes from the sled, and bring it in?" Osnat wondered why she hadn't said *my people* when discussing Norma.

"I'll get the clothes, but I want you to remember something: if you lose control of your cruelty, it will conquer and destroy you. A strong person is one who controls her inclinations, not the other way around."

Strange advice from her husband's butcher. She gave her mother a quick hug and crawled into the crowded little shelter. She went up to Eric and waved her knife in front of his face. "I won't hesitate to take out your eyes one by one, or cut off any part of you and make a meal of it. My friends will confirm that just yesterday I destroyed twenty of your children. There's nothing left of them but ashes."

Eric tried to back away, but he was already against the wall.

"You thought you were finally getting out of your vehicle, but then found yourself trapped in a building, which was worse. You thought you were getting out of the building, but found yourself trapped in these lands, which was way worse. You thought you were finding help, but you found me instead. That's infinitely more horrible for you."

Aarluk came in the door with the children's clothes, handing them to Osnat. She put down the knife and waved the small garments in front of Eric's face. "You have felt my power; you can see what I'm capable of. Obey me, and you will live. Think of disobeying, and your suffering so far will seem like a stroll in the park."

Eric's hands shook, as Norma's eyes shot upwards.

"Park...? Here?" Norma asked, her lips trembling. She looked at Aarluk, at Haran, at Ijiq before turning her eyes back to Osnat. "Who... what are you?"

"I am your life; I am your hope. I am Tunniq. I am Osnat, Olive Tree clan; my father, Leopard clan."

Norma gasped, and then stumbled forward, falling tearfully in Osnat's lap. Haran raised his arm to remove the threat, but Osnat motioned him off. Without thinking, she ran her fingers through Norma's hair, calming her. Everybody else stared silently, waiting.

Osnat motioned again to Haran, who hauled Norma back by her shoulders, sitting her against the wall next to Eric.

"How long is it since you've eaten?" Aarluk asked as she took the clothes back from Osnat.

"We caught and shared a fish a long time ago," Eric responded, still trembling.

"If you eat a lot now, it will kill you. We'll give you some broth. That will give you some strength."

"How many are you?"

Norma looked confused by Osnat's question. "Two."

"How many people are alive? How many survived the winter?"

"Oh." She did some quick calculations. "In our group, maybe fifty."

Osnat raised an eyebrow. "Our group?"

"We were arguing about the best way to survive after the scouts all failed. Most of the people from later..." Norma nodded towards Eric, "...went off following the esker. A group of us took to the woods, where we managed to build shelters and catch the occasional animal. Another group took its chances with the bears at the caves. We've had no contact since we split up."

"What happened with the scouts? How did they fail?"

"The ones that returned came back empty-handed, having found nothing or no one to help. Most didn't come back at all." Norma suddenly flinched, as she understood. She leaned forward, put her hand on Osnat's knee and whispered, "Where's your husband? Where's Simon?"

All time, all motion, stopped. Even the vapor rising from the pot of boiling food seemed to freeze. Osnat's lowered her eyelids, as in her mind she ran towards the people in the distance, she and Simon ecstatically waving their arms. They had found help, they would live...

"My husband and I both died after being captured by cannibals."

15 EARLY BRONZE AGE 5

Qimiq pulled the frantic puppy from the water. He stroked its head, easing its panic. Another few minutes, and it would have probably gone still. He gave the dog a bit of dried fish, more to calm it than to assuage its hunger. Too much food to an overheated animal wasn't good. And besides which, it would be a waste.

Qimiq looked at the small barrel in his skiff. He had gathered a handful of blue Fire Snakes, about a third of what he needed. A beautiful oil-fish glided slowly by the side of his boat, its bright green stripes practically an invitation to lift it out of the water. Qimiq declined; he couldn't afford the distraction and didn't know what its scent would do to the snakes he had trapped. The fish would have made a wonderful feast, or provided enough lamp oil to last for days. Some women liked wearing the skin of the oil-fish as a festive collar. When dried out, the green stripes remained, while the rest of the skin turned a dull orange. It was a sign of success, of wealth, of contentment.

Qimiq was neither content nor wealthy. His plot against the Far Marsh people had been a success, but the results were a disaster. His cousin Balthan had disappeared after assassinating Asenath, probably for fear of what the Chief would do to him. He was no doubt also terrified of Sheyds. He had been frightened while the foremost Sheyd trapper was around to protect him. Now he had killed her.

Maybe Asenath had punished Balthan after he killed her. She was so powerful that even Aua, the strongest Sphere Traveler, was forced to bow down to her. The day before she died, she was said to have grabbed a man off the street with invisible ropes and cut off his head without touching him. If she could do things like that, why should death stop her from taking revenge? And even if she couldn't, what was to prevent the Academy students from avenging her death? They were physically puny, but their powers had to be strong. They might have cursed Balthan, or maybe all the Marsh people for that matter, bringing sickness or starvation down upon them.

Look at what had already happened. Qimiq had figured out how to avenge his son, retaliate against the Far Marsh people, take over their villages, and become wealthy. The result however was the destruction of most Marsh villages, and the deaths of too many of their people. Instead of being wealthy and respected, his people were now virtually slaves to the Madai. The Clay People's curses were powerful indeed.

The little dog at his feet looked at him with big, round eyes. Qimiq lifted it up by the belly, bringing its face to his. He ruffled its head, and let it lick his cheek.

"Let's keep hunting." He picked up the end of the stick attached to the dog's collar and tossed the puppy back in the water. Attaching the stick to a peg on the skiff's gunwale, Qimiq scanned the surface for any sign of motion that wasn't from the dog's frantic paddling. They lost a lot of puppies trapping Fire Snakes, but there were few alternatives.

Gathering snake venom was difficult, but it was the only thing keeping the Low Marsh people from being slaughtered by the enraged Chief. The poison was for weapons, Taiku had said. Qimiq hoped they wouldn't end up pointed at his people.

Most of the men of his village were out harvesting snakes. The women were extracting venom, and the children were playing with the bait for coming hunts. Hopefully there hadn't been any accidents.

A faint motion in the water pulled Qimiq's attention to the right. In a single smooth motion, he dipped the woven reed net, sweeping it up and capping it as he lifted the snake out of the water. His life depended on getting the cap in the exact right position.

Smiling at its blue color, Qimiq gingerly added it to the collection in the barrel, and turned back to the puppy, debating whether to give it a brief rest as a reward. He started to lift the stick, when he realized the puppy wasn't splashing. He saw the reason biting the puppy's paw, and grabbed at it with the net and cap, but not carefully enough; he almost let the snake's head out. He frowned: two Fire Snakes shouldn't be so close to one another.

A dead puppy wouldn't attract as much attention as one that was splashing wildly, but maybe he could catch a few more snakes anyway. He made sure the trap to the barrel was tightly closed, and resumed his scan of the reeds and waterways, lightly jiggling the dead dog.

Something about the lily pads caught his attention. They usually floated in familiar patterns; now they were askew. As he bent to examine a twisted stalk, a small blue snake opened its mouth and bit the puppy. Qimiq snatched his hand away and grabbed at his net, fumbling for the cover. The snake let go of the bait as soon as it realized it was attached to something. It dove, and Qimiq caught it half in the net, half over the side. He shoved it with the edge of the cover; the snake tore at the cover with its fangs. Qimiq pushed the snake's head back with the pole he used to propel the skiff, and slammed the net's cover in place. He winced as he heard the wooden handle cracking on the boat's gunwale. This was the end of his snake hunting for today; it was almost the end of his life.

More snakes glided past his boat: red, blue, green... Where did they come from? Was this more Clay People witchcraft? It was probably connected to whatever was wrong in the lily pads. Qimiq turned, and headed back towards his village, towards where the snakes seemed to be coming from.

Something alien; large boats probably, appeared to have pushed their way through, tearing up the carpet of lily pads that covered much of the marshes. Qimiq surmised that at times the strangers had to get out of their boats to pull them through by hand. He estimated that there were a few vessels, ripping through whatever got in their way. If proportioned like his skiff they could be large enough to hold as many as ten people. Qimiq could see where their keels snagged under the water. Whoever came in here didn't have an easy time of it. These weren't marsh boats; these weren't marsh dwellers. These were strangers, probably hostile.

Qimiq had heard of the stories told by the refugees: vast hordes of men sweeping overland, consuming everything they touched. Qimiq had discounted the stories, figuring the travelers as vagrants trying to stir up sympathy; probably misfits who were banished from their communities.

The torn reeds, the uprooted lily pads suddenly made the refugees' stories palpable, as Qimiq's grimness turned to fear.

Another blue Fire Snake swam by his boat, shaking its head as if trying to get a bad taste out of its mouth. Fire Snakes often did this when they had just released their venom at something too large to swallow. Qimiq paddled around a stand of rushes, just keeping his skiff from crashing into a young man standing in the water to his waist, his left hand in a fist, his right arm touching the water. Terror was huge in the man's eyes, in his frozen limbs.

Qimiq quickly pulled out his knife, and made a shallow slash on the man's chest, a little above the heart. Taking some anti-venom from his bag, he rubbed it into the wound. If he got it right, the paralysis would stop spreading, and reverse itself within a few hours. That would give him sufficient time to figure out what to do. He carefully hauled the man over the front of his skiff, the barrel of Fire Snakes between them. He removed the knife from the man's belt, the long sword from the scabbard over his shoulder. Scanning the reeds nearby, he spotted a stand of saw-grass. Cutting off what he needed, he bound the stranger's hands and feet together behind his back. Saw-grass was barbed. The more it was disturbed, the further the tiny points pushed themselves out. Any movement would cause his prisoner tremendous pain.

"Make any noise, I open the cover and let the snakes out. Understand?" The man's eyes showed that he did.

Qimiq paddled cautiously towards home. He didn't want to blunder into any of more of these people.

He stayed concealed in the narrow, crooked channels. It wasn't long till he spotted the man's boat, which was the size and shape he expected. What he didn't expect was that it was filled with women and children from home. Cloth blinders covered their eyes; ropes binding their hands behind their backs were tied to the gunwales. His younger sister kneeled motionless, tears running down over bruises on her cheeks. Three men stood in the water at the sides, cursing loudly as they tried to drag their deep-water boat through the shallow marsh.

Had he simply seen a boatful of women and children from his village or clan, Qimiq would have waited silently till they passed before continuing homeward to find help. But his younger sister was his responsibility. When she would be old enough to have children, he would be the one to support them, to teach and protect them. He could not abandon her.

Qimiq knew how to travel soundlessly through the reeds and waters; even other Marsh people weren't able to detect his approach. He smiled, remembering Balthan's shock when Qimiq popped up in front of him on a recent quiet dawn. His smile faded as he contemplated how since then all their lives had become an unceasing, high-pitched scream.

He took an extra strip of saw-grass, tying his skiff to a bush to keep it from drifting. Carefully removing the barrel of snakes from under his prisoner's face, he loosened the wedges that held the cover in place. A couple of moments in the water with snakes struggling against it, and the barrel would open. The movements of the men struggling with their boat would attract the snakes. He gave the barrel a soft push, to be borne toward his foes by the gentle current.

Struck within a few minutes by an invisible weapon, the men stopped struggling. Qimiq waited a bit longer for the venom to dissipate, and then approached quietly with his skiff. He loosened their frozen grips on the gunwale; they fell over into the water. His sister and the others wept in relief as he untied them and removed their blindfolds.

His sister explained. "Seven boats arrived at our village a little after mid-day. They grabbed everyone they saw. Father demanded they leave. One of them pulled out a sword and cut his head off. They blindfolded and tied up the women, then threw us into boats. We hadn't gone far before the keel started getting snagged in roots and sand. The attackers spent most of the time in the water dragging the boat and cursing. I spent the time praying for Fire Snakes."

Qimiq thought about his father, a rough man who never spared a beating, who loved his children and would stare down death to defend them. Now the job was upon Qimiq to defend his siblings.

"Is there anything we can get rid of to make the boat lighter? I don't want any of you in the water; there are too many Fire Snakes around. I think the ones we've been keeping in the village have escaped."

She considered this. "That must be what killed our captors."

The women looked at him in disbelief as Qimiq quickly recounted how he had killed the attackers, keeping one prisoner alive. He expected praise, not a punch in the mouth.

The face of Tamsyn, his young cousin on his mother's side, was redder than the small moon. Tears and fury coursed from her eyes. Qimiq gingerly put his fingertips to his bruised lips. His cousin's frail looks belied her strength. Too many people wanted to drive her and her sister out of the village, frightened by the dark powers of identical twins, and the odd moles on their wrists. Tamsyn used the magic of strong limbs, a sharp mind and lots of combat practice to stay where she wanted.

"Why would you give him anti-venom after what they did to us?" She massaged her knuckles as she spoke.

"There's no time for me to explain. See if there's stuff we can get rid of, or things we want to keep."

Tamsyn addressed Qimiq again, this time gently. "Do you want to know what happened to the people of our village?" She opened a large, heavy bag at the bottom of the boat, and pulled out five heads, the necks cleanly severed. She placed them one by one on a bench along the side of the boat. The five men had gone out hunting for Fire Snakes at the same time as Qimiq.

Qimiq quickly splashed his face with water, trying to cool off the burning in his mind. Everyone in the boat was turning green. He took a stick and whipped it down on his prisoner's ear. The bloody mark it left didn't wipe out the trace of a smirk.

Tamsyn gently returned her older brother's head to the bag, then the others. "Who will teach, who will take care of my children?" Women unfortunate to be born before any male siblings usually ended up as spinsters. Today Tamsyn had violently been thrown into that lot.

"We have to get back home. Check the other things in the boat."

They dumped the water, the colorful strips of dried meat, and the biscuits crawling with little black spots.

A wooden chest was filled with marvels. There were a few swords, higher than a man's waist. Nobody understood how anyone could make a sharp blade that long. There was a strange bow, with a slotted, greased wooden block for the arrow to lie on. The arrows were unlike anything they had seen: short, thick wooden bolts, with sharpened metal points. A pile of inscribed parchments lay under the weapons. The chest of marvels was clearly valuable.

Now that they felt a little safer, the children in the boat cried for home. Qimiq lifted a couple to the back of his skiff, comforting them. Two of the women grabbed the oars on either side of the large boat. Qimiq led them through the deeper channels, not following the usual route. Everything usual about his life was over.

Taiku, the man who had enslaved his people, was the best person to deal with this. First Qimiq would take something from the chest for himself. Then he would bring everything else to the Chief.

16 EARLY BRONZE AGE 6

Taiku's home was attached to the Lagash Meeting House. It had a single large room, a small vestibule, and a broad courtyard surrounded by a high, stone wall. The building was usually full of soldiers, administrators and petitioners. This night it was empty, dark except for the dying fire in the hearth of the sitting room. Taiku had eaten supper by himself and sent all his servants away. He sat at a table, nursing his willow tea.

A highly polished clay bowl sat on the table in front of him. Most Sheyd-trap bowls were made to deal with specific, named targets. This one was unusual; Asenath had made it to protect Taiku against all demonic foes. He was too important, she explained, to have to wait for a bowl to be made if he needed one. Too much harm could come to Lagash if he was preoccupied with Sheyds.

Taiku lifted the edge of the bowl off the table with one hand, running the other fondly over the engraved surface. He had protected Asenath, but it was his foolishness that led to her needing that protection. Now that she was dead, he consoled himself, he could do her no more harm.

Cannibals. Aua told Aleku he was protecting her from cannibals. How could a cannibal hurt someone with no body? Were there cannibals in other Spheres? Was the Abode of the Dead as painful as the Abode of Life? Taiku had certainly done his share of inflicting pain in this world, but he did so to prevent worse horrors. What more horrible thing could he do to his friend now?

A knock disturbed his brooding. Taiku quickly scrambled to greet his visitor, and flinched as he realized how he could do worse: Simon,

Asenath's son was at the door. His violet eyes evoked his mother's, and his smile was the same one Taiku had loved for so long. He invited Simon to join him at the table.

Simon eyed the bowl that Taiku had been playing with. "May I?"

Taiku lifted it gently and handed it to the boy.

Simon smiled. "I thought I'd find this here."

Taiku didn't respond.

"My mother spent more time on this bowl than any other. She mixed the clay more precisely; made sure it was perfectly shaped. She never let me see who it was for." Simon raised his head and looked intently at Taiku. "Bad times are coming."

Taiku was startled by his intensity. "Why do you say this?"

"My mother was certain of it."

"If Asenath says something is certain, then it is. I will protect you."

"I know," Simon said. "There's something else my mother was certain of, and that's her faith in you."

Taiku sighed. "Then maybe your mother wasn't always right. I've made some serious mistakes."

"Of course you have. My mother's faith wasn't that you never take a false step. It was in your ability to understand what has to be done. You recognize your mistakes, she said, but don't drown in them."

Was this a mistake by Asenath? Taiku was indeed drowning in what he had done to her.

"How are you and your sister doing? How about the students at your Academy?"

"Dinah and I are being looked after by the community. Thank you for the food you sent."

"And the Academy?"

"It's difficult. Those who are more advanced teach the others. We've sent a carrier pigeon, requesting a new Academy Head."

Taiku played some more with the bowl in front of him, as he digested this information. His fingers paused over a dark, round area on the side.

"What does it say?" he suddenly asked.

"What?"

"What does it say in this circle on the inside?"

Simon took the bowl back from Taiku, reached for a lamp and brought it closer. "Made for Protector, Friend Taiku... made by Asenath, daughter of Samuel, mother of Simon, mother of Dinah. In his able hands we entrust the well-being of the Ebers of Lagash."

Taiku paled. He didn't deserve, nor did he want this trust. "What does the rest of it say? The part that traps Sheyds..."

Simon held the bowl up, examining the outside text.

"Upended, overturned, quelled are all Sheyds, all those without merit, all rock-spirits, and Liliths, and Mekelats, and idols and goddesses, and barren ones, and pregnant ones. This is the suppression by which heaven and earth is suppressed. You are all suppressed, whether your names are mentioned or not. All those who dwell within his house - and who kill and harm and appear in hateful shapes which are not good. I Asenath, daughter of Samuel, performed a sealing act by the name of me and in the merit of the names of those before me. It is buried in the threshold of the house of Taiku son of Asahel; it is buried by my hand, and I seal it against you - this is the seal that is intact, with which are sealed heaven and earth."

"Then it's no good. Your mother didn't have a chance to bury it."

"It doesn't have to be physically placed in the ground to work. You create as your heart resonates through your voice. It's words that seal the Sheyds away."

Taiku sat silently, his hands resting on the table. Simon watched his eyes, watched the quiet, which was interrupted only by the occasional crackle from the fire.

Taiku rose and put another log on the flames. It ignited quickly from the glowing embers around it. "Are you and Dinah still living at your house? Who cooks your food, washes and mends your clothes?"

"We take care of ourselves."

Simon stood up and walked over to where Taiku was standing next to the fire. "Chief Taiku, I'm here to bring you a message. My mother knew that her trip to the Marsh village might cost her life."

"Why didn't she call on me to help? At least to send some soldiers with her!"

"I wasn't about to question her judgment, so I didn't ask." Simon sniffled, and wiped his eyes with his sleeve. "I do wish though that she'd made a different judgment." He wiped his eyes again. He tried to continue speaking, but his lips were trembling too much. Taiku wrapped his arms around him as they leaned their heads on each other's shoulders, trying to hold back tears.

"What's your message?" Taiku finally asked, moving back.

"Actually, you already have it: "In his able hands we entrust the well-being of the Ebers of Lagash." The community and the students at the Academy will do whatever you require of us, whether it's to study or fight. Chief Taiku, by written direction of my mother you are the leader of the Ebers of Lagash."

Taiku stared at Simon, his lips trembling. "Your mother is lost to this world. I give you my oath that I will never do anything that could endanger you or Dinah."

"Only the dead are out of danger, and then not always. We're exposed to it now, from Ja'ix. My mother judged that you're our best hope for survival. I told you already that I don't question her judgment. I don't think you do either."

Taiku walked back to the table, lifted the bowl, and looked again at the inscription that he couldn't read. He put it down, walked over to the fireplace, and poked at the logs. The flames rose higher, reflecting against the wood he had added a few moments earlier. The room was getting hot.

The Chief leaned against the mantle, his face furrowed in concentration.

"You've already been a tremendous help with the wood-obsidian weapons you designed. Keep working on those."

"I'm glad you approve."

"You used a pigeon to send for a new Head for your Academy, right?"

Simon nodded.

"You use pigeons to communicate with other Eber communities, right?"

"Yes. We're spread out over much of the world. We want to know how our families, our people are doing in different areas. Is there anything they need from us, like a teacher? Is there anything we can do for them? We've even arranged marriages by pigeon."

"All Eber communities use pigeons?"

"All that I know of."

"If you sent a message to a community a day's ride from here, they could send one to the next community over?"

"Yes," Simon said. "Actually, you're reminding me that I have another message for you from the Tungus horse breeders. The horses you requested are on the way; lots of them. A group of riders and our new Academy Head started out about a week ago."

Taiku smiled for the first time since Simon arrived. "I need the students at the Academy to do some trapping, but not Sheyds. I want you to find out where Ja'ix is. Determine where he's been, how fast he's moving. Use your pigeons; use your communities to cast a net over the world. We'll calculate his movement and position from the information you collect."

Taiku stopped his pacing and put his face close to Simon's. "But keep the messages simple, and don't write in the regular script. Use the kind you put on the bowls, which only Sheyds and Ebers can read. That way, if Ja'ix's people get hold of a pigeon, they won't understand what we're doing."

He straightened up. "I declare the Academy a military center; you're all my soldiers now. I leave you and the other students to work out the details of your task.

Once again, he wrapped his arms around the young man. Taiku would protect Simon and Dinah. Nothing would come before that. He prayed that Aua would protect their mother from cannibals, whatever they were.

17 MODERN AGE 5

Saima couldn't sleep. He found Linda in her common room, sorting pottery and parchments that Tammy had knocked out of place when she fell over. The shard he had used to stab John sat by itself on a table. Linda was wearing a white button-down robe and thin white gloves, her luxuriant black hair gathered in a tight bun.

Saima watched her pick up a piece at a time, examine it, write a few notes, and put it on a shelf. She was oblivious to his presence, her back to him while she worked.

"Can I help?"

She turned to Saima with a grin. "It will probably take me the rest of the day to go through the collection to put it in order. Afterwards, we can 'help' each other. Shower again?"

Saima reddened. "Let me help you with these." He waved his hands towards the pieces.

"It's complicated. Some of the pieces seemed to have jumped from one shelf to another, as if they had minds of their own. Things are supposed to fall down; not sideways, down and then sideways again. Especially not sideways, up, and sideways again. It's a bizarre mess." She pointed at some bones lying on the floor. "Don't touch the snake skeleton. It's toxic."

"What do you mean?"

"The first few people who touched it died within minutes, as if they'd been poisoned. After that, it was kept in a special unbreakable glass case."

"Where's the case now?"

"I threw the broken pieces of glass in the trash. I have special forceps for handling the snake. I just have to figure out what I'm going to do with the bones when I pick them up. The simplest thing would be to incinerate them, but I suspect this snake had some special ritual significance. It's too important to destroy in a fire."

"Thanks for the warning." Saima walked over to the shelves and reached for a random pottery shard.

"Gloves," Linda said. She smiled as Saima reached his arm awkwardly behind her for the box of gloves, carefully avoiding touching her. They both yelped as the piece he gently picked up crumbled into tiny flakes.

"That was five thousand years old. You destroyed something that cannot be replaced."

"I was barely squeezing it."

Linda sighed. "That was one of the coarse-grained pieces. The finer pieces are stronger."

"The one I used: which type is it?"

"With the blood? Fine texture. Why?"

"It was bloodied before I stabbed a person with it, maybe hitting bone. It got soaked again in blood and it's still intact."

"You said that happened in the aurora. I don't understand what you meant, but maybe that's what protected it. The piece might have been destroyed if you had been in normal space. I had the blood analyzed. It's John's, but it's not human. I can't explain. There are also traces of human blood, but so decomposed they must be from when the bowl was first used. "

Saima frowned as he considered this. "Where did you get all these things?"

Linda's lips quieted. Her eyes focused on him as she dropped her hands to her side. She took a deep breath, glanced around the room, and then put her eyes back on Saima.

"You won't believe it. You'll be angry."

"Tell me."

"Will you still trust me? Will you continue to stay at our house?"

Saima had asked only to distract her from her ire at his destroying a piece. She had now made the question vitally important.

"Let's turn it around. Do you trust me enough to answer?"

She looked into Saima's eyes and then back to the wall of pottery. One hand rummaged aimlessly along the shelf, adjusting positions, turning pieces over, and then turning them back to how they had been.

"Come sit on the couch with me." She sat down, legs crossed, her robe riding up her thighs. Saima sat beside her. She immediately put her head on his shoulder and sniffled. Saima wrapped an arm around her, telling himself it was to comfort her. His other hand rested on her knee.

"My research wasn't getting any interesting results; I wasn't learning anything that hadn't been covered before. So, I sent a team of students to the Dead Lands." She squeezed his hand. "They excavated these pieces."

Was she expecting a profound reaction, perhaps shock, or anger? Saima squeezed her hand in return.

"So, do you still want me as your host?"

"Explain your actions."

"I'm the head of the archaeology department at the university. Any student who's going to become a career archaeologist has to obey whatever instructions I give him. I sent ten of them to the Dead Lands to dig. It took them three years to find and excavate a promising site."

She looked at Saima expectantly. He still had no idea of what this meant.

"And...?"

"Four of them died in the Dead Lands. Three more died within months of coming home. The last three are permanently damaged: one blind, the other horribly crippled, and the last one lost his mind. All because they followed my orders." She blinked, fighting tears.

Saima wordlessly removed the hand from around her shoulder, removed the other hand from her knee.

They sat together silently, Saima trying to grasp what this was all about.

"I sacrificed them to advance knowledge."

"Did you know it was so dangerous?"

"I sent them to the Dead Lands!" she stood up and shouted. "I know what the word 'dead' means!"

"You knew it was dangerous and you sent them anyways?"

"Yes."

"Why?"

"It's a big hole in the archaeological record. For centuries scientists have been curious about what happened in the Dead Lands."

"Why didn't the curious scientists go?"

"They didn't want to die for curiosity."

"Was it that risky?"

"It wasn't risky; it was certain. Nobody survives the Dead Lands. Everyone knows that!"

"I'm a northern savage, remember? I never heard of the Dead Lands till you just mentioned them."

Linda put the back of her hand to her mouth. "I'm sorry, Saima! I forgot you're not a regular person."

"I'm a regular person, just not from the regular place. What are the Dead Lands?"

"A dreadful wasteland where the air and the ground are poisonous. According to some it was destroyed by debris from a collision in space: an asteroid, or something like that. Maybe there was a war, but that in itself wouldn't make the place toxic. There are stories of the odd lost travelers' reports, describing remnants of towns; farms, graves, and other signs of long-ago life. We excavated around the remains of a trading center, at a river delta. Legend says it's the place where civilization first flourished. Now it's an arid wasteland devoid of life. Some scientists believe the changes happened no more than five thousand years ago."

"That's a long time ago."

"Not from the perspective of a planet. A world changes very slowly from our perspective, but that's because we have such short lives. A planet's life is much longer.

Saima considered her words. "It's not always slow change. A rock formation on a cliff near my home looked like the face of an angry old man. It came down suddenly and changed my world very quickly."

Linda laughed. "Old people's faces do sag sometimes. But you're right: some changes happen quickly. I'm certain a sudden catastrophe struck the Dead Lands. That's why I sent the students to investigate."

Saima's heart flared at Linda's joke. Remembering his dream from the utility room, he fought the temptation to put a spear through her breast. Not that he had one at hand anyway.

"I never considered the planet changing. In my home the changes are seasonal."

"Are you sure, Saima? Is every winter as cold as the previous? Are the summers always as hot?

"We expect regular variation. The stone face falling off the cliff was a small change, even though it killed my wife."

Linda blanched. "Saima, I'm sorry, I didn't... I know you're angry about the Dead Lands."

"Why should I be angry about them? I don't understand sending students to die, but you people do lots of bizarre things."

"I thought—"

"Trees!"

"Trees? What are you talking about?"

"It's too cold in our lands for any vegetation, except moss or tiny bushes. But there was a time forests grew in the river valleys below the escarpment. It means our home was once a much warmer place."

"It would mean your people adapted to the change in climate."

"We knew about trees from before we were sent to our present home. My father is from the Olive Tree clan."

"My students found lots of dried olives in the Dead Lands."

"Maybe I should go there."

"Do you want to die? Don't even think of it."

***

The hatch of the police wagon slid open roughly, groaning as if it didn't really want to move. There was a notification from Police Central. Tammy entered her destination, pressed "go," and then "listen." The hatch hissed closed behind her.

"What did you and the northern savage do, that you sent everybody out of the room? The official report will show you broke the Codes. Jackson will hear about that; it will cost you. Make sure you bring in the suspect. He needs re-education." Finer was a trusted Lieutenant, but the Superintendent's message confirmed that Police Central still monitored everything she did.

The message was legitimate. Finer could lose her job, or worse for the violation. Saima might be exiled. Maybe her, too.

She touched the reply button. "I have a plan. He trusts..." Finer stopped speaking as she realized the wagon was still on the ground, not moving. All the readouts were dark.

She pushed the reply button again. "For the record, I'll bring him in when I'm done with him. I'll explain in person." She leaned over and spoke into a baffle next to the hatch: "Police Central."

Still no response.

"Police Central. Engage." She leaned over to put her eye in position for the blue light to scan, and held herself in place.

Nothing.

"Police Central." She spoke again into the baffle, keeping her eye at the ready. Still nothing. Finer sat up, raising her eyebrows. She repeated it, louder.

"Recorder Depository..." No response. "Central Facilities..." Tammy Finer took a deep breath. "Home..." The wagon was silent, except for the sound of its occupant's breathing.

She touched the concentric-ringed communicator on her collar: "I'm stuck on the ground; my wagon is not responding."

"Tammy Finer," it replied.

The Detective opened a door under the control panel and looked for the large red "reset" button that was supposed to be somewhere there. There was a big green button, but that was all. She pressed it, and fell back in her seat as an iridescent, blue-green dragonfly the size of her fist flew out from underneath.

The wagon shuddered. A noise, like escaping gas came from a baffle on the control panel.   All the dials lit up, but in green, rather than the usual blue, red and orange. A green mist was settling over everything. Finer leaned closer to the baffle to inspect.

Something unsubstantial, feeling like a fist of compressed air slammed into her chest. It knocked her from her seat, painfully twisting her leg and bouncing her head on the floor.

Panting, she carefully put a hand to the back of her skull; no blood. Concussion? Not likely. She flexed her leg; no break.

Detective Tammy Finer closed her eyes and inhaled deeply. She held the air in her lungs for a couple of seconds, and then slowly let it escape through pursed lips. She blew a quick last puff through her mouth and opened her eyes. The wagon was filled with a pale, moldy mist. Finer stood up, pressed the emergency release on the hatch, and then tried kicking it loose. Nothing. She put her mouth to the baffle: "Emergency." The wagon remained still.

The transparent wagon shell was slowly becoming translucent. Soon she would be sealed in, blind to the outside. If the wagon was reverting to its opaque high-efficiency state it could mean that all outside air would be cut off. How long would it last if it wasn't being refreshed?

Finer sat down, cleared her thoughts, and struggled to calm herself. She was police; she could deal with this. She shuddered as she felt the soft, green mist seep through her skin. It terrified her. She unbuttoned her coat and grabbed her sword, meaning to fight off whatever it was. She had a death grip on the hilt; the blade vibrated to her trembling. She shut her eyes and moaned.

She drifted. The place was familiar. That was odd, because there was nothing to recognize: no features, no walls, no dimensions. There was just whiteness.

It wasn't through her eyes that she knew where she was. It was the pain that touched her. John's feet and fists had kicked and beaten her in this place. That is, if it could be called 'place.' There was no violence here now, no John. The emptiness was excruciating, more painful than the assault. Finer felt like she was being absorbed into the emptiness.

How was this happening? She was fading, disappearing... Finer battled the growing panic in her stomach. She was a trained warrior. She couldn't let this overwhelm her.

But how to resist? There was no enemy to battle. She gripped her sword tightly and spread her feet in a fighting stance. She looked to the right, to the left. There was nothing to swing at, except a swirl of green smoke that caressed her fading body. She put the sword back in the scabbard.

How did Saima save her the last time? He had stabbed her assailant with a piece of pottery from Linda's common room. How did he get it? Finer shut off her thoughts, except for an image of what she wanted. She reached out frantically and grabbed. To her surprise, she held a shard of pottery in her hand. She swung viciously, though she had no target. The clay crumbled into dust, which slipped out of her hand and was carried off by the mist.

There was no panicking. You had to exist to panic, and Finer was vanishing into oblivion. There was no fighting, either. You had to be, to fight. There was just a pain in her toes, in her fingertips, and the thin smoke dancing around her, dissolving her. What color smoke was she? No color; nothingness is undifferentiated. Her toes, her fingertips were disappearing; there was vague warmth...

The sudden, searing pain on her cheek pulled her body back to her; she gingerly touched her screaming skin with her fingertips. She was in pain, but in the Abode of Life. She opened her eyes, and looked into Linda's worried face.

"You have to get moving!"

"What..."

"Give us your arms."

Finer moved her hands a little forward, as Saima and Linda grabbed her arms and pulled her up.

"Walk!"

Finer shuffled towards the hatch. They pulled her out of the wagon, and half-dragged her into the house, sitting her on a chair in the vestibule. Saima kneeled in front of her, taking her hands; his face was creased with concern. She shivered.

"Bring hot soup," Linda ordered Alex. "We have to get some warmth into her."

Finer's lower lip trembled. Tears formed in her eyes as her nose dripped. Her breath came in little gasps.

Saima put his palms on her cheeks, and wiped the tears away with his thumbs.

"Nooo!" she screamed. She stared at him, and then sighed in relief.

"Tell me."

Finer put her head on Saima's shoulder.

Alex walked in with a tray holding a steaming bowl of soup. "Bring her into the dining area, so she can eat more comfortably."

Saima reached to wipe her eyes again. She stopped him and wiped them herself. She eyed him cautiously. "What did you do to me?" She softly touched her lip with her tongue, tasting blood.

"First I shook, then I slapped you. I slapped your cheeks, hard to bring you back. Sorry I cut your lip. You were being dragged away from the Abode of Life."

Linda appeared with some ice wrapped in a cloth. Saima held it to Finer's bleeding lip.

"That was dangerous, but thank you," she whispered. "I'm glad you came when you did."

"Linda and I were discussing her pottery fragments. She's working on a difficult project—"

"I know about it," Finer spoke through her bruised lips. "I had to deal with her student who refused to go to the Dead Lands."

Saima turned in surprise to Linda.

"I told you, students have to obey me. One girl tried to quit. I told the Student Union to handle it. You're not allowed to resign. They called the police."

Finer moved the ice pack from her mouth. "She refused counseling, so I had to deal with her."

Saima moved closer and kneeled beside her. "By 'deal with her' you mean..."

"I gave her a goodbye kiss," she said, a blank expression on her still-pale face.

The tray almost dropped from Alex's hands. He managed to get hold of it again as his back arched, his eyes widened. "Are you—"

"Yes, I am" she hissed through swollen lips. She drew a breath and shivered. Her eyes went longingly towards Alex's tray.

"Let the Detective have the soup while it's hot," Alex said. "I don't want her upset."

Saima and Linda reached to take Tammy's arms, but she waved them off. With Saima ready to grab her, she shuffled her way to the dining area. Alex hurried in with the food, and quickly withdrew after putting it on the table. Detective Finer sat down and tentatively lifted the spoon to her lips.

She felt life come back to her as she took a few mouthfuls. "This is—" She suddenly dropped the spoon and stared straight ahead, gritting her teeth.

"What is it? What's wrong?" Alex said as he took a step away.

Finer wrapped one hand around the fingers of the other and rocked gently, breathing hard.

Saima kissed the top of her head. "This is good. If your fingers weren't in pain, it could mean they were dangerously frostbitten. If they hurt this soon, you'll be fine. Wrap your hands around the soup bowl. You should take your boots off, too."

He climbed under the table to help her, and sat there for a few minutes, softly massaging her feet. Her teeth came unclenched, her breathing softened.

"You told me before you're here to get something that was lost. Is it me, Saima? That's twice you've rescued me. When do I get to save you?"

Saima came back up and took the chair facing her. "Stolen, not lost. You're neither. You're busy with your dog mission, aren't you?"

"I don't have a mission anymore. It disappeared in the wagon. I'm resigning." She pressed her communicator.

"Tammy," it answered in her own voice. She twisted her face in frustration.

Saima took her hand. "Don't resign. Help me."

"What was stolen?" Linda said. "What are you looking for?"

"I don't know."

This brought silence to the table. Linda, Alex and Finer looked back and forth from one to another.

"Let me show you something." Saima bent forward, kissed Tammy's thawed fingertips and strode from the room.

"Can I have more to eat?" Finer said.

Alex went to a cabinet and brought out a plate full of crackers. Linda dropped a fistful of green-flecked cheese balls onto it.

Finer looked at the cheese, and then up at Linda.

"Mint farmer's cheese. Is that good? We have other kinds."

"Farmer's cheese is okay," Finer spoke as she popped a ball into her mouth. She chased it down with some crackers. Alex brought her a glass of water.

Saima returned with two fragments of pottery in his gloved hands, which he placed carefully on a napkin.

Tammy took another cracker and more cheese before draining the glass. Saima stood silently beside her.

When she looked up again, Saima unfolded a piece of paper from his shirt pocket. He handed it to Alex. "What's this?"

Alex held it in front of his face, moving it forward, backward, trying to get it into better focus.

"I don't know. It looks like Linda's writing." He passed it to her. "Why did you write on this instead of your regular notepad?"

Linda frowned as she studied the document. "It's from my regular notepad. This is part of my original inventory of boxes that were delivered from the Dead Lands. I've been looking for this for weeks." She looked at Saima. "Where...?"

"Remember when the generator was making noise? It was this paper flapping behind the grill of the cooling fan. I wondered why you use a green notepad."

"This paper was white when I wrote on it."

"The paper is green. Your wagon was covered with green dust when we went to get you out."

Finer's eyes flickered. "There was a green glow over the control panel just before I was hurt." She pushed the cheese plate to the side.

Saima scratched his arm, and paced back and forth a few times. He stopped, picked up a cracker, put it down and resumed pacing. Finer reached for one of the pieces of pottery, but Linda intercepted her hand. "You have to wear gloves..."

"You shouldn't have been able to reach me," Saima said.

"I didn't; you reached me when I was stuck outside the Abode of Life with John, and again when I was in trouble in the wagon."

"You shouldn't have been able to reach me in the northlands. Not you personally, but anyone. Touching the Edge of the World normally burns your skin off. I was terrified when we flew out."

"What are you talking about, the edge of the world? The world doesn't have an edge," Finer said.

"The northlands are surrounded by an impenetrable green curtain. Everyone there is, was cut off from the rest of the world."

Linda fiddled with one of the pieces of pottery. "If you're now able to leave the northlands, the curtain has ripped. But if you're really from the Olive Tree clan, I think you Ebers are originally from the Dead Lands."

Saima leaned in closer. "Continue."

"You said your father was Olive-Tree clan. My students discovered that olives were a staple in the Dead Lands. Are there olives across the Edge of the World? Another thing: you were drawn to the Dead Lands pottery shards, having no clue what they were. You used them to rescue Tammy. How did you know to do that?" Linda put her hand over Saima's. "The northlands are surrounded by a green curtain, which is torn. We're having all kinds of problems, and most of them have to do with the color green. Green note, green mist, dust.... As bizarre as it sounds, I think that the holes in the curtain are pieces that got ripped away and are now causing havoc here. We've never had so many things break down before. There's got to be a connection."

"How does that connect with the Dead Lands?" Saima put a fingertip in his mouth and nibbled at the corner of the nail.

"I don't know, but I'm almost certain that the Dead Lands were once your home." Linda pointed at Finer, who was munching on a cracker. "Why didn't you die in the wagon?"

She frowned, and washed the cracker down with water. "Because you and Saima saved me?"

"Yes. I don't understand how."

"What do you mean?"

"When we realized your wagon was still sitting outside, we ran out to investigate. It was covered in green dust. We wanted to check if you were inside but couldn't see through. Saima tried to force open the hatch. As he was pulling at it, a piece of pottery I had put down on the wagon started to slip."

"When the piece slipped, the wagon began to vibrate, as if it was trying to lift off. As soon as I put it back on the wagon, the vibration stopped."

"The dust disappeared, the wagon became transparent, and we saw you slumped in the chair. We tried the hatch and it opened right away, as if it hadn't even been closed properly. I've tried to contact the Committee to report the incident, but we can't reach anyone."

Finer stood up suddenly and put her hand to her mouth. "General Failure Alert!" She jabbed at her communicator button, but it just repeated her name. "That's why nothing's working! All wagons within a day's travel are supposed to be heading to the Central Facilities."

"What's a General Failure Alert?" Alex asked.

"What are the Central Facilities?" Saima asked.

"When the systems that run our city start malfunctioning, they go into a default mode. I don't know what most of it means, besides chaos. I know we're in trouble." Finer took a few breaths to calm herself. "The Central Facilities keep our city alive. Our water, energy, wagons, the communicators, all the records, everything is controlled through the Central Facilities. It never malfunctions."

"Never malfunctions?" Saima said. "When's the last time you were in there?"

Alex chuckled. "No one has been in the building for hundreds of years; the doors are sealed. There are stories about the place. It's said that many years ago thousands of people were forced into the Facilities and never came out. According to the legend, one day they'll return and lay waste to the world. I wrote a poem about it."

"They never came out?" Saima asked.

"I have to go now." Finer pulled at the sleeves of her jacket.

"What do you mean? I'm not letting you leave, Detective Finer."

"And how do you intend to stop me?"

Saima smiled. "You're stranded. You can't take a wagon."

"A General Failure Alert can lead to total chaos. I have to do something!"

"Unless you know what to do, why don't you sit down for now and think things through. You still need to recover your strength."

Finer looked around at Saima, at Alex, at Linda. She sat back down.

"We'll go to the Central Facilities together," Saima said to Finer. "There may be answers there. Maybe records." He frowned. "Maybe Sheyds."

"Before that we should check out the Old Post for clues. That's where you said you started from."

"What clues?"

"About the dog. As a Detective, it's my responsibility to—"

Saima glanced out the window, and then flinched. "Why are there so many rats outside?"

The others looked outside. Dozens of rats ran back and forth outside the low window, peering in.

"Rats?" Linda looked out the window, and put her hand over her mouth. "We've never..."

Finer stood up and grabbed Alex's arm. "Take me outside."

Alex froze.

"Oh, don't worry; I won't kiss you goodbye. Let's go, before I change my mind."

It was quick. A brown light from Finer's weapon cooked the rats enough to stop their movement; not enough to keep them from shrieking.

"Finish them off. I can't stand this noise." Linda hands were over her ears.

"I've neutralized them. The Codes say we're supposed to have respect for all life. By what right can I kill them?"

"We're human. They're rats. Do it," Saima said.

"Police are supposed to help the injured."

"Help rats? You want me to be your teacher, remember? Your first lesson is to know the difference between animals and people. Besides which, you injured them in the first place. End their misery."

Finer sighed and vaporized the few closest to her. She waited for her weapon to recharge and moved on to the next group.

Linda pinched her nostrils against the stench of roast flesh and burned hair. "Why are there rats? I've never seen any before."

Saima pulled her hands away. "Someone, or something is sending you a message. It's best to pay attention."

Brown grass showed around the wagon, where the snow cover had been melted. Finer took Saima's arm as they went back into the house. "I'm pleased you've decided to take me on as a student."

Saima groaned to himself. Now he was stuck with a decision he hadn't made, with an apprentice he didn't really trust.

18 MODERN AGE 6

The route from Alex and Linda's home back to the Old Post was quite scenic in the daytime. Low, spiral communities dotted the landscape. The cobblestones, mosses, and trees of each group of homes were laid out almost identically, on slightly different terrain.

The door to the Old Post was locked. There was no response to Saima's knocking.

Saima eyed the Police Detective at his side. "Once we've come all the way—"

"Move." Finer nudged him to the side, activated a device on her belt, and pushed the door open.

Saima walked slowly around the large room, searching. He wasn't sure for what. The floor was recently washed, the tables cleared.

He sighed. "Nothing."

"Come look at this." Finer was at the counter at the far side of the room. A hummingbird hovered over a body lying flat on the floor, picking at the flesh of his exposed heart with its elongated beak.

Simon grabbed at the bird. It evaded him easily, and escaped out the door.

Finer pressed her fingers against the man's throat. She lifted and released an arm. "He's been dead for a while. Do you know who he is?"

"That's the kid who was here when I was attacked. He brought food out from the kitchen."

"Is he the one you fought with?"

"No. He just smiled and watched the action. What are you going to do about him?"

Tammy motioned towards the door. "Come with me."

She spoke into a little baffle by the entrance: "Lieutenant Detective Tammy Finer. Present Security Panel." A blue light scanned her eye; a panel lit up, showing the interior of the club.

"Tell me when you see your foe." She turned back to the baffle. "Lieutenant Detective Tammy Finer. Visual rewind, sixty to one time ratio."

Saima was stunned to see himself and Tammy walking backwards out of the Old Post, followed by the door closing, the room empty. "What is this?"

"The logs."

"Everything is recorded?"

"Yes. But only high-ranking police can get to all of it. I have limited access. I couldn't access it remotely because of the General Failure Alert."

He turned back to the panel and watched as an hour went by every minute. Finer paused as it showed the staff about to leave.

"Is your attacker one of them?"

Saima shook his head. He pointed to one of the staff. "That's the one on the floor now. Why didn't we see his death on the recording?"

She shrugged. "Lieutenant Detective Tammy Finer. Resume rewind."

The staff cleaned up, then sat around the messy tables, talking.

Saima, facing the door, walked stiffly into the room. If not played backwards, he would have been running out. A knife was in his hand.

"Lieutenant Detective Tammy Finer. Visual rewind, one to one time ratio."

He was on the floor. He was falling, standing, circling... Saima was wrestling someone, being overpowered. But there was no one visible except the kid now on the floor, who was watching the fight with amusement.

"Can we hear him? Do the logs include sound? He was muttering the whole time we fought; something about traps."

"We should be able to."

Had Mekelat only been in his imagination? Finer couldn't see anyone with him, the staff didn't see anyone with him. Saima couldn't see his adversary in the recording.

"I'm not crazy," he said.

"I can see you're being pushed. Your opponent must have been a big man to be able to shove you around like that. Any idea why we can't see him?"

"He looked like he would break if someone blew on him. He was at least a head shorter than me, and his skin had a sickly, silver pallor."

"And he was still getting the better of you..."

"I remember his eyes. They were bloodshot, but not red bloodshot; they were green..."

"Lieutenant Detective Tammy Finer. Pause." She leaned an arm against the wall. "Green?"

Saima pointed to the panel, putting his finger over his invisible opponent. "You're right. I didn't think of it before; a green man, who's stronger than he looks."

Finer's eyes went to the panel, then back to Saima. "At least we know what he is."

"He said that he was going to pay me back for everything my daughter did to him."

"Saima, you never told me you have a daughter."

"I don't."

Finer tilted her head, her eyes wrinkling with pleasure. "We'll have to do something about that." She sat down at a table. "Either he knows the future, or he's crazy. What else can you tell me?"

"Sheyds are a legend my ancestors learned from the Tunniq. They're insubstantial beings, whose trapped souls make up the Edge of the World. They're jealous of the people who are solid. That's all I know."

"We should speak to the Tunniq, then."

Saima sat down across from her. "Can't. We wiped them out long ago."

"I see." She reached over and pulled Saima's hand away from his mouth. "Is that when you started biting your nails?"

He put his hands flat on the table, his cheeks turning a slightly red as he looked downward. He tried to smile.

Tammy put his hands over his. "Don't be—"

Saima lifted his head. "What's that smell?"

Finer sniffed and screwed up her face. "Where did it suddenly come from?" She sniffed again, walking towards the back of the room. "It smells like dung."

"Burning dung. We use it for fuel sometimes."

Finer stood. "I'll check the toilets."

"The smell is stronger this way." He walked cautiously towards the kitchen.

Saima tried to push down the unease in his stomach as he examined the ovens, cook-tops, sinks. The smell was stronger in one particular direction. He opened a cabinet door under one of the cook-tops.

"Detective," he shouted. "What's the inverted pyramid hanging from a box in the kitchen?"

"What? I'm coming..."

"It's about two spans high, with a couple of thin pipes coming out its sides. That's where the smell is coming from."

Finer came into the kitchen, wrinkling her nose in disgust. "The pyramid? That's the standard service coupling to the Central Facilities." She went and peered under the cabinet. She straightened out, a sour look on her face. The scent of damp, smoky dung was getting worse. Tammy was turning green.

"I think we should leave, Detective."

"I want to see the diagnostic read-out on the unit. I want to know what's going on."

"We're being hunted, Detective. There is something after us; we have to get out of here."

She took a deep breath and bent down again to the cabinet. A hissing noise, like pressurized gas came from outside the kitchen. Tammy stood up and pulled Saima's sleeve. "Let's go."

The Old Post was built with a grey-stone exterior, and vertical simulated cedar-plank interior walls. That was the original construction, at least. At the moment, the interior walls were made of vertical strips of fire, each plank a separate flame. The tables, whatever they were, slowly melted to the floor as Saima and Tammy ran for the blazing door. Saima's foot caught on the leg of the corpse; he tripped and slammed unevenly to the floor. He rolled over, wincing from pain.

Finer reached down, and grabbed him under the arms, yanking him to his feet. She pulled a weapon from her belt and adjusted a knob, aiming at where the door used to be. "Go," she said as a momentary gap appeared in the wall of fire. She ran through, pulling Saima behind her. "Keep running."

The smell of burning dung dissipated as they headed towards the river. Tammy was no longer sprinting for maximum speed. Her gait was relaxed, and she breathed easily.

Saima needed to rest. Wincing, he leaned his head against a birch, rotated his sore arm, and tried to catch his breath. She massaged his shoulder blades, easing the pain. "We'll walk a bit."

He tried to respond but was too winded. Saima played the events back in his mind. They didn't make any sense, except for one. Mekelat was a Sheyd. He had been part of the Edge of the World, and was surly after thousands of years of imprisonment.

"Maybe your daughter went back in time and did something to him." Finer jolted Saima out of his brooding.

"Is there a way to travel like that?"

"No. It's logically impossible. Maybe your foe doesn't exist in time. That might be why we couldn't see him fighting you at the Old Post."

Saima considered this. Its implications were overwhelming. "His name is Mekelat. Maybe we better run some more."

Finer smiled, grabbed his sleeve, and took off at an easy lope. "At least you found who you were looking for."

"He found me," Saima said. "It's like he laid a trap, knowing I'd come back."

"What now? Will he follow us to the Erbils'?"

Saima stopped. "Where?"

Tammy stared at him for a moment. "Alex and Linda's home. Erbil's their family name."

"Is 'family name' like 'clan?' Anyways, I think we're safe there. Something's been keeping Mekelat away from their house. He didn't approach even though he attacked you in your wagon. I think he's the one who sent the rat message."

"What are you going to do?"

Saima stopped to catch his breath, and to consider the question. "I don't know."

They were back at the river. Finer had been nervous about crossing the ice on the way to the Post, and Saima had teased her about it. She was still nervous. This time, Saima was also; not about misjudging what was under his feet. The problem was that nothing in his experience could help him deal with a Sheyd carrying a five thousand year old grudge.

"I want to cross where the slope to the river is gentle; where there's an open view in all directions, in case we're attacked again."

"I want to cross where the ice is solid," Finer said. She pointed to an area a little to the right. "Is that good? We can see around the bend."

"We'll find out." Saima took her hand, leading her down. He was surprised to again find an area of ice so thin you could see the wavelets lapping at it from underneath. He hadn't spotted it when they had started across. There were also large bird tracks he hadn't seen before. Saima was almost surprised, but definitely relieved when he and Finer made it to the far bank. They quickly ascended, and sat quietly on a large rock, catching their breath.

He surveyed the skies around him as they rested. "What are the biggest birds around here?" he asked Tammy.

"I hate birds."

"Are there any large ones here?"

Finer shrugged. "Loons, I suppose. The occasional duck or goose."

"No, that's not it. I mean something really big, maybe half the size of a person."

Finer made a sour face. "Ugh. Do you have them in the northlands?"

"You have them here, judging from the tracks we just passed."

"I didn't notice. Do you want to wait, to see if it shows up again?"

"No."

"What, then? Keep going?"

Saima nodded, and took Tammy's hand. They held on to each other as they ran the rest of the way to Alex and Linda Erbil's.

***

"I don't think supper agreed with me." Saima put down his fork and rested his arms on the table.

Linda ran through the meal in her mind: soup, grilled fish, and tea. She turned to Alex and Finer. "How about you? Are you okay?"

They nodded. Saima was starting to pale. He put his head on his arms and trembled. Finer reached over, putting her hand to his forehead. "He's got fever." She leaned closer to his face. "Can you walk? I'll bring you to bed."

Saima tried to lift himself; Finer pulled him up. Once he was standing, she wrapped his arm over her shoulder, supporting his weight.

Alex frowned. "Should you be doing that?"

Tammy's brow furrowed in concentration as she tried to understand his question. She forced a smile when she did. "I'm in control of myself."

They all followed Saima to his room, lying him down on the bed. Finer turned to Alex. "I think he'd like it better if you undressed him rather than us. Maybe give him an alcohol rub to bring down his fever."

"I made an oath not to touch him. I think he'd prefer if someone else did it."

"Alex likes young men and boys," Linda turned to Finer. "Saima considers that disgusting."

"Oh. What about you?"

"Alex treats me well, and just as he finds other entertainment, so do I. He encouraged me to have sex with Saima in the shower." Linda spoke matter-of-factly. "Since I've been intimate with him already, I'll take care of him now. Why don't you and Alex go entertain yourselves? But first bring me a damp towel, and fever medicine."

Alex looked like he was about to be nailed to a wall.

Tammy's smile came on its own this time, without forcing. "Come on Alex, I told you I'm in complete control of my venom. I can use just the right amount to keep you strong."

The assurance seemed to frighten him even more, but he didn't resist as Finer grabbed his hand and pulled him out of the room.

Linda quickly undressed Saima. Alex came back in with the towel and medicine as she was pulling off socks. He handed her the supplies, looked at Saima, and fled. Linda heard Tammy intercept him.

The discussions, the banter, being undressed barely registered with Saima. One bite of the fish had tasted slightly different, but he had ignored it until his stomach started bubbling. That had been the first sign, but soon his head was pounding, he was losing all his strength and shivering as if stranded in a winter storm.

It wasn't just the bubbling in his stomach. Somewhere, he sensed that someone was rubbing him with a foul-smelling liquid. He would have objected to the intimacy, but he had no strength to care, never mind speak. His whole body felt detached as his thoughts drifted away from his shivering and sweating.

He dreamed. Orpah was looking for the bear cub as Alex raced to attack her. Spear at the ready, she aimed at his leather case, when suddenly Tammy's visage came tumbling down the side of the mountain, burying them both. A boy stood unmoving, naked in the snow; a finger poking him in the chest, on the shoulder, on the back, a hand lifting his foot... In a far-away part of Saima's mind he groaned; Alex was having a bad influence on him, that he was dreaming of naked boys.

Now he was standing on a rooftop in the hot sun, clipping shirts to a rope. This was the last of the laundry, and there was no more room on the line. In the far-away place in his mind, Saima knew that this wasn't any part of his life experience, but then, dreams didn't have to be. A short muscular man with a small, flat face, and slightly slanted eyes came up the stairs to the roof, stared silently for a while as if in deep thought, and then bowed, his hands sideways in front of his face. Saima was sweating profusely; he didn't know if it was from the hot sun or his fever.

"I'm here for the sake of your daughter, my Teacher," the man said, with a look of utter solemnity.

"I'm not your teacher; I've never seen you before. I've never been in such stifling heat."

"We've met, in the aurora. Your daughter is my teacher."

"I have three sons." In that place in his mind that was watching himself dream, Saima got an inkling that this was an important discussion, that this was an important man.

"Your daughter isn't manifest now. She is my teacher across five thousand years. I stayed outside of the Abode of Life to protect her after she was assassinated."

Saima had no answer to that; he had no question whose answer would help him make sense of such a statement.

"Know Simon, that your daughter, your grand-mother is skilled at trapping Sheyds. They tried to take vengeance on her when she was killed, but I wouldn't let them harm her. We took soldiers into the paths between Spheres; I stayed on to keep watch.

"You understand correctly what has happened. The Sheyds were trapped in a curtain for five thousand years, but that time is over. They want revenge and control. You must trap them once again. They're already hunting you. Mekelat tried to drown you at the river; he tried to burn you at the Old Post."

Saima felt utterly lucid in his feverish dream. "How do I trap Sheyds?"

"Read the verses that I arranged for your host to dig up for you. Turn them; twist them till they're legible."

The man furrowed his brow, exaggerating his strange eyes even further. "Simon, it took great effort for me to be able to reach you; I shouldn't be able to touch the Abode of Life. I'm not a Sheyd. I've watched you and all your grandmothers from the aurora. John, the boy you stabbed when you rescued Tammy, made the Old Post smell of dung to warn you. He's grateful for how you helped him move on. Now you have to expel the poison and use what I've told you. I am pleased to see you, and I will be pleased if you leave in health."

The roiling in Saima's stomach intensified. He felt the dampness of the sweat on his skin. Someone was rubbing his back, repeating his name, sounding worried. The bubbling inside him was feverish lava, frothing and burning. His head rang as all thoughts melted away, like flakes of snow in a hot soup of pain.

A hand on his forehead. Another hand rubbing his stomach. Saima coughed. The volcano inside him erupted as he vomited all over his pillow, all over Linda's arm. Gasping, he lay on his side, trying to piece himself together. His stomach was no longer consuming him from the inside. He opened his eyes to Linda's worried frown, to a gentle kiss on his forehead. Her hair was brushing over him, picking up his filth. She wiped the back of her hand on a clean bit of blanket.

"Better?"

Lifting his head a bit off the pillow, Saima nodded.

"Your eyes were all over the place. You looked startled, even frightened. Bad dream?

"Probably. I don't remember my dreams. I'm sorry about the mess on the bed." He slowly sat himself up, and saw what he had done to the floor. "I'm really sorry about the carpet. I'll clean it up."

"I think you better clean yourself off first," Linda said, laughing. "The floor can clean itself." She pulled the linens off the bed and threw them into a chute in the wall. "Come on, we both need a shower."

Saima sighed.

19 EARLY BRONZE AGE 7

A continuous fire of green wood and manure had been burning all day inside the Meeting House. Nothing could survive the smoking; the windows and vents were sealed. Even Taiku's living quarters, attached to the far side, was part of the cleansing process. After the last embers had grown cold and the air was once again breathable, a troop of children armed with brooms went through it, sweeping the bugs, rodents and small birds off the stone floor.

Benches were positioned in a "U" around the room, leaving a stage for the dancers at the top. A thick curtain decorated with the totems of the various clans hung over the dancer's entrance.

The Madai clan leaders were meticulous with preparations for the War Dance. The care they lavished on Taiku's Meeting House bespoke the fact that he, not they, ran Lagash. If other peoples besides the Madai came to the Dance, they would be acknowledging that he was their Chief as well. Taiku and his soldiers stayed away for now, leaving his subordinates to their tasks. Usually the War Dance was the prelude to the Games: soccer, lacrosse... This time, the game was deadlier.

There were six clans among the Madai: Leopard, Fox, Gazelle, Cheetah, Olive-Tree, and Monkey. The Elam clans had the same totems, perhaps implying a common origin, long lost. There was no question as to whether Elam and Madai were members of the same clan. They weren't. If anything, there was resentment about infringement on their respective totems' honor. Taiku hoped to reverse that.

A person always married outside his clan, with the children belonging to their mother's group. In the occasional fights between clans, a man could end up killing his wife's brothers or father, becoming a blood-enemy of his children. For now though, the six clans were dancing together. In the scale of balanced opposition, they were supposed to be uniting against a larger enemy. If Taiku's plan worked and the Elam joined the Dance, together with the refugees they could be a formidable force.

It wasn't that many years ago that what was once called the 'Winter Dance' was part of the actual preparation for war. Taiku renamed it because too many had forgotten what the ceremony was really about. The bad odor that now filled the air would help set the mood. If the Madai and Elam didn't go to war against each other at the Dance, then together they would go to battle against a common foe.

The Marsh People generally stayed out of the Madai's way. Occasionally they would rent a water buffalo to a farmer for a few days, or come to trade. Mostly though, you'd see Marsh People in Lagash when they came to ask the Ebers to trap Sheyds. The Ebers always told them to look for other solutions to their problems, but as the Madai all knew, the Marshers were lazy. They preferred to blame someone or something else, not wanting to take responsibility for their own circumstances. Now that Taiku had made them utterly dependent on him for their survival, their past indolence was at an end.

The Clan totems were a leopard skin, fox pelt, gazelle antler, cheetah tail, olive branch, and a small monkey skull. These were now set out in different sections of the Meeting House; low wooden dividers separated each area. If this didn't cause a riot at the outset, it would be an important victory. By separating each clan into a different area, he'd be forcing Madai and Elam whose clan shared the same totem to sit as one.

The milling crowd of Elam in the square fronting the Meeting House grew silent as it divided itself in two, making a path for the Sphere Travelers: Geordi, carrying his own drum, and Aleku, carrying Aua's drum, made of human skin. That Aleku was carrying it confirmed that Aua wasn't expected to return. The Elam delegation followed them in, after which two soldiers took positions by the main door. All the access points had guards; some visible, some hidden.

The soldiers checked their weapons. If the Elam objected to the seating arrangement, the fighting would start now.

There was grumbling, some raised voices from inside the Meeting House. But they quieted down waiting for the Dance to begin. The guards moved aside, and the Madai delegates went in. They had been warned not to contest the arrangements. As the Leopard Madai seated themselves beside the Leopard Elam, the Gazelle Madai amongst the Gazelle Elam, there were exclamations of surprise, but not much else.

Taiku followed the last of the Madai in, sitting with his Cheetah clan. A few eyes followed him, but most were focused on the curtain that the dancers would emerge from. There was a sour mood in the room, mostly from the close quarters of people between whom there was mutual disdain. The leftover stench of the smoke rubbed on nerves that were already abraded.

Aleku and Geordi sat near the curtain, their drums beside them. Two more men kneeled by the Dance Drum, a hollowed-out log. Another held a reed whistle, while a couple of women held palm-sized wooden rattles, each intricately carved.

Thick fabrics dimmed the light coming in the windows. Smoke from the women's pipes twisted its way up to the ceiling, as the sweet scent of tobacco mixed with the sour smell of the smoke used to clean the building. The odor of nerves and sweat mixed into the thick air as the drums and rattles began to clamor.

The first dancer slipped out from behind the curtain, his head down, elbows bent, his back to the delegates. His coat and pants were made of dark deerskin, interrupted by bands of short, white feathers. He bounced a few times on one leg, darted his face to the side, bounced on the other leg, all the while moving slowly towards the center of the dance floor. His folded arms rose and fell like the wings of a frightened bird, desperate, but unable to fly. Bits of down fell from his clothes as his body spasmed, as the rattles clattered, as the drums pounded. From time to time he'd turn his head sideways and stare at the people, the huge eyes and distended mouth of his wooden mask both terrifying and afraid.

The leather fringes on his mask were swaying, his feathers flying as the whistle started to play. It had only two notes, but they became part of the song, part of the drum beats. His movements held all eyes, as if they were tied to his limbs. He squatted, he rose, he spun... A foot tapped the floor, as if digging a hole, then abandoned it as the dancer sidled towards the delegates. The bird-monster trembled as he twisted and bent, stared and hopped to the syncopated, staccato beat. All hearts were bound to his movements; all hearts answered the primeval call to violence, which cried out through a rich, wordless language.

Though everyone remained silent as the bird-monster retreated behind the curtain, you could touch the sense of relief in the room. After each dance there was usually some light-hearted performance to relieve the tension.

Taiku stood up as he heard shouts. The War Dance was solemn, even the humorous parts. There should be no break in the decorum. Everyone's eyes were riveted to the curtain, which was moving as someone struggled against it.

The fabric tore from the rope holding it up as a youngish-looking man fell against it from behind, crashing to the floor. His hands and feet were bound. No, his hands were bound tightly behind his back, but he had only one foot. The other leg had bloody bandages wrapped around a stump at the ankle. The man's wrists were bleeding too, as the tight saw-grass abraded his skin. A cloth gag was wrapped around his mouth, a blindfold over his eyes. His face was smooth, untroubled by a beard.

More noise, as two of Taiku's soldiers charged in, holding onto Qimiq's arms. Qimiq, in turn, put his foot on the chest of the man on the floor.

"Everybody, sit down," Taiku shouted. The decorum had dissolved into pandemonium. Soldiers moved among the crowd, encouraging everyone to be calm. The excitement, the shouts, the muttering faded.

Taiku knew Qimiq as a person who kept away from Lagash. Unlike the other Marsh People, he never blamed his problems on Sheyds. If Qimiq interrupted the War Dance, there was a good reason. Looking at the prisoner bound and bleeding on the floor, Taiku's breath halted as he realized what this probably meant. He motioned to the soldiers to release Qimiq's arms.

"The bag." Qimiq looked at one of the soldiers who had just released him. The man went towards the door, and retrieved a large, heavy looking sack.

"Gently," Qimiq ordered as the bag was placed on the ground. "Please," he said, pointing to his prisoner. The two soldiers put their boots on his chest.

Qimiq reached down into the bag and lifted out a young girl's head, putting it gently on a bench. He lifted out more heads, and placed them all facing the assembled delegations. When he finished emptying the grizzly sac, he turned towards Taiku, but spoke loudly enough for all to hear.

"The Marsh People demand vengeance; we demand protection. Me against my brother. My brother and I against my cousin. My cousin and I against my far cousin. The Low Marsh against the Far Marsh people. The Low Marsh and Far Marsh against the Dry-landers. The Marsh people and Dry-landers against the Elam. Our horizon against the far side of the horizon. Our world against the next. Our God against all Gods."

"What is this?" Taiku asked.

"Our God against all Gods. Ja'ix sent this man to spread the message of the Envoy of the Master of Spirits; Jaix's message."

Was it the horrible smell of smoke in the room? Was it the severed heads that made Taiku nauseous? He thought he had months, a year to prepare. He had to protect the refugees who had come to Lagash. He had to protect the Ebers. As Chief, he had to protect everyone. He wasn't ready.

He turned to the drummers. "Resume the Dance."

Qimiq reached down, to return the heads to his sack. Taiku put a hand on his arm.

"These people deserve to see the rest of the Dance, to know they will be avenged. Bring them to sit with the clans."

Taiku turned to the people and raised his voice. "We will honor our dead with a war in their name. As Chief I declare that the people of Lagash, be they up in the mountains, in the village, the marshes or the Abode of the Dead, will be paid in the blood of their enemies."

Until that moment, Lagash had referred only to a small town on the delta of the Klee-Dekel River. Now it was a much larger territory, with Taiku as its ruler.

Most of the delegates in the Meeting House were too distracted by the severed heads, by the prisoner, to notice how the Chief had just transformed their world. All of them were standing to honor the dead whose heads were seated among them, but more to keep their distance from the gruesome objects.

"Are there any objections to Taiku's declaration of war?" Vlad met the gazes of each of the clan leaders: the figurehead Madai men, and the powerful Elam Clan Mothers. All nodded their agreement.

The Winter Dance had once been a call to arms. As the peoples of the valley had settled down, tilling fields and grazing pastures, the Dance became more of a drama, a ritual. The calls to action were forgotten as soon as they were over, everyone having enjoyed a good community get-together.

Now hearts were pounding, foreheads sweating as the people filed out of the Meeting House. Many of the older villagers who had felt ill at ease with the taming of their world, shivered as they remembered slitting throats, burying their dead.

In those days, wars were fought by everybody; one group of people against another killing anybody and everyone they could, whether a nursing baby or a well-armed warrior. More than a few people coming down the river had tried to take the rich pasturelands along the Klee-Dekel for themselves. Many traders had tried to wrest control of the village and its docks. Desert caravans raided for slaves or women. Legend told that the Madai had wiped out every one of the previous inhabitants of the area.

So the older Lagashans didn't see the impending violence as a change. Rather, it was just another part of the rhythm of the world, cycling between calm and rage.

The curtain had been removed; the heads replaced in Qimiq's sack. All the clan leaders stayed behind on Vlad's instruction, as the other delegates left the Meeting House.

Taiku addressed the Elam Clan Mothers. "The six of you will be my Council of the Clans. You need to move your homes closer to the village, so I can protect you. He turned to the Madai clan leaders: "The Clan Mothers will tell you about our discussions. Go home now." The Madai clan leaders had lost their jobs to the Elam Mothers.

Taiku had wanted to unite the Madai, Elam and Marsh Peoples. He had wanted to merge their clans. He wanted everyone to take seriously the threat looming from over the horizon. The unity he had expected to take months to achieve had been instantly pulled into place by the curtain yanked down by Qimiq's prisoner. What had also been ripped away was the time Taiku needed to prepare for the coming war. The soldiers encouraged the last of the stragglers out the door. Taiku turned to Qimiq, motioning him to sit. "Tell me about your prisoner."

20 EARLY BRONZE AGE 8

His name was Shor. He was about sixteen or seventeen years old. He wasn't certain, because he had lost track after being captured by Ja'ix.

He came from a fishing village full of pagans, people who refused to acknowledge the Master of Spirits. When the soldiers who rescued Shor from his family explained the Truth, the villagers laughed. Naturally, they had to be purified. The boys who weren't old enough to have been irreversibly corrupted were taken away to be taught and trained.

It took some time, but Shor eventually got used to watching the purifications, ignoring the horror of entire communities being burned to death. When he was old enough, he was given the honor of gathering wood for the fires. Then he became one of the people herding the unbelievers into buildings to be set ablaze. And finally, he was given the honor of throwing the torch.

After that, he received a letter from Ja'ix, congratulating him and naming him a soldier of the Master of Spirits. Shor couldn't read, but Omer, the leader of his unit, read it out loud for him and his comrades. The next day they took all the girls from the hamlet they were raiding and celebrated on them instead of their usual goats.

Because he was from a fishing village, Omer presumed that Shor knew his way around sea travel. He was a somewhat correct, enough that of the twenty-eight boats that had set off, Shor's was one of the five that wasn't lost at sea. Although he had been captured and his comrades killed, Shor told his captors he was content. Shor was certain that the other four boats traveling alongside his were safely on their way home. The prisoners and the information they had come for would help Ja'ix spread his message.

The dust kicked up by the people leaving the Meeting House hung in the soft beams of light coming through the now-uncovered windows. The prisoner lay on the floor, blindfolded and trussed like an animal ready for roasting. The gag had been removed so he could respond to all the threats of torture, but except for the story he had already told Qimiq, he didn't speak.

The Olive Tree Clan Mother suggested cutting off the prisoner's fingers one at a time. Qimiq pointed to Shor's missing foot, saying that the painful amputation hadn't gotten him to talk. Other Clan Mothers had their own suggestions: rats, pulling off his nails... Taiku listened to all the suggestions, immediately dismissing ideas that would make it impossible for him to speak. They needed information more than vengeance.

"When's the last time he ate, or had something to drink?" Taiku said.

"We gave him some water after we cut off his foot. That's all. The women he captured weren't feeling too friendly towards their prisoner, but I knew you'd want him alive."

"You did well. This man's our guest now, and it's our obligation to treat him properly. We have to feed him and let him regain his strength. Maybe then he'll fulfill his duty as our guest."

The Clan Mothers, Qimiq, the soldiers bit off their angry responses and waited. Shor's lips curled upwards in a slight smile.

"We're dealing with a formidable opponent here. He came on a long journey, battled his enemy, was poisoned by a Fire Snake, had his foot chopped off, is tied up like a goat, and still is strong enough to refuse to answer our questions. He's even able to smile."

The smirk on Shor's face grew.

"We'll put him in the Stone House, feed him and let him rest. We must respect him for the bull of a man that he is." Taiku paused. "Tomorrow we'll turn him into an ox."

First a look of puzzlement, then Shor's smile disappeared as he realized what Taiku meant.

Zaytea nodded her approval. "Maybe he's not helping us because we cut off his foot—."

"I cut off his foot after I captured him. Why do you say "we?""

"You're the one who captured him. You're of Lagash. We're all people of Lagash now, with Taiku as our Chief. The Olive Tree clan is the leading clan, and as its Clan Mother, I'm the Chief's consort. Together, we rule and protect all of Lagash."

Taiku flinched and stared at his "consort." He didn't expect her claim to joint rule; he certainly didn't expect her claim to marriage. She was a beautiful woman, with long black hair touched by grey; the latter perhaps a reflection of her responsibilities. Her brown eyes, small nose, and delicate lips belied the power she wielded over her people. She was rumored to be a distant cousin of Asenath; smart, able to bend the wills of the other Clan Mothers to hers. Zaytea ruled the Clan Mothers, the Clan Mothers ruled the Elam, and Taiku had just set them over the Madai as well.

It couldn't hurt. He had never considered marriage, feeling that his obligations as Chief precluded those of a husband. But if Zaytea was stepping into this willingly... Never mind willingly. He wasn't being offered a choice about sharing his power, his bed, or his life with her. If he contradicted her, it would humiliate Zaytea, and he would lose Elam support. And then he would have to pay for his earlier humiliation of the Madai clan leaders. Taiku had no choice in this marriage.

"What do you suggest?" he asked.

"As you ordered. Feed him, and let him sleep tonight. If my idea doesn't work, then tomorrow I'll cut off his testicles and harness him to a plow myself."

The only thing that Taiku's grandfather Muuad ever feared was his wife. Taiku understood this more clearly now.

"Vlad, see to it. I'm going to spend time with my consort." He took Zaytea by the hand and pulled her out.

***

Shor was blindfolded and gagged, with cloth stuffed in his ears. Smell was his only sense that wasn't impeded, which was unfortunate. The room still stank of smoke. It irritated his throat, scratched at his lungs. Occasionally he would break into fits of useless coughing. There was nothing though to cough out. Before they had gagged him, one of his earlier coughing fits had caused him to vomit up most of what he'd eaten during the last half day. He'd been famished, unable to resist the endless supply of meat, dates, olives and wine. Now it was on his face, on his neck, his chest... He couldn't wipe any of it off because he was tied, face up, on a wide bench. He could only turn his head a bit from side to side because of the barbed grass holding him down.

There must have been some kind of laxative added to the food, because he had soiled himself. The only measure of time he had was that his excrement and vomit had started to dry. They were itchy, but he barely took note of it.

An ox, harnessed to a plow. He had planned to plow the girls he captured, but eunuchs don't do such things. Before he had been taken by Ja'ix, Shor had dreamed of hauling nets in a sleek fishing boat, the smell of brine in his face. Maybe his comrades who had been lost at sea were the ones who were really blessed. They died as men. Shor was going to die as a castrated beast of burden.

Still, he would die in service to the Master of Spirits. Ja'ix taught that such a death was worth more than the most vainglorious life. He would have women, beautiful beyond the boundaries of desire after death. They would all flock to his bed. Shor imagined his heavenly harem, the pleasure they would give him.

If he died a eunuch, would he remain one after death? What's the reward given a man for whom women are useless? Not only a eunuch, but a cripple. What joy would there be? A crippled eunuch, covered with vomit and waste. Never mind the women. Would he want to be with himself?

Or perhaps death purified. Would passing from this realm restore his manhood, his missing foot? Would it cleanse him of his filth?

"Did you have a good meal? Are you well rested?" Shor was startled by a woman pulling the cloth out of his ears. He couldn't answer because of the gag. It wasn't a voice he recognized from the previous day.

"We're going to clean you up, ask some questions, and then give you fresh clothes."

Shor felt the hands pulling off his pants. The person undressing him smelled like a woman, but he couldn't be sure, because his own stench was much stronger. The fingers making light contact with his thighs felt thin and feminine. A knife cut through the cloth, and the remains of his garments were yanked off. The blade cut through the fibers holding him in place, and Shor gingerly move his head side to side.

The feminine hand took his. "Stand." With surprising strength, she hauled him up. He gingerly put his weight on his remaining foot, resting a hand for balance on the bench. "Stay still," she ordered.

It must have been a bucket of water; no, maybe a few buckets emptied on him at the same time. He struggled to catch his breath. Some of it seeped through the blindfold, irritating his eyes. Some went up his nose. A bit went through the gag over his mouth, easing the taste of vomit. He sucked it gratefully.

Strong hands grabbed his arms. Another hand scrubbed him all over with a brush, removing the dried filth from his body. He heard someone breathing hard. Was it from the exertion of scrubbing him down? Was it excitement over seeing his exposed body? Shor imagined a face to go with the female; a body to go with the delicate fingers that had removed his pants. He started to breathe harder.

He felt those hands on the sides of his legs again. The voice, sounding like it was below him, breathed warm air onto his excited flesh. "Hold your legs apart."

Shor re-balanced his hands, carefully keeping any weight off his stump. He felt her hands on him. She was pinching the top of his testicles quite hard. The pain was exciting, but in the back of his mind, he knew that this was not good. He struggled to enjoy her hands, but fear was taking over.

"Keep yourself excited as long as you can. When we tie a bull scrotum, it takes anywhere from ten to fifty days till it drops off. I don't know how long it will take with you, or when it will be too late to untie it."

He reached down with one hand, and felt the string tied to the top of his scrotum. He immediately brought his second hand down, almost tipping over as he hurried to untie it. Strong arms grabbed his wrists, pulling them away and keeping him from falling over. He felt the woman's hand again on his private parts, making sure the string was tight.

"You're still a man, and you'll probably remain one for a few days. The quicker you talk to us, the better your chance of not becoming an ox." She stood up and reached behind his head. She untied the gag from his mouth.

Shor's rapid breathing was fear now, rather than excitement.

"Tell me something. Ja'ix murdered your family and everyone in your village. Rather than seeking revenge, you came here to do to us what he did to your home. Why don't you help us avenge the death of your people?"

Shor leaned heavily on his arm, trying to demonstrate strength to these non-believers. "My home was full of pagans. Purifying the village was actually a kindness to them, because they refused to purify themselves. When we kill everyone here, you'll hate us for our cruelty, but after your death, your spirits will thank us."

There were angry growls from around the room.

"Impale him now! In his filthy bottom and out his mouth!"

Shor had helped his comrades do that to all the children in a small village, forcing their parents to watch. If having it done to him was the price of his dedication to Ja'ix's Truth, so be it.

"No," the woman's voice answered. "We need him to talk. And if he doesn't, we can use him to pull a plow."

"You aren't scaring me. You can't be crueler than us. I know all the tricks to inflict agony. The worse you do to me, the greater my reward in death."

The hand was on his scrotum again. "Losing this won't kill you, my friend; just change you."

Shor swung blindly, grabbing for a hostage. His fingers touched skin, but the woman sidestepped quickly. He lost his balance, and fell painfully on the floor, bashing an elbow and knee, his head bouncing on the wet stones.

The people in the room had taken a collective breath as Shor swung, but before he could regain his senses, several sharp metal points were pressing against different parts of his anatomy.

"You've fallen right into the filth we washed off you earlier, and your head is bleeding. If we don't take care of it, you'll get an infection."

She wasn't standing as close now. Shor took some satisfaction at having frightened her off.

"Get up on the bench."

He reached out a hand, for someone to help him.

"Get up." The metal points pressed harder into his skin. No one took his hand.

He felt around for the bench, pulled himself to his knees, and then up. His head was pounding from where it had bounced on the flat stones of the floor.

"Lie on your back."

Abrasive reeds were tied around each of his shins, fastening them individually to the bench. Another cord went around his neck, and his wrists were bound tightly together in front of him. That might be useful; maybe he could swing his arms. But then the fibers tying his wrists were being fastened to something else. Shor flinched as he felt a tug on the cord strangling his scrotum. If he moved his arms, he'd pull it tighter.

The voice was next to his ear. "I'm going to wash the dirt off your injury now. It may hurt. Hold yourself still." Shor braced himself, paying extra attention to keeping his arms motionless.

A cloth rubbed softly against the side of his head, near the temple. A finger gently applied some kind of lotion, which felt cold. The hand lightly brushed the hair off his forehead.

"I don't want your cut to get splashed with dirt while we wash you off again. I'm going to take off your blindfold because it's dirty but keep your face covered with a towel."

She took a breath and continued. "Now listen carefully. It's important that your eyes remain covered, so shut them tightly when I remove the blindfold. If you open your uncovered eyes even a crack, I'm under orders to immediately dig them out with a spoon. I don't want to do that, so... You can open them again after I put the towel over your face. Please appreciate; I'm trying to avoid unnecessary harm. Do you understand?"

It was not pleasant being strapped to the bench. It was frightening to have one's hands tied to one's genitals. But this woman seemed to be on his side; in a way she was protecting him.

"I understand. Thank you." Shor offered the best smile he was capable of.

"You're welcome. If you'll be as kind to me as I have been to you, maybe we'll take that string off you on time for you to stay intact. Now shut your eyes."

Shor obeyed, grateful for the warning. He felt her fingers untie the blindfold as the towel was quickly draped over his head. He felt the bench moving a bit, as his feet were elevated slightly. He relaxed the muscles of his face.

"You can open your eyes. I'm going to wash you off again. This time stay clean. There are limits to our patience."

The warm water on his foot, on his legs, was soothing. He could hear the voice breathing softly near him. His muscles relaxed, his eyes drifted closed, his anticipation of torture faded. Shor's chest rose and fell in rhythm with the voice. The pouring water was like the touch of her fingers, kneading his skin, massaging his fears. As the water climbed his thighs, Shor's anticipation excited him. He had drifted off to his own world now, and didn't care who was watching.

"Shor, if you're uncomfortable while we're washing you, let me know."

"I can't move my hands without hurting myself."

"Don't move them, my friend. Maybe we'll be able to untie the string later. I wouldn't want you to lose what you have."

"Can—"

"Shh." The voice put a gentle finger over his lips. "Don't say anything. I'm going to wash you more. If the water makes you uncomfortable, just ask me nicely to stop. Remember, nicely. If the others think you're angry or demanding, they won't let me help you. A lot of people want you dead."

He relaxed. The water felt good on his neck, where the saw-grass had scraped it earlier. It felt good on his ears, just a slow, relaxing trickle. He took a slow, deep breath as it moved over his face.

The sudden pain tore him awake. His scrotum felt as if it had almost been ripped off by the unexpected jerk of his hands towards his face. Shor tried desperately to breath, but couldn't. He felt he was standing, face upwards, under a torrential waterfall. The water filled his nose. When he tried to gasp through his mouth, he sucked in more water. Breathe! But he couldn't. There was no air, just water. He tried to thrash his head, but it wouldn't move. A vise of some kind was holding it still. Shor was drowning, dying. When he tried to swim to the surface of the water a terrible pain in his groin stopped him. How could he drown? He was from a fishing village. His heart was exploding; it had never raced so fast. What had she told him to do? Ask her to stop!

He tried to yell. No, that was no good. The others wanted to kill him. Ask politely. But you needed to breathe air in order to say anything, and all he was breathing was water. Please, please, let me breathe... he couldn't get the words out of his mouth. He was dying, and he couldn't even tell her that he needed help.

Relief, life... air. The cloth lifted off his face as the hand gently stroked his cheek. He stared into a pair of beautiful, chestnut eyes above a small nose. The voice spoke from a delicate mouth below it.

"How are you, my friend? I'm still worried about the wound on your head. We have to make sure it's clean."

Shor took in the sweet air, his chest rising and falling as he tried to calm himself enough to say "stop, please."

The towel went back over his face before he could speak. The waterfall, the drowning, the panic resumed. He had survived it once. How long could he hold on? He grabbed desperately for air, but water was all he could find. He pictured himself as a fish, the first fish he had ever caught. It flopped around in the bottom of the boat, trying to breathe the alien atmosphere. Now it was being avenged as Shor was dying, strangled like his first victim. *I'm sorry for what I did to you, fish. I understand now how you felt.* He started to cry. Not for the children he had impaled, not for the people he had burned alive. He cried breathlessly for the fish he had killed by removing it from the water.

The roar of the falls stopped. The towel lifted from his face. The woman spoke to him, her voice urgent.

"Shor, the others say that we need to keep cleaning your wound. I think it's enough, but they're insisting. I told them we should listen to you, but they'll only let me stop if you answer their questions. I told them you would. Will you?"

Shor tried to calm himself; he had to think.

"No, wait," she yelled at the others, as the towel came down once again on Shor's face. Would they ever pull him out from the waterfall? How many times would they drown him, before they finally let him die? And now they weren't even listening to his friend.

A new fear came to him. Would they drown her next, as punishment for trying to help him? If he could breathe, he'd protect her. Then after he saved her, he'd look after her as her husband, or maybe as her draft animal. Whatever she wanted. If he could breathe, if his heart didn't explode out of his chest.

The towel lifted again. With a mighty effort, he quickly spoke one word: "Ja'ix." It caught their attention. He sucked deeply at the air, slowing down his racing heart.

"I'm part of the navy. Twenty-eight boats set out. Five made it across. A few of us came from fishing villages, so we knew our way on the water. The others were afraid, but our leaders told them that if they died at sea, they'd get their reward in the afterlife sooner."

Shor paused to catch his breath. "Please don't hurt her. What do you want to know?"

The woman with the voice smiled, which relaxed him. He was protecting her from these pagans.

"Why did you attack Lagash? What was the purpose of taking those people?" A man behind him asked.

"We need information. We're capturing people from all over the world. We use their knowledge to draw maps. With them, we know the best travel routes. We learn where the biggest cities are, which ones are defended, which have the most riches."

"Maps?"

"A skilled map-maker can prepare a wondrous representation of the world, just from listening to people's descriptions," Shor explained. This was good. Talking about maps meant they weren't drowning him. He had to tell them more.

"What if someone gives a bad description?" she asked.

"That's why we take many prisoners from the same area."

There was silence. He couldn't take a chance; he couldn't afford the silence. "Ja'ix learned that the mountains of the continental divide go north for a great distance. He's sent thousands of his meanest men to try to go around the top and come down the other side." What else to tell them? He couldn't make things up, because they'd hurt her if they found out he tricked them. It was good that Omer had told him all these things before he started his mission.

"Many thousands of men are traveling towards the mountain pass that leads to the headwaters of the Klee-Dekel. They're going to come down the valley, floating their supplies and equipment on barges."

There was fear in her eyes. Had he not told them enough? Were they going to drown him and his friend now? He'd better continue.

"A smaller force is coming from the east, from the road along the sea. They're going to arrive first, to make you think that's the main attack. While you're diverting resources to the road, the main army will come in from the north, along the river valley. Lagash is an important target for Ja'ix, because it controls trade on the river and along the coastal road." He looked at her face; she had a broad smile on her beautiful lips. He felt a tug at his groin. Her fingers were on him, unwinding the cord connected to his wrists, which could have abruptly made him into an ox.

She gently squeezed his testicles. "My name is Zeresh. You're my property now. Keep me happy if you want these to stay."

***

Qimiq and the other were ready to resume their Fire Snake harvest, glad that Taiku seemed to have gotten over his anger at the Marsh People. The Chief was pleased about Qimiq's prisoner. He was intrigued by the box of treasures captured in the boat, especially the parchments, which he had sent over to the Clay People to decipher.

The Marsh People no longer viewed their arduous task of collecting Fire Snake venom as punishment for the death of Asenath. Their homes were vulnerable, and making poison was part of defending themselves. The men harvested snakes, and the women fashioned weapons to deliver the poison.

Qimiq would have liked to be bitter. His people had died in the attack, not the Madai or the Elam. He had to brush that feeling aside, though. He had instigated the events that had led to many more deaths. Ja'ix's hand on the marshes was nowhere near as heavy as his. Besides which, the Madai, Elam and Marsh populations were all one now, citizens of Lagash. What had Qimiq started that day when he had talked Balthan into going to war? His complaint was a few mutilated animals. Qimiq felt as if he had been duped by Sheyds. Where was Asenath, now that he needed her?

He spotted Tamsyn walking towards him, cradling his bait in her right arm. She was scratching the puppy's head, rubbing its snout, talking soothingly to it like one would talk to a baby. She ran a finger over Qimiq's lip.

"I'm glad the swelling's gone down. In the darkness of the Meeting House, nobody noticed where I hit you."

"Maybe you shouldn't be so fast to attack. I had a reason for giving that man anti-venom. The information Taiku gets will help us."

"You're right, Qimiq. You did have a good reason. But you're wrong about not attacking quickly. Maybe you should learn to defend yourself better."

His cousin was a problem. People associated her with evil, because she was an identical twin. Often, she acted in a way that seemed wicked, such as punching him in the face right after he saved her life. People avoided her, made the stupidest accusations against her. Some considered her and her twin worse than Sheyds. They were relieved when her sister Anahita disappeared a couple of years earlier. Tamsyn had been heartbroken; the joy of the people around her made her bitterness more intense.

"I wasn't ready. I had just saved you. If I'd have expected your attack, you wouldn't have been able to touch me."

Tamsyn suddenly grabbed Qimiq's right shoulder and swept her foot behind his ankle, knocking him off balance and landing him instantly on his back. She planted a foot lightly on his neck. "Don't move," she warned him, but with a smile. Removing her foot, she extended a hand to help him up. He eyed her warily as he rose. The puppy was still cradled comfortably in her arm.

"Why did you attack me now?"

"When you have a real enemy, he's not going to tell you before he attacks. You have to know how to deal with an unexpected assault. If

Taiku's plans to protect Lagash depend on being warned before an attack, we should all kill ourselves now. It would be safer."

Qimiq stared at his cousin. She had a slender build, of medium height. Her long eyelashes promised softness, a promise that was belied by the ferocity in her deep, blue eyes. Her lithe body, her fluid way of moving, reminded people of a snake lying in wait.

"How do you expect to find a husband, Tamsyn, if you're always attacking?" His voice was gentle, not because he wanted to mollify her. It was gentle because she was his cousin, and though she didn't need his physical protection, he felt that her spirit was fragile, like a fine ceramic bowl that could easily shatter.

"It would have been difficult enough when my brother was alive. People are afraid of my 'dark powers.' Who would have a person like me? Now that there's no one to support my children, what reason could there possibly be for someone to marry me?"

Qimiq stifled a sigh. That would be telling her that she was right, which she was, but he didn't want to confirm it.

"Reason?" He raised an eyebrow. "You, obviously."

Tamsyn didn't stifle her sigh. "That's nice, but what does it mean?"

"There's no one like you in all of Lagash. When your sister was here there was someone who looked like you, but her character isn't the same. You're exciting. The way you threaten everyone with your fierce attitude, with your so-called dark powers, arouses all the men. Do you know how many dream of giving you their child? They all want you to beat them to a pulp, and then sleep with them. That you're beautiful enhances the challenge."

Tamsyn thought about his words, and then grinned. "I'm sorry Qimiq, you're my cousin. I can't open my legs for you even though I just beat you up."

"Well, you didn't really beat me up; you just had me on the ground. I'll settle for a hug."

She stepped closer as Qimiq wrapped soothing arms around her. She rested her head on his chest, taking the comfort he offered.

21 THE EDGE OF THE WORLD 7

Osnat sent Eric ahead before entering the woods where the survivors lived. She wanted to be announced. More than that, she didn't want anyone to talk to her unless she spoke to them first. Haran stayed at their shelter, while Osnat, Aarluk and Ijiq went with Norma.

"Are all your people Sphere Travelers?" Ijiq ran his hand along a tree, fingering the blackness where it had been burned off its stump. Logs cut by fire leaned together to form conical shelters, lined by a patchwork of ragged skins, snow and fabric. The Tunniq knew only stone axes to shape wood.

Osnat caressed the charred stump. "In a way, yes. We have devices that channel power, which we can control very precisely."

"Could you have channeled the power to end the storm more quickly than Aarluk?"

"No. Aarluk is stronger for that kind of thing. But I'm going to use our power to bring the mountain down on our village."

Aarluk patted her shoulder.

Gaunt faces peered at the newcomers through eyes filled with despondence and fear. Osnat recognized some faces: a friend, a cousin, a co-worker from the other side of existence. She greeted no one, nodded at no one. She stifled the sob that tried to escape her throat when she saw Dina, her brother's wife, her skin blackened and scarred by frostbite. She didn't pause to ask her about Shelah.

"Why do so many houses have pieces missing from the walls? Do people raid each other for logs?" Ijiq asked.

"There were many more people alive when we built these. The latest storm took about half of us, including the last surviving children. It took Rachel, Dina's baby." Norma shot Osnat a look.

Osnat blinked, but no more, on hearing of the demise of her niece. "What do you do with the deceased?"

"We can't bury them. We don't have the strength or the tools."

"Do you eat them?"

Norma spat angrily. "We're not cannibals. We built a special place for the bodies. Scavengers try to get them, so we guard the area. We've caught a fair bit of game that way. It's embarrassing, but we use the dead to attract food."

"Better than using the living. What do you do with their clothes, with their lighters? Was anybody able to bring anything else useful with them?"

"We divide the clothes among us. We've collected all the lighters. The people from later didn't expect to come here, and most didn't bring anything useful with them. A few knives, some lamps, fusion spanners, a cutter, and stuff like that. A teacher had bunch of children's books, but she took her class with her to the esker. Another woman had a fancy turquoise knife; she went with it to the caves. There are some waterproof containers. We've put the more interesting stuff in them."

Osnat masked her excitement about the tools. "How do you divide the food you catch? Is it everyone for themselves?"

"We take turns eating. There's a list. The person at the top of the list gets food, and then goes to the bottom of the list, and waits till everyone else is fed. Sometimes it's a day between meals; usually a lot longer."

"What if somebody gets sick? Do they get priority?"

Norma took a deep breath, which she released slowly. "If someone gets sick, they die. If someone gets weak, they die. This wasteland sucks the strength out of you. There's not enough food. To give it to the sick is to waste it on the dying. That brings an earlier death to those who might otherwise survive."

While Osnat had been struggling to keep a neutral expression on her face, Aarluk and Ijiq felt no such obligation. They were both smiling broadly, choking down laughter in a weak attempt to match Osnat's stern demeanor. Norma was appalled. Osnat felt her soul splitting in two, her heart broken by the horrible choices these people had been forced to make. At the same time, her mother's chuckling was infectious, and a grin started to creep onto her lips. "Why are we laughing?"

Aarluk and Ijiq couldn't control themselves anymore. They roared. Osnat couldn't control herself either. She didn't laugh, though; she turned red with embarrassment at the idea of laughter in the midst of such anguish.

People came closer to get a better look at this alien vision: humans laughing. It was something from a past life that they hadn't experienced for a very long time. Hollow, intense eyes stared at the round, laughing faces. Thin bodies leaned on dead trees, on walking sticks; some leaned on each other as they listened to the extraordinary sound of happiness. A few smiles crept onto the emaciated lips of the watchers. A few giggles, a few grins spread among the group. Joy, laughter, was harder to find than food. It was a precious commodity, not to be wasted.

Osnat pressed: "So...?"

"I told you about a winter village near here, which had to be abandoned."

Osnat nodded, vaguely recalling the discussion.

"It was a place where people gathered. There's plenty of food around, though we wouldn't have chosen to live among the trees. The people here now died because of ignorance."

"Can we feed everyone here?"

"Not by ourselves, but we can teach them to feed themselves. There's a bigger problem, though."

"A bigger problem than them starving?"

"The sun is starting to show itself during the day. Soon the surface of the snow will melt, and the rags they're wearing on their feet will soak through. Their feet will turn black without proper boots. And in the spring rains they will get sick without good coats."

"Can we provide them clothes and boots?"

"Not fast enough."

"Can we teach them to make their own?"

"Not fast enough."

Osnat thought about this for a moment. The laughter faded from Aarluk and Ijiq, but smiles remained etched on the faces of the onlookers, as they hung desperately to that small taste of happiness.

"I guess we'll just have to be careful." Osnat smiled also.

"Careful?"

"We'll have to be careful when we bring the mountain down on our village so that we don't bury anything we need under it."

Aarluk grinned. "You're thinking like us now. How are we going to do it?"

"I don't know. There are a lot of smart people here. We'll work it out."

Osnat turned to Norma, who was standing a little off to the side, wondering. "How many of the people here are from later? Have they been cooperating?"

"There are maybe ten left. At first, they were very difficult, complaining about everything and demanding that some silly codes be followed. Some didn't even want to kill animals, saying they have just as much right to live as humans. Most of them changed their mind quickly. As the sun disappeared and the weather grew colder, they abandoned their codes. But they were still helpless, not used to thinking for themselves. They were dependent on us; many of them were resentful. They complained we were bossing them around, even though they would have died quickly otherwise. I think a lot of the people who marched off to the esker did it just to get away from the Ebers."

"Who are they? Where do they come from?"

"A place on the Opinaca River. They don't have a name for their home, or even for themselves. Their technology is a little more advanced than ours, but they don't know much about it; I can't use it to date them. They're from later time; a hundred years, maybe five hundred. All I can tell you for sure is that they dislike us."

Osnat was disgusted, but not surprised. Before the Trail of Tears, the Ebers were resented for their accomplishments. These people took the same attitude as their presumed ancestors, who had exiled Osnat's people to this place. There was a certain grand irony to their being here. "It's time," she said to Norma. "Please get everybody together."

As Norma went off to gather the little community, Osnat considered the feeding list. Being sick was a capital offense here. Being weak was also punishable by death. Not punishment actually, but the same consequence. In some ways, the Tunniq weren't so different from the Ebers. True, Eber violence hadn't been ritualized and the killing was passive. Nonetheless, the results were the same: the weak died, the strong lived. How could they deny food to the weak? Wouldn't the proper course of action be for the strong to help the feeble?

And then what? More people would die of hunger. It's worse to let two people die when one could live. Sometimes kindness entails nastiness.

And who was she to complain about meanness? She had done her best to terrorize Eric and Norma. Even Aarluk thought she had gone too far. There was larger problem, though. The Ebers took their oaths seriously, but a forced oath wasn't binding. She could give orders, but the moment she told them something distasteful, they might decide that they weren't really bound by any vow.

Norma was soon back. "That's everybody."

"Thank you, Norma. I release you and Eric from your oaths of obedience."

Norma paled. "What...?"

Osnat smiled, and gently touched her face. Looking around at everyone, she raised her voice. "I'm sorry you suffered so much. I'm glad some have survived. I hope you live through the spring, when your rags will be useless against the melting snow and rain. My friends and I are leaving. We'll trade you some meat for your extra lighters, and then we'll be on our way."

Silence. Everyone stood, not even staring, just looking weakly at the person who had embodied their hope for survival. That hope had just announced it was going away. Were they so weak that none of them could say anything? Was their will so completely extinguished? Osnat had expected an outcry against her abandoning them, demands that she stay to help. There wasn't even a murmur. Just numb stares, except for Norma and Eric, to whom she had given food, strength, and a promise. They were glaring angrily at her.

Her sister-in-law approached. "I'm sorry Simon was killed, Osnat. With my child gone, you and I are the last of our family. I don't expect to be around much longer. I hope our baby lives," Dina said softly, pointing at Osnat's belly. Osnat's heart was exploding with grief as she kept her face calm. She wanted to touch Dina, to hug and comfort her, but she knew that if she did that, if she even spoke a gentle word, she'd break down. This wasn't working the way she wanted. She wanted them to plead with her for help, freely and desperately offering oaths. Her own idea of her awesomeness wasn't as widely shared as she had anticipated.

Norma was furious. "I gave you an oath. You said would give us food, shelter, warmth. You promised us life!"

"I gave you some food. I warmed you up. And you seem to have decent shelters. There are too many of you. There are only four people on my list to share food with. If I change that to fifty-four, it puts my life in danger."

Eric pointed at her, murder in his eyes, but Osnat didn't give him a chance to speak. "I have a dangerous task, rearranging the geography of the village where we live. If I succeed, I'll have extra clothes, which I can bring back and trade with those of you who are still alive."

Eric's angry burst of energy quickly dissipated. "What do we have that you would trade for?"

"I'd like some more lighters, and I'd like the things that the people from later brought with them. Maybe I'll hire some of you to work for me."

"Take us with you now, to help you rearrange the geography. We're good people, and we don't need much to survive. You can just give us your scraps."

Osnat hid her embarrassment at making someone beg her for help. That wasn't how she had been brought up. "It's a dangerous place. There are people who would cut off your hand and gnaw at your fingers while you watch. I can't afford to have to have you in the way."

"I promise not to get in your way, Osnat. Was I ever in your way?" Dina's bony hand pressed her face gently. Osnat removed it, kissing the twisted fingers. Two of Dina's fingertips were missing, a mass of grey scars in their place.

"I'm going to war, Dina; a war of extermination against a people. No one is coming to take us back across the Edge of the World to our former homes. The only people I can have with me are those who are completely loyal, who have sworn to obey me without question."

"I trust you, Osnat. I listen to you."

Osnat turned her back to Dina, and looked up at Ijiq. He wiped the tears from her eyes, and dried her cheeks with his mitt. He put his hand on her shoulder and gave a light squeeze as she turned back.

"I listen to you too, Dina, but that's not enough. I need complete obedience. If I tell you to gouge out a baby's eyes, I need to be able to count on your doing it. I know you're older than me. I know you have more experience than me in many things." She noted Dina's eyes flicker to her stomach, and remembered with a start that Dina was an experienced midwife. "I would rely on your wisdom, your love. But I'm not the person you knew. I was murdered by cannibals. Before that I was raped by them."

"How did you get away?"

"I didn't," Osnat said as she held her hand out towards Aarluk and Ijiq. "This is my mother and rapist; Simon's murderer. Her name is Aarluk, and this is her husband Ijiq. I'm alive because of them, and they trust me in anything I ask. Back at our tent outside the woods is Haran. His family has sworn to kill me, but he will do whatever is necessary to keep me from harm."

Osnat looked at the eyes of all the people watching her. There was no consternation, no bewilderment at her bizarre declarations. It must be because of their weakness. Or perhaps after having suffered so many shocks, nothing could surprise them anymore. As they stood watching each other, Osnat realized that she was doing poorly at anticipating other people's reactions. If she was like that in a battle, she would lead a lot of people to their deaths. Maybe they really would be better off without her. She could give them her extra food; give some hunting advice...

A tall man with faded red cloth wrapped around his head went and stood beside Ijiq. "My name is Seth, Olive Tree clan. I'm a structural geologist. I can help you rearrange the geography. I give you my oath of unquestioning obedience."

Nobody reacted, nobody moved. Aarluk looked at Osnat, then stared angrily at the crowd. Osnat crossed her arms over her chest, glaring, looking impatient.

"I'm Peter, Cheetah clan. You have my oath of unquestioning obedience."

"Kenny. I swear to obey."

"My name is Carol. I'll do whatever you tell me to."

One by one, men, women, Ebers, people from later all went to stand by Ijiq and Aarluk. They gave Osnat their oaths, each one becoming a burden on her shoulders. She kept the panic out of her eyes as she realized she was no longer just carrying one baby; she was carrying the lives and futures of these people. She breathed heavily, wondering whether that was balance to the fact that she was also carrying the destruction of a different community.

Aarluk reached out, and gently turned Osnat to face her. She spoke softly. "You're almost there."

"How can you tell?"

"I'm your mother. I know these things."

"I need a hug, mother."

"Now's not the time. Feed them, and the memory of this meal will tie them tightly to you."

"It wasn't long ago that you told me that if we fed others, it wouldn't stop them from trying to kill us."

"Osnat, you are on both sides of the Edge of the World. You are going to use this to protect your people."

Only her mother could understand her so well. Osnat turned back to the people now sworn to her. "I, too, give you an oath. We will make a new life here. I also give you my oath that one day we or our children will return and get back what was taken from us." She raised her stone knife above her head. "I declare war on those who try to stand in our way. I declare war against those who have stolen our lives in the past, and against those who may oppose us in the future. If we have to be ruthless, we will not hesitate."

She put her knife away.

She looked around for objections. There were none. "This is what I, Osnat, of the Olive Tree clan, declare. You are bound to obey."

No cheering, no hugs... Norma and Eric smiled.

"Understand though, the seriousness of your oaths. Anybody who violates it will be killed, upon my word." Osnat struggled to keep her knees from trembling. "We're going to feed you now."

Once again, they tasted happiness. This time it was their own.

***

There were fewer people alive at the caves. Osnat, Aarluk, Haran and Seth were greeted by a shower of rocks when they approached. It took a while for Osnat to convince the cave dwellers that she hadn't come looking for a meal. About a month ago, a Tunniq hunting party from further north had taken away three men and a woman. While the cave survivors looked better fed than the people who had lived in the woods, there was madness in their eyes. They hissed and spat at their visitors, refusing to come out. Aarluk explained that they had been dragged alive to the Abode of Confinement; it was not possible to bring them back.

Osnat nodded, and was turning to leave when Seth asked, "May I try?" Before she could answer, he pulled a small flute from his rags, and started to play. Osnat listened, trying to place the familiar tune. When one of the cave dwellers started to sing the lyrics, she realized it was the battle song of the Vultures Games League Alliance. The Vultures had won the national lacrosse title just before the Trail of Tears, and were widely expected to win soccer as well, giving them the overall championship. Osnat herself belonged to the Auks Alliance. She used to feel embarrassed at being associated with such a non-descript bird, but there was no choice in the matter; you inherited your Games League Alliance from your father. A few more voices joined the song.

Another voice started up, countering with the Auks' song, and Osnat joined in. She walked over to the singer, a middle-aged cave dweller, and put her arm around her shoulders. They sang together, provoking of a chorus yet more Alliance songs from most of the remaining voices in the cave. Aarluk and Haran had never looked so astonished.

When Seth finally put his flute away, he again turned to Osnat, asking "May I?" She wanted to jump on and hug him. She nodded instead.

"The Games are different here," he addressed the cave dwellers. "The Alliances are different. There are only two: Life and Death. Osnat is the Captain of Life. All of us who live in the woods are with her. You have a simple decision in front of you: Life or Death. If you want to be with our Alliance, make an oath of complete, unquestioning obedience to our Captain. We have to return to our camp in the woods. If you're joining us, gather up your belongings and come outside to take your oath."

Only four of them remained behind, too deeply a part of Death.

She now had about as many people sworn to her as there were at the village she was going to destroy. All were depending on her for their very lives. All were feeble from hunger and cold, weak from the crushing horror of their life, from the utter obliteration of the existence they had known. Osnat wanted to hug them one by one, comfort them. But if she was going to do a good job as their Captain, she had to be like Aarluk, stomping off and abandoning her charges in a blizzard so they could learn to find their way on her own. Human kindness in this cold, cruel land would surely bring about all their deaths.

They spent the next couple of days feeding people. It was several hours between meals, so people's stomachs had the chance to adapt to larger portions.

Osnat took one of the abandoned huts as hers, instructing people to restore the gaps in the walls. Aarluk provided a few pelts and other furnishings to make it comfortable. Smoke drifted lazily upward from the small fire in the center, escaping out a small gap at the top.

Osnat interviewed each of the survivors, noting any potentially useful skills. The butcher and carpenter were already plying their craft, adapting to new materials, and working without their regular tools. The architect, having won many awards for the beautiful homes he designed, said that the shelters he built here gave him more satisfaction than anything in his previous career. The pharmacist was helpless without any medicines to dispense. The mortgage broker didn't find business much worse in her new location than her old; recent decrees limiting interest rates and the ability of lenders to exercise their liens meant that very few loans were taking place. At least now she didn't waste any time at it.

Osnat masked her excitement at the presence of a fusion technician and a discovery physicist. These people had the skills, along with Seth, to bring the mountain down as Osnat planned, yet save the clothes and equipment.

"Are you pregnant from the rape?" Dina was the last person she sat down with.

"What difference does it make?"

Dina put her hand under Osnat's coat, feeling her belly. "I want to know when the baby is due."

Osnat closed her eyes and concentrated, trying to cleanse her emotions of the image of her husband being brutalized while all those men took their turns with her. "Simon and I were going to wait. When the Collective Council went crazy just before declaring the Trail of Tears, we felt something horrible was coming, and decided not to delay. It was maybe a week before we went through the hoops; I think that's when I became pregnant. It may have been when I was raped."

Dina removed her hand. "I'm sorry. Who raped you? Your mother? I don't understand."

Osnat clenched her teeth.

Dina took her hand. "Really, I'm sorry. Talking about it can help. It wasn't your fault."

The ice in Osnat's eyes was replaced by fire. She angrily grabbed Dina's wrist. "I know there was nothing I could do to avoid being raped! I know there was nothing I could do to avoid Simon being butchered and served as a festive meal, and there was nothing I could do to avoid being sent on the Trail of Tears! But I'm not going to be a victim anymore, Dina. Do you understand that? I'm going to be the one to have victims."

"Is this what you want to become of you, Osnat? Is this the person you want to be?"

"It's who I am." Osnat took a deep breath, calming herself. "The person you knew before was murdered by cannibals. You're questioning the essence of my life. Don't. The conditions of the oath apply to you as much as to anyone else."

Dina looked away. She started to rise, but Osnat was still holding her wrist, and pulled her back down. "In answer to your other question, it was Aarluk's idea to rape me. She was the first; then a few more, from Haran's family. My mother might be the father. Maybe one of the others. So tell me, when is the baby due?" Osnat released Dina's wrist, and sat quietly, looking at her. The first time her brother had brought his future wife home, Osnat had been awed by Dina's flawless appearance. She tried now to see around the patches of blackened skin to her beauty. The flawless heart was still there, filled with concern for Osnat.

Dina was in tears. "I've lost my baby; I've lost my life." She lifted her eyes. "If I wasn't at the edge of starvation, my breasts would be engorged with milk. If I wasn't at the edge of starvation, my daughter would be alive."

"Really, what you want to know is if I'm carrying one of ours or one of theirs."

Dina nodded.

Osnat pulled off a mitt and cupped her hand to Dina's cheek. "I thought that I was pregnant before I was raped but wasn't certain. Now I know I'm pregnant, but not sure by whom."

"He's your baby, Osnat, and you'll love him no matter what."

"He's...?" Osnat asked.

"I sense a boy. I don't have any of my diagnostic equipment, but I can tell by touch; my senses are more reliable than equipment. You have a boy, and he'll be with us in around thirty or forty days unless you push yourself too hard, in which case he might arrive earlier, or not at all."

"I won't push myself. All I have to do beforehand is kill everyone in a village, take all their clothes, equipment and food, then bring a down mountain on the remains. Oh yes," she added. "I also have to feed and clothe everyone here. Forgive me if I'm a little testy."

"I told you before, Osnat, I have faith in you, whether you're comforting or threatening me. My husband loved to tell me stories of his little sister, whom he admired so much. His feelings for you are part of me. There isn't much of him left, and I hold on to what I can."

The fire flared again in Osnat's eyes. She was Tunniq, she was a murderous cannibal. How dare this woman treat her as if she was part of the other side of existence? Her brother had been a tease, making her miserable at times. More often, he was a rock, supporting her, encouraging her, even when she didn't understand how much she needed that support. He had never threatened to kill her. Osnat imagined herself holding a bone spear, standing in the middle of a river calmly telling Shelah that she was going to have his liver for supper if he didn't help her back to shore.

She couldn't kill Dina, though. That would be killing the last of her family... last except Aarluk, of course.

22 THE EDGE OF THE WORLD 8

Osnat had not seen the young woman before. The crack in her lip, the bruises on her face explained the constant darting movement, the hunted look in her eyes. Her long blond hair was filthier than most. She was one of the people from later, one of the cave dwellers who had been captured a month earlier. Haran introduced the man who arrived with her as Zimri, one of Puah's sons from a previous husband. He had fled to another encampment shortly after receiving his name.

Zimri in turn introduced the young lady as Wendy, his wife-to-be. She stank of fear.

"Stop trembling. You're safe for the moment, if you agree to follow my orders." Osnat was revolted by her own harshness to Wendy, whose heart was clearly frayed; no, shredded.

Aarluk growled, "Agree to follow her commands, or leave."

Zimri nodded his assent.

Osnat walked up to the man. "Why are you here?"

"To be married!" Looking at the blank expressions on the faces around him, Zimri continued. "Since I had never had a woman before, I was told I could be first with the woman we captured. But when I pulled Wendy's pants down, she started to cry. Sex is supposed to be pleasant, so I asked her why she was unhappy."

"I told him," Wendy said tearfully, "that I was saving myself for my husband. He shrugged, said he would be my husband, and then raped me. After he was finished, every other man in the village raped me."

"I keep my promises. After everyone was finished, I told her she was my wife. She was crying and crying; some of the men had hurt her. She insisted on being brought back to her people. I want my wife to be happy, so we're here."

Haran put his arm on Zimri's shoulder, giving it a friendly squeeze. "He's alright," Haran turned to Osnat. "He's not nasty enough for his family; his brothers would have killed him long ago."

Wendy's trembling was getting worse. Her breath was coming in short, noisy gasps. Zimri was frightened. "Help her!"

Osnat stood up, and slapped Wendy's face, hard enough to make it sting. "That's enough."

"I was gang-raped," she whimpered.

Osnat shrugged. "So was I. Get over it."

Wendy stopped trembling, her breathing calmed. Her eyes stopped their darting movement, as they focused on Osnat.

"You? Who...?"

Osnat nodded towards Aarluk, standing behind her. She folded her arms over her chest, doing her best to look impatient.

Wendy looked around. She opened her mouth to speak, but no words could get past her lips.

"Everyone here has taken an oath to obey me without question. You have to do the same if you want to stay. Decide."

"I swear to obey you without question in order to protect my wife, even if it costs my life," Zimri said.

Wendy stared at him, her mouth open, her forehead furrowed, before turning to Osnat: "I give my oath to obey you."

"Do you accept Zimri as your husband?"

Wendy stared at him again.

Haran slapped Zimri on the back. "You really enjoy having her," he grinned.

"Only if it makes her happy. I won't ever touch her again if she doesn't want me to. If that pleases her, I'll be content."

"Do you offer your oath to care for and protect Wendy, to make her happy?" Osnat pressed.

"Yes, yes..."

"Do you accept his oath, Wendy? If you do, you're his wife."

Wendy looked at Aarluk, then to Osnat, then to Zimri, and whispered "I accept."

"Congratulations. Tell me, do you have any skills? What's your training?"

"I'm Captain of the Hummingbird Alliance lacrosse team."

Osnat smiled to herself. Wendy must be a lot tougher than she seemed at the moment.

Broad smiles were on the faces of everyone who had watched the unexpected celebration. "Haran, please find them a house where they can be together."

He took their hands and led the newlyweds out.

Osnat turned to Norma, who had been standing quietly to the side. "Did you think three days ago that you'd witness a wedding?"

"I didn't expect to be alive now, I was so hungry. I was sure that I'd pass out on patrol, or that Eric would do something stupid that would kill us."

"He does stupid things?"

"He's a 'Harmonizer.' When someone caused a lot of discord, they were sent to a re-harmonization camp where they were taught to stop being disruptive. Eric was one of the counselors there, and thinks all problems can be solved by teaching people to be friendly. When a boy was cornered by a polar bear, Eric yelled at him to think peaceful thoughts. If the kid had started running right away, he might have lived. When he examined the boy's blood on the snow, Eric said he could feel anger in it, so it was the boy's own fault that he died. Not the bear's. Certainly not Eric's."

"What kind of discord would get a person sent away?"

"Refusing to share, insulting someone..."

"Insulting..." Osnat repeated. She wondered if maybe the people from later had been sent here to learn from the Tunniq how to be civilized.

"Like calling someone fat, or stupid; refusing to have sex..."

Osnat shook her head in disbelief. Maybe being exiled was a better fate then remaining would have been. She dismissed that thought.

"What about Eric's oath? What if I order him to kill?"

"I wouldn't count on him."

"Norma, you have to tell me who else does stupid things, who I can't count on. Such people put all our lives at risk."

"Eric's the worst. Harmony is his life's mission, no matter how much destruction it leaves in its wake."

"Thank you for the warning. Keep your eye on people for me."

Osnat sat down on the pelt floor, and leaned on an arm.

Norma sat down next to her. "The cave-people said four people were captured by Balthan. What about the other three? Can we do anything?"

Osnat shifted uncomfortably. The question had been at the back of her mind since Wendy and Zimri walked into their camp. She turned to Aarluk. "What about the other three?"

"A crazy old man named Balthan runs that camp. Since names are hard to get these days, he insists that they be taken as soon as a boy is born. One of the women at Balthan's camp should have given birth not long ago, so there are only two captives left."

"Are you sure she gave birth to a boy?"

Aarluk squatted on the pelt in front of her. "This woman has given birth many times. Only once did she have a girl, so I'm sure there are two captives left."

Osnat jumped, and hauled Aarluk up by the shoulders. Her usual calm expression was replaced by excitement, even glee. "What did you just do?"

"I told you that one of the captives is dead."

"How do you know that? Did you travel between Spheres, and the dead man told you?"

"Since the woman gave birth to a boy, and Balthan demands that names be given..."

"How do you know the woman gave birth to a boy?"

"Since she gave birth mostly to..." A smile pierced her face, as it dawned on her. She began to chuckle. "The woman who gave birth probably had another boy."

Aarluk was laughing, but her face was red from embarrassment. Osnat hadn't thought that she was capable of that. "What's next Aarluk, now that you use probability? Propositional logic? Or maybe I'll teach you calculus."

"You've corrupted me, you realize."

"Well, you've influenced me, so...."

Norma barely muzzled her rage. "Aarluk tells you a captive has been killed, and you're laughing about epistemology. Please explain to me what the birth of a boy has to do with killing, and why it's funny."

Aarluk wrapped an arm around Norma's neck. "Do you want her to suffer before she dies?"

"Don't hurt her." Osnat wiped a mitt across her eyes, and then fixed her glare on Norma. "There aren't lots of opportunities for laughter here. Don't let any go to waste." She turned and stalked out of the shelter.

Seth was waiting for her, leaning on a tree. "Can you tell me more about the geography you want to alter?"

Osnat motioned with her head, and kept walking. She needed to clear the tangled underbrush from her mind. They were practically out of the camp when she turned to him. "What's your experience?"

"Rivers, mostly."

"Rivers?"

"I'm sure your mother can get as much information reading animal tracks as we get out of books. I read rivers."

Osnat was about to point out that her mother was an accountant, when she realized who Seth was talking about.

"With a bit of research, I know the land formation, what minerals are likely to be there, the weak points...," he said. "In a recent assignment I had to find the best way to re-route a river that ran through a gorge. I looked at the river. I looked at the gorge, and told my clients how they could collapse its sides, at the same time creating a new path for the river to follow." Seth's eyes sparkled with pride. "They thought the project would take years. With my guidance, it took a few months. On the next contract I bid on, my price was more than double my competitor's. I got the project anyways, because my reputation is so good."

"What was it?"

"To get easy access to an ocean-shelf deep gas deposit." Seth stopped, snared by memories. "I had my insurance company post a performance bond to guarantee I'd complete the job. I wonder if they paid out or fought it."

"Why? What happened?"

"I came here instead. Osnat, I'd be grateful for a contract."

"We won't pay you more than your competitor's asking." Osnat enjoyed the business banter. She had not only been an award-winning scientist; she had a singular talent for negotiating rights for her products. She had made a lot of money by insisting on short-term initial licenses. Once a product was well known, the value of a long-term contract was a lot higher than when it was new.

It was a tough business model, and it made her some enemies. On losing the product rights to a competitor, one manufacturer swore vengeance on Osnat. Jackson, the manufacturer's uncle, was Secretary of the Collective Council that sent her here. He pushed the Trail of Tears through despite widespread opposition and questionable legality. Was her exile retribution for an unhappy business deal?

"If I continue to live, I'll consider that satisfactory payment." Seth's face turned serious. "I'll need a helicopter, of course, for an aerial survey. A gravity corer, radiation detector, and so on." He counted the items off on his fingers as he spoke.

"My policy is that all contractors have to provide their own equipment." She smiled, "And what about a performance bond?"

"My oath to you is my bond," he said.

Osnat leaned over and kissed his cheek. "There's your contract."

"I'm honored. What do you want me to do?"

"The job has gotten a lot more complicated now that I've discovered all you people alive."

Seth arched his eyebrows.

Osnat explained her promise to Aarluk and Ijiq.

Seth's oath kept his lips sealed as Osnat continued outlining the terms. "We also have to be careful how we kill them. Stabbing would ruin their clothes."

"Excuse me, please." Seth stepped quickly to the side, turning his back to her. He coughed, took some loud, deep breaths, and stepped back to Osnat. His eyes were red.

"Let's head towards my office." She ignored his discomfort and started walking through the snow. "We have a fusion technician and a discovery physicist here. Your contract will be easier to fulfill if you work with them."

"You have something in mind?

"The escarpment above my village has small valleys punched through intermittently, with lots of cracks and overhangs. There are veins going through it. Many are luminous."

"Luminous? What color? Is that why you offered to trade for lighters?"

Osnat was pleased that he understood, doubly pleased that he hadn't objected to the grizzly assignment. "Mostly yellow and rust-colored, some blue. The fusion technician can work with the lighters. Go speak to him and the physicist." She waved her hand, sending him off. Osnat trudged the rest of the way back to her office alone, her feet sinking into the snow, her heart sinking deeper into her memories with every step.

She pulled aside the pelt door to her current office, where Aarluk and Haran were waiting patiently. Osnat's nerves were itching. She pulled her coat off over her head, flopped down on the hide floor, and shut her eyes. The cold air on her skin was refreshing.

Aarluk sat behind Osnat, kneading her shoulders, working powerful hands down the muscles of her back. Osnat's nerves relaxed as her thoughts drifted off.

She was practically purring as she rested her head on Aarluk's lap. "You're a good mother," she said, reaching up to touch her cheek. Aarluk smiled, running her fingers through Osnat's hair, gently massaging her scalp.

"The first time I saw you" Aarluk said, "I knew that I wanted to keep you close to me."

Osnat reached for Aarluk's other hand, kissed her fingers, and fell into a light sleep.

She woke to a whispered conversation between Aarluk and Haran. She shivered, wondering how long she had been lying on Aarluk's lap.

Sitting up, she slipped her jacket on, flinching at its stiff, cold touch against her skin. She moved closer to the small wood fire.

"Are we going to rescue the captured cave-dwellers," Osnat asked.

"You're not going to rescue anyone. Zimri, Haran, Ijiq and I can take care of that. Will you be safe with these people?"

"They're afraid of me, and they desperately need me. What about you? There are only three of you."

"Four; Zimri will help us."

"That's still not enough. If you're killed, many more people here will die. I'm not going to take a chance to save two captives."

"Are you planning to give Wendy back when Balthan comes for her? In a few days he'll realize that Zimri and Wendy went for more than a little trip."

"He's going to come here? He'd be willing to attack us to get back a captive?"

"Not attack," Haran said. "Massacre. They know of a helpless group of people at the edge of starvation. Balthan will bring some men from his village in order to take more captives, and then kill everyone he doesn't want. He'll probably have extra sleds to carry all the bodies back."

Osnat raised an eyebrow.

"For the feast," Haran raised his voice.

Osnat stood up, startled. She untied the door and stepped outside.

To her surprise, the 'feast' was looking back at her. Bits of the discussion were loud enough for people to overhear, and they were curious. There was life in the eyes that gazed at her; there was the energy of anticipation. They were still afraid of her though, so no one spoke.

"How would you like to be the main course at a banquet?" Osnat asked.

"Be the main course?"

"If you don't like that idea, get ready. Those who would dine on our flesh are coming."

She went looking for the butcher, who was trying to learn how to use the stone knife he got from Ijiq. After being exiled, he taught himself to use a tight-flame lighter that Jacob, the fusion technician, had modified. There was a certain satisfaction to cutting rabbit meat with a physical blade. He would probably enjoy it less if he had to use the stone knife on a walrus or bear.

"We need thigh bones." Osnat had always bought packaged meat, never having to deal with the people who cut the flesh. She had pictured butchers as broad, muscular men with fierce expressions. This one was thin, with patchy skin and nervous eyes. Maybe he had been broad before the Trail of Tears.

He was eager to fill the order. "I can give you rabbit bones. How many would you like?"

"You can't kill anyone with rabbit bone," she glared at him. "We need them long and thick."

Osnat knew that except for the occasional polar bear, the woods-dwellers had lived mostly on rabbits and small scavengers.

"How long do they have to be?"

She measured out her thigh with her hands, and held them up in front of her. "About that long. We need at least twenty."

His chest heaved as he angrily sucked air through his mouth. His emaciated body exaggerated the effect. "Which bodies should I take? My father is at the bottom of the pile; my wife, near the top. Should I take children, too?" His eyes were steady now, anchored by a blistering rage.

Osnat pushed down her rising stomach. "Children are too small."

"It's true, what you said." Eric had been listening to the discussion. "Finding you was infinitely more horrible than being stranded here. We were dying, but at least we were dying as humans."

"Your death can be easily arranged, if that's your preference." Osnat turned back to the butcher. "I want long, heavy bones. Choose the bodies accordingly. The femurs will have to be dried, so try to find tall, big-boned people who died earlier."

"Why don't you help us choose who to cut up?" Eric asked. "You can watch us dismember our friends and family, since it seems so important to you."

She wiped all the expression off her face and gazed sideways at Eric. "I watched already. The last I saw of my husband, his severed head was on the lap of a naked, aroused teenage boy." Osnat took a step towards Eric; he moved back in alarm. "I will be thrilled if only the dead are dismembered." She turned, and walked into the woods, taking a long way to her shelter, so she wouldn't have to deal with anyone else.

What was she going to do with thighbones? Would her own people use the weapons against her, in retaliation for desecrating their dead? And who anyways, were her people?

Osnat had to be careful when she pushed their minds over the cliff of what used to mean sanity. She had to be careful that they didn't turn on her for shoving. She would tell Aarluk she needed to be guarded.

23 THE EDGE OF THE WORLD 9

Panic gripped Osnat. She tried to yell, but the hand over her mouth prevented it. Was the intruder going to kill her? Another hand clutched her arm. She shook off her dreams and pulled her eyes open a crack. Eric's face was right over hers. How did he get into her house? She had perimeter alarms, guards. Where were the police when she needed them?

His lips were moving but she couldn't hear anything. He must have drugged her.

Eric kept indicating something to the side, as he mouthed the same word over and over. Osnat's hand reached down and touched fur instead of the wool blanket she expected. She turned her head and saw the skin-covered log wall. With a start, she realized that she wasn't deaf; she could hear yelling outside. She shook the last of sleep from her mind, pulling herself back from her Simon, from her soft, heated bed to the cold world of wakefulness. To the world where someone was promising to kill everyone and dine on their flesh. Osnat looked again at Eric, and realized what he was mouthing: "Balthan," who had come sooner than expected to take Wendy and Zimri back.

Osnat nodded her comprehension, and Eric released her. She lifted her head and saw Wendy sitting on the floor, her knees drawn up to her chin, her arms clasped around her legs. Zimri was comforting her.

It didn't seem to be helping. Wendy looked even worse than when she had arrived. Her skin had a blue pallor, the color of death. Her eyes bulged.

Osnat listened. Haran was outside addressing Balthan, saying these people were too powerful to destroy. The other speaker, Balthan she presumed, laughed, saying they were barely worth the effort of killing. Balthan then started describing Wendy, saying why the men wanted her alive. Wendy turned her face towards her husband. She looked like she was fighting desperately for control.

Eric offered thighbones to Osnat, Zimri and Wendy, and whispered "Be ready."

Zimri smiled, but his eyes were fierce. "I don't need. I have Wendy's knife. Today it's going to remove a lot of heads." He pulled a turquoise-hafted steel dagger from his sleeve, displaying it proudly.

A grating, humming sound suddenly filled the shelter, as the walls trembled. Wendy stared at the knife in her husband's hand and grunted. She shuddered, then snatched the weapon. The shelter quieted as she somehow pulled the grating sound into herself.

"It's for hearts." She pulled the blade from its leather scabbard and jabbed the point into her fingertip. Using it as a paintbrush, she drew quick red lines from the corners of her mouth, from the corners of her eyes. The contrast with the blue pallor of her skin was frightening. She painted her lips, and then stuck the brush in her mouth, coating her teeth.

"This is what we're going to do." Eric startled Osnat. She had been completely absorbed by Wendy's ritual.

"We'll go out there without weapons, to show that we're not afraid. I'll talk to Balthan, and explain—"

Wendy stood quickly and shook her head, "No. I'll deal with him myself."

Osnat lifted an eyebrow in question.

"Osnat, use your strength to make sure no one interferes." Wendy was out the door before anyone could argue. Osnat followed, wondering what "strength" Wendy was talking about. Eric and Zimri trailed the women.

Osnat took in the situation. Balthan had several men with him. Empty sleds were behind them, the dogs lazing on the ground, still attached to their traces. Zimri went to stand beside Haran, facing the visitors. A couple of the people from later stood next to Osnat's shelter. Everyone else had disappeared behind the long-dead trees.

Balthan was somehow out of place; there was something about him that didn't belong. He had a primordial aura, an ashen appearance and odor, a seeming frailty that said he should have returned to dust long ago. Small, raised red dots on his face looked like mosquito bites, but it was too cold for insects. He smelled of dampness, he smelled of heat and rot. He smelled horrible.

Haran greeted Osnat with a proud smile. He extended his arm towards her: "Our Chief."

Balthan turned, a sneer in his ancient eyes. But as soon as those eyes caught sight of Osnat, he flinched. He breathed deeply as he took a step towards her. Haran, Aarluk, everyone moved to protect Osnat, but instead of attacking, Balthan fell to his knees, looking up at her, his hands sideways in front of his face. He kissed the fingertips of one hand, brushed the tears from his eyes, and wiped his runny nose with his sleeve.

"Protector! I'm sorry I killed you. You were always kind to me; you always helped when I asked. I regret the pain I let into the world when I murdered you. I should have listened to your words. I've been trapped by Sheyds through my own choices. My heart has been hardened, and I can no longer choose differently, as you had advised me to. Forgive me for what I've done to you. Forgive me for what I'm doing. Thank you for all you've done."

Osnat was dumbfounded, her thoughts churning. What words? What kindness? Her foe was a madman. Did he expect her to protect him?

Balthan rose swiftly to his feet and stalked over to Wendy. Wrapping one hand around her throat, he lifted her off the ground with a strength that belied his feeble frame. Balthan whispered something to her that no one could hear, and she smiled. Haran, Zimri, everyone moved to protect Wendy, but her eyes went to Osnat's alone.

Osnat wasn't sure if it was what Wendy wanted her to do, but she did it anyways. The men trying to rescue Wendy froze on the spot, unable to move. Balthan's men had also stepped forward, but they too were unable to budge. Had Ijiq told Wendy about the invisible ropes? What if Osnat misunderstood? Her heart was pounding in her head; it would explode if it got any louder.

Wendy's blue pallor deepened as Balthan squeezed her neck. Zimri was in a frenzy, unable to help his wife. He would probably kill Osnat if he knew she had caused his immobility.

Osnat had never felt her heart beating so loudly, even when she and Simon had been captured. It was a deafening, rapid thumping. It took her a few moments to realize that the sound was coming from Wendy, whose face was now a deep blue, with bright blood-red trails. Her huge eyes seemed to gaze out from the sides of her face. Osnat felt the sound vibrating up through her legs; the ground was resonating to Wendy's heartbeat. A few people tried covering their ears as the thumping saturated the air. They were all inside Wendy's heart; the whole world was its chambers, pumping her blood, pumping her passion. Every thought, every breath, every motion of every person was now part of Wendy's divine will for vengeance.

The Captain of the Hummingbirds suddenly pounded at Balthan's chest with the turquoise-hafted steel dagger she pulled from her coat. His jacket, his skin, and then his ribs split apart. She opened the chest wider with her hands, reached in, and yanked out the still-beating heart, undamaged by the knife. She tore off a valve, put it in her mouth and started chewing. Balthan's hands were frozen around her neck. She peeled them off, landing on her feet as he folded to the ground, a death grimace on his face. "Balthan is a sacrifice to me," she proclaimed.

Osnat struggled to keep from gagging. Eric was ashen. Others were pale, sweating, or supporting themselves on trees.

Rocks, clubs, everything on the ground was vibrating, bouncing as if to the footsteps of an approaching giant. Nobody covered their ears anymore; the thumping of Wendy's heart penetrated their whole bodies. In the presence of Huitzil, the Hummingbird Master of War, there was only one source of desire, one source of intent.

She walked over towards the closest attacker, Nimjo, but spoke to all of them: "Your hearts are free; you have your own will."

Huitzil waved the remains of Balthan's heart in the faces of the attackers, pulled off another piece, and put it in her mouth. She looked over to Osnat. "Release them."

With a flicker of thought Osnat did so, relieved that she had understood Wendy properly.

Nimjo turned to Zimri. "Why are you fighting me?"

"You hurt my wife."

"So? We've hurt lots of these people and you never complained. Should I remind you what you did to some of the pairs we captured? We'll have no problem making a feast of everyone here, though they are kind of boney."

Osnat flinched. Nimjo was discussing pairs of scouts, like Simon and her. Zimri pointed to the Master of War, his wife. "What about her?"

"We won't kill her if you want to bring her home."

Wendy put a hand on Zimri's shoulder, and gently pushed him to the side. Her nemesis towered in front of her, a full head taller, probably twice her width, and maybe three times her weight.

He smiled broadly as he stood before her, licking his lips in anticipation. "I like it when my prey fights back."

The wings of some hummingbirds beat ten times a second; the wings of others fifty. No one could tell how fast Wendy's hands moved, but it was somewhere in that range as she yanked out the man's eyeballs, skewered on her index and little fingers. Nimjo's brain was still processing what happened as Wendy's foot slammed upwards into his crotch. Her fist crashed into his chin as he bent over in pain, severing his tongue. Nimjo staggered back, spitting the blood from his mouth. He charged blindly, fists first. As he reached her, Wendy ducked to the side, stabbing her knife into his back. She jumped on him as he collapsed, severing his spine. She slashed open his ribs and chest with another thrust of the Hummingbird dagger, and ripped out his heart.

Osnat was right: Wendy was tougher than she seemed.

The attackers were on the receiving, rather than the giving end of the slaughter. Some tried to run, while others struck out with bone spears, stone knives, whatever weapons they could bring to hand. A man running backwards tripped before he could take two steps. Ijiq grabbed his arm, put a foot on the side of the man's chest and yanked, ripping the man's sleeve, tearing apart the flesh of his shoulder. The frail- looking butcher quickly wrapped a thin, transparent cord a few times around a Tunniq neck, and pulled it tight. The rope went through the flesh like an over-ripe fruit. Aarluk used a femur to destroy the face of a man running towards Osnat.

Wendy had her steel Hummingbird knife, but all the other weapons were stone, bone or wood; none particularly sharp, none particularly lethal. Most of the blows were struck to maim.

Balthan had counted on Wendy's people being feeble from hunger and despondency. His crew had counted on not having to fight, and were severely outnumbered by people who although not physically strong, had regained their hope for life. The cries of men having their necks slashed and eyes gouged joined the sound of the beating of the Hummingbird heart.

The butcher, unable to do another head, had to satisfy himself removing hands, slicing thighs through to the bone. One attacker had almost made it to his sled before Seth intercepted him. The two grappled, holding onto each other's arms. It was a contest of brute strength between a person who had been living on the edge of starvation and his well-fed opponent. One a geologist, the other a seasoned hunter of both animals and men.

Seth's rage served him well, but it wasn't enough. A punch in the mouth staggered him backwards. While the other fights were two or three against one, Seth was on his own. He grabbed the thighbone club he had dropped and swung it at his opponent's head. The man's arm broke it in two, and the weapon fell from his hand. Seth was now isolated and unarmed against a much stronger opponent. He backed away, and smacked up against a tree as his opponent closed in for the kill.

The man raised his stone knife; the weapon paused halfway down. Seth pushed himself away from the tree and kicked fiercely at the man's crotch.

The hunter didn't respond. His eyes, his mouth were open, he was breathing hard; his knife remained up in the air, ready to strike, but not doing so. Seth dove and grabbed the broken femur. The man didn't budge. Seth rose to his feet, not taking the time to wonder. First one eye. Splinters of bone tore off and stuck out of the eyeball as Seth pulled back. He quickly went for the other eye, and then slashed at the cheek. The man stood, immobile, blind, bleeding. Seth stabbed him in the throat; he remained standing; his knife raised.

This was arduous. Osnat could have immobilized all the attackers, letting her people hack and stab them to death. The trick was to have them find their own way, without letting them get killed.

She saw Eric slip back towards the trees. He had almost made it when a bone weapon slashed through his cheek. The pain froze him to the ground. Osnat was deciding whether to let him die when a stone axe felled his assailant and saved him.

The rest of the attackers were beaten, bleeding, or dead. Huitzil motioned for everyone to back off. The invaders that still had life left put their hands protectively over their chests. She walked over to each one and with a foot uncovered his heart. "Do as I command, or have your heart annihilated, so that you never return to the Abode of Life."

The beating noise was slower now, louder, shaking the ground, shaking the trees with each thump. Some of the dogs were panting, fear pinning their ears against their heads. Dirt and snow fell from branches; a few of the shelters collapsed as their logs shifted. But they barely made a sound compared to the thundering of Wendy's heart.

She kneeled beside each invader, stabbing him through the throat. None resisted.

Huitzil handed Osnat a bloody piece of Balthan's heart and motioned for her to eat. In the back of her thoughts, Osnat realized she no longer felt the thumping, was no longer surrounded by the heartbeat. She was now an element of the sound. The silence of the thick, dense air was stifling. Osnat put the soft, dripping flesh in her mouth, not surprised that it was still pulsing. She chewed and swallowed small pieces, feeling its vibrations inside her. Her legs grew weak from nausea, and she sat down in the snow.

She looked over at the person who had called her "Protector," whose heart she was chewing. He no longer smelled of dampness and heat. It was hard to see, but it almost looked like he was smiling.

Wendy knelt in front of her, the blue of her skin fading, the thumping dissipating. She wiped her knife clean in the snow, dried it on her coat, and then carefully placed it in its scabbard. She gently put her hands on Osnat's shoulders. The two women held onto each other's arms, filled with quiet sorrow for what they had lost, more for what they had gained.

***

"We have a problem," Ijiq announced.

"Was anybody killed?" The sudden reminder of her responsibility crashed into Osnat's thoughts. After the death of Balthan and his men, Ijiq, Haran, Zimri and Aarluk had gone to wipe out the rest of his village.

"All of them, as you instructed. But Zimri said killing the baby would be an insult to Stanley, the cave-dweller whose name it had. We've brought the new Stanley back with us."

"I meant were any of our people hurt?"

Ijiq shook his head. "The women hurt my ears with their screams."

"Are the captives alright?"

He nodded.

"Then what's the problem?"

"Do we let the baby starve to death? It's hungry, and its mother is dead."

Osnat put her hand on her belly, feeling the life moving inside her. Was she ready to nurse? Would she be taking milk away from her own baby? "Maybe I can feed it. Bring Stanley here, and get Dina."

Aarluk had been waiting outside; she entered and handed the baby to Osnat. Osnat looked at the tiny face and wondered why its life was more worthy of protection than anybody else's. It was young, it was adorable, and it was helpless. But its helplessness could endanger others, which she would not allow.

Dina's eyes watered as soon as she saw the infant in Osnat's arms. She took it, and began to make cooing sounds as she rocked it gently in her arms.

Osnat got right to business. "It's hungry. If I try to nurse it, will I be harming my baby?"

Dina hesitated. "I don't know. A mother's first milk is different. It's better not to deny it to your baby."

"So, we should let this one die?"

"No. Give him to me. Now that I'm getting more to eat, maybe I can produce enough milk to keep him from starving."

"His name is Stanley." Osnat handed the baby to Dina, who hesitated, looking sideways at Aarluk.

Aarluk nodded. "I'll wait outside."

Dina took off her jacket, and put the baby to her breast.

Osnat smiled. "From now on Dina, you'll get two portions of food, for yourself and the baby. You'll see, with this new life we stop dying; we start living again."

Dina nodded, not able to join in Osnat's enthusiasm. Stanley was not getting anything from her. "We killed his mother."

"We're going to do a lot more killing," Osnat said. "There are many Tunniq encampments. We're going to destroy them all."

Dina shivered. The baby was sucking hard, and she could feel dampness on her nipple. She did not like discussing mass murder while nursing. "Not Stanley. We may have killed the woman who gave birth to him, but I have to take care of him."

"No, not Stanley; he's one of us. Just as Aarluk is my mother now, you're his." Osnat took a long breath.

Dina nodded, softly rocking her new child.

"I once had another mother..." Osnat's eyes were to the ground. "Her name was Naomi, and she had a son, my beloved Shelah." Osnat looked up. "You're mine, Dina; always."

"I loved Naomi from the moment Shelah introduced me to her."

Osnat's eyes narrowed. "Aarluk's my mother now."

"I hope she gives you as much love as your mother that I knew."

"Aarluk? She's a man, with male desires. Sometimes I'm very uncomfortable in her presence, especially when I'm undressed."

"Why do you put up with it?"

"I'm Tunniq. They do everything in front of each other, whether to relieve their bowels or their sexual urges. It's really awkward when she and her husband are having relations. I don't think Ijiq enjoys it. Whenever he and Aarluk are apart, he goes after other women. Aarluk doesn't care."

Dina was no more comfortable with this discussion than with planning a slaughter.

"Have you done any scouting, Dina? Have you ever been away from these woods?"

Dina shook her head.

"This is a vast land. There are endless stretches of rocky plains, broken by rivulets; stands of long-dead trees, separated by emptiness. Above the escarpment, the terrain makes even this place seem friendly. Further inland is the glacier. The Tunniq say that one day it will reach the sea. When that happens, everything here will be crushed underneath. We have to leave before. We can't go south, because that's where the Edge of the World is, trapping us. To the north are more Tunniq villages, filled with people who consider humans as just another meal."

Dina stared hard into Stanley's eyes, avoiding Osnat's gaze. She couldn't escape the soliloquy.

"This is a land of death, Dina. We rescued two people by killing many more. The only semblance of life that exists here is viciousness and cruelty. There's some laughter, some joy, maybe the occasional kindness, or rather what seems to our mistaken eyes to be kindness. I can't explain to you why Aarluk took me in, taught me how to kill animals, how to kill people. What's more, she taught me how to want to kill people." Osnat took a breath before continuing. "I want to be cruel. I want people to be terrified of me. That's who I am: Osnat, Olive Tree clan, now and always was, Tunniq. It just wasn't revealed before. Just like Wendy... Huitzil, the Hummingbird Master of War who eats living hearts. It hadn't been revealed, even to her."

Dina rocked the nursing baby, trying to shut out Osnat's story. It wasn't working.

"People are terrified of Wendy now. Almost as much as they're terrified of me."

A cruel smile formed on Osnat's face. "There's one person I've frightened the most, who would rather die than face the horrible Osnat, savior of her people, scourge of the Tunniq. But this person can't allow herself to die, because she made some promises. She has to deal with Osnat; there's no escape."

Dina listened intently. She knew everyone was terrified of Osnat.

"Do you know who this victim is, who lives in absolute terror of what I'll do next?"

She realized who Osnat was talking about. It was indeed terrifying.

The baby had fallen asleep. Dina shifted it to one arm, slid over to her sister-in-law, and put her other arm around her. She placed Osnat's head on her shoulder. In one arm she held a Tunniq newborn; with the other, her husband's younger sister, at the moment another Tunniq child. "Shh, my sweet Osnat. Don't be frightened. I'm here with you..." She rocked both of them as she swayed gently back and forth. The scourge of the Tunniq closed her eyes as Dina combed her fingers through her hair, soothing her.

24 EARLY BRONZE AGE 9

"I don't have to justify my actions to you, dear sister. I am the Olive Tree Clan Mother, and the Chief's consort. When I tell you something's dangerous, like playing with that boy's genitals, you don't argue."

Zeresh glared right back, wagging her finger for good measure. "I didn't say it's not dangerous. It's a lot less risky though than naming yourself Taiku's consort. I did what I did to protect all of us."

The Clan Mother's glare wilted in face of the truth of Zeresh's argument. Zaytea had used her position to bully Taiku into sharing power. Now the information her sister extracted had given her a great deal more.

Zaytea glanced around the empty room. All her furniture was on a cart bumping its way down to Taiku's house, except for the Olive Tree Clan chest next to the wall. Her new husband would soon come to take the two symbols of authority over the Elam: his wife and the chest. Once at his Meeting House, they would be symbols for all of Lagash.

"Why was he at your mercy after a few minutes? The trickles of water on his face couldn't have hurt so much."

"I gave his testicles hope, so he had something to protect."

"And the wet towel?"

Zeresh smiled. "That's something I learned a long time ago. I once got into a fight with another child, and wacked her on the head with a stick, making her bleed. I had a towel with me; we were supposed to go swimming together. As I cleaned her wound, I realized I was on to something."

"She must have been furious."

"When I stopped the water, the girl was too grateful to be angry. She told her parents that she fell."

"You tried this once on a playmate, and then used it on a captive soldier? Are you insane?"

"No, dear, I tested it again, and you should be very happy I did."

Zaytea folded her arms over her chest.

"Do you remember the family that gave most of their flocks to us and then moved away, beyond the mountains? We became rich, and you became Olive Tree Clan mother soon afterwards."

"Yes, I remember."

"The leader of that family was a letch. I was visiting his daughter Abijah in the upper pastures. She wasn't there, but her father came into the tent where I was waiting and demanded to have sex with me. That I was so young seemed to excite him. I agreed immediately, on condition I could first wash the dirt off his face. He let me tie him up, thinking I was going to do something special. It was, but not in the way he expected. I didn't stop until he took an oath to never to have sex with young girls. Then, to make life difficult, I made him take an oath not to have sex with goats or sheep. I was impressed by how fast he agreed. Then I told him that since he couldn't have sex with his animals anymore, he might as well give them to us. I left him a few so his family wouldn't go hungry."

Zaytea's mouth was agape. It took a few moments, but she finally found her tongue. "What about Abijah, your friend?" She took a deep breath. "It seems that I owe you a great deal."

Zeresh's eyes were closed, as she seemed lost in her thoughts.

"I haven't heard from her since." Zeresh flinched and shook her head, as if shaking off a frightening dream. "You can repay me by convincing Taiku to abandon Lagash. It will be destroyed."

"What! That's not going to happen. We're getting—." A knock at the door cut her off. Her husband had arrived to escort her to her new home.

Zeresh pulled her sister closer, speaking quietly but firmly. "Don't ever tell anyone about how we got those flocks. If anything I do with Shor seems disgusting, remember why I'm doing it. Please, tell your husband we all have to leave this place."

Zaytea shook her head and opened the door for Taiku. He didn't say anything as Vlad and Jared took the Clan chest. He reached under his jacket and pulled out a silver wire necklace, from which hung a rough turquoise, about the size of an olive. These were rare jewels, signs of great power, of danger. The only other turquoise she had ever seen was on Huitzil's knife. Taiku clasped the wire around her neck, the stone hanging between her breasts. He crooked an arm; she took it with both hands. This was even more perilous than she had expected.

* **

Ner let Zeresh into the stone prison where Shor was dozing lightly. She sat down on the chair on the far side of the room, too far for him to reach from the low pallet he was chained to. The chamber pot was clean, as she had insisted; Shor had to feel that he was benefiting by cooperating. She took a couple of jars and a towel from her pack.

He must have been sleeping lightly. He opened his eyes and rolled over on his side, smiling at her. She returned the greeting and walked over to examine his stump.

"I want to make sure your leg's not infected, and that you're not turning into an ox. How do you feel? Have you gotten enough to eat? To drink?"

Shor lifted his arms over his head, stretching and yawning. As she looked over his muscular body, she considered that he was like an overgrown child: trusting, affectionate, but with aspirations of deadliness.

"I've been well fed, thank you. I feel okay; a little tingly where I lost my foot."

"I have an ointment for your stump that will make it heal better. It may even make it grow a little bit."

"First you cut it off, then you make it grow back? You people are confused. "

Zeresh put a hand on his knee. "I didn't say your foot would grow back, just your stump would grow a bit of flesh and skin, to heal better."

She carefully pulled off the cloth protecting the bandage. She didn't like what was underneath: redness, and a festering smell. She took another cloth, poured some water over it, and cleaned the wound as best she could. Walking back to where she had laid out her things, Zeresh took a deep breath of clean air. She picked up a jar filled with a yellow cream, took a fresh cloth, and kneeled beside the exposed injury. The ridges in the flesh, the chips in the bone showed that the amputation wasn't done with proper cutting instruments. It must have been a slow, excruciating process. Just thinking of the pain made her wince, and filled her with greater respect for this boy, who just a few days later was smiling, and treating her as a friend.

He didn't flinch as she rubbed cream into the injured flesh. Though the ointment contained ingredients to deaden pain, just the sensation of touch on raw flesh must be agonizing. He might be young, but he was responding as a hardened man. And he wasn't bad looking.

"My leg was hot before. Now it feels cold, refreshed... What is that cream? If it does what you say, we could probably save a lot of our troops with it."

She continued to gently massage the cream on to the wound. "I don't know. The Ebers make it."

"Get it off me!" Shor suddenly sat straight up. He was sweating; terror rounded his eyes. "Get that Eber poison off my foot!"

Zeresh looked up in surprise.

"I've never been touched by anything Eber. I don't want to be contaminated by their dark magic."

"What are you talking about? What magic?" Zeresh had Eber family, distant cousins.

"The Ebers draw from the powers of the dark sky to carry out their wicked plans. The stars above us, the trees in the forest, the stones on the ground all demand that the Ebers be destroyed. Don't put their evil on me."

"What do you mean 'powers of the dark sky'?" She was taken aback. Many people considered astronomy akin to witchcraft. Could that be what Shor was talking about? She took a calming breath. It was superstition; probably nothing. Zeresh had kept her studies secret.

Shor was working himself into a frenzy. "Get the cream off," he screamed.

"It's starting to get infected. This cream will save your leg, maybe your life!"

"I don't care! I won't be touched by Eber magic. It's my leg."

"I'll wipe it off, but you're being a fool." She reached over and slapped his thigh, hard enough to hurt. "Now, what do you mean by magic."

Zeresh decided to cooperate with his bizarre concern. He was wrong though about it being his leg. It belonged to his captors. Since she was in charge of the prisoner, the leg belonged to her. She took another cloth and began to blot the ointment.

Shor closed his eyes to concentrate as he calmed himself down. "Let's say you wanted to open the door. You would use your hand to pull the handle. With magic, you could open it from the far side of the room without even touching it, using dark powers to do the work for you."

Zeresh had never heard anything so absurd.

"You have me tied to the pallet," he continued. "An Eber can hold a person prisoner without rope, just by casting a spell."

She stared. No one had really wondered how Asenath had captured the man trying to climb onto her roof. Everyone just took it as one of those things that Asenath and the Ebers could do, like make ointments and trap Sheyds.

"How are we going to heal your leg without Eber ointment?"

"I don't know. Make some yourself."

"The Ebers are the only ones who know how."

"See? They control you because you depend on them. They probably use their dark powers to keep you from the truth." Shor had a triumphant smile, as if he had proven his point.

"We depend on each other. We don't need to learn to make their ointments."

"Let me explain." Shor gently took her hand, peering into her eyes. "The Master of Spirits controls the world on behalf of the Source of all Power. There are things that make sense to people. Many other things are beyond understanding. In those, the Master of Spirits dwells. The Ebers have broken into that dwelling and stolen from him." He beckoned her closer and spoke softly: "Ja'ix plans to avenge the theft and return the stolen goods."

"Return them?" Zeresh tried to look serious.

Shor smiled proudly.

Zeresh returned the smile. Ja'ix's plan could be useful. "I've removed all the ointment I can. There may be a bit left, but don't worry: the Ebers here aren't so powerful. They can't work their magic with just tiny amounts."

"I'm happy you understand."

"Shor, things that are stolen have to be returned. From what you've told me, this ointment really should be in the hands of the Envoy of the Master of Spirits." Zeresh looked around, as if making sure no one was watching. She put a hand on Shor's thigh, brought her face close to his, and whispered. "If I bring some of the ointment, along with other Eber magic, could you take me to Ja'ix, so I could return what they stole?"

"Would you be willing to do that?"

"If you had two feet you'd be able to bring them on your own. But since you have only one, I have to come along to take care of your injuries."

Shor looked at her, uncertain.

Zeresh patted his knee in assurance. "Your leg isn't your only wound. You almost lost your manhood yesterday. I want to make sure you're not becoming an ox. You didn't try to loosen the string, did you?"

"I don't want anyone to cut them off."

She took his scrotum in her hand, massaging it, examining the redness around the top. She released it, and rubbed the inside of his leg. "I see that you haven't lost anything. I'm pleased."

He reached over and put a hand on her breast. "You'll be more pleased if you have sex with me now. I want you to be my first."

She lifted an eyebrow. "Your first?"

"To do it willingly. My older comrades told me that it's much better when the woman wants it. I've penetrated lots of women, but it was always by threatening to penetrate them with my knife."

Zeresh calmly removed his hand. "It's not the time for that now. I'm not ready."

"When will you be?"

"I hope you don't die of gangrene first. I'd like to have a brave, strong young man like you."

"You know where to find me," he grinned.

Zeresh stood up and walked over to the door. "I have to check the injury, where you bloodied your head, to make sure it's clean. Lie on your back." She picked up a bucket of water and walked over to her prisoner. He saw what was in her hand.

"What are you going to do?" he asked, agitated.

"Nothing I haven't done before. Now listen carefully." She looked him straight in the eyes. "I said that I'd like to have a brave, strong man. You're not going to panic because of some water. I'm not going to tie you up like I was instructed to, but you've got to stay perfectly still while I wash your head, or we're both going to be in trouble."

"You're going to follow instructions or you're both going to suffer." Ner stormed in, grabbed Zeresh's wrist, and handed her a fistful of saw-grass. "Use this!"

Zeresh sighed to her prisoner. "I tried. Be the man I think you are and we'll both be safe."

She bent over his groin, carefully tying a cord to the one around the top of his scrotum.

Ner shoved her roughly aside after she completed her task. "Give me your wrists," he ordered Shor, binding them tightly together. "Put them over your crotch."

Ner tightly connected the bindings on Shor's wrists to the rope on his testicles. Any pull, any twitch of his arms would cause intense pain.

"You've done enough, Ner. Get out."

He glared at Zeresh, who held her ground.

"You can watch through the door if you don't trust me. Get out." She put an assuring hand on Shor's chest.

Ner grumbled as he left.

She wiped the perspiration off her forehead, then reached over and wiped Shor's glistening face. "Be strong. Don't move at all. I have to clean your head. We can't let them get angry at us." She kissed her fingertips, which she then touched to Shor's lips. She placed the towel over his face.

The first time she had done this to him, she had used a couple of cups of water. This time she was going to use the whole bucket, slowly.

By the time Zeresh finally removed the towel from Shor's face, his whole body had turned to jelly. She cut the ropes; first the one binding his wrists to his testicles. She inspected the latter: there was not much blood. She dusted them with powder to keep them from chafing. She pulled her prisoner to a sitting position and hugged him. His arms were limp by his side, his head a dead weight on her shoulders. She could feel his heart racing against her breast, pounding so hard she felt it would burst out of his chest and come crashing through hers. She stroked her fingers through his hair, whispering soothing sounds in his ear.

"I... I..."

"Shh, you don't have to speak. Just answer my questions when I ask."

Shor nodded weakly, and kept his head on the comfort her shoulder. His heart was still pounding, but it wasn't threatening to leave his body anymore. She held onto his shoulders and released the embrace.

"Shor, when you attacked the marshes, why did you capture those women and kill the men?" Zeresh was certain the explanation would be simple: people to rape.

He gathered his breath. "We need Asenath."

Zeresh's heart felt like it would burst out of her chest.

"What?"

"A few months ago, we captured a man with a bunch of ancient parchments. He told us one of them described how to turn a person into a Fire Snake."

"That's crazy!"

"We thought so too, and demanded he explain. He refused, no matter how much we tortured him. As he was dying, he said there was only one person in the world who could decipher the parchments. He expired before we could force the name out of him."

Shor paused for a breath.

"We spent a week searching for the man's wife. We told her we would kill her baby immediately if she didn't reveal who her husband had been referring to. She named Asenath and told us where she lives."

"Then what? If you were after one woman, why did you take so many in your boats?"

"We figured that if we captured one person and tortured him to give up the one we wanted, she'd have time to flee. It was safer to take all the women. Unless Asenath was one of the women in the boat I was on, then she's on her way to Ja'ix now. The problem is that the parchments were in my boat. Do you think Asenath will need them to make a person into a Fire Snake?"

Zeresh stood in surprise, and walked over to the other side of the room. She had to work this out.

They had come to capture Asenath; they didn't know she was already dead. How had those people known of her at all? What's the point of turning a person into a Fire Snake? It would be much easier to capture the snake itself. The Marsh People were doing even better, extracting the venom so you didn't need to depend on a dangerous animal to do your killing. Would a person turned into a snake keep his human memories, his loyalties? If so, he could be a very lethal weapon.

Zeresh understood how dangerous the Fire Snake parchment was. But she also knew it wasn't the most frightening part of the collection in Shor's chest. She had that, and was the only person who could understand it.

Zeresh sat down again beside him and stroked his thigh. She needed everything from him. "Tell me about the soldiers going north around the continental divide." Zeresh was skilled at playing emotions like a musical instrument. She was not however, a military interrogator. What should she be asking?

"I think Ja'ix wanted to get rid of them. They're brutal."

Zeresh wondered what could be brutal to people like Shor and Ja'ix.

"They had invited me to join their society. I was afraid to refuse, but was more terrified to become like them."

"What are they?"

"The Cannibal Society. They slice off and eat a piece of the shoulder of everyone they capture. If they seize someone who's impressed them with his fighting skills or strength, the person who captured him cuts off the prisoner's head, and adds the prisoner's name to his." Shor paled at his own words.

"Why does Ja'ix allow it?"

"Because they're very effective. The Cannibal Society is a powerful storm that blows away all resistance in front of it."

This didn't make sense. If they're so effective, Ja'ix would want to keep them close. "Why north?"

"We have no maps from there. It's unknown country. Ja'ix is bringing the entire known world into the service of the Master of Spirits. He's also bringing the unknown parts."

With a start, Zeresh realized that as she had been concentrating on Shor's information, he had been working on getting her fingers further up the inside of his thigh, his hand lightly over hers. She couldn't inhibit his talking, so she'd better not inhibit his desires. Shor's body was no longer jelly. She wanted him to want to keep talking.

***

Zeresh pushed herself up from beside the pallet where her prisoner was snoring. She walked quietly to the door, which Ner opened.

"Did you get everything?" she asked. In addition to being a skilled fighter, Ner had an infallible memory. He would hear something once, and it would be a part of him, which he could recall at will. Some people playfully called him "the recorder."

"I have it all. Get another soldier to take over here, and we'll give our report to Taiku."

Zeresh grabbed his shirt in her fists and pulled him close. "He does not have to know how I got the information. If anyone ever finds out, you're a dead man. Make sure you give a full report before you blab, so nothing critical will be lost with your demise."

Ner crossed his arms over his chest. "I can't tell anyone what I don't know. I erased all the irrelevant sounds from my mind."

Zeresh was satisfied with the assurance. "You did well," she said.

Ner shrugged. "You did much more. We should give our report."

25 EARLY BRONZE AGE 10

Eighty men; actually, eighty boys and men stood in four rows of twenty each, all gripping their macanas, the flat oak staffs with embedded obsidian blades. Once Taiku conscripted the Eber Academy, texts had been put to the side.

A light breeze stirred the dust in the courtyard where they practiced. There was no wall around the enclosure, other than the lines of tall birches that formed its perimeter. The people who inhabited this region before the Madai believed the trees were the gateways to other Spheres, and so the grounds of the Academy had been considered sacred. If the trees were gateways though, nobody knew anymore how to open them. Visiting other Spheres was therefore done in the traditional way, by Travelers such as Aua or Aleku.

Taiku, and a half dozen of his soldiers watched the patterns the students were practicing defending against a mounted attack: a waist level horizontal swing, followed by a reverse upwards thrust. After every set, they would drop to the ground for five push-ups, a short pause, and then another set with the macanas.

The horizontal swing was to sever a horse's forelegs. The reverse upward thrust was to chop into the rider, who should be off balance as his horse stumbled. The push-ups were because these Eber students needed to develop some muscles if they were going to be able to chop through anything.

It wasn't too long ago that they had watched in horror as Tanayt Asenath used a macana to sever the head of a donkey. They didn't assume that if a woman could do that, it would be easy. They knew her wisdom enabled her to wield the weapon effectively. For Asenath, strength did not only reside in the muscles. For the students, the best path was push-ups.

"We would prefer more realistic exercises. We don't have horses to train on," Simon explained.

Taiku folded his arms. "And if you did? Your mother told me that you're not permitted to inflict unnecessary pain on animals."

"If brutalizing a thousand animals would save one human life, we would do it."

"How about torturing a thousand enemies, to save one of your people's lives?"

Simon bit his nails: "Like Ja'ix is doing? The terror reduces the number of battles he has to fight, and likewise the number of soldiers he loses. Aren't our Elam women torturing a prisoner now?"

"If it were up to you?"

"Chief Taiku, we rely on your judgment."

"You're avoiding the question. Would you torture someone if it helped save the lives of your own people?"

"Yes. I wouldn't be happy about it."

Taiku frowned. "I thought with all the studying you people do, you would have smarter answers."

"Being too clever can be very foolish. Sometimes pure violence is the smartest response to a problem." He pointed at the students, struggling to lift their chests off the ground. "This is one of those times."

"Will they be ready on time?"

"If we have enough of it. This brings me to what I want to discuss with you. I received my first response from our "net," as you call it. Ja'ix's assault on Mattara was a disaster. He's been stopped at the entrance to the valley, and suffered heavy casualties. He's dug in for a siege."

"A siege! How? If he's stuck at the valley entrance, then he couldn't have surrounded the village. You can't lay a siege from one side."

"The information has to fit on a parchment small enough to attach to a bird's leg. There's no detail. It said "Ja'ix halted at Mattara valley, lost many, trying siege." I can't tell you more."

The Chief should have been pleased with the news. Instead he started pacing back and forth. After a few moments he asked "Have we heard anything from Samarra? It's closer."

Simon didn't answer. Taiku turned towards him.

The attack had been quieter than the light rustle of leaves in the wind. Taiku's soldiers were on the ground, not moving. A woman stood hidden behind Simon, a knife at his throat.

"Surrender immediately or he dies now."

Taiku was stunned into silence.

"Well? I count to three, and then kill him."

What could have happened? Had he already lost? He didn't see any foe, except this woman's knife arm. He couldn't let Simon die. He had promised.

"One."

"Two."

"I... no..." Taiku tried to speak.

"My cousin insisted on telling you something important. She wanted to do it in her own way." Qimiq appeared out of nowhere. "I want to make sure no one gets hurt. You're not under attack." He stepped among the prostrate soldiers.

A handful of Marsh people came out from behind the trees, as Taiku's men began to stir. Tamsyn removed the blade from Simon's throat. "I'll make this up to you," she whispered. She waved her dagger at Taiku before putting it away. "Some lessons need to be learned at knife-point. Three."

It took Taiku a few seconds to understand what had just happened. It took a few more seconds for the feeling of utter hopelessness to transform into irredeemable rage. "How dare you do that to me? How dare you threaten Simon!"

"You deserve to be embarrassed. I was able to destroy you before you knew you were under attack. The only thing that prevented the defeat of Lagash today is that we're on the same side."

Taiku's anger burned hotter. "You caught me by surprise. If I had been ready for you, the knife would have been through your throat."

"If Ja'ix attacks before you're ready, will you ask him to wait? I know you're making grand preparations, but he may not feel bound to your schedule. You must be ready right now, or we're all dead."

"You're right: Ja'ix isn't bound to my schedule, but I happen to know his. He's laying in for a siege at Mattara. By the time he gets to Lagash, if he gets here at all, we'll be ready."

"You just said the siege story doesn't make sense."

"The Clay People don't lie." He wondered how long Tamsyn had been silently stalking him.

"Maybe. Do they make mistakes?"

Taiku looked at Simon. "There are decisions I wish they hadn't made."

Simon wiped the sweat from his forehead and quieted his shaking. He nodded in agreement, as he stepped over to Taiku. "Ebers lie. We make mistakes. We get tricked. Some of us trick others or each other. Our studies, our way of life gives us a discipline that makes us resistant to those faults, but not impervious. Don't make us into something we're not. My mother wasn't perfect; she knew it, and didn't consider it a flaw. No humans are."

Taiku's thoughts drifted to Asenath, to the time they spent together, the understanding they shared. Their friendship was perfect, regardless of what anyone else could say. He glared at Tamsyn. "It seems you don't trust my judgment."

"Why are you worrying about whether people trust you? Did I hurt your feelings?"

"I'm getting Lagash ready for war, and you're getting me angry."

"Never mind getting ready. Be ready, now. I don't care about your moods. This is about the survival of Lagash."

Taiku's nostrils flared as he took a step forward. "Tamsyn, I know what I'm doing. Lagash only has room for one Chief. If you think you know so much, kill me and take over. Otherwise stay out of my way."

"Alright. Draw your sword."

That wasn't the answer Taiku expected. He gaped at the slender woman with the fierce blue eyes. She was serious.

The Eber students halted their practice. Taiku's soldiers moved closer. Qimiq was perspiring, despite the cool breeze. Everybody formed a wide circle around the combatants.

"Give her your sword," Taiku said to one of his people.

She took the hilt, examined the sickle-shaped blade, and then tossed the weapon to the side. "Useless," she muttered.

Tamsyn calmly beckoned to Taiku to come at her. He stood wondering how he got himself into this situation, when Tamsyn abruptly turned her back on him. This was ridiculous. How could he attack an unarmed woman from the back? Such a victory would be humiliating. No matter what the outcome, he would lose. Perhaps the simplest thing to do would be to have his soldiers behead her, so that it would be another capricious act of violence, rather than an unfair fight.

The pain on the side of his face was stunning. He hadn't seen anything come at him, and was trying to figure out what it could possibly be as his shins were swept out from underneath, pitching him towards the ground. He swung his sword arm, but a wrenching pain in his shoulder halted the movement. He was face down in the dirt, his sword ripped out of his arm, which was pulled excruciatingly behind him. As he tried to grasp what had happened, he realized that Tamsyn had a blade to the back of his neck. She drew it slowly across, just deep enough to trace a thin line of blood.

"You're dead. I'm Chief now, according to your terms."

Taiku prepared himself for his end.

Tamsyn hissed softly: "Here are my orders. I'm taking over the training of the Eber students. I am going to teach these feeble scholars to kill using weapons, brains and discipline rather than power. You are going to provide me with straight wooden practice swords for each of them, about an arm's length longer than those useless metal weapons you carry now. Everything else, you're in charge of. I'm appointing you Chief, but on condition that you're ready to fight now."

Taiku's head was spinning.

"Don't be embarrassed," she whispered. "I've only lost one fight in my life, and that was to my granddaughter."

Tamsyn had no children.

The knife lifted from his neck at the same time that he smelled dust being kicked up. A blade clattered to the ground, stabbing him lightly in the side of his calf as it bounced. He felt the warm blood on his leg, but it was too much for the small jab he felt. He twisted around to see one of his men lying on the ground, a huge gash in his thigh; it had spurted blood over Taiku's own leg. Taiku jumped up as others rushed in to neutralize Tamsyn.

"Stop." He thrust his arm into the air. "Tamsyn's worth more as a soldier than any of you. From now on, except for Vlad and Zaytea, you're all under her command."

"She tried to kill you!"

"If I tried to kill him, he'd be dead," Tamsyn casually responded. "Take care of his injury," she then barked, pointing to the gashed thigh of the man who had attacked her from behind. She pointed to a couple of the Eber students: "Now, unless you want to be the ones on whom I demonstrate how to quickly break arms."

One ran to get a cloth for a tourniquet; the other to get salve to clean it.

A wall of soldiers stood between Tamsyn and Taiku, protecting him from a danger that had already passed. He pushed through impatiently, grabbing one of the men by the arm. "Bring Zeruiah, Vlad and my wife to the Meeting House." He looked over at Tamsyn. "Join us there. I'm fulfilling your condition."

Taiku turned to one of the Ebers. "Go find Ner and Zeresh. See if they're through with the prisoner. I want to know what they learned."

"I have to speak to you about the documents in the chest Qimiq captured." There was something about Simon's urgent whisper that grabbed Taiku's attention.

"Come with me," Taiku said.

"I can't tell if those parchments were composed by humans, but there is something very diabolical about one of them. It says how to make a human Fire Snake."

Taiku continued to walk up the slight incline towards the Meeting House, stepping very deliberately, his eyes fixed forward.

"I doubt if it's true. It's too fantastic," Simon added.

"It's true. Your mother told me about it."

Simon stopped, staring.

Taiku grabbed his arm and pulled him over to the shade of a large tree. "Simon, there's something about your mother I don't think you know. To you, she's a mother, a mentor. To everyone else she's a teacher, a sage, an incredibly beautiful woman, someone respected to the point of awe. To me she was all that, and something else: the perfect friend. We grew up playing together, challenging each other, learning from each other.

"When we became old enough to bear children we had to distance ourselves. It wouldn't have been appropriate otherwise. Before then she told me many things, including something she heard from her father about a box of ancient documents that had been stolen from the Academy library, possibly by Sheyds."

"How could they do that?"

Taiku let go of Simon's arm. "She didn't know; her father didn't know. She said the documents explained how to make a person into a Fire Snake, how to destroy the people of a village without touching it, how destroy everything using the tar seeps. Another said how to make a transparent wagon without wheels that can fly through the air at great speeds. There was supposedly one document no one could understand, that discussed altering the sky."

Simon digested this as he picked idly at the thick bark of the old tree. Sap leaked onto his fingers, which he scraped off with his teeth. "We've gone through the first scroll, about the Fire Snakes. It took a long time, because we were sure we didn't understand it properly. The second document, about how to destroy the people of a village, starts with gathering particles of nothingness, created where lightening hits the ground. We have no idea what that means. The other documents in the chest are more ordinary: inventories, marriage contracts, things like that."

"I'm only interested in the first. Can you do it?"

Simon wiped his finger on his shirt. "You want to make a person into a Fire Snake?"

Taiku didn't respond.

"She has to volunteer. I won't try it with anyone who doesn't want."

"She?"

Simon nodded. "It has to be done once, to a woman. Every female child she has who survives will then be a Fire Snake, and those women will also bear Fire Snake daughters. Most will be still-born."

"I want a few Fire Snake women. We don't have time to wait for their children to be born. Get started. What do you need?"

"Fire Snakes, anti-venom, and volunteers. There's also an ointment that we have to make that will entice the snake to consummate the marriage."

"Do what you have to. Find at least five volunteers."

"Five? You want me to find five women to allow a Fire Snake to enter their wombs? People here are already suspicious enough of the Ebers. If I start looking for volunteers for that, everybody will blame the Ebers if anything goes wrong. They'll consider us sorcerers."

"We're at war. From what I've heard, the Ebers will be the first to be slaughtered if we lose. You're Eber, but you're also Lagash. Do it. That's an order, given on the authority granted me by your mother."

"What about Tamsyn's training?"

"Skip it. See to the Fire Snake women. Gather whatever you need. Get it done."

Taiku turned from Simon and strode away. His gloom deepened as he recalled the discussion about the stolen box of documents. He and Asenath were children at the time, and the box sounded like a treasure trove of mystery. "I want to become a Fire Snake," Asenath had declared. "Imagine. I could kill someone with my tears. No one would dare make me cry. When I would kiss someone goodbye, they would really be leaving. And my daughters would be deadly."

Taiku had objected. "It's too dangerous! What if you swallow your spit accidentally?"

"If the venom is already in me, it must mean that it can't hurt me." She saw the fear on his face and added "I could protect you, just like you always promise to protect me. I would never hurt you."

She had hurt him. First by dying needlessly. And then by understanding what he had done to her. A Fire Snake kiss would have been much less painful. He had forgotten that long-ago children's discussion, filled with mystery and wonder. Now the mystery was back, dripping with pain, rather than cloaked in wonder.

Finding Zeruiah, Vlad and Zaytea standing at the Meeting House drew Taiku back from his memories. After some discussion, they all agreed that the best place to stop an attack from the north was at Sipress Pass. Once a southbound army would reach the bend near the woodlands, there would be too much open ground to protect.

Zaytea suggested digging out a section of the road, letting it fill with water from a stream. This would slow down an attacker, giving defenders an opportunity to strike. Zeruiah suggested catapults on the south ridge.

"What about the river itself? If Ja'ix could send boats through the marshes, he can certainly get boats downriver."

"I have some ideas, but they will take time."

"Tell me."

"We'll divert the river entering the marshes. When the water level goes down, no large boats will be able to enter. At the same time, we harvest the saw-grass from the marshes to make a net that stretches above a narrow part of the Klee-Dekel, at Sipress Pass. Zaytea told me that there's a twist in the river just above a narrows. We put the net there, and station archers and catapults beside it. When the enemy hits the net, we attack. We have it on pulleys, so we can raise it for friendly vessels."

"They would have to be very large catapults if they're to launch rocks heavy enough to damage troop-carrying boats." Trajectories, logistics, launch sites ran through Taiku's mind.

"We're going to launch urns with tar, not stones. We'll burn their boats."

"It will take weeks to make the net. What do we do until then?" Zaytea objected.

"Ja'ix is besieging Mattara. We have time." Taiku tried to assuage her fears. "We'll start by sending a group of people to guard the river-bend and dig out the trail."

Zaytea walked to the back of Taiku's chair, and put her hands on his shoulders as she addressed Zeruiah. "Take some refugee women and get them working immediately on the tar bombs and net. Tamsyn, Simon, you may also leave now."

They looked at Taiku for confirmation. He nodded.

He felt his wife's fingers slide down from his shoulders to his chest as Zeruiah and the others closed the door behind them. He was tense, tired. Too many things were rattling through his mind. Taiku felt Zaytea against his back, her breath against his neck. He wanted her to stop, but that would bring a host more problems. He looked for someone to walk in.

As if on cue, Zeresh barged in trailed by Ner. Zeresh looked at how her sister was leaning, and raised her eyebrows. Ner was red-faced at first but then pleased to note Taiku's look of relief.

Zaytea wasn't happy. "So?" she asked.

"He told us locations of their soldiers, strengths of their forces, battle plans, and their now-spoiled plans to use Eber witchcraft to create monsters."

Taiku was taken aback by the last bit. Before he could challenge the remark, his wife had her own question.

"How long did you have to keep him between your thighs to get all this, dear sister?"

Zeresh turned red. Taiku and Ner turned red.

Zeresh composed herself. Her report was too important. "A long time. He's a young man, quite eager. He was grateful to me for trying to protect him, and he satisfied me with his body and information. He didn't begrudge me that I tortured him."

Taiku fumed. "I'm not interested in your sex report. Tell me the locations of their soldiers, strengths of their forces, battle plans. Tell me everything."

26 MODERN AGE 7

Saima stared out the window of the Erbil's common room as the Finer's wagon was hauled away. She had already left, and the explanation of why she was going made him apprehensive. The only part he understood was that she wouldn't be back soon. They were supposed to go to the Central Facilities together, but he would have to wait.

Saima and Linda had just about finished re-sorting the pottery fragments. It was an impossible job to complete, because it was utterly subjective. A fragment that might go in one group could just as easily go in another. Despite all the energy they invested, they didn't feel they had made much progress towards understanding the collection. Alex occasionally made suggestions, pointing out obscure similarities.

"When you told the police that you're a member of the Olive-Tree clan, I was thrilled. It meant that—"

"I'm not part of the Olive-Tree clan," Saima said. "That's my father's clan. It's more of an affiliation. I'm Leopard clan."

"I don't understand the difference, but alright. When I heard "olive-tree," it said to me that my work was going to take an enormous leap forward. I thought that redemption for the suffering of the students I sent to the Dead Lands was at hand. But now I'm just as frustrated as I was beforehand. No one can read the fragments; we don't know any better what they are."

Saima gazed at the fire, its programmed rhythmic flares, its timed crackles and hisses. He stepped closer to Linda, reached over, and put his hand gently on her arm. "Maybe we do know, and we don't realize it."

Linda took his hand, and gently kissed his fingers. She looked up to his eyes, dampness in hers. "Tell me then, what are we missing?"

Saima put his hands on her face and wiped away the tears with his thumbs. In the back of his mind, he heard Tammy screaming "no" when he had done the same to her.

"The pottery controls Sheyds. We've used the pieces twice for that: first, when I stabbed John, and then when we got Tammy out of the Wagon. And they're connected to me," he said.

"Sheyds? Connected?"

"They're what you know as demons. You said you think the Ebers are originally from the Dead Lands, where you got the pottery."

Linda digested his words for a few moments. "You're drawing a lot of conclusions."

"I might be wrong. But let's assume that I'm correct, and try to understand the markings based on their being used to control Sheyds. Your community seems to have ground to a halt in the last few days. If the Sheyds were as bad in the Dead Lands as they're becoming here, people would have taken them pretty seriously."

"So, what do you propose?" Linda asked.

"I have no idea."

"That's a big help."

Saima and Linda picked up pieces of pottery in gloved hands, turned them over, peered at them and put them down, trying to see something different. Saima's idea quickly led them to the same place as their prior approach: nowhere. Alex watched them silently from the side of the room. A glass of water sat on a table. He jiggled it gently, letting the room's lights catch it at different angles.

Linda frowned at Alex's head lying on the table, the glass just in front of his eyes. He'd give it a little twist, and continue to watch. She walked over and stood behind the glass, her arms folded across her chest, waiting.

Alex lifted his head. "What's the pattern of water?"

"What?"

"What pattern does water have?" he asked.

"Alex, you may be bored, but we can't be distracted."

"On the contrary," Alex said. "You're not making progress because you're focusing too hard. You need to be distracted. Indulge me."

"Alex, we—"

"Okay, I'll indulge you," Saima interrupted. "Water has no shape. River water has a different pattern than seawater. Rain has a different pattern than a glass of water."

Alex lifted his glass off the table, holding it at eye level. "And even a glass of water's pattern differs, depending on how you look at it. The observer creates the pattern by his act of observation. Two observers; or maybe two different kinds of observers see different patterns while looking at the same thing."

"I'm distracted, Alex. Can we get back to—?"

"No, please continue," Saima said.

"What if two creatures with different natures looked at the same glass of water from the same perspective?"

"What do you mean by different natures?"

"Let's say a Sheyd and a human. Both looking at the pattern of water would see something distinct. Both looking at markings on pottery would see something different."

"And...?" Linda's ire was cooling down.

"These pieces were made to deal with Sheyds, so you have to see what a Sheyd would see."

"We're human. How can we do that?"

Alex frowned. "Humans made the bowls in order to do something to Sheyds, so it must be possible."

Something familiar clawed at the back of Saima's mind: a faint memory, a dream...

Linda turned to Saima. "When you first started talking about dimensions and Spheres I was amused, then annoyed by your puerile mysticism. Then I started to wonder..."

He smiled. "Puerile mysticism is part of who we are."

Saima walked over to a shelf and chose a small parchment. Linda set it on a glass table with switches and dials on the side. They all stared. "We're looking at two dimensions. A Sheyd wouldn't read it this way," Saima said. "Let me try twisting it or something."

"No. That might damage it. There's a better way." Linda squeezed her lips together in concentration, and then adjusted some dials at the side of the table. A holographic image of the manuscript hovered above. She reached over to the image, grabbed an edge, tilted it upwards and stared. Using a knob, she flipped it over, turned it on its side, and then rolled the projection into a cylinder. She looked around at Alex and Saima, who both appeared frustrated.

"Project it normally."

She did so, peered at it for a moment, and sighed.

"Maybe the letters are just tilted. Can you pull them straight?"

Linda tugged at a corner of the image.

Saima signaled her to stop, as he walked slowly around the hovering text; words, ideas that had been engraved many thousands of years earlier. The letters were somewhat disjointed, but the text was legible. He read slowly:

"If a person wants to know of their presence, let him take sifted ashes and place them around his bed before going to sleep. In the morning he will see marks in the ashes like the footprints of a large rooster."

The bird tracks at the river. He continued to read.

"If a person wants to see them, let him bring the placenta of a female cat, a black cat which is the daughter of a black cat that is a firstborn girl of a firstborn cat. Let him burn the placenta in a fire, grind it, put some of the ground ash in his eye, and he will see them. He should place the rest in an iron tube and seal it with an iron seal, so Sheyds won't steal it from him. And he should close his mouth so that he will not be harmed."

Linda stood up quickly. "The Psychology Lab has lots of cats for research. I can push them to give us what we need."

"You experiment on cats? I thought you people forbid cruelty to animals."

"Of course. But the Lab is doing a multi-generational project on bad luck and black cats. They might have what we need." Linda touched her communicator.

Why he didn't need the ashes to see the bird tracks, or the placenta to see Mekelat?

"No luck. A Harmonizer freed all the cats. Why would anyone do that? Those animals were treated well."

"To keep the Sheyds hidden," Saima said.

Alex pointed at a corner of the document. "Look at that part of the text: Library of Samuel, Head of Academy, Father of the House of Judgment of Arbil." He grinned at Saima: "Well, this proves you're connected to the pottery."

Saima reddened. "I'm 'Saima,' not 'Samuel.'" He looked over at Linda. "You've been redeemed."

Tears welled in Linda's eyes; her mouth opened slightly as she pondered this. She looked as if a wattle and daub wall of frustration had been torn down.

Saima waived his arm at the shelves. "Can you project the pottery shards like you did this manuscript? If you tilt the images in the same way, we may be able to read them."

She dried her eyes with her sleeves. "It won't be the same. The text you just read tells us how to detect Sheyds. Sheyds don't need to know how to see Sheyds. That document was written for people."

"Then why wasn't it written plainly? Why did the writer compel us to tilt the letters?"

"I don't know. Bad handwriting?"

Linda pressed a button on the side of the table, the projection flashed and then faded. A page appeared on the tabletop beside the ancient manuscript, a printout of the now readable instructions for spotting Sheyds.

Alex handed her the piece of pottery that had been used to stab John. "I'll bring everyone a tea."

Linda put the piece on the table and activated the projector. The markings seemed to be cut along multiple planes. She twisted, rolled, folded and flipped the projection. The image and the markings were clearly visible, but the words remained concealed. No manipulation was working.

Alex returned from the kitchen with a teapot and three cups. "I think a break would be helpful."

Linda pouted, but took the proffered drink anyways. "I expected that once we deciphered one, the rest would be easy."

"The pottery's different," Saima said.

Linda sighed.

Alex brought some chocolates and dried figs to the table. "What other fruits have clans? Is there a pear clan, or a date clan?"

Saima sipped his tea and considered the question. "The Olive-Tree clan is the only one I know that's not an animal. Keep in mind that the clan is named for the tree, not the fruit. The other three clans are animals: Leopard, Fox and Gazelle. There may have been more long ago. There's also the Cannibal Society. Their members are across all the clans."

Linda and Alex both flinched. Linda swallowed before asking, "Have you, um... ever eaten human flesh?"

"I'm not part of the Cannibal Society, and no, they don't eat human flesh. I can't explain the name."

Alex sipped at his tea. Saima picked up a few grapes, and put them in his mouth, one at a time. He walked over to the projection table. "Can you enlarge it? No distortions. Keep increasing the size till we see something."

Linda made some adjustments, and soon the image was covering most of the ceiling. They walked around the room, peering up, looking for something comprehensible hidden in the markings.

Linda pointed to a small area surrounded by a circle. The text was clear, albeit incomplete: "Protector, Friend Taiku... Asenath, daughter of Samuel, mother of Simon, mother of..."

A thick silence filled the room, as they gazed upwards. After a few minutes, Alex turned to Saima, and hugged him. "You disagreed before when I said the manuscript was yours. Are you going to argue about this,

Simon, son of Asenath?" Alex was delighted. "I hope the hug isn't a violation of my oath."

"Your hug is okay. My name is Saima, not Simon. Osnat is my mother's sister, not my mother."

"Saima, Simon... ".

"Who's Taiku?"

"He's is listed as protector, not family. Let's assume he's the person who needed this anti-Sheyd device. It can't be the name of a Sheyd. Simon or Asenath would have been the ancient maker of the anti-Sheyd device.

Saima walked over to the stack of parchments, and thumbed through them. He pulled out a tiny one, less than half the size of his palm. The writing was small and twisted. He put it on the projection table. "Do this one."

Linda enlarged it, flipped it, and spun it on its side... Nothing intelligible.

"How about if we just look at it?" Alex suggested.

"And do what?"

"Enlarge and project it upwards. Linda, you try to make sense of the individual markings. Saima, you look at the whole thing at once; trying to sense patterns. I'll try to read it like it's a poem, and see what words come to me."

His wife gave him another sour look.

"Well," he answered, "do you have a better idea?"

She sighed. "All right."

The archaeologist, the savage and the poet sat on the low sofa and gazed at the image hovering before them. After a while, Saima's eyes started to droop, and he slipped into a light sleep. "Turn them, stretch them till they're legible..." he dreamed.

He forced himself awake. "Linda!"

She gave a start. She had been half-asleep as well.

Alex cut Saima off. "I can't tell you the words, but I know the emotion in this document: fear."

"Look at the space that curves around the markings," Saima said. "What if they're spaces between lines of text? Can you adjust the projection, so the spaces are straight?"

She bent to the controls, fiddling for a while. The image shuddered, as Linda tried to get the required effect.

"Stop!"

The lines of text were straight, but still illegible.

"Try a different axis. Turn it on a vertical plane."

This was stretching the projection table's ability. Linda concentrated, working methodically. Finally, the markings began to move as she wanted. At thirty degrees, she stopped.

"Ja'ix in Samarra in days. Destroyed Mattara, killed all Ebers, others join or die. Tens of thousands of soldiers, crossbows, death-hoops, mounted, marching. Anywhere safe?"

Linda and Alex hugged each other, elated. Saima put his knees, then his face to the floor.

27 MODERN AGE 8

Two cut-stone towers stood in the river, about a hundred paces from each shore. One blue, one gray, each spanning the width of the old bridge. Rising from the river, the huge stones were twice as tall as a man. Two parabolic arches on each tower allowed people and vehicles to pass through. At the roadway, each had a service door near the railing, rusted in place and locked with an ancient metal device.

Most human footprints on the bridge went straight from one end to the other. Nobody bothered to go to the side, to gaze at the river. Until a few days ago, hardly anyone used it; wagons flew people straight to their destinations. The bridge was a relic, an abandoned piece of scenery to most people. But since the General Failure Alert, the movement of the goods necessary to life depended on the land-bound vehicles that used it.

Some vehicle tracks, some footprints, paw-prints had been preserved on the surface ice by the quick drop in temperature; the same chill that was keeping most people indoors. Lieutenant Detective Tammy Finer, dressed for the weather by someone to whom this would be a warm spring day, leaned against one of the chest-high railings running the length of the bridge. It was said that long ago these railings were electrified, rendering unconscious anyone foolish enough to try jumping over. Those were bad times, full of strife. People despaired, and killed themselves regularly. It was back then that the police, after expelling the causes of discord, began to devote most of their energy to restoring harmony, rather than punishing wrongdoers.

Finer wondered about Saima. Did he want to be rid of her? His insistence that she not cross the river ice added hours to her journey. She had won his trust; enough for him to work with her. Did her departure destroy that? She had to report to Police Central in person; her communicator didn't work. She had told Saima the truth. Not all of it, because she didn't think he wouldn't understand; she was certain that she didn't.

She tried to focus on the report she was going to give, but the meandering animal tracks tugged at her concentration as she walked. An icy breeze reminded her to walk faster. Though she was dressed for the cold, it was still winter; she didn't want to get frostbite again. Saima knew more about cold weather than anyone around. It wasn't all he understood better, and that bothered her. She was a Detective, Class L; he was just a northern savage.

General Failure Alert, Sheyds... Maybe it wasn't just the paw prints that distracted her from her assignment. The animal tracks stayed mostly towards the center of the bridge, occasionally curving off towards the rail. Rats, cats, rabbits, dogs... She wasn't sure. The dog she was investigating had died cruelly, but quickly.

She looked at the huge footprints. She couldn't tell rabbits or rats, but these had a little bump, and three points splayed out in front of it. Birds; large birds came to mind, like the ones Saima had noticed at the river. Lieutenant Detective Tammy Finer's report flew from her mind; her hand flew to her mouth. She started to run, following them.

As she came to the blue stone tower, the strange tracks took a sharp left to the tower's door. It was as if the birds had gone inside, but the rusty lock was still in place. The door looked like it hadn't been touched in centuries. A few tracks seemed to be partway through it; that wasn't possible.

Finer pulled out her scope to check inside. When it didn't detect anything, she ran a diagnostic scan. It was working perfectly. Either there was nothing in the tower, or the stone was interfering with the signal.

The bridge was a revered historical structure. In its early days, a truck carrying something powerful and highly unstable crashed into a fusion generator on the side of the tower. The explosion blew away much of the bridge, which was subsequently rebuilt. The quantum signature of the remaining tower was altered, turning it blue, and emitting a strange kind of radiation. Wagons were programmed to avoid the area, for fear they would lose their guidance stream. Although a useless relic for centuries, the bridge had been preserved as a heritage site. Only the barest minimum of maintenance was allowed, to keep it from falling apart.

Opening the tower door without Committee approval could be a violation of the Codes. Forcing open the locked, rusted door on her own initiative would definitely be a violation. She could lose her job, and be sent to a re-harmonization camp. On the other hand, she was still on assignment, investigating the death of a dog. She was trying to come to grips with a possible General Failure Alert, among other things. Something mysteriously passing through a locked door merited examination.

Finer stared at the door, her hands clasped in front of her face. She pulled her cutter from her utility belt and held it over the lock; the blue flame sputtered and went out. Maybe that was a sign telling her to put it away, leave the door alone and continue walking.

A sign from whom? The tower's radiation might simply have damaged her equipment. She frowned, licked her lips and re-started the cutter. The flames sputtered, but held enough to start making their way through the ancient metal. The cutter had been designed for much more sophisticated materials, so even at partial power it didn't take long to slice through the lock's hasp.

The heavy door, rusted closed for so long, should have resisted any movement. Finer was startled when it pulled right open, sliding as if on well-oiled hinges. Inside the walls were the same blue stones as outside, but covered by slimy, black mold. She was astonished to find another door on the opposite side of the room, leading out. She hadn't seen it before. Why would it be camouflaged? She gave it a little shove, expecting it to be locked. It swung right open, and Finer stepped back out onto the bridge. She looked at the door from the outside; it appeared just like the one she had entered through.

Powerful arms wrapped around her from behind, immobilizing her arms. Thick hands clamped her mouth shut.

"Don't make a sound. If they kill you here, you'll never get back," a man's voice whispered.

In addition to being upset about being caught unawares, Finer was embarrassed about being caught unawares by an idiot. People who are killed generally don't get "back"; they don't get anywhere. Who was holding her? And what "they" was he talking about? She started gathering saliva in her mouth, when she realized that the fingers holding her face were carefully avoiding her lips. Her only hope was to drool saliva down her chin onto him. But this man's posture showed that he knew what she was, and was smart enough to prevent her fighting back.

"If you make noise the Sheyds will find us," he continued to whisper. "Your venom can kill me because I came here alive, like you. But it won't bother the Sheyds, and they can hurt you badly. Then you won't be able to help Saima. I need you, and Saima needs both of us. Do you understand?" The man eased the pressure on Finer's chin enough for her to nod. She still couldn't tell who was holding her.

"If I go back to the Abode of Life, I'll be stuck there. Now that you're here, you can do the job and bring a Sheyd-trapping bowl back to Saima. He's the father of Asenath, my Teacher and Master, whom I have sworn to protect. My name is Aua. I arranged for you to come here. If I let go of your jaw, will you talk without spitting on me?"

Finer nodded again, and he released her. The man was short and powerful looking. Her first thought was that he must be terribly cold; he was dressed in a thin cottony shirt and pants with open sandals; she was bundled up in layers of thick cloth. Aua knew what she was, who her friends were, and, it seemed, could also read her thoughts, judging from how quickly he let go when she decided to trust him.

"You must be freezing. Don't you have a coat?"

"You're not where you think you are. There is no hot or cold here; no substance, no molecules to vibrate. You can be bundled up, or in thin cloth."

"I know where I am: the bridge across the narrows of the Opinaca River." Her rising voice made it into more of a question than a firm declaration.

"You were, Detective, but not now. You're on the original bridge, one part of which was carried to the pathways between Spheres when a wormhole device exploded after hitting a generator. People thought it was a terrible accident, but it wasn't. I caused it, so there would be a way for you to come here now. Think of it as reverse time engineering."

Finer stared at him, her mind filled with a knotted multitude of questions. Aua leaned against the railing and spoke softly. "I'll answer everything, but we have to be on our way."

She moved closer him. "On our way? What do you—"

Putting a thick arm around her waist, Aua shoved Finer through the railing. Her shock at going through the ancient metal was displaced by her anticipation of breaking her skull on the ice below, or going through it and drowning. She looked at Aua, whose arm was still grasping her firmly. She had made a split-second decision to trust him, and now had a split second to live.

"There was a hooped transport device which no one understood. The Collective Council decided it was too dangerous to have in a populated area, so it was to be brought into unoccupied countryside. I turned the driver's stomach just as his truck passed the bridge generator. He lost control and crashed. The explosion sent one end of the bridge into the pathways between Spheres, though to people in the Abode of Life it looked like it had been destroyed. Amazingly, the cab of the truck was blown clear, and the driver barely had a scratch on him. When the bridge was rebuilt, he was buried alive at the base of the tower, which had turned blue from the explosion. The Collective Council figured that the driver's durability would become part of the bridge."

Aua's story was mesmerizing, but illogical. How could he turn a stomach? How could he arrange something hundreds of years ago, and be with her now? Time didn't work that way. And how could she be listening to such a long story when she had just a split second to live? She hadn't hit the ice, and was dry.

"We had to get off the bridge. The Sheyds would have attacked. I don't mind fighting them, but you have something more important to do." He smiled at her. "We're not going to hit the ice or drown."

Finer realized she no longer had the sensation of falling. She was moving, but there was nothing, no markers by which she could discern her passage. She didn't know up from down, before from later. "Where are we going? What do I have to do?"

"We're going to my home, to take something of Simon's."

"I'm police, I don't steal... Where's your home?"

"You're bringing it to Simon, its owner. If it makes you feel better, leave something in its place; maybe your pipe or your lighter. I'm from Lagash, on the Klee-Dekel River."

"We're stealing... taking it from Saima and bringing it to Saima?"

Aua nodded. "You've been playing with pieces of Sheyd-traps in Linda's collection. Simon needs one that's intact, and someone who can read the inscriptions to him. I'll teach you."

Her opinion of him was rising and falling like a bouncing ball. "I never heard of the Klee-Dekel."

"You know it as the Dead Lands."

The sensation of movement stopped. "Why are you bringing us there? Everyone who goes there ends up dead or damaged! Saima's not there anyways."

"He's not there on the day we jumped off the bridge. He's there when we'll be there. It's a time when the lands were full of life, before you decided to destroy them."

Finer fell silent, turning this over in her mind, trying to make it fit the way she understood the universe. She couldn't, especially the part about her deciding to destroy the Dead Lands. "How will we get there?" was the only question she could get past her lips.

"By desiring it. There are no wagons on the pathways between Spheres. Your will is freed of the confines of everyday physics. Just now when you feared going to the Dead Lands, our movement stopped. Now that I explained it to you, we're on our way again. We'll be there before you're able to understand."

She resumed her silence. Every explanation was baffling her more.

"When you get to Lagash, you can get a Sheyd trapping bowl, and then go home through the tower."

Finer needed more help. "Those pottery shards at Linda's are for Sheyds?"

"Sheyd traps. They're why the Sheyds avoid Alex and Linda's home. A few shards are forgeries. Some of the Marsh People tried to make their own traps."

"Who are the Marsh People?"

"They lived in the river delta outside Lagash. It was one of the Marsh People, Balthan, who murdered Asenath."

"She's dead? You said before you were protecting her."

Aua nodded. "Saima needs to get control of the Sheyds. He needs to return to the northlands, so she can be born."

"This person Asenath; you talk about her in the Dead Lands, in the northlands and here in the modern world as if she's one person. People don't live for thousands of years."

"There is much to existence that transcends everyday experience. Your confusion is from how you understand time. Think of it as laid out like a landscape -a timescape, with everything that's manifest or not yet manifest there together. If you understand this, then five thousand years separating my Asenath and your Saima are irrelevant. Because of the hatred the Sheyds have for her, their desire to destroy is intimately bound up with Saima, and thus with your mission. If they succeed, they will become solid and take control across the timescape."

Finer considered what Aua described as her mission. It was of a different magnitude then investigating the death of a dog. It was also different from all her other assignments, in that she had to make the decision herself.

"What do I have to do?"

"Travel with me."

Tammy took hold of the timeless man's sleeve. "Let's go. Tell me when we're there."

Aua nodded.

They weren't moving; they weren't traveling. It was more like the shape of existence was being warped, rolling past them. Finer watched life, watched events, generations go by. Cities changed to farms, forests to fields, fields to desert and waste. Nothing seemed quickened as it rushed by. The blue sky shifted to azure, and then cobalt blue. The air warmed, chilled, and warmed again. Finer coughed as her breath curdled with the stench of tar, smoke and fear. Just as quickly, it cleared.

Finer abruptly clutched Aua's arm tightly and screamed in horror. Aua suddenly was alone. Just as quickly, she was by his side again, her forehead covered in sweat, her eyes moist from tears.

"You shouldn't have kissed him," Aua said.

"It was too horrible. I had to."

They continued on in silence.

28 EARLY BRONZE AGE 11

"Y ou can't."

"Why?"

"Well, for one thing, you're a virgin. A virgin can't consummate this marriage."

Dinah struggled to keep the tears out of her voice. "It won't difficult to find a man to have relations with beforehand. I'm reputed to be ravishingly beautiful."

"Do you really want to be had like that?"

"No. But if it's necessary, I'll do it."

Simon sat straighter in his chair. "Mom will be furious."

"Mom's dead."

"I know. But she's still watching us."

Dinah wiped a tear from the corner of her eye. "She's watching, and she won't like it. But it's us in the Abode of Life now. Mom wants us to be able to act on our own, not simply do what we think she'd choose."

She pleaded with her brother. "You know I have to do this. I have to be the first, before the other four that Taiku has demanded. Otherwise people will accuse us of witchcraft. And besides which, the Ebers could use Fire Snake women."

"The people who want to accuse us will find any excuse."

"True, but consider: is my blood redder than theirs? Is my life more valuable than any other woman's? If you're going to ask others to do their part, you have to ask me first."

The tip of Simon's middle finger flew into his mouth, and he started gnawing the skin around the nail. "It could kill you, you know. Either when you open your legs for it, or after it's in your womb and the anti-venom wears off."

"I know."

"You have to consummate this marriage lying naked on the ground with your legs apart, in front of a crowd of people."

"I read the manuscript."

"And if you're still alive after a day you have to take a human lover to make you pregnant."

"I read the manuscript."

"I'm scared. First Dad, then Mom... Will I lose you now? Why can't we be ordinary people? All we'd have to do is put food on the table, a roof over our head. Why do we have such responsibilities, that Mom has to die protecting Marsh people, and you become a Fire Snake? I'd rather be a Madai farmer, or an Elam goat-herder."

Dinah ran her fingers soothingly through her brother's hair. "It's futile to ask why. The question is what are we to do? And we're really better off than others, even though our lives are more difficult."

Simon put his head down on his folded arms.

Dinah sat down next to him, tears trickling down her face as she leaned her head on his shoulder. Human sacrifice was forbidden to the Ebers, but this was coming close.

They were in the library of their home, at the table where Asenath used to study. It was a room of joy, of the happiness that comes from insight and understanding. What kind of joy would today's insight into their obligations bring Dinah? She was a private person, modest. The ritual for becoming a Fire Snake violated her sense of being, her sense of who she was. She dreaded the human physical contact, which she heard was initially painful and bloody. With a husband she loved, it would be one thing...

And the snake. It was to make a home for itself in her womb, eventually becoming part of her body, part of her. Anti-venom was good for a few hours. She would take some before the ritual started, so if it attacked right away, it wouldn't harm her. It was after the anti-venom started to fade, when the creature was ensconced inside but still not part of her that was the danger. If something caused it to exude venom, she would die without any warning. Was this how she's better off than others?

***

"You're in a good mood, Vlad. Did some beautiful virgin proposition you?" Zaytea asked.

"Yes. She insisted, even after I tried to brush her off."

Taiku put a hand on his brother's shoulder. "Very nice. Maybe you'll get married and have children."

"I don't think so. Anyways, that's not the reason I'm in a good mood."

"Well, share the happiness with us."

"We got a report from the west. The horses you ordered from the Tungus will be here in a day or two. There are hundreds, with more following."

Taiku was stunned. He had expected at most one or two hundred all together.

"That's not all," Vlad said. "The Tungus have concluded that they're best off if Ja'ix never comes close to them. They figure you're their only chance of keeping him away. They're sending us hundreds of fighters."

Taiku's joy vanished just as quickly as it had appeared. Another group of people depending on him.

Zaytea beamed. "We're developing a nice empire here."

Taiku exploded. "We are not building an empire! We're trying to keep a tyrant from destroying Lagash."

"Oh? What do you mean by 'Lagash?' A month ago, it was a town on the road, at the start of the Klee-Dekel River delta. Now it's a place that stretches from the sea to the mountains. It's not just a collection of houses, but it includes marshes, woodlands and hills. Its people are the Madai, the Marsh and Elam, plus a growing population of refugees," Zaytea said.

"You left out the Ebers."

"Ah yes, them. I'm not sure what they are. Are they loyal to Lagash? Or will they join our enemies?"

Vlad put a restraining hand on Taiku, who had clutched his sheathed knife. He turned to Zaytea. "The Clay People put themselves in the Chief's hands of their own initiative, before the Elam or Marsh People. They were making weapons for us while your people were entertaining their goats, and the Marsh People were busy killing each other. Your sister may have slept her way to information about those parchments that Qimiq captured, but thanks to the Ebers we're able to use them. As a result, we're the ones who will have human Fire Snakes, not Ja'ix. The Clay People have made a lot of sacrifices for Lagash. You'd be wise to think carefully before you say anything bad about the Clay People if you plan to remain as my brother's consort."

Zaytea looked at Vlad, then her husband in surprise.

"I have a suggestion for where to keep the new horses," she said. "There's a grassy area west of the village, bounded by a fast-moving stream. It would be easy to fence it off. It's large enough to support them, at least until we can make other arrangements."

"If an attack comes along the road, it would be an easy target," Vlad said.

"Ja'ix is expected from the north or east. Either way, the village is between his approach and this pasture. Give me the word, my husband, and I'll organize some refugees to get a fence up."

Taiku's mind wasn't there. He was recalling his last discussion with Simon about Fire Snakes. He was thinking of his position as head of the Ebers. He was remembering eighteen-point-two.

He snapped himself back to attention. He knew the place Zaytea was describing.

He turned to his wife. "I don't know if we have enough refugees to do everything."

"Maybe you should count them, like you did the Marsh People after Asenath was killed."

"That was an Eber suggestion. Not only was it their idea, but they did the work, without complaining. The Marsh People didn't like it, but I now have a list of every single one of them. And you know who killed the Eber leader, don't you? But the Ebers didn't try to take vengeance. Do you know why? Because of their loyalty. I'll be very happy if I can count on my consort as much as I can count on the Clay People."

Zaytea flinched. She silently looked at Taiku's eyes.

Taiku squeezed his fingertips against his temples. "Counting the refugees is an excellent idea, my dear. In fact, I think we should take it a step farther. Let's count everyone: the refugees, the Elam, Ebers, Marsh and Madai people. We'll have a master list of all citizens of Lagash. Go now, ask the Clay People to take care of it for us."

Zaytea didn't move. Taiku took her hand in his, and kissed her palm. "Go now, my wife."

He watched the doorway as she left. He picked up a split log, and placed it on the fire. It was warm inside; there was plenty of light coming in through the window, and more than enough flame on the fire. Taiku pointed at the kettle. Vlad filled it, and then hung it over the fireplace. Taiku took some dried willow leaves from a box, and put them in a couple of mugs as the water came to a boil. He didn't really want a hot drink, but it was the best chance he had to calm himself down and ease his headache.

"You need her."

Taiku turned his gaze from the dance of the flames. "I agreed to take her as my consort, but she's jealous of a dead person."

"True."

"If Zaytea puts all her energy into competing with Asenath, I'll be married to a shadow. We'll both be miserable."

"What will you do?"

"Hope she learns to be satisfied being Zaytea to me, rather than Asenath."

Taiku sat down at the wood plank table as Vlad took the kettle off the fire and poured the tea. Vlad opened the jar of date honey, adding one spoon to his cup, three for Taiku's sweet tooth. Taiku's forehead glistened with moisture, reflecting the leaping flames from the fireplace. Eyes closed, he put his elbows on the table and folded his hands together, resting his chin on them. Both men sat quietly, listening to the flames, listening to the heat as they sipped their tea.

"Did I appear weak by letting her pin me into this marriage?"

Vlad shook his head. "How many wars do you need to fight at a time? Naturally the person who leads the Elam clans is ambitious. Otherwise, she wouldn't be the leader. She used the same skills to wedge herself into being your consort. Work with it."

"I've been trying, but I've got everyone giving orders and making demands. Maybe if I execute a few people, I won't get so many arguments."

"You need them. Pick some people and make them your Council of Advisors. The ones you appoint will be honored, and will owe their elevated position to you."

A smile finally crossed Taiku's face, as he lifted his head. "You're my top Advisor. Ask Dinah to recommend a scribe."

Vlad stiffened at the mention of Dinah. Taiku pretended not to notice.

***

Forty pairs of eyes watched uncomfortably as the small blue snake disappeared into Dinah. She lay on her back, her breath slow and deliberate. Her naked body, even her hair was smothered with a viscous yellow lotion, which was starting to dry and crack in the sun. The crusty material must have been horribly itchy, but Dinah didn't scratch, or even twitch. Her wrists were cuffed, tied to stakes planted firmly in the ground. A rope around her neck kept her from lifting her head. More cuffs were around her ankles, holding her legs immobile and open.

This was for her protection. The parchment explained that if the snake in her womb felt threatened, it might attack. Even though Dinah had taken anti-venom, her insides were exposed to sharp fangs. And as the anti-venom faded, she had to avoid provoking the snake to exude any kind of fluid inside her. Movement was the most frightening thing to a snake ensconced in a dark, hot womb.

Vlad sat beside her, alternately holding her hand, stroking her hair, wiping her forehead. Occasionally he gave her small sips of water through a reed straw.

Taiku sat at her other side, watching Dinah, watching Vlad. He should have realized that Dinah would have been the first volunteer. He should have realized that once again he was bringing destruction to his friend; this time through her family. The ritual wouldn't necessarily kill her, but the public exposure, the humiliation of the ceremony was in itself a kind of death. Most of the women of Lagash were modest in their dress. Many married women kept their hair covered when outside their home. Taiku imagined that once this ordeal was over, Dinah would not want to live anymore amongst people to whom she had been so horribly exposed.

Many people attended the beginning of the procedure, but left shortly after it had started. They all knew Dinah and were too distressed by what was being done to her. They couldn't watch, even though they were told the Fire Snake demanded witnesses for consummating its marriage. Nobody spoke. They just sat for a while, and then left.

Ner and Zeresh also attended the ceremony. While Ner was upset, Zeresh was fascinated. Tamsyn sat across them, clearly annoyed by the other woman's treating the event as a spectacle.

It had started at mid-day. By the time the yellow moon had reached its height in the night sky, the only people left with Dinah were Vlad, Taiku, Zeresh, Tamsyn and Simon. Zaytea occasionally came by to refill the water bladder, or to offer snacks to her husband and his brother, which were refused. A night chill was in the air, and she offered them blankets. They refused these as well.

The drying lotion on Dinah's skin did not offer any protection from the cold. Her exposed skin was developing chill bumps, as her body struggled to keep itself warm. She was lying on animal pelts, keeping the ground from draining warmth from her body. But the light night breeze was sapping what little heat Dinah had. She was starting to shiver.

Dinah's eyes were closed. She was supposed to stay naked, not be covered by anything except the lotion. Zaytea came up quietly behind Taiku and whispered something in his ear. He nodded, and she quickly ran off.

A few moments later, she was back with a crowd of people. She ordered them into a tight circle, standing shoulder to shoulder, completely surrounding Dinah. Another group sat with their backs to the first group, their knees together, leaning against the legs of the people standing. They couldn't cover Dinah with any material, they couldn't build a shelter of any kind around her, and they couldn't use fire. But at least they could block the night wind. Dinah was still shivering, but it was very slight. Hopefully it wasn't enough to cause her death.

As Dinah had undressed, she slipped her mind away from touch, from smell, from sight. She knew what was going on; she felt the hands apply the goo to her body. She felt the hand that applied the special "marriage cream" to attract the snake to enter her. She stretched out her arms and her legs as she was supposed to, offering no resistance as they were tied in place; no objection as the choke rope was fastened over her neck. She smiled at Vlad as he took her hand. She didn't feel his fingers through her body, but through the closeness they had reached when lying together.

She felt the snake as it made its way inside her. It didn't hurt, not like when she was with Vlad. She didn't try to communicate with it; that was proscribed by the manuscript. She could feel the snake though, as it curled around inside her, exploring, testing...

She was sitting by a spring, a bubbling brook coming from a Rock made of pure light. Her mother had told her about this place, explaining that it couldn't be found by searching; she would come across it when she was ready. Occasionally she dipped her hand in the water and took a sip. A gentle breeze warmed her skin. It was a comfortable place to be, much better than where she was located in place and time.

A rustling sound caused her to turn. Her father Jacob stood above her, a slight frown on his face. Dinah was surprised to see someone from the Abode of the Dead.

"I wanted you to live."

Dinah realized that she could no longer feel the snake. The sensations from her body had faded.

"The anti-venom didn't last. The snake salivated and paralyzed your heart."

Dinah had also wanted to live, but there were no regrets to be had here.

"Come, my daughter." Jacob extended his hand, and Dinah got up.

As the day brightened, as dew blanketed the ground, Vlad was breathing hard, and sweating heavily. He looked ready to kill, to destroy; anything to vent his rage. He continued to stroke Dinah's hair, though her body lay still. No rising of her chest, no movement of her eyelids. No shivering, no chill bumps.

No one wanted to move, because that would mean acknowledging her death. By continuing as they had through the night, it was as if Dinah was still alive. It was almost mid-day again when Zaytea dispersed the circles that had been guarding her. One of the Eber women wrapped Dinah's body with a blanket. Vlad's powerful arms scooped up the result of Lagash's attempt to fashion a human Fire Snake, holding her close to him. He spoke softly to some of the men who had gathered, instructing them to dig a grave right away.

Taiku was about to leave with Zaytea, when she pointed to Vlad. Seeing his brother holding Dinah's body, he went instead to join the gravediggers.

Within a few hours, the ground was ready for her. The crusted, cracked lotion had been washed off; she was wrapped in a clean burial shroud. Vlad cradled her in his arms, rocking her back and forth. It was time to leave; the Ebers preferred private funerals. Practically all of Lagash was there.

"We've suffered a casualty of the war to defend our families and our community. We will suffer many more," Taiku addressed the people. "Me against my brother. My brother and I against my cousin. My cousin and I against my far cousin. The Elam against the Madai. The Elam and Madai against the Marsh People. All the people of Lagash: Elam, Madai, Marsh and Eber against the far side of the horizon. Both sides of the horizon against Ja'ix. Our world against the next. Our God against all Gods.

"Never forget what Dinah sacrificed for us. Never forget what her mother sacrificed," he said. "We must prevail; for their sakes, if not for ours. They are forever part of us." Taiku turned and walked away, gesturing with his arm for the others to follow. They did, leaving Simon and the Clay People to their private sorrow.

29 EARLY BRONZE AGE 12

The sound of the front door moving stirred Vlad from a deep sleep. He sensed dawn was breaking from the faint light in the window, but was not awake enough to sense trouble from his door creaking open while he was still in bed.

There were certain sounds to dawn: crickets, birds... But the only sound Vlad heard was the soft padding of unknown footsteps towards him. An alarm tried to ring in his mind, warning of potential danger. But its sound was muted, as if a heavy blanket had been thrown over his consciousness. Vlad felt himself relax, instead of tensing as he should have.

Small, thin fingers explored the hair on his chest, moving upwards and then down. Vlad breathed deeply with anticipation as the covers were pulled off him, and Tamsyn lay down at his side, her naked chest against his. In the back of his mind, he was puzzled; he had never been close to her. No one had, as far as he knew; she was too dangerous. In the front of his mind all such thoughts were obscured, as he absorbed the smoky pleasure of the moment.

He saw Tamsyn lift her head for a moment, eyes towards the window as if listening to the utter silence outside. She turned back, put her lips on his, and climbed onto him.

***

The rumble of thunder on a cloudless dawn woke Taiku from a restless sleep. It was an endless pounding, shaking the ground under his house. He threw on a robe and stepped outside.

Two bright moons and a hint of the sun shone down on a stream of horses thundering through Lagash. Some had riders, others just following their tethers. They were lean and muscled, their eyes intense. Vapor rose from their nostrils as they steamed forward through the village dawn.

It wasn't the spectacle of the powerful beasts that held everyone's rapt attention; it was the riders. They were standing as they rode, mimicking the stance of an archer turning from side to side targeting his foes. They weren't holding the reins. Their feet were secured in little cups, connected by something over the back of the horses. No one in Lagash had ever seen such devices.

Zaytea came up beside him, taking hold of his arm. "The fence was put up quickly. I sent instructions ahead for them to ride through Lagash before setting up camp."

Taiku turned to look at her.

"I want the entire village to know there's help. People are frightened. Despair could defeat us before we even start to fight."

He continued staring.

"Lagash is too big for you to handle everything yourself. I acted."

A smile broke the stare. "You did well. Look," he pointed.

People were coming out of all the homes to see the spectacle. Soldiers quickly ran over to protect Taiku.

"These riders can shoot while in motion. An archer no longer needs a chariot and driver to move quickly," he said.

This was tremendously important. Ja'ix had chariots. Taiku didn't. They were fragile, difficult to build and costly, but they gave an army a tremendous advantage. Those little leather cups hanging over the sides of the animals, enabling riders to fight while in motion, nullified that advantage.

The parade of charging horses was almost past Taiku and Zaytea's house when a few riders broke away from the line and came to a halt in front of them. They dismounted quickly, and, at a nod from Zaytea all except one went to a knee before Taiku, their hands in front of their faces, palms to the side. The wrinkled skin of faces crisped by desert riding could not camouflage the alertness in their eyes. All were dressed in identical beige coveralls, with loose, layered gauze shirts and woven reed headdresses.

"I am the Tungus. I am two hundred seventy, and soon I am more. I'm an army to fight alongside you, if Lagash agrees." The man at the center of the kneeling riders was tall and wiry, with a thin face and small nose.

The Tungus People understood themselves as a collective first, and only then as individuals. Taiku's father had once sent him away with some Tungus traders; he had become familiar with their strange sense of self, their strange way of talking.

Zaytea took a step forward, but Taiku put out an arm, keeping her back. "Lagash is whole, from the mountains to the marshes. Are you part of this whole?"

He could sense the quickening of his wife's breath. A normal response to any of the other peoples in the region would be to invite them into your house, drink tea, negotiate... That would work with individuals who were part of a stratified leadership structure.

The Tungus speaker pointed towards the rider who had not gone to one knee. "He is not part of your whole, but he claims to speak for part of you."

Taiku looked over at the rider, who was looking off to the side, disinterested. Eber.

"I'm not concerned about him. Is the Tungus committed to the defense of Lagash, according to my words?" Taiku pressed the point.

"I am."

Taiku's mind raced. Should he try joining them to Lagash? They had a reputation as vicious but loyal warriors. If the Tungus became part of Lagash, he would be responsible to defend their home as well, including the long stretch of land in between them. It was hot, sandy terrain, stretching in a slow curve along the side of the sea. Not valuable for anything except where it led to.

He turned towards the man on his knee before him. "I am pleased that you are whole with me. May I be strong together."

The man rose, smiled, and grabbed Taiku's arm. "Yes, I'm strong."

Taiku surmised from their saddlebags that the Tungus People had brought everything they needed along with them. He turned to Zaytea. "Who of I will show me to my home field?"

His guest smiled. He took hold of Taiku's other arm as well.

"Taiku, my friend, you're going to hurt your queen's ears if you keep trying to talk like me. You honor me by doing so, and it's for this that I stand with you. We are in Lagash, and we shall do what you require of us, including speaking like you. I, separated, am Zakhor." He let go of Taiku.

Taiku smiled back. "What I require are a few thousand fighters in addition to the ones you brought." He let Zakhor's "queen" remark pass without comment, though he could see that his wife was intrigued.

"A few thousand fighters? You just sent for horses. I brought you many of each."

"Ja'ix is pressing closer. According to a report I just received, he's besieging Mattara. Either the reports aren't true, Ja'ix is an idiot, or he has a tremendous number of fighters. We have to be prepared in case it's the latter."

Zakhor took a few moments to digest this. "Alright." He turned to the man beside him, who had already pulled out a quill, a small jar of ink, and a paper. Zakhor dictated: "All."

The man retrieved a pigeon from a small cart, fastened the message to its foot, gave it a drink of water, and released it to the sky. All eyes were on it as the bird circled above them before taking off for the south. Taiku wasn't sure, but he discerned a fleeting look of concern on some of the Tungus' faces. He put it from his mind as Zakhor turned back to him.

"We have over five thousand fighters ready. They'll be here in a few weeks. The Master of Spirits will never be our master. Our best chance is to be one with Lagash."

Taiku turned back to his wife. "Have this man escorted with honor to his campground."

She in turn beckoned towards a nearby group of women.

Zaytea turned to Zakhor. "Our Clan Mothers. They are the esteemed guides of the people of Lagash. They will escort you."

Zakhor nodded his approval. He motioned with his head and eyes to the man standing off to the side, the one who had not gone to his knees with the others. Zakhor, the other riders, the horses all rode off as one, following the Clan Mothers. The Eber was the only newcomer left.

Taiku folded his arms and waited. The last contact he had with a leader of the Clay People was when she reached out from the grave to appoint him as her replacement.

He told himself that just as his wife shouldn't try to compete with Asenath, he shouldn't hold this man up to her standard. He must be a good person. Otherwise, he wouldn't have been sent.

Vlad approached, with Tamsyn trailing slightly behind. Taiku looked at the two of them in surprise. He knew his brother didn't trust her. Nobody did; they feared her.

Later. First, he had to greet the new head of the Eber Academy.

"Welcome to Lagash. I am pleased to see you, and I will be pleased if you leave in health."

"Thank you. I am pleased to be here, and will be pleased to remain a long time."

"We will defeat Ja'ix, and you will be safe. All of Lagash, including our Ebers, is working towards that end."

The man frowned.

"I am Chief Taiku; this is my consort Zaytea, also Clan Mother of the Olive Tree Clan, head of all the Clans. Vlad, my brother, is my First Officer, and the embodiment of Huitzil, Master of War. Tamsyn, at his side, is a member of my Council of Advisors and is training the Eber students to fight."

The man appeared annoyed when Huitzil was mentioned. That appearance changed to serious consternation as Tamsyn's role was explained. He directed his words to Taiku.

"I mean no disrespect, but it is not part of the Eber way for men and women to touch or even talk directly to each other if they aren't husband and wife. I cannot address your wife or your fighter woman. My name is Baryon. My father is the leader of the Ebers who live in Samarra. His brother leads in Mattara. The best way for the Ebers to defeat Ja'ix is to work harder at our studies. The students will immediately cease any military involvement and resume their real obligation."

This was stunning. Grown men and women not talk to each other? Tamsyn stepped between the two men, her back rudely to Baryon.

"This man's not allowed to speak to me. That's too bad. There's something he needs to hear. You gave me the task of teaching the Eber students to fight. I'm not finished, and their training won't stop until I am. Anyone who tries to interfere is my enemy. Do you understand, Chief Taiku?"

Baryon was tall, with dark penetrating eyes. Those eyes met Taiku's over the head of the woman who stood between them. There was questioning in those eyes, maybe fear.

He kissed Tamsyn's cheek, hoping this wouldn't be a problem for his wife. Baryon irritated him, and he wanted to return the favor. "I was appointed leader of the Ebers by the engraved order of Asenath. You will continue to carry out my instructions."

Baryon didn't rise to the bait. He reddened somewhat, though. "Truly, we appreciate the protection you provide to our people, and the leadership you have provided the Lagash Ebers. Now that I am here, I can relieve you of the latter responsibility."

Taiku reddened with anger. "Your people? Everyone who lives in Lagash is my people. That includes the Academy. And it is through being their leader that I can best effect their protection."

"You mistake me, Chief Taiku. Whether in Mattara, Samarra, or the oases of the Tungus, all Ebers look to you as our best chance of surviving the coming scourge. I now understand the importance to you of training the students, and as their leader, I won't interfere. I simply ask that it be completed expeditiously, so that they can resume their studies."

Taiku drew a deep, calming breath, as Zaytea turned to Baryon. "You may have appeased Tamsyn's concern, but you haven't appeased my husband or me. Asenath was a friend, a valued advisor and guide for my husband. She spoke to all of us; she listened to everyone. She wasn't just head of the Clay People; she was effectively the protector of the hearts of all the people of Lagash. If she could listen to men, you will listen to women."

That solved one problem for Taiku. His wife seemed to have dropped her competition with the dead. He picked up where Zaytea left off. "As I recall, a written appointment can't be overturned by one person. Rather, a decision is required by the "House of Judgment," and that requires three unbiased judges. Are you willing to leave the decision in the hands of your fellow Ebers?

"Chief Taiku, I didn't come here to compete with you. Nor do I want you to feel that I'm trying to diminish Eber loyalty to Lagash. Asenath had her own way of doing some things, which are unfamiliar to other Eber communities. I did not expect what I've heard from you today. I disagree with the role you've assigned to the Academy students, and I'm upset that this woman is teaching them how to fight. I certainly hope they don't have physical contact with her."

Tamsyn grinned in response.

"I am bound to these people," Baryon said, "and they to me in ways that I cannot explain. We both know that Asenath's appointment of a non-Eber to lead the community was a temporary measure until a replacement could be sent."

Taiku beckoned to a couple of soldiers. He whispered instructions and they quickly strode off, in different directions.

One returned almost immediately with a chair. He placed it behind Baryon, offering him a seat. The soldier took a small water flask from his belt and offered it as well.

Baryon accepted both and drank thirstily. Taiku, Zaytea, Vlad and Tamsyn stood in a semi-circle in front of him, looking down. Other soldiers approached, completing the circle from the rear. Taiku watched Baryon's eyes, to make sure he sensed the implicit threat. It wasn't clear.

The second soldier returned within a few minutes, walking briskly with three of the Clay People. Taiku turned to them.

"Thank you for coming so quickly."

As Taiku and the others turned, the Clay People saw who was sitting in the chair. They immediately lowered their eyes, though there was joy on their faces.

The oldest looking one, a craftsman named Ruben, raised his hands in front of his face, kissed his fingertips, and spoke. "Teacher! Welcome to Lagash. We are pleased to see you, and will be pleased if you leave in health."

Taiku didn't give Baryon a chance to respond. "I asked you to come quickly because I want to hear your understanding of certain Eber traditions."

Ruben beamed. "Teacher Baryon has a world-wide reputation for his detailed knowledge of our traditions."

"No, I want to hear it from you."

Ruben frowned, and looked at the ground. "It is disrespectful to express one's opinion in the presence of a master. Please, present your question to Teacher Baryon."

"Ruben, I must ask you, not him."

Ruben didn't respond. He stared intensely at his sandals. The other two people with him also examined their footwear.

"Ruben, I accept what you say about Baryon's expertise. I'm not looking for a conclusive answer; I need your opinion. Afterwards, we can ask your Teacher if you're correct." He turned to Baryon. "Is that acceptable?"

He nodded.

"Okay, Ruben?"

"If Teacher Baryon says it's okay, then I accept it."

The Clay People all called Asenath "Tanayt." When Asenath was first addressed that way, Ruben explained to Taiku that it was a very exclusive appellation, reserved only for the wisest of sages. Baryon, on the other hand, was being called "Teacher."

"Tanayt Baryon, I intend no disrespect by asking my friend Ruben for his view. You can of course correct him if he's wrong."

"Thank you for addressing me as Tanayt, but it's not a title for me."

"Oh? Explain, please."

"I am male. Tanayt is a feminine form of the word "Taana." It's rarely used in its male form, but that's way more often than the female form. Many people question whether there can be such a thing as a female Taana."

"So, I call you "Taana Baryon?""

"No. The title is reserved for the wisest, most exalted leaders. I do not come close to deserving it."

Taiku turned to Ruben. "What would it take to overturn a decision by a Taana?"

"It would take a ruling by three Taanas of equal or greater stature."

He looked back to Baryon. "Is Ruben correct?"

"Yes."

"Ruben, did Tanayt Asenath deserve the title?"

"Many people objected to her being called 'Tanayt,' arguing that only a man can be a Taana. But nobody questioned that her wisdom was at the level of a Taana."

"Do you agree, Teacher Baryon, that Tanayt Asenath deserved the title?"

Baryon looked at the faces around him. He had just lost this fight, but his eyes were sparkling with pride. "It was my father who first called her Tanayt. It caught on so quickly because of the esteem people have for both of them. It would take a ruling of three people of the level of Asenath to overturn your appointment as leader of the Lagash Ebers. There isn't even one such person in the world today. You've been given authority according to Eber traditions, and you've acted properly within that authority. On the other hand, the Eber community here owes me respect and obedience. I don't want that obligation to be in conflict with you, but would nonetheless like to resume the regular studies at the Academy as soon as possible."

"What do you suggest?"

Baryon smiled and stood up, handing the water flask back to the soldier. "As I said earlier, all the Ebers in the region look to you as their best hope for survival. You mentioned a Council of Advisors. May I be your advisor on Eber affairs? I would then be head of the Ebers, but subject to your authority."

"And what about your desire to take them away from their present tasks? They're not just studying how to fight; they're also making weapons and gathering intelligence for us."

Baryon turned to Tamsyn. "Would it interfere with their responsibilities if I could have the students for an hour a day, first thing in the morning?"

"I'll do better than that. Tomorrow noon, I will become a Fire Snake. While I need the students to attend the marriage, the entire transformation takes a full day. You may have them for that period."

Everybody looked at Tamsyn in shock.

Stunned, Baryon asked Taiku "You found the stolen parchments?"

But Taiku had more important concerns that moment. "Are you crazy? We just lost Dinah trying to do that!"

On hearing this, Baryon was aghast. "Dinah? You mean Tanayt Asenath's daughter? She's dead?"

Taiku nodded, and Baryon fell to his knees, in tears.

Vlad was livid. "Why did you do that to me?" he yelled at Tamsyn. "First Dinah, and she dies. Next you, and you'll die."

Baryon now looked confused as well as aghast. Tamsyn, however, was unperturbed.

"Vlad, if there's something important that you have to accomplish, and you get hurt the first time you try, do you give up?"

"Dinah didn't sacrifice herself so that others could throw away their lives copying her," Vlad raged.

"Dinah didn't sacrifice herself. She took a chance with something dangerous that needed to be done. It didn't work, and she died. Many people already consider me a dangerous snake, so it's less of a transformation."

Zaytea extended her hand to Baryon, who took it and pulled himself up. Tears rolled freely down the sides of his face. "At my father's suggestion I had corresponded with Tanayt Asenath about Dinah. In two or three years her mother was going to suggest she marry me."

He sighed and nodded to Zaytea. "Thank you for the hand up."

"Why me?" Vlad shouted. "Why did you have to use me? So I can have two dead women?"

Tamsyn grabbed him behind the neck, pulled his lips to hers, and kissed him hard.

"Enjoy that. It couldn't injure you. The next time our lips meet, I'll have the ability to end your life with a kiss. I'm not going to die tomorrow, or the day after. Others will."

"How can you know that for sure?"

"I do."

***

It was cold. Nothing else. Just very cold.

Well, it was miserable and cold.

And something else. Balthan was terrified. As long as they considered him useful, the soldiers wouldn't cut him up and throw him into one of their big pots, like they had done to so many of their captives. And those were the lucky ones. A few had been boiled alive.

When they had started their long march northwards, the soldiers' practice had been to slice off and eat a small piece of the shoulder of everyone they captured. But as supplies were used up, as the forests grew thinner and game scarcer, they decided to make better use of the prisoners trudging in front of them. Would the Cannibal Society soldiers remember that Balthan wasn't their captive? That he had come of his own accord, offering Ja'ix information about Lagash and its defenders? In truth, it wasn't completely of his own accord. He had been thinking of it, but his bird-footed friends had quickly finalized the decision for him.

"Balthan, you've been trapped by Sheyds," Asenath had told him. She was so arrogant! And correct. He was furious at the men who fired the arrows at her back, even though they were following his instructions. When the ravens started circling overhead, he took an arrow and shot at one of her assassins, somehow killing both of them. At that very moment, he spotted the bird footprints on the beach and the grinning Sheyds that were now his masters. The Cannibal Society members didn't hold him prisoner. His captors were much crueler beings, and his fate would be much worse than even the ones boiled alive.

When he had first arrived at Ja'ix's camp, he had been interrogated for days. He was then handed a stick of charcoal and a large paper, and told to draw a map of the entire region around Lagash. Balthan had never before tried translating the images in his mind into lines on paper. He produced messy scrawls that made no sense. After a couple of days, he was told he had outlived his usefulness. He begged for just a few more hours to produce a readable map. The soldier in charge replied that he was going to relieve himself, and that Balthan was to produce a useful drawing by the time he was done.

At that moment, Mekelat touched his mind, connecting the images in his head directly to his hand. He didn't think about drawing maps. His hand printed them directly, his arm a device operated by Sheyds.

Balthan was the only one who could see them. The Cannibal soldiers knew there was something strange surrounding him, and kept their distance.

"Your life is mine," Mekelat advised him.

In an instant, he became a slave. In the same instant, he mastered the art of reproducing the pictures in his mind as lines, shading, curves and angles. He spent days filling in details of the landscape: topography, vegetation, roads and bridges... He drew all the houses he knew, identifying their occupants. He drew the Eber Academy, its courtyard, each individual birch tree.

After providing this information, he had been confident that Ja'ix would keep him nearby as a trusted advisor. But instead he was sent north with the Cannibal Society, further and further from the home he had hoped to one day return to in triumph, as a conqueror and liberator. As a hero.

Mekelat moved to the woods and beckoned to Balthan. A pigeon came from the sky, landing on his shoulder. Balthan reached over, and pulled the little scroll from the pouch, showing it to Mekelat, as he had done before.

"All," he read. "We can't have that. Pull out your pen." Balthan threw the scroll to the ground, pulling a pen and a small blank parchment from his sleeve. Mekelat directed him to make a series of marks, carefully indicating angles, lengths, spacing and curves; Balthan was the handle of Mekelat's pen. When he was finished, he put the new scroll in the bird's pouch. Mekelat touched the birds head, and it soared back into the air, carrying a new message.

"What does it say now?"

"'None; danger, betrayal.' Taiku won't get any more Tungus reinforcements."

Were the Sheyds working for Ja'ix? At first he had thought so, considering all of Mekelat's help. Sometimes, though, the Sheyds had other ideas. A rope bridge over a river caught fire when it was packed with soldiers. None of them ran; they stayed and burned. Few survived.

Mekelat had grinned as he fell back into the line of troops beside Balthan.

"I was testing my blow-torch. I need to thin some ice on the Opinaca River. Do you like the way I held the soldiers still as they burned? Asenath's got her rope trick. Mine's glue."

Balthan didn't respond.

"Do you know why I haven't killed you?" Mekelat suddenly asked.

"No."

"My daughter thinks you're cute. Do you know why we're tormenting you?"

Balthan shook his head.

"How many times did Asenath trap Sheyds for you? Ten? A hundred?"

"I don't know. More than twenty."

"Come with me." Mekelat broke off from the line of soldiers. Balthan followed, running towards the back. Normally such an act would be punishable; it looked like a soldier was trying to retreat. But Tunney, the Cannibal Society's ranking officer, saw wisps of green smoke curling and twisting around Balthan as he ran by. He knew better than to interfere.

Mekelat stopped at the supply carts. He pointed to a large pot.

"How would you like to be in that?" It was one used for boiling prisoners.

Balthan didn't respond.

"It isn't too bad. There's place for your legs if you fold them. And once you're cooked, it's over."

Balthan averted his eyes.

"Imagine instead being forced into a bowl not much bigger than a human thigh. Imagine being kept there for an eternity. Would you like that?"

Balthan continued to silently avert his eyes. A wave of pain abruptly slammed his insides. His body emptied as he doubled over and vomited. He gasped for breath as the pain and nausea slowly dissipated.

"Well?"

Balthan forced his eyes up to Mekelat. He quieted his breathing and tried to remember what he was supposed to answer.

"I asked if you'd like to be trapped in a tiny pot for an eternity."

Balthan shook his head. It came together now; he understood why he was being tormented. Asenath should have warned him that he was making the Sheyds suffer when she trapped them. This was her fault.

Mekelat smiled.

"You feel you're innocent, that it's Asenath's fault. It doesn't matter what you think. You have a special responsibility for our suffering. As long as you live, you're ours. And you'll live until we decide it's time for you to die."

An idea lit Mekelat's eyes.

"That's not fair, though. You killed Asenath after she was so helpful to you. I bet she's so angry that she'd like to take a bite out of your heart. I'll tell you what: if you die fighting her and she takes a bite of your heart, you'll be free of us." Mekelat was quite pleased with this formulation. "Of course, she'll also expect an apology."

This implausible scenario didn't upset Balthan or cause him to lose hope. You have to have some hope in order to lose it. As Asenath had fallen to the ground that day, Balthan had quickly realized that he was utterly and completely doomed.

30 THE EDGE OF THE WORLD 10

Balthan's village wasn't large, but it provided enough clothes and furs that the survivors now had proper garments. A cold wind was enough to blow away any objections to how they were obtained.

Dina's milk had been slow coming back, and people didn't think Stanley would survive. Some considered him a symbol of the slow death that they were all having. When he started to show some energy, it cheered everyone.

Nobody except Zimri and Osnat were willing to be around Wendy now that she had been revealed as Huitzil, Hummingbird Master of War. Osnat insisted she be treated the same as everyone else, with no special comforts to appease her divine anger. Osnat didn't try to understand Wendy's transformation; there was no useful paradigm in her experience to apply.

Like everyone else, Aarluk, Ijiq, Haran and Zimri had been terrified when Wendy's heart had encompassed the world, but it didn't contradict their understanding of existence. The Ebers, and especially the people from later though, lost confidence in the laws of nature. For them the real terror was Huitzil shattering of the rules of reality.

Wendy explained why her victims had lain down on the ground, allowing themselves to be stabbed in the throat. Everyone has the ability to Travel between Spheres. A Sphere Traveler can cannrol it. Such Travel gives the heart the ability to return to the Abode of Life as a newborn child, grow old, die, and come back again. When Wendy threatened to destroy her enemies' hearts, she threatened to erase them forever from the cycle of existence. This was much more terrifying than mere death.

The whole group was heading towards the sea-ice, now starting to crack and heave from the warming currents from the south. It was the season to hunt the vast flocks of auks migrating to breeding grounds atop the escarpment. The birds first stopped to feed at the edge of the ice; that was the time to catch them. Osnat hoped they would cooperate with a member of their Games Alliance.

It was slow traveling with a large group of people who had spent the winter dying in the woods. The landscape was barren to them, nothing like the buildings, streets, or forests they were used to. Endless snow turning to endless mush was all they discerned. Osnat was astounded; the country was alive to her. She could orient herself by the smell of the sea blowing over the land, by the curls of the wind, by the ripples in the sodden snow they trod on. Osnat could feel the landscape.

When Aarluk had first taken her out to the sea ice, Osnat had expected it to be flat, like the Opinaca River in winter. But the sea was buffeted by conflicting currents and fierce tides. It had been uneven when she first went seal hunting with Aarluk, but was still easily passable: you rode over some small ridges, climbed over humps.

It might have been the same place, but it was a different world. Huge white-blue boulders thrust upwards, higher than a man. Pillars stuck out at awkward angles; the floor lay broken and tilted. It was as if a city had suddenly fallen from the sky and smashed itself to pieces on the ground, defacing it with the frozen rubble they had to climb over. The shadows cast by the spring sun were a ghostly population.

Most of the people waited on land. They weren't able to hunt, and there was no reason to have them struggle over rough ice. Ijiq used the opportunity to teach them chores like fixing boots, icing the runners on a sled, or attaching traces to a dog team. Osnat, Aarluk, Wendy, Zimri and Haran went to harvest the auks.

"It's hard to imagine knocking a bird out of the air with a rock," Wendy said.

Zimri smiled happily at his wife. "The birds are fast once they take to the sky, but they're slow getting off the ground. That's when we catch them, throwing our bolas as they take off. When they settle down again at the edge of the ice, we go after more."

"Do bolas kill the birds?"

"No. We keep them fresh until we're ready to eat them. Many people enjoy eating the auks while they're still alive. There's a certain cleanness to the meat that way."

The idea of eating a live animal made Osnat's stomach rise. "Maybe I'll try that."

Osnat and Wendy had been told to ride the sled along the ice. Osnat because of her advanced pregnancy; Wendy, because she was... what she was. Zimri ran alongside, pushing the sled over steep obstacles, guiding the dogs. But even with all of his work, the two women did more walking and climbing than riding; the sea ice was simply too uneven. The ups and downs on the sled nauseated Osnat; she was concerned about the bumps and sudden drops harming her child. One thing she refused, of course, was to stay behind with the others.

She felt ready to empty her stomach, and maybe her womb when Zimri suddenly ran to the front of the dogs, cracked his whip in the air, and brought them to a halt. Aarluk and Haran were ahead of them, crawling on their stomachs, hiding.

It was hard for Osnat to crawl on her belly, but she managed to stay low while getting to their hunting blind. Aarluk pointed ahead to the countless birds on the rough ice. Osnat could smell the water lapping beyond them. She could hear the auks talking, a low cacophony, like an orchestra tuning its instruments before a concert. One voice was a little louder than the others: te-aw, te-aw, te-ee. It seemed to be saying 'danger, stay back.' Did it know hunters were approaching, and was warning the other birds? Or was it warning the hunters? Osnat admonished herself not to let her imagination carry her away.

Zimri gave each of them two bolas, made of three ropes tied together in the center. The ends of each of the six strands were tied around small rocks.

"Wait until the right time to throw them," Haran said. Wendy was on edge. She had spent a lot of time being hunted this past winter: first by bears, then by Tunniq. She was not used to being the hunter. Osnat squeezed her arm in encouragement.

Zimri disappeared to the side, using the broken ice as cover to sneak up on the birds. The nausea in Osnat's stomach from the sled ride was replaced by a gnawing feeling. Zimri's path took him too close to the open water.

He charged, yelling at the birds, which started flapping their wings and running towards the hunters. Aarluk and Haran stood up quickly, their arms spinning their bolas.

"Now," Aarluk commanded. Ropes and rocks headed towards the birds, which were just getting airborne. Aarluk and Haran released their second bolas as Osnat and Wendy got their first swinging over their heads.

Osnat and Wendy let their bola's fly. Aarluk and Haran grabbed the last two bolas and sent them spiraling through the air.

It was over in moments. The birds were all off the ground except for a handful struggling to move their tangled wings. The birds taking off had been so thick in the air that aim wasn't necessary. You just had to throw the bolas fast enough to land among the rising flock.

"Go help your husband," Haran told Wendy. She grinned like a child carrying a prize as she walked, birds in hand, back alongside Zimri.

They set to freeing the bolas. Osnat and Wendy followed the others' example, and cracked the birds' wings as they untangled them. The auks screamed vainly in terror and pain.

Aarluk smiled. "That was good. Try to release the bolas quicker next time."

Osnat looked back to where just moments ago, the surface had been thick with auks. To her surprise, the birds were already returning, settling onto the ice. By the time the hunters had laid out their weapons, the flocks were back as they were before.

Again, Zimri chased the birds, and Wendy helped gather them. Again, each bola successfully snared a target. Wendy was amazed that after a winter of such hunger, food could be so easy to gather. She and Osnat laughed with delight as they broke the birds' wings.

The next time, Aarluk went to flush the auks. After the bolas had ensnared their prey, Haran sent Osnat to help her mother. She dutifully trotted down towards the edge of the ice. Aarluk had already picked up all the birds in back, so Osnat gathered the two closer to the blind. The ice was yellow and black, thick from droppings.

Osnat headed back with her catch, surprised to see Zimri and Haran waving their arms frantically, gesturing for her to return. She looked back, puzzled, and saw Aarluk running.

"Hurry," Zimri and Haran yelled.

Osnat realized that Aarluk was empty-handed. She dropped her birds, and ran towards the blind, not giving herself time to figure out why.

"Don't stop; jump!"

As Osnat got near, she saw a sickening gap between the ice she and Aarluk were on, and the ice the others were on. She put her head down, pumped her legs harder, and ran faster. The gap was growing quickly. She could see little caps on the waves between her and the shore.

She didn't stop to think; she just leaped. Arms reached out and caught her, dragging her to the ground, her boots just skimming the waves. Exhausted, she scrambled quickly out of the way to give Aarluk room to jump, and turned around to watch.

The gap was now twice the length of her body. Aarluk stopped running, and just stood, looking at them. Osnat was about to yell, but Haran put his hand over her mouth. "She's dead," he said.

Osnat yanked his hand away and screamed. "Mother, jump! I need you."

A smile seemed to form on Aarluk's lips, but it was hard to tell across the growing chasm.

Osnat focused her gaze on the gap separating Aarluk's ice flow. "Run across," she screamed. "Now, or it will be too late!"

Aarluk yelled something back, but she was already too far for Osnat to make out her words.

The birds were returning again to the ice. "Te-aw, te-aw, te-ee."

Osnat didn't dismiss the warning. "Let's get away from here."

Zimri nodded and tugged at his wife.

Wendy pointed at Osnat. "She's losing her mother. We have to do something!"

Zimri grabbed her hand, pulling harder. "We have to get away from the edge of the ice, or we may lose ourselves. There's nothing we can do. Aarluk's dead."

"She has all those birds. She can live on them until the ice flow touches land."

Haran shook his head. "She's been pulled to sea by a warm current. The ice will melt before she has the time to eat them all. Let's go, now!"

"Why didn't she come when I told her?" Osnat was distraught.

"Because then she would have drowned immediately in the icy water," Haran explained.

Osnat put the back of her hand to her open mouth as she realized they didn't know what she had done. Just as she had imprisoned the Simon who had stolen her husband's name by putting invisible ropes around him, so she had built in invisible walkway bridging the ice floes. Aarluk, thinking she had no chance, didn't run across when Osnat had screamed at her. She had saved her mother by making the walkway, and then killed her by not telling her it was there.

She stood up and took Wendy's arm. They walked, they clambered alongside the sled. Osnat's heart was being consumed. She felt that the city that had smashed itself down to create this landscape had actually landed on her.

"Why did we come for these stupid birds if it's so dangerous?"

"Not having food is dangerous," Osnat said, stopping to rest against a large pillar of ice.

"There has to be a safer way!"

"Wendy, forget life on the other side of the Edge of the World. You're not there. Nothing here is safe."

"It's not fair!"

Osnat grabbed Wendy's wrist. "You, more than anyone else, should not be talking about fairness. Erase that concept from your mind. You'll be a lot happier."

"But it's—"

She glared at Wendy. "No more."

"Keep moving," Zimri ordered. "We'll stop when we get to land." He grabbed the back of the sled, and leveled it with the top of a waist-high slab of ice as the dogs pulled forward. He clambered to the top and extended his arm to help the women. As he hauled her up, Osnat thought back to the employment contract she had negotiated with her lab. It gave her two years paid maternity leave, which she could take as soon as she got pregnant. The contract exempted her from climbing over broken sea ice. She thought of her marriage contract with Simon, which exempted her from cleaning and cooking. It didn't say anything about hunting, or eating birds that were still alive.

"It's not far." He pointed ahead to where the ice sloped sharply upwards.

She could smell the water lapping up through small fissures as they made their way forward, climbing over jagged projections of ice, over rough, cold boulders.

Osnat clambered onto the back of the sled as soon as they were on level ground. She wanted to catch her breath. More than that, she wanted to catch her thoughts, which were running much faster than the struggling dogs. Zimri was trotting near the front, ready to crack his whip to stop them when needed. Osnat was jealous. Zimri could stop the dogs, but she couldn't slow down her mind, which was racing wildly towards a cliff.

They soon arrived back at the camp where the others waited. Everything was loaded on sleds, ready to continue their journey. Osnat spotted Ijiq staring at her sled's light cargo of birds, staring at the people with it. She saw his expression fall.

Osnat walked over to him. She put her head on his shoulder, put her arms around his neck, and wept. She wept for losing her job at the lab. She wept for losing her parents, her friends. She wept for her husband, for the brat Simon she had stranded in the snow. She wept for the children by the esker, for the thousands of people buried on the other side. For all those whose bodies were piled up in the survivor's camp. For her brother Shelah, for her niece Rachel, for Dina's suffering. For the gang rape of Wendy, for her being a war deity. For Balthan, having his heart cut out and destroyed. For the cave dwellers they couldn't save. For Aarluk. For Ijiq. Especially for Osnat.

31 THE EDGE OF THE WORLD 11

They camped on a broad part of the esker, near the escarpment. The elevated surface would provide dry ground if the weather suddenly warmed. Its windward side attracted rabbits, who found easier access to forage through the snow cover. A nearby stream teemed with fish.

Dina's milk had come in. The regular meals, together with Stanley's constant sucking, had revived her breasts. There was love in her eyes for the baby in her arms. There was resentment there too, for the child that had replaced her own.

Osnat's baby's head was down. If Osnat wanted to reshape the world before he arrived, now was the time to do it.

Dina declared that Osnat shouldn't travel; her main activity should be resting in her tent. Haran stood a fierce guard against anyone who wanted to disturb her. People brought their concerns to Ijiq or Norma. If they felt it was important, they'd bring it to Osnat.

"What do you want to do? Kill everyone, take what you need, then bring down the mountain?" Ijiq asked Osnat.

"Yes."

"Bad plan. Falun and Miriaq could probably tear your head off with their arms. They're experienced fighters. Even if we defeat them, we'd lose a lot of people, and the clothes would be ruined from the stabbing and blood. Haran will never allow it, anyways."

Osnat raised an eyebrow.

"If Haran has to tie you up and sit on you to keep you from danger, he'll do it," Ijiq said.

"Not even the dead are out of danger."

"That's talking like a Tunniq."

"I am Tunniq: daughter of Aarluk, Protector of Balthan, eater of his heart, soon to be slayer of our village, and a mother."

"Soon to be dead Tunniq, eater and slayer if you raid our home. Then you won't get to be a mother."

Osnat sighed and leaned her head on Ijiq's shoulder. He was one of the few Tunniq who had never terrified or disgusted her. Though Aarluk was no longer around, Osnat continued to live in his tent. He had never declared himself Osnat's father. Their relation was close, but without a name.

Ijiq was right, of course. A raid would be suicidal. Was there an alternative? Eric had insisted that they negotiate a way to live in harmony. This angered Wendy, who as Master of War wanted everybody fighting to the death. She was definitely itching to murder Eric, but Osnat discouraged such behavior.

Killing Eric wasn't necessarily a bad idea. His idea of harmony had let a boy get mauled by bear. Apparently, it wasn't the only stupid thing he'd done. There was enough death around without his harmony.

Instead of killing Eric, Osnat sent him to do what he wanted: negotiate peace.

"I'm not pleased." Wendy was speaking as Huitzil.

"He's not coming back. He won't even have a chance to say what he's there for." Osnat looked at Ijiq, who nodded in agreement.

"Why did you send him, then?" Norma fidgeted uncomfortably.

Osnat shrugged. "He insisted."

"My turquoise knife was sent to me in order to kill him. Please, Osnat; it's time. I've waited too long. If he's still alive he has to die, painfully."

"It's too easy to get into the habit of making people suffer simply because you can. If you lose control of your cruelty, it destroys you."

Osnat gnawed her lip as she remembered who told her that. "What do you mean your 'knife was sent to you?'"

"I'm a Master of War. I'm appeased when beating hearts are offered to me. My goodness is through death and bloodshed." Wendy pulled out her knife, along with a folded, creased paper. She passed both to Osnat.

Osnat carefully opened the note. "Rand Eric is extremely dangerous and must be killed. By order of Police Superintendent Detective Tammy Finer." Then, in different handwriting, "Eric is dangerous. Kill him. Saima, son of Jako, Leopard clan."

Osnat froze. This could mean too many things, or nothing. She tried to run through the possibilities in her mind, but there were so many that her mind got tangled, and ground to a stop.

"Breathe!"

Wendy was rubbing her back. Ijiq's frightened eyes were staring into hers, while Norma squeezed her hand. Osnat took a gulp of air, and then gasped, catching her breath. Her thoughts went back to the last part of the note. Its implications were too stunning.

Composing herself, she motioned the two women closer. "There is a man named Tuli in the village. He has a boy who's old enough to receive a name. Tuli is sick, unable to feed his family, never mind go out on a raid. Eric will solve the problem of Tuli's son."

Osnat watched Norma puzzle out what this cryptic explanation meant. When she took a sudden sharp breath, and put her hand over her mouth, Osnat knew Norma understood what would happen to Eric, what had happened to her Simon, and why they had to destroy the Tunniq village.

Osnat turned to Huitzil. "If Eric somehow comes back alive, we'll use the knife to cut off and eat a mouthful of his flesh every day till he's dead." So much for her mother's admonition.

Norma fled in horror as Wendy nodded her approval.

"Tell me about the knife and note. Why didn't you kill Eric right away?"

"They appeared in a box at my feet a moment after I came through the hoops. I gave the box to David. I haven't killed Eric because of my oath to you. You discouraged murder, so I was waiting for the right moment."

Osnat handed back the knife. "When did Huitzil join with Wendy?"

"When I got this." She slipped it into its sheath. "I didn't know until Balthan attacked us." Wendy's heart was beating loudly again. "Eric is in pain."

Osnat frowned. Eric was a danger, but not because of malice. Did he deserve to be painfully killed? His good intentions had caused a boy's death. He still had those same intentions, and felt authorized to follow them through. He wasn't dying to atone for the past, but to protect the future.

The order to kill him came from Police. That made it suspect. It was Police who had forced the Ebers through those accursed devices to this place. But the explanation came from a member of her father's clan, whose name was similar to her husband's.

On the same piece of paper. Does that mean they're together? Does it mean that her family is somewhere back on the right side of the Edge of the World? The box with the note and knife arrived after Wendy, so it probably went through the hoops after the people from later. How much later? Minutes, days, millennia? How long does this barren exile last? Or is it already over?

"Wendy, do you know Saima, son of Jako, Leopard clan?"

She shook her head. "No. We don't have clans."

"Please tell me again how you ended up stranded here."

"There was a General Failure Alert. The wagons landed inside the Central Facilities, trapping us. When the food ran out, people started to panic. There were rumors that some children were murdered and eaten. The only escape was through the hoops."

"What caused the General Failure Alert?"

"I don't know. When I was Balthan's prisoner, I told him what happened. He laughed, and blamed it on Sheyds that escaped from their prison."

You could hear a heart pounding, but this time it was Osnat's, not Wendy's.

"Ijiq, what did you tell me the Edge of the World is made of?"

"Sheyds, trapped there for five thousand years."

Osnat chewed her fingertip as she mulled this over. If Sheyds had escaped from their prison, from the Edge of the World, that meant there were holes in it. The Sheyds' escape meant their escape. It meant it was possible for Simon, Saima, to go home one day.

She took a deep breath and turned to Wendy. "Do you know Police Superintendent Tammy Finer?"

"Lieutenant. She's the Left Attacker on my lacrosse team. She says to kill Eric, so with your permission I will, if he's not already dead."

Osnat was elated: Wendy knows Finer, and Finer knows Saima. Eventually her family will leave this place.

***

"It's ready. We'll wait for Osnat's instructions."

Haran nodded at Jacob and set off back towards camp. He had never before been this close to the Edge of the World and was relieved to be getting away. As a Sphere Traveler, he felt the anguish of the demon souls from which the green curtain was woven. Non-Travelers would feel it only if stupid enough to touch it.

David, Jacob and Seth were agitated, but Haran didn't know whether it was the Sheyds, or the demonic work they were doing. "Death in a Box," the three of them called it. They had altered a few of their strange lighters, and combined them with parts from another device they had found. The four of them had climbed the escarpment, and gone a little south of their village, right up to the Edge of the World in search of "tritium." It was something mysterious, which you couldn't touch, see or smell. Somehow, David, Jacob and Seth knew they had found some, and placed it into the small box.

David explained the device would make a loud noise; there would be a flash of light. Some rocks could fall, some dust... and then every living thing below the escarpment would be dead. If not immediately, within days. Safety was in being high up, or at least a day's travel away.

The plan was to ignite Death in a Box while they were up on the escarpment. They would wait for residual radiation to dissipate, go down and take what they needed. Then another bomb would bring down the mountain on the remains.

Destroying the people he had lived with most of his life didn't bother Haran, but he didn't look forward to the task of getting everyone, especially Osnat, up onto the escarpment. She wanted to be the one to activate the Death in a Box. She insisted on being the person who killed everyone who had feasted on her husband's flesh. Well, not everyone. Haran and Ijiq had been among the diners.

Osnat was ready to give birth any day. Climbing the escarpment on a bumpy sled could be enough to make it happen. What if the baby came too soon? On the other hand, if they didn't get her up, they would have to delay setting off Death in a Box. That might give the villagers time to escape, or worse yet, attack.

Haran's thoughts wandered as he made his way past the top of the steep gorge nearer the village. The people who remained with Death in a Box had enough supplies to last several days. He wasn't happy about leaving them, though. What if a bear attacked? What if someone from the village happened to find them?

"Brother!"

A hunter can't afford to let his alertness slip, or he risks becoming the prey. Haran looked around, saw Falun was alone, and attacked.

Falun was surprised. Haran had left as a reluctant hostage. Now he was striking out as one of the enemy. Haran was counting on that surprise, because Falun was stronger and faster than him.

It wasn't enough.

Falun was furious that the brother he wanted to rescue attacked him. He grabbed Haran's wrist and bent it backwards, forcing him to his knees. He extracted the knife from his hand and wrapped a thick arm around Haran's neck. "Osnat is a powerful witch. I'll lift off your head, and free you from her curse."

Falun looked one last time into his younger brother's face, and affectionately touched his cheek with his fingertips. He opened his eyes in sudden pain as he took a deep breath, giving Haran the opportunity to slam his elbow into Falun's face. Falun doubled over in misery, hand on his belly, and then vomited. Haran didn't stop to wonder as he picked up a large rock and brought it down on the back of Falun's neck. Falun's legs went limp, his arms flopped uselessly. Haran rolled him onto his back, and propped him against a boulder.

"Help me, brother. I can't move."

Haran took out a water bladder, and poured some slowly into his brother's mouth, making sure he didn't choke.

"I can't feel my arms or legs. What will happen now? I don't think my wife will be interested in taking care of me."

Haran spotted a large boulder a little way down the gorge, which would give Falun shelter from the prevailing winds. He hooked his arms under his brother's shoulders, dragged him over and propped him up. He took off Falun's bag, and placed it in easy reach. He looked back at his brother, and realized he had no reach. Haran rummaged through the bag, surprised to find Falun's horn trumpet. He used that only when hunting people.

"I'll bring someone who will know what to do. Stay alive, my brother." He took off towards the esker, to warn Osnat. His first thought after he paralyzed Falun had been to bring Osnat to kill him herself. Upon finding the trumpet, his quest became keeping Osnat and her people from being killed. He hadn't seen any other tracks on top of the escarpment, which meant either he wasn't paying attention, or no one else from the village had climbed up.

He should warn David, Jacob and Seth, and have them take a defensive position. But what would that accomplish? They weren't fighters. If attacked, they would die. Hopefully they would hide Death in a Box if they saw attackers approaching.

And what about the rest of them, out on the esker? Would they spot attackers in the distance? If Osnat was killed while Haran was away following her instructions, would Aua punish him? Aua had warned him that his task was to protect Osnat.

Could Aua do anything to help them? He had told Haran that he was strong in the pathways between Spheres, but powerless in the Abode of Life. At most, he could... Haran couldn't remember what it was that Aua said he could do. He was tired. He had been running for hours, and was now scrambling down the slope leading to the esker. Going down was harder than going up, and he had to concentrate.

He trotted into the camp. Everyone seemed to be going about their business; they hadn't been attacked. He stopped outside Osnat's tent, composed himself, and entered. Osnat was limping back and forth, a grimace on her face, her right hand pushing on her hip. Haran turned to Dina.

"The baby is facing forward, which will make the delivery long and painful. If she walks maybe it will turn the other way."

Haran took a breath. "They're coming for us. We have to climb the escarpment right away. They may attack here, or go after David, Jacob and Seth. If they get the box, we're in trouble."

Osnat gritted her teeth. "Someone's coming on a sled pulled by four dogs. I think it's Miriaq. He's close."

Haran was astonished. "I'll go to him."

"No. That would delay our climb. There's already a rope around him, tying him to me."

Haran thought back to Simon's feet, fastened to the ground in their village. He thought of Balthan's men, of himself, when they tried to kill, tried to defend Wendy.

"Falun is waiting for you to come kill him."

"He's waiting...?"

"Near the top of the gorge closer to the village. He can't move."

Osnat looked astonished. "What did you do?"

"I hit the back of his neck with a stone. He's paralyzed."

The faintest flash of disappointment crossed her face as she nodded. What did she think he had done?

Osnat gasped in pain, and started panting. Haran reached under her jacket, pressed one hand against the small of her back, the other lightly massaging just under her belly with his fingertips. "Take even breaths. In... out..."

Her breathing steadied, she stopped wincing. Haran removed his hands. "I'll tell everyone we're moving?"

"Please leave." Dina's words were polite, her tone insistent. "I want to see if the baby has started to come. If it has, we have to wait."

"It hasn't," Haran remarked, as he left. "We should be ready to go when Miriaq gets here."

He went in search of Zimri, told him about David, Jacob and Seth being on their own on top of the escarpment, and recounted his encounter with Falun. Zimri proposed that he go defend the men on the escarpment.

"Take your wife with you," Haran said. "She'll make sure that Death in a Box is safe."

The people in the camp quickly set to taking down their shelters, piling their things onto sleds. Ijiq and Haran made sure they were properly loaded, so they wouldn't fall off when the sleds tilted precariously. They explained to everyone how to get the sleds up over rocks and slush. The plan was to stay on the snow-covered southern slope of the gorge near the esker, and then once on top turn straight south, towards the Edge of the World. The explosion, David had explained, might rip a hole in the green curtain that trapped them. If so, Osnat wanted to be close enough for all of them to run through.

This made Haran nervous. He had no experience with Sheyds, but Balthan had recounted stories about how Sheyds had trapped and tortured him. It was enough for Haran to know that if the Edge of the World tore, it might free some of them. To his mind, the smartest thing would be to get as far away as possible. But Aua had instructed him that once they started up the escarpment, he was not to leave Osnat's side for longer than a heartbeat; otherwise he would no longer have one.

Norma organized everyone for the climb. Each sled had a minimum of four people, one on either side at the front and rear. Except for Osnat, nobody was riding. Haran marveled at the careful planning, at one person telling all the others what to do. He could understand them listening to Osnat, but Norma was just another one of the helpless people that they had rescued.

Osnat stood beside her sled, holding onto Dina's arm. She managed to smile, though she was clearly uncomfortable. Dina had given her an intimate examination, which brought her to the same conclusion Haran had already reached. Haran was surprised; as a midwife, she should have been able to tell. And why didn't Dina arrange the sled better? They had made a bed for Osnat, but a flat surface wasn't a good position for her kind of pain. Haran rearranged the things so that she could lie facing forward, with a pile in the center supporting her chest. That would take pressure off the spine and keep her from staying in one position too long. She couldn't be allowed to get stiff.

Haran helped her on. "Put your knees down here, with your feet behind you."

She gave him a quizzical look, as she knelt, her back ramrod straight.

"No, you'll cripple yourself if you travel like that. Lean forward over this pile. Stretch your arms out and hold onto the sides of the sled."

She bent forward, with her stomach pressing on the pile.

"Pull yourself back a bit, so that your breasts are resting on the things, and your belly is right behind it."

Osnat looked up at Dina, who shrugged. "Haran knows sled travel."

She adjusted herself accordingly.

Ijiq was on the other side of the sled from Haran. "Let's go."

"No!" Osnat pointed to a man standing alone just to the south of the esker. Miriaq.

Ijiq gave a little shout, ran ahead, and Osnat's dogs followed. Haran made sure the other sleds' dogs stayed put, and then ran to catch up. Norma trotted behind him.

Miriaq's eyeballs were ready to come out of his head, he was straining so hard. He had shed all his clothes, perhaps remembering Simon's nakedness when he had been tied down by invisible ropes. Unlike Simon, Miriaq wasn't excited, but enraged. He glared at the approaching sled.

It stopped right in front of him.

"Are you ready to give birth to my baby?"

"You're so sure it's yours?" Osnat's pristine hatred pushed her discomfort aside.

"Every woman I give my seed to gets pregnant, and gives birth to a child who looks and acts like me."

"You think my baby is going to be ugly and stupid, like you?"

"I know it will be."

"Can I rely on you to get the baby a name, if you're so sure it's yours?"

"If you'll come back with me, I'll make sure he gets a name. But Puah will probably kill you for what you did to Simon."

"How long did she wait before killing him?"

Miriaq pointed his arm at Osnat, accusing. "Simon was useless, frozen to the ground. She wrapped some blankets around him to keep him warm, but he wouldn't stop crying. Puah finally stopped it, because the noise kept her from sleep."

Puah had killed her own son for crying too much, and they held Osnat responsible. Well, she was, actually.

Norma squeezed Haran's arm and trembled. "Don't look, if it's going to bother you," Haran said.

"What's going to happen?"

He didn't answer.

"I'm not going back with you," Osnat said. "I'm not interested in having Puah kill me. But you will provide a name."

"Fine. But you'll have to come to me when the child is old enough."

"I'm not going where you're going. But I'll have the name." She took a stone knife from Ijiq and stepped closer.

Miriaq sweated, his body trembled as he looked at the knife. Osnat reached between his legs and started to massage.

His brow furrowed. "You want it again?"

Osnat slashed down with the knife, sawing roughly to sever his manhood.

"I didn't like when you stuck this in me without asking. I'm going to stick it in you now, and I'm also not asking."

Miriaq's mouth was open in shock. Osnat shoved his penis between his teeth, and with a thought bound his lips together. Haran held Norma upright as her knees buckled.

"Are you having a good day, Miriaq? As good as the day you first met me? As I remember, you were hunting for a name for a boy...."

Blood was pouring from between Miriaq's legs onto the wet snow. His mouth was clamped shut; his arms sewn to his sides. The only thing that moved was the hair on his chest, waving gently in the breeze. He had control of his eyes, but they were frozen wide open by terror, stirred together with hate.

"You offered to provide a name for my son. I'm going to take you up on that now."

When Falun had butchered her husband, he had first stuck a spear tip through Simon's throat, killing him. He was dead when Falun had started removing his head. Osnat didn't bother with that nicety. Nor did she bother afterwards to release Miriaq's mutilated corpse from the invisible ropes that held it in place. She tossed the name onto the snow, and then kicked it away.

"You should remember what your mother told you, Osnat."

"What are you talking about, Ijiq?"

"If you lose control of your cruelty, it will conquer and destroy you."

"I remember mother's words. I remember everything she said and did the first time we met. I remember every word she spoke when she and Falun butchered my husband." Osnat climbed back onto the sled, leaning forward as Haran had instructed her.

Ijiq ran beside the dogs and yelled at them. They started trotting back to the rest of the expedition.

32 THE EDGE OF THE WORLD 12

The gorge leading up from the esker was a smooth, though sometimes steep climb for strong legs on a healthy body. For a person riding a sled, it was like being in a small boat on a wind-tossed sea. The constant jarring tilts would have made Osnat nauseous, but she was in too much pain to notice. She was grateful to Haran for putting her in the pitched-forward position; otherwise she'd be bouncing up and down on her spine. She still had to get out occasionally when the sled tilted too far, or where too much barren rock stuck out from the snow cover. Ijiq, Haran and a few others stayed beside her sled, helping her along.

Osnat had never given birth before. She'd heard about it, that most of the time the pain was manageable, could be mitigated through medication. Sometimes though, it came early and could not be driven away except through surgery. Midwives usually refused to cut unless the mother or baby was in danger. They were certainly in danger here, but giving birth was just a small part of it.

Falun. At last, Osnat would get to avenge her husband. That was thoughtful of Haran, leaving his brother paralyzed rather than dead. Osnat tried to distract herself from the pain by thinking about how she was going to exact vengeance.

What she had done to Miriaq was too gentle. Should she cut off Falun's testicles as well? Stuff them in his mouth? Maybe she could make another orifice and place them there. She could demonstrate to Falun how the principle of 'least action' applies. Nature always finds the most efficient course from one point to another, whether the orbit of a planet, the path of a photon, or the trajectory of justice. Perhaps she could make an orifice and take something out; something that wouldn't kill him. Does the conservation of angular momentum apply, ensuring vengeance is equal to the avenged? But what about plastoquinone, the electron carrier? Could its task in photosynthesis be replaced with something that would result in 'synthesis' without the 'photo,' without light?

What did dark synthesis, angular momentum or 'least action' have to do with making Falun suffer? Why was she ruminating about that? She had no interest in growing anything inside him. Retribution was the only harvest she wanted.

Even better: she would be nice to him. She would pull some intestine out of his belly, just enough to stick into his mouth so he could be his own feeding tunnel! Osnat knew quantum tunneling was a factor in enzyme reactions. But what about restraints? Quantum tunneling depended on many things, such as temperature, a particle's mass...

Did enzymes actually evolve to complement tunneling? Her Thesis Supervisor thought so, stirring a great deal of outrage. Many people called the idea 'heretical,' saying he was violating the consensus of the scientific community. Most of his students left, for fear of academic reprisal. To Osnat's mind, the evidence was inconclusive. That it stirred such outrage made it undeniable though that scientific truth had become a religion, subject to laws of blasphemy. Osnat stayed with her Supervisor out of loyalty, and a refusal to be bullied. When he was expelled from the university, Osnat also left, taking a position at a private innovation laboratory. Jealousy of her achievements there, coupled with anger at all the money she was making eventually led her to this place, led her to consider whether to put Falun's genitals or intestines into his mouth.

"You have to get off the sled. The terrain here is too rough. Put your arm over our shoulders," Haran said.

She reached for him, as Peter grabbed her other arm. She stepped to the side, leaning heavily. Ijiq went to the front to guide the dogs. She took a deep breath and stepped forward, struggling to put one foot in front of the other. It was difficult to focus on anything but the agony in her back. Her right foot went into a slight hole, which threw her off balance. A cry escaped her lips, together with the remnants of lucid thought.

"It's not far till you can ride again," Haran said, as they kept a firm grip, holding her upright.

Her thigh was damp. No, it was wet.

Haran stared at her. Osnat stared back. She was too overwhelmed to think this through.

"We're turning north when we get to the top of the escarpment. We keep going till we're away from this gorge," Haran said.

That meant turning away from the Edge of the World. That meant someone else would detonate Death in a Box. She tried to argue, but had no strength. Peter and Haran were carrying her arms over their shoulders, dragging her toes, rather than helping her walk.

"Ijiq, when we get the sled up, you'll run and tell the others to detonate. Osnat can't do it."

Dina caught up to them, carrying Stanley in the back of her coat. She looked at the misery on Osnat's face. "Why are we changing plans?"

"Her water broke."

"We have to stop now!"

"We can't."

"The baby might be coming now. I have to check if she's dilated. We have to put up a tent, so we can have some privacy."

"Look at her eyes, Dina. The frightened child is the mother. The baby will wait; we'll stop when we can."

"What?"

"He won't try to come out now."

"We need a clean room, running water, and a birthing bed. We need medications against infection, and something to ease her pain!" The tears ran down Dina's cheeks as her lips trembled.

Haran turned to Osnat. "We won't lose the baby. I know you're in too much pain to understand what's happening. We'll make sure your child is well. Aua has spoken to him, and he understands he has to wait."

Osnat turned her glazed eyes to him, trying to understand the words of assurance.

"Have you delivered babies?" Dina didn't bother to wipe her tears.

He resumed moving up the slope with Osnat. "Many. Not one of them died from a complication of being born."

"Who taught you?"

"Nobody. It's something we just pick up, like learning how to hunt."

"You all know how to hunt. Do you all know how to deliver babies?"

"Some people are better hunters. I'm good at babies. Osnat told me you are, too. We'll work together."

The terrain leveled out. They put Osnat back in the sled, pitched over her support. She screamed as they positioned her. She panted heavily, moving her lips, trying to form words. Haran brought his ear close.

"Get a gun and shoot me. Do it."

He turned to Dina. "What's a gun?"

"It's a weapon. You push a button, and it kills the person it's pointed at. Why?"

"Nothing. When we're on top, I'm going to try to speak to the baby directly, to ask him to face the other way. You'll reach in with your hand to help."

It wasn't nothing. Why wasn't Haran shooting her? Aua was going to punish him for that.

"Ijiq," Haran called.

Ijiq turned.

"Osnat says do it."

Ah, he'll have Ijiq shoot her; Aua wouldn't let him do it himself. Ijiq nodded, and took off, presumably to get his gun. She hoped it wasn't too far. If Death in a Box had been nearby, she'd set it off now to get rid of the pain. Anything to get rid of the pain. Falun and his enzymes! What did she care about him now? Miriaq. Was it his baby? She screamed at the thought. Had to get rid of it.

If only she could get some plastoquinone for the pain. Why was it so hard to breathe? She strained to take in some air. She tried to lift herself up, but her hands were glued to something, and that something was tossing her around, keeping her from losing consciousness. Tilting side-to-side, rocking, bumping... If she'd have the energy, she'd throw up.

Think of something pleasant... She pictured her wedding table again, the silver utensils. Why was someone digging at her kidneys with a fork? The stabbing pain went all the way through, and out her back. Something had taken hold of her hips and was trying to rip them apart. Osnat tried screaming. No, that required air, and she had given up breathing; it must have been months of agony since she had taken a breath. I'm going to kill you, Miriaq, for doing this to me...

Water, she was desperately thirsty. Ask Aua for a drink. She had to find water. Her sanity, if not her life depended on it.

There were hands on her back. Follow the hands, they will lead to water. They had to; she had no idea how else to get a drink. The pain eased a little. Ah, the hands were protecting her kidneys from the silverware. She followed the hand, the warm fingers, catching little bits of air. She heard water, a stream. They were traveling alongside a stream leading down from the glacier. No, she was hearing a different stream, a brook. It wasn't coming from the glacier; it was coming from a Rock. A brook, pouring from a Rock made of pure light. Osnat listened to the water gurgling and bubbling. The stabbing continued, the ripping at her hips went on, but the stream pouring from the Rock came and flowed in front of the pain, its waters pleasant and soothing. Her breathing slowed; her heart returned to its place. The hands held her over the brook, and she drank.

Osnat opened her eyes. She was in a tent, lying on some furs, her trousers off. Haran squatted beside her, one hand on her belly, the other stroking her hair. She recognized his hands: they had carried her to the water. His eyes were open, but they didn't spot Osnat. He was seeing in another Sphere.

The fork was still digging at her kidneys; the pain was slashing through her back. Dina's hand was inside her, tapping at something. Dina too, was in that other Sphere, but not with her eyes: with her finger that was gently and constantly tapping. It was a soothing rhythm. Osnat closed her eyes again, and let the tapping join the orchestra of her senses: the fork, the stabbing, the slaked thirst, and now the tapping. There was movement inside her, movement to the music. Her child was dancing. No, not dancing; turning... turning around.

Dina's hand came slowly out, along with the fork. There was still the stabbing, but it was different now, a tightening of her muscles. There was a memory of the pain as it receded, like the waves slipping off a beach back into the ocean.

"Stand up."

Haran put his hand on her belly, sensing. Dina's scarred fingers were next to his.

"How should I breathe?"

"Whatever way feels comfortable."

Short shallow breaths were best when the waves of pain flooded back, regular breathing between.

"Walk."

"Where?"

"Back and forth inside the tent. The baby will be here soon."

A wave came in and receded. "Where are we?"

"Your baby was facing forward, pressing on your spine. Your water broke while we were climbing the escarpment. We're on top now, in a birthing tent. The baby's turned."

A large wave washed over Osnat. It took her breath away, but not her thoughts.

"Falun?" she asked.

"You'll deal with everything when your son is out."

A large wave dropped Osnat to her knees.

Haran put a pile of folded skins in front of her. "Rest your chest on this. Fist your hands, put them over the side."

Dina sat down behind her and prodded gently. "He's coming."

***

Ijiq stopped to check on Falun, who greeted him as a beloved friend. Ijiq gave him some food, a drink of water, and encouragement.

"You'll be outliving the rest of our village. They'll all be dead very soon."

"I know. When is Osnat coming for me?"

"It may be a while. She's having her baby."

Falun showed no surprise. "Puah sent Miriaq to offer to take care of it."

"Yes, we met him. Osnat thanked him and accepted his offer. I have to go now, to detonate Death in a Box. I'll pass by afterwards, and if you're alive I'll give you some more food."

Ijiq wasn't far past the second gorge when he spotted blood. It was splattered, like a fight that had tumbled around. Ijiq sniffed. It was mostly, but not all human blood. He climbed onto a little rise to look. A bear cub carcass lay not too far off, near the remains of a human arm and some torn innards. He went over for a closer look, and saw the limb of a boy who probably was old enough to have a name. Tuli's son... That must have been a sorrowful death, being pulled apart by a bear. At least the boy managed to inflict some sorrow on his attacker.

The boy's tracks came from where David, Jacob and Seth were waiting with Zimri and Huitzil. Ijiq quickened his pace.

It was good Ijiq had no hostile intentions. They were so absorbed in arguing with each other, that Ijiq was able to approach undetected. It was good also that they were fighting with words, rather than weapons. Otherwise, there would have been a lot more blood on the ground.

"Hello," he announced himself.

He hadn't run up completely undetected. While four of them jumped, Huitzil calmly thanked him for coming.

"Did you also let the boy approach you without being seen?"

Jacob sighed morosely. "We're arguing about what he said."

"Well, your argument is over. Detonate now," Ijiq said.

Huitzil smiled.

"It's not so easy. He made a request," Jacob answered.

"He's dead, so it doesn't matter. Osnat says do it."

"Why did you kill him?"

"I didn't. He came between a bear cub and its mother. The mother bear took everything except his arm."

The three Ebers paled. Wendy grinned, and gave her husband a kiss on the cheek. "I told you: Huitzil does what she has to."

"You sent the bear?" Ijiq asked.

"I'm sorry I questioned you." Zimri was proud of his wife.

"Then this is yours." Ijiq reached into his pack and withdrew a bloody pelt. Unfolding it, he handed the boy's lacerated heart to Huitzil. "The bear must have left it for you."

The three Ebers averted their eyes.

Ijiq wasn't moved by their discomfort. "What are you getting sick about? You're about to destroy an entire village, and you're disturbed by Huitzil sending a bear to kill one boy?"

Jacob spoke. "He brought a message. They want us to spare some of the younger women. They would send them up to us as gifts."

"We could use them. We have a lot of men, which means some of our women will have to take more than one husband. But that's not your concern. Detonate Death in a Box now. Stop delaying!"

"They know we're going to kill them. Eric didn't even ask for his own life."

Ijiq looked at Zimri and shook his head. "Eric?"

David spoke this time. "The boy. He seemed proud of his name."

"Of course he's proud of his name. He just got it."

This took some time to sink in. The Ebers turned ashen as they understood. "Our Eric?"

"He's my Eric now," Huitzil answered, waving the torn heart in her hand. "Since he belongs to me, I annul his question, and order you to detonate Death in a Box immediately."

"No."

"I am Huitzil, Master of War. I command you to detonate Death in a Box now."

"We don't answer to you."

"You will answer me with your deaths." Wendy pulled out her knife.

David, Jacob and Seth looked at each other, sweat rising on their foreheads.

"You need us."

"Not if you refuse to detonate. It means we have to kill them one at a time. The people below us will all die, regardless of what you do. The difference is that they'll suffer more, a lot of their clothes will be ruined, and your people will get cold and sick. Most of your people will die."

"We're not responsible for the killing you do."

"Not doing what you must will also be murder, no matter what your excuse." Huitzil raised her arm as her heartbeat thundered through the air.

Ijiq reached out and stopped the downward motion of her wrist. She turned towards him, small flames coming from her eyes, blood leaking from the corners of her lips onto her blue skin.

"I know how these people think. Wait," he whispered. He let go of her and turned to the three men whose hearts were about to be ripped, still beating, out of their chests.

"You sent out scouts such as Osnat and Simon, who approached us for help. If we had responded peacefully, we would have all benefited. Rather, we answered as Tunniq, because that's who we are. If you want to live, you must destroy the Tunniq. It means you have to become murderers; it means you have to become us."

"Are our lives more valuable than yours? You're people, like us." Jacob said.

"No! We're not like you." Ijiq grabbed Huitzil's wrist once again, this time pointing threateningly with the knife it was holding. "Osnat orders you to detonate. When you first met her, she promised war. This is it. Your oaths are now payable."

The pounding of Wendy's heart was relentless. It echoed off the Edge of the World and danced up to the sky behind them. Could they hear it in the Tunniq village below?

Jacob squeezed his fingers to his temples in concentration.

Ijiq pointed at them one by one. "You must obey your Tanayt, Osnat." Aua had told Haran the title was important.

"What did you call her?" David's eyes opened wide.

Jacob jerked backwards as if he had been kicked. "How do you know she's a Taana?"

"I know."

"Do you have any idea how dangerous a Taana is?" David ignored Huitzil's knife hovering near his heart.

"The last one was killed thousands of years ago." Jacob paused to collect his wits. "They're incredibly powerful."

"Like Aarluk?"

Jacob shook his head. "If three Taanas suggest something to the Source of Blessing, he's likely to follow the suggestion. If four insist, there is no doubt the Source of Blessing will comply."

Ijiq thought furiously about the implications of this. And if four Taanas decided that the world should be destroyed, it would be?"

Jacob looked at Seth and David. "If even one Taana says we have to destroy this part of the world, it has to be done."

Huitzil touched her knife to David's chin. "Osnat is a powerful Taana. She's given her order. Obey."

Everyone was wrapped in the pounding of the Master of War's heart. Jacob took the cover off the box. Seth prepared the basket and rope to lower it over the edge, while David used a pole to keep it away from the wall. Seth threaded the rope over the notch they had fashioned at the end of the pole. They were ready.

Jacob touched something inside the box, tied the cover on with dog sinew, and placed it in the basket. Seth lowered it gently.

The rope went slack as the basket touched ground.

"Run back," Seth ordered. Letting the pole fall, they scrambled away from the edge of the escarpment as they heard a single, muted 'pop' from below.

Nothing else. They waited, holding their breath as they felt a rumble, like a small caribou herd stampeding through the rock under their feet.

A small cloud came up from below the escarpment. Like an alien beast rising from the depths, it turned its ghastly mushroom head to look at them, and then blew out towards the sea. The prevailing winds coming off the glacier carried the invisible death away from them.

There's a particular kind of crystalline sparkling sound made by a sheet of thin ice, or a piece of fine glass when it shatters. But the noise that came right after was neither of these. It was much too loud, as if the entire sky was shattering. The sound didn't approach like a wave, building up to a crescendo and then receding. The crushing, sparkling noise was abruptly upon them, wrapping them, ripping everything from their minds.

And then it was gone. Not just the sound, not just the cloud. The Edge of the World was gone, destroyed by Death in a Box. As their senses returned, the people looked out at existence on the other side, wondering what to do next. David took a tentative step forward before Wendy's fist slammed into the side of his face. He stared at her for a second before he fell to the ground.

"It's not time," she said.

Zimri, Jacob and Seth also fell to the ground, their hands over their ears as another sound enveloped them, this one the sound of thousands of screams coming together in agony. Only Huitzil managed to stay upright as patches of the curtain that closed off their world were roughly stitched back together in a jumble of pain. It was the agony of Sheyds, who thought for a moment that they were free.

"Did it work?" Ijiq asked.

"It detonated. If we isolated the tritium properly, then it worked." Jacob turned to David. "What do you think?"

David was still on the ground, hands wrapped around his bent knees, eyes downcast. "My biggest fear was that it would detonate. I should have carried the bomb down myself and died with them."

Ijiq reached down, grabbed David's forearm, and yanked him to his feet. "How do we know if we succeeded?"

David winced as he rotated his arm, testing if it was still in its socket.

Ijiq grabbed David's face tightly in one hand. "I've learned some things from living with your kind. You should have learned that people who indulge their feelings are usually dead people." Ijiq opened his hand. "People who indulge their feelings also cause other people to die. I'm not interested in your self-pity. Did we succeed?"

"The only way to know for sure is to go down and look around," David finally answered.

"Let's get going."

"No!" David protested.

Ijiq's patience was running thin. He grabbed David's face again and lifted him off the ground.

"No, he's right, put him down." Jacob took hold of Ijiq's arm.

Two of them? Wendy and Zimri would have to make sure he didn't rip these foolish people into pieces.

"We can't go down; it's dangerous. We'll end up as dead as the people below. We have to wait a few days for the radiation to dissipate," Jacob said.

Ijiq lowered his arm. "Let's go to our camp, then." He started off, not looking back. Jacob, Seth, Zimri and Wendy quickly gathered their things.

"I'm not going to destroy any more." David folded his arms on his chest and spread his feet.

Wendy walked up to him, bent her knees, and casually flipped David onto her shoulder, his head facing down. She started walking. Zimri shoved Jacob and Seth forward, causing Seth to fall. He looked at David riding upside down on Huitzil's shoulder, stood quickly, and followed.

They passed the remains of the new Eric. The Ebers wanted to stop to investigate, but Ijiq ignored them. When they came to the first gorge, it was Ijiq who wanted to detour, but the Ebers wouldn't let.

"We don't know how high the radiation went up the gorge. Going to check on Falun might kill you. We shouldn't even be near the mouth of the gorge."

"Tunniq aren't afraid of death."

"What about Osnat? She needs you alive," Jacob said.

"You keep going till you're away from the danger. Zimri, keep them moving. I'll catch up."

"Didn't you listen to what I told you?"

Zimri herded them forward.

"Falun!" Ijiq yelled as he stood over the top of the gorge.

Silence.

"Falun!"

Ijiq didn't see any radiation. He had been told that you could only detect it from the damage it caused.

"Falun!"

The gorge was neither gentle not straight. Ijiq hoped this would work in his favor as he ran from rock to rock, trying to conceal himself from the undetectable hazard.

"Falun!"

"Ijiq!" finally came the reply.

Ijiq took in the scene below him. Falun was leaned up against a rock, smiling, about two-thirds of the way down the gorge. A little further down was Eric's crushed head, a leftover from the bear's meal. The bear was off to the side, its white corpse dotted with blood-red stains.

Ijiq quickly ran over to Falun and gave him a drink, followed by a meal of dried fish.

"Look! I can move my fingers now." Falun's fingertip quivered slightly. "The bear was running down the hill, with Eric's head in its jaws. I shouted at it as it ran right past. The bear was almost all the way down before it turned, and started running back towards me."

Falun paused to take a breath.

"I heard a "pop," and felt a sudden, dusty wind. When I opened my eyes, the bear had stopped below me. Its eyes and ears were leaking blood. I yelled at it to put Eric down. It obeyed, and opened its mouth. I expected it to roar, but it moaned instead." Falun looked quite pleased with himself. "I must be a powerful Sphere Traveler."

"I'll bring you to Osnat's camp if you agree not to harm anyone."

"I'll do whatever I can to help her."

Ijiq slung Falun over his shoulders and trotted back up the gorge.

***

"She's resting." Haran sat outside the tent, refusing everyone access. It was Ijiq's tent though, so he was an exception. Osnat was half-asleep, the baby lying on her chest. She turned and smiled weakly.

"We have a strong baby," Ijiq declared, grinning. He ran his fingers gently over the infant's back, over Osnat's cheeks. "You kept your promise to your husband."

Osnat came fully awake. "What—"

"You promised him that your baby would live. I told Aarluk that I would protect her grandson and find him a name. I will also keep my promise."

She was too weak to question him.

"Death from the box came part way up the gorge. Jacob says we have to keep Falun alive for a few days to learn if he's been damaged by it. Falun says he'll do whatever he can to help you."

The newborn shivered, and Ijiq gently picked him up, cradling him in his arms. "You're going to be a great one," he told the infant. "People will fear you. Women will flock to your bed, and animals will beg you to hunt them."

Ijiq looked at the side of the tent, and then moved over quickly, shifting the baby's position just in time for it to relieve itself on the snow, rather than the furs.

"Now you must learn to tell your mother when you need to go, just like you told me."

Osnat was still too weak to ask. Everything that Ijiq did or said gave her another question.

The baby whimpered. Ijiq slid himself over and put the baby's mouth to her breast. It sucked softly, while Ijiq gently stroked Osnat's arms. She fell into a light sleep, feeling at peace, wondering how her war was going.

33 MODERN AGE 9

The shadows were late-afternoon long when Detective Tammy Finer stepped out from between two birch-trees into the dusty courtyard and groaned. She had wanted to avoid any contact with people, but a slender young woman stood staring at her, just a few paces away. Dressed in loose pants and a suede pullover, she was leading a goat on a bronze-studded leash. Finer tensed. There was something about this woman that felt dangerous, a threat.

As if in response, the woman, without taking her eyes off Finer, bent down to wrap the goat's leash around the leg of a table. She straightened up, and launched herself.

Finer used her forearm to deflect the kick to her cheek, and the woman fell off balance to the ground, not anticipating that Finer would defend herself. She swiftly rolled over and stood again, holding her fisted hands loosely in front of her. A jab with her right fist was a decoy, and Finer was thrown onto her back by a kick behind the knees. The woman wasn't the only one to have underestimated her opponent. Finer rolled hastily to the side as her attacker jumped at her. Both women stood quickly, arms in front, circling each other.

Finer jabbed towards the woman's head with her left fist. Her arms went up defensively, and Finer dropped fast, wrapping one arm around the inside of the woman's right thigh, another behind her left knee. She quickly straightened, throwing her opponent on her back. The woman's right hand shot up into Finer's jaw as Finer moved down to pin her opponent. Her head rang; she tasted blood in her mouth. The woman took advantage of Tammy's momentary distraction to shoot to her feet, grabbing onto Finer's ankles, yanking her down again. Finer kicked, just managing to free herself. She rose quickly and stepped backward.

Not quickly enough. The two were the same height, and apparently matched in skills. But the woman was wearing loose fitting clothes, and Finer was swathed for winter in thick layers of cloth. As if in answer to Finer's thought, the woman lifted herself on her toes, and then swiftly brought her right foot straight into Finer's injured jaw. Finer didn't step back this time; she staggered.

It was time to end this. She had a job to do, and fighting this young woman wasn't part of it. Finer lifted her bent right leg in the air, bouncing on her left foot, her arms wide to the side. Her attacker kept on circling, her eyes, her expression not changing in response to the strange stance.

Finer dropped her right foot to the ground at the same time that she twirled her body and kicked upwards and sideways with her left foot. As she expected, the woman blocked the kick with her fist, but wasn't ready for Finer's arms sweeping in from the side. The woman was pinned, back to Finer, the latter's arm wrapped around her neck, the woman's left arm immobilized behind her back.

"You're dead. Don't move," Finer said.

"You're good fighter, but not good enough. I have my knife in my hand. You're dead."

"I have my saliva, which you've now mixed with my blood. I spit on you, you're dead before you can use your blade."

The woman had no answer to this, but held her knife still.

"Let's have a truce for a moment. I won't spit on you; you don't stab me. Agreed?"

"Okay."

"Can we take this farther? I want to do my business and leave. If I let go now, will you attack me?"

No answer, just steady breathing from her captive.

"Well?"

"You're a Sheyd. Only a Sheyd could come through the gateway from another Sphere. I never heard of it, but I'm guessing that only a Sheyd could kill someone by spitting on them. A Sheyd, or a Fire Snake. You don't look like either. I will kill you, whichever you are."

"I'm not a Sheyd; I'm a person, like you. But I'm also a Fire Snake. If I want you dead, you're dead."

The woman had no immediate answer to this as well.

"What's the goat for?"

"I'm selling it to the Ebers."

"Can it be replaced?"

Finer loosened her grip a little. The woman nodded, as best she could.

Finer spat through her injured lips at the goat, which was tethered off to the side. She missed, hitting the leash. Some spit dripped onto a chipmunk that had been darting its head back and forth as it had watched the bout. It immediately stopped and fell over. Tammy licked her lips, gathering saliva and blood in her mouth. The goat bleated as the mixture landed in its eye. It took a half step backward. Its head froze in mid-turn as its legs folded, and it collapsed on its side.

Finer let go, and the woman turned around to face her. "What are you? What's your business?"

"I'm Detective Tammy Finer. Aua brought me here to take a Sheyd-trapping bowl to Saima."

Mention of the Sphere Traveler seemed to ease the woman's hostility. "Aua? Where is he?"

"He can't come himself. He's the same Aua that you know, but he's in the pathways between Spheres, Traveling between times."

This should not have made sense to anyone.

"What about Simon? The Ebers are the ones who make the bowls. Why would you have to bring him one?" She paused. "Simon in another time?"

Tammy nodded. "Yes. There is a terrible destruction coming; this place will be obliterated. The knowledge of how to trap Sheyds will be lost, and they will become uncontrollable. I need to bring a bowl to Saima, so he can learn how to trap the Sheyds again."

"What about the marshes? Will my home be destroyed?"

"This whole area will die. The air, the ground will become poisonous."

The woman merely frowned in response.

"We have pieces of Sheyd traps, but need a complete bowl in order to figure them out. If my Saima doesn't get the knowledge he needs, the Sheyds will be unstoppable."

"Will we, will the Marsh People survive the destruction?"

"I don't know."

"The Ebers will?"

"They must." Finer looked at the woman's brown hair, looked at her deep, blue eyes, noticing the long lashes. "There are Sheyds that want to become solid, complete. If they succeed, they'll gain control in every time. Even the existence you have here now will be threatened." Finer wiped a sleeve across her forehead. "I know this makes no sense, and you have no reason to believe me. It doesn't make sense to me either, but I trust Aua. Will you help me?"

The woman didn't hesitate. "You're the only person I've fought whom I haven't been able to defeat instantly. I'll get you a bowl. Do you have anything to leave in its place?"

Tammy dug into her pockets, pulling out her pipe and lighter. She hesitated before extending her hand "This is all I have on me. I hope they don't cause trouble."

"Stay here; keep out of sight." The young woman picked up the dead goat, the pipe and the lighter, and carried them to the Academy, just beyond the courtyard.

Finer waited, enjoying the fresh scent of the air, the strange, un-designed landscape. She marveled at the redness of the moon, and how early it was showing in the sky. She contemplated having a friend from across five thousand years.

The woman returned soon afterwards, holding a clay bowl in her hand.

"This was supposed to be for Balthan," she said as she placed the bowl on the table.

That was the name of Asenath's assassin, from Aua's story. "Thank you."

The woman nodded. She scratched idly at her arm, pulling up her sleeve a bit. Tammy stared at the dagger-shaped mole, and then pulled up her own sleeve, exposing her wrist to the woman.

"I should say thank you, grandmother. I guess we survive the destruction here."

The young woman reached for her face, this time not in combat, but with surprised affection. "I'm Tamsyn."

She pulled back. "Someone's coming. Quickly."

Detective Finer nodded, picked up the bowl, and ran back between the birches.

Aua looked at the bowl in her hand, at the blood on her lips.

"It was supposed to be for Balthan."

"I heard the discussion."

"Do you know what happened to him?"

Aua's smile was of irony, not amusement. "Balthan was trapped by Sheyds. They—"

"What! Sheyds trap humans? Do they put us under clay bowls?"

Aua laughed. "No, no... They entice people to trap themselves. People who always try to evade responsibility build their own prisons."

"What finally happened to him?"

"Asenath rescued him by taking a bite from his still-beating heart." Aua chuckled at the astonishment on her face.

Finer looked at him warily. "Can you keep me away from her? I don't want anyone chewing on mine."

"You meet her."

They traveled on in silence, Finer thinking about her apparent grandmother, and about Asenath, who saves people by chewing their hearts.

As they approached the bridge, Aua gave her some parting instructions on how to get past the Sheyds at the tower. They likely knew what she was carrying.

"The bowl offers some protection, but don't brandish it at the Sheyds. They'll try to trick you into breaking it. Don't bother with your weapons either; they won't affect them. If you have to, use this." He handed her a ceramic dagger.

She examined it, and then slipped it into her belt. "Can I really protect against Sheyds with a knife?"

"The best is to seal them away. Say the words on the bowl out loud, using your name as the one doing the act."

Finer looked at the strange markings on outside of the bowl. To her surprise, they were perfectly legible. She recited:

"Upended, overturned, quelled are all Sheyds, all those without merit, all rock-spirits, and Liliths, and Mekelats..."

Aua folded his arms over his chest, smiling as she finished the recitation. "You create as your heart resonates. Your words form the seals that hold the Sheyds away. The bowls hold the resonance in motion, even when the speaker is no longer present."

"Didn't you say only the Ebers could trap Sheyds?"

"They're the most experienced. Anybody can make a trap, for themselves or for Sheyds.

Aua's expression turned serious. "I want to tell you something. There's a good chance that you will remember absolutely nothing of me or of this trip once you go back into the bridge tower. Write a short note on your hand, telling yourself what you have to do."

She reached into a pocket and came out empty-handed. "I must have lost my pen during the fight."

"Burn a note on your hand."

"Have you lost your mind?"

"I gave up my body in the Abode of Life, not my mind. Think of what's important, and decide. Not too long ago, your priority was a dead dog."

She gently rubbed the fingertips of her right hand against her left palm. "I must be the one who misplaced her mind." She pulled out her cutter, set it to the lowest power, then wrote 'bowl to Saima.' The pain was tolerable; the smell of burnt flesh not so much. "How do I contact you?"

"Travel between Spheres without the datura. Use a real drum."

"I'm a fraud at Sphere Traveling. I've never done it without drugs."

"Saima will teach you."

They were both standing on the bridge, by the door to the blue tower.

"Go now. I am pleased to see you, and will be pleased if you leave in health." Aua pulled open the door and shoved her inside.

Finer was soaked; she stank of urine, as if someone had poured a pail of it on her head. In fact, someone had as she passed through the tower door. She felt a hand grabbing at her crotch, others squeezing her breasts. Bony fingers were in her hair, pulling. It was terribly dark, after the brightness outside. Horrible laughter. Something hard was in her hand. What was it? She couldn't remember, but knew it was vital.

She was freezing. There was an icy wind blowing through the cracks in the doors, and she was drenched. She hardly noticed the silver hands groping her, she was so cold.

Doors. There were doors on opposite sides of the room. She had to go out the door that she was facing. That was critical. She shivered. There was something she was supposed to say, but couldn't remember what.

"Uncomfortable, dear? Let me warm you up." A blue flame hissed from a torch. "Would you like me to warm up your breasts? Or should we get right to business? Open your legs and I'll make you hot."

"Upended, overturned..." she mumbled. That's how it started. It must have been right, because the creatures all stepped back, looking at her cautiously. What came next? She couldn't remember. The Sheyds smiled, as they realized she wasn't continuing.

A rough tongue lapped at her palm. "I don't like what it says on your hand, Detective. I'm going to have to remove it."

Finer blinked. What did that mean?

A couple of hands pinned her arm down against a shaky wooden table. A different creature's arm lifted high above her, holding a gleaming, sharp steel cleaver.

Finer remembered the ceramic knife, yanked it free, and slashed the arm holding the steel.

Pandemonium broke out as she slashed and danced around the little room. A couple of Sheyds were already on the floor, inert deflated bags of silver skin. The others laughed, and ran through the door Tammy had just come in. Finer looked around, took a deep breath, and read the message on her palm. She shuddered, and hurried out the opposite door.

Lieutenant Finer stood in the bright winter light. She was still drenched in urine, and she was still freezing. She had to get moving. Police Central was too distant. Back to Saima, or home? She was about halfway between them. Too far from either to walk before freezing to death. She looked at the bowl.

Running wouldn't do. What about a wagon? She would probably be in trouble if there was another General Failure. She would definitely in trouble if she didn't quickly get somewhere warm. Hopefully the bowl she held would keep the Sheyds away.

Why did she think that? The message on her palm simply said that she had to get it to Saima. There were no good choices here. She pressed the communicator on her collar. It glowed lightly. *Wagon, stat.*

In less than a minute, a police wagon was gliding onto the bridge. She'd quickly go home, wash, get her backup weapons, and complete her new mission: to deliver the bowl to Saima. She clambered in, set the destination, and closed her eyes.

Finer lived in a forest of tall apartments. Its designers felt that the residents should feel like squirrels, happily gathering acorns for the winter. Buildings were proportioned accordingly and named after trees. Lobbies were modeled after rot holes, and could be five or fifteen stories off the ground. The 'trees' used to have branches, but after a few collapsed, killing most of their inhabitants, nobody wanted to live in them anymore. Eventually the branches were pruned off, leaving the appearance of a dead forest, waiting to burn.

Finer's apartment was on the seventeenth floor of a mock diseased elm tree. A particular nasty fungus spread by a voracious beetle had devastated real elms around the world, at the same time produced fascinating patterns on the bark. The designers mimicked the blight on the building's outer skin.

As a Police Detective, Tammy Finer was entitled to her own simulated-fungus landing shelf, saving her the trouble of waiting for elevators. She quickly showered and changed into a starched olive-green jacket over a tight red sweater, and a crisply pleated knee-length skirt. She pulled on her boots, replaced her weapons, inspected herself in the mirror and was satisfied, except for the swelling on her lip. It looked as if she had been punched. She turned up the lights and looked closer. Her lip was split, and as she ran her tongue over it, she realized it was a fresh injury. She put her hand to her jaw and felt the bruise there. How did she get hurt crossing a bridge? She didn't remember falling. Had she passed out? Finer didn't remember getting up, either.

And why had she come home smelling of urine, as if someone had emptied a bucket of it on her head? What was that ugly fruit bowl on her table?

Her fingernails were cracked. She examined her hand: "bowl to Saima" was scorched into her skin.

It was no fruit bowl. She stared at the markings on it. They looked familiar. They looked important. They must be, if someone had burned a message on her palm to make sure she delivered it. She placed the bowl on a high counter, and sat on a stool, so that her eyes were level with the text. She stared. She saw gibberish.

Detective Class L Tammy Finer, a five-year veteran of the police, took a drink of cold water, wiped her eyes with the back of her hand, sat back down on the stool, and cleared her thoughts. She closed her eyes to erase the gibberish from her mind. She couldn't, so she switched her thoughts to the place, if it was a place, where John had assaulted her. She positioned her memory of the markings on the bowl against this empty background.

"Upended, overturned, quelled are all Sheyds.... I Simon, son of Jacob, performed a sealing act by the name of me and in the merit of the names of those before me. It is buried in the threshold of the house of Balthan, it is buried by my hand, and I seal it against you - this is the seal that is intact, with which are sealed heaven and earth."

Tammy opened her eyes, surprised. She read the words again, aloud.

Amid all of Finer's confusion, there was one area of clarity: she had to follow the instructions on her hand without delay. She quickly put some ointment on her lips, put the bowl in a protective bag, her weapons in place, and ran back to the wagon.

There were four messages from Police Central. She entered her destination, pressed "go," and then "listen." The messages were all from the Chief.

The first two were general notifications: "All police are to report immediately to Police Central," and "Jackson has ordered all northern savages to be rounded up and brought to Police Central."

She didn't expect either of those. Well, she didn't expect the latter that soon.

The next one was personal. "Detective Finer, you're now the highest-ranking member of the police who is still functioning. Almost all high-ranking officers are on stress leave. You're hereby promoted to Class 'S,' Superintendent. Jackson confirmed the appointment. It means that the only action you can be reprimanded for is fraud. Other than that, you have a free hand."

"Pause."

Finer had risen rapidly in the ranks, from Constable to Detective, to Lieutenant Detective. Getting to 'Captain' was something she had dreamed about. Now she had bypassed that and gone straight to Superintendent. What happened to everyone else, to the Chief, the Captains, and the other Class L Detectives? Why weren't they functioning? Somehow, "Superintendent" was less meaningful now. Chasing dead dogs was less meaningful. Finer had a different agenda, and now she had the authority to pursue it.

"Resume."

"I have an important mission for you. Thousands of people are missing since the General Failure Alert. They may be trapped in the Central Facilities. Find them."

This would take her where she was already planning to go with Saima.

"Communicate with Chief."

"On extended stress leave," was the automated reply.

"Communicate with next in command."

"Next in command- Superintendent Tammy Finer.

The Chief had run away, unable to cope. He left her to deal with the descending chaos.

Her wagon set itself gently down in front of the Erbil's home.

Alex eyed her up and down as he opened the door. He frowned at the vehicle at the end of his walkway.

"You traveled by wagon," he accused. He motioned for her to come in.

Saima and Linda were standing in the common room, both looking a little displeased that she was back already. It implied something had happened. These days, that probably meant something bad.

"What happened at Police Central?" Saima's voice was a mixture of relief and surprise.

She placed her bag carefully on a shelf and took off her jacket. A projection of a clay fragment hovered above a table.

"I had somewhere else to go." It was Finer's turn to accuse. "Why did you distort the image like that?"

"The texts on the fragments of pottery were written in a script which we can't read," Linda said.

"They would have been legible to the people who wrote them."

"They're not here, Detective," Linda said.

"What's wrong with your face?" Saima asked.

"You don't like my face?" Tammy pouted, pretending to be insulted.

"Your lip is cracked, and your jaw is swollen. It looks like you were in a fight."

Finer gently rubbed her jaw. She remembered a foot hitting her chin...

"But of course, you're still stunningly beautiful," he said.

She licked her lips, and lightly touched his arm. "That's what I like to hear, Saima. I won't kiss you now, but I'm very tempted."

Alex jumped a couple of steps back.

"You can kiss me all you want after we figure out how to control the Sheyds," Saima said.

"Really? Then let's get started." She waved her hand towards Linda's collection. "There's how."

"We know that. It would help if we could read them."

Tammy hesitated. She spotted the box of gloves for handling the pottery fragments, put one on, and took the shard off the projection table. She sat down on the couch, looked at it for a moment, and then closed her eyes, reading silently in her mind: "Leopards are dancing on my arm... accidents, bad things, the mouth of the world... I close and double close the great tongs of creation..."

Finer opened her eyes, and read it again, this time out loud. The others stood around her, staring down.

"Let me select another one." Finer went over to the shelves, looking for something to catch her attention.

Something did: a leather ribbon, about two spans long, with a barely discernible stain and a small, decorative bronze stud.

"What's this?"

"Part of a leash, I think. Why?"

"I don't know. Why do you think it's a leash?"

"There's goat hair on it."

"What's the stain?"

"I don't know."

"Please send it to the lab right away. Have them study it, top priority." She spat into the palm of her glove, and then removed it. "Have them study this, too. Don't touch the wet part."

Saima approached her. "What's this about, Detective?"

She shuddered. Her eyes flickered with uncertainty as her poise evaporated. She walked over to the fireplace, leaned her forearm on the mantle and looked at the carpet where she had recently rolled upon the fragments, on the texts she was now reading.

"I don't know. I traveled very far today, but I can't tell you where. It was as if I was in the pathways between Spheres, but I my injured lip proves that whatever happened took place in the Abode of Life. While I was there, I took someone's life. I don't know who. I saw him, I kissed him; he died."

Alex shuddered.

"I killed a goat by spitting in its eye, and I fought a woman who gave me this." Finer gingerly touched her lip, as she tried to assemble the vapors of her memory into something coherent.

"What did—"

"Listen; I brought something important back for you, Simon." She reached for the bag, held the bowl in front of him, and started to read:

"Upended, overturned, quelled are all Sheyds, all those without merit, all rock-spirits, and Liliths, and Mekelats..."

Finer paused, and looked directly in Saima's eyes as she finished the recitation:

"I Simon, son of Jacob, performed a sealing act by the name of me and in the merit of the names of those before me. It is buried in the threshold of the house of Balthan, it is buried by my hand, and I seal it against you - this is the seal that is intact, with which are sealed heaven and earth."

"My father's name was Jako," Saima said softly.

"Simon, son of Jacob, I have an important message for you: you have to resume sealing acts." She placed the bowl in his hands.

"How?"

"That, I can't tell you. But I do know this: our life here is over if you don't."

"That's not a harmonious way of thinking," Linda said. "Jackson wouldn't approve."

"There are thousands of people missing since the General Failure Alert. I suspect they're not feeling too harmonious either."

"The wagons we saw... If not for the shard we put on your wagon, you'd be missing, too, Detective." Linda reached for the bowl. "May I?"

"Who's Jackson?" Saima asked as he rotated it in his hands, looking at all the markings. "I can't make out a word." He passed her the bowl.

"Where did you get this? It's the same material as my shards," Linda said.

"My grandmother gave it to me five thousand years ago, in the Dead Lands."

"How...?"

Finer's memory through the door of the bridge tower was shredded. A kiss, a kick, a scent lingered in her mind, but she could not assemble the scattered pieces into a coherent tale.

"I don't know. I had help, but I can't tell you more."

Linda ran her fingers along the lettering of the bowl. "Did your grandmother teach you to read this?"

Tammy squeezed her eyes tightly closed. She didn't remember who taught her. The image of the man she had kissed to death came to her. She leaned her forearm on the fireplace mantle, trying to shake the vision.

Linda handed her a small document. "Can you read this?"

Finer wiped her eyes and took the tiny parchment. She peered closely. There were just two words.

"Three days."

"And?"

"That's all: "three days.""

Linda handed her a coarse-grained pottery fragment.

Finer frowned. She looked at it, she closed her eyes, opened them. She held it at an angle, she held it sideways. "It's gibberish."

"Maybe it's a different script?" Alex said.

"No. It's as if someone who didn't know how to write imitated someone who did."

Linda rummaged through the pieces, selecting more to show Finer. There were hundreds of fragments on the shelves, and it seemed Linda was going to have her read most, if not all of them.

Alex rescued her. "Have you eaten anything since this morning?"

Tammy shook her head.

"You must be hungry. I think you've earned the kisses that Saima promised earlier. Why don't you collect them while I prepare dinner?"

"I'm starving, actually."

Alex set about preparing a quick stew and salad, piling some crackers on the side.

"Am I also going to die after kissing you?" Saima put down the parchment in his hand.

"Of course. Unless you plan on killing yourself first."

It took Saima a moment to digest this. "No, no. I mean will I die as a result of kissing you?"

"No. Why?"

"Alex is terrified of you. You said that you kissed a man and he died. It seems there's something deadly about you."

Finer grinned, despite her sore lips and jaw.

"I'm police, so you knew that anyways. You just don't know how deadly." She leaned over and gave him a quick peck on the lips. "I'll collect the rest of what you owe me later."

"I don't owe—"

"I'm actually exhausted, Saima. And I really need to eat something. Why don't you go figure out sealing acts meantime? Save the kisses."

"What?"

"I have some police business that I have to take care of."

"I have no idea what sealing acts are. Can you tell me anything else about the bowl? Where it's from, how it works?"

"Saima, I'm going to have something quick to eat, and then I want to be alone. Alex, why don't you bring Saima to his room?" She licked her lips and narrowed her eyes.

Alex flinched, grabbed Saima's arm, and started pulling.

Linda quickly put a glass of juice next to Finer's plate, and left the room.

Detective Class S Tammy Finer downed her meal alone. She pushed the plate to the side and picked up her napkin, holding it ready.

"Dim lights." She folded her arms on the table in front of her, resting her forehead on them. It was time, she decided, to weep for the things she had done, for the things she was going to do. The tears didn't come.

Saima didn't resist being led out. Was that how his ancestors left? One moment the police offering kisses, the next sending them away? There was no doubt about the threat behind her demand.

She was right, though. He had to figure out 'sealing acts.' Saima went to his room and sat down on the floor, back against the wall. "Dim lights, lock door."

What are 'sealing acts?' What was Finer up to, suddenly asserting herself? When he had first met her, she seemed easy to control, especially after he guided her back from the place between Spheres. His mind drifted to her swaying hips, her naked writhing. He stared at her breasts as she strutted across the room, growling like a leopard. She hissed at him, her tongue darting. Tammy crouched at the base of the cliff, taking aim while the dog Bella cried for protection. Her spear flew into Saima's breast.

With a start, he shook himself awake. There was light breathing beside him. Tammy was sitting on the floor watching him, her arms around her bent knees, back against the wall. It took him a moment to remember that he had been alone in what was supposedly a locked room.

"How did you get in? The door was sealed."

"I didn't become Police Superintendent because of my blue eyes."

Saima was curious. "How did you—"

"You don't need an explanation."

"I think I deserve it, though."

"'Deserve' is a hollow apology for desire."

"What are you talking about, Detective?"

Tammy sighed and turned to him. "I always thought the world was fair. I no longer believe that. I've seen the Dead Lands when they were full of life." She stood up and paced. "Saima, the Sheyds will try to destroy everything. Did you figure out what you have to do?"

"What about your Codes? I thought they provided all the answers."

"The Codes keep us from life. Saima, I'm the Police Superintendent now. I have no idea what I'm supposed to do." She rested her cheek against his shoulder.

Saima stroked her hair. "Maybe that's why the Sheyds are here: to stir you to life, by making you think for yourself."

Tammy dabbed her eyes with a tissue. "When I was in Lagash a woman attacked me the moment I appeared. If she'd have done that here she'd have been sent to a re-harmonization camp. But her attack was the most precious gift she could give me... In addition to the bowl, of course."

"Lagash?"

"In the Dead Lands."

"Why didn't you kiss her to death?"

"It's not right to kill your own grandmother." Tammy pointed to the mole on her wrist. "She had one of these, and she won our fight. The only reason she didn't kill me was that I'm a Fire Snake, which gave me an unfair advantage."

Saima's head spun. Fire Snake?

Tammy gazed into his eyes, and then sighed. She took his hand in hers, as they both listened to the stillness.

"What's a fire—"

Tammy put her wounded palm to his lips.

He examined the burn, and then kissed it lightly. "There. All better?"

"What are we going to do?" she asked, putting her hand on his thigh.

"I need to know what..." He put a fingertip in his mouth and started to gnaw. "I have to investigate the Central Facilities. It's important, going by what you said. What do you think?"

She smiled at him as she took his hand from his mouth and placed it on her leg. "I understand." She brought her lips close to his.

Saima grimaced, and then stood. "Lights on full."

Finer shaded her eyes with a hand, peeking out as her vision adjusted to the sudden brightness.

"Did I hurt your eyes? Sorry."

She stood up, ignoring Saima's proffered help. "You have an important task. I have an assignment."

"You promised to work with me."

She offered a tight smile. "If you're sure you want to, we'll leave for the Central Facilities at daybreak. Get some rest."

34 EARLY BRONZE AGE 13

The Klee-Dekel River begins its flow southward high in the Koryak Mountains. At the start it's narrow enough to jump over, but it runs strong and swift, avenging its narrow confines upon anything that enters it. The river grows quickly as it's joined by underground streams, becoming wide enough to travel by small boat. These flow from beneath the Mountain of Destruction, named for the caves with large deposits of saltpeter.

Some people argued that the mountain was unfairly labeled. Why should something used to help crops grow be considered destructive? There were fragments of old stories about saltpeter and fire, but no one could piece them into a coherent tale.

The mountain kept its name. Barrels of saltpeter were regularly transported to Lagash where farmers purchased some; more were loaded onto wagons to be transported east, south and west by road.

Taiku had convened his Council of Advisors. The population of Lagash had grown quite quickly, with most of the new population consisting of refugees and Tungus soldiers. Many more of the latter would be arriving soon, and they would have to be fed. The provisions they had brought would not last forever.

"Suggestions?"

"We could give land to refugees to clear," Jared said. "It will increase the food supply."

"It would take at least a season to get the first crops from the ground," Vlad said. "We need it sooner."

"The Marshes dry up more every day," Qimiq said. "Fish are stranded in the remaining pools of water. If we could stop spending all our time on Fire Snake poison, we would gather the trapped fish. If we don't harvest them, they'll rot where they are. Let our people have them."

Baryon rose. "The Tungus consider sun-dried fish a great delicacy. They travel to the coast from time to time, and buy large quantities, which they prepare according to their own tastes. The Marsh People could show them where to find the fish. Tell the Tungus that we're honoring them with the gift."

Taiku turned to Qimiq. "How long would it last them?"

Qimiq clenched his fists under the table. "How should I know?"

Nods signaled agreement to Baryon's proposal.

"Will the Elam sell more of their flocks, so we can feed the refugees some meat? They're working hard; they need to keep up their strength." Jared was the Councilor responsible for refugees.

"We need to keep our dairy and breeding animals. We plan to survive the war." Zaytea had married a Madai, but hadn't become one.

The Advisors one by one gave reports on their areas of jurisdiction. Taiku considered the information, asking the odd question. After hearing from them all, he put his hands on the table to rise.

Baryon rose again. "May I?"

The others sat back down, muttering.

"I've heard before about your tar seeps," Baryon said. "I hadn't realized how extensive they were, or how badly they smell."

"You're free to leave at any time, if you don't like the odor," Zaytea said.

Baryon looked at Zeruiah: "Do you have saltpeter and cardate?"

"All saltpeter comes from the Mountain of Destruction, and passes through Lagash. Some merchants offer us cardate, but I don't know if we have any in the village now. Why?"

Baryon hesitated, and then spoke softly. "Have you ever used a pomegranate to kill someone?"

Now the Councilors were silent, staring in surprise.

Zaytea snickered. "I once threw a pomegranate at a man, and it stained his clothes red. He thought he had been stabbed, so he died."

Baryon shook his head. "I'm not talking about the tree-fruit. I'm speaking of a manufactured pomegranate with metal seeds, which explode outward in a ball of fire, penetrating the flesh of anything within a few paces."

The Councilors were silent again.

"Your seeps smell bad because the tar contains lots of sulfur. When mixed with saltpeter, powdered charcoal and cardate, the combination can create a fiery explosion. Add small pieces of sharp metal to the mixture, and anyone close by will be badly cut up."

Again silence. But this time it didn't take long to turn into an uproar as all the Councilors shouted out questions, objections and accusations. Accusations that Baryon was either a fool or a liar. He assured them he was neither, explaining that he had never seen one of these exploding pomegranates, but had studied a document from the east, which described them in detail. "If Ja'ix has conquered the lands the document is from, he may already have pomegranates."

The previous uproar was a sea of tranquility compared to the reaction to this declaration. Taiku banged on the table. "We have to stop saltpeter from going east, towards the lands that Ja'ix has taken. From now on, the traders can only sell it to me."

He turned to Baryon. "Other tar seeps don't smell as bad as ours. Does that mean they won't be as good for making pomegranates?"

The discussions whirled around ingredients and design for the pomegranates. They decided that Baryon would work with Ruben and a few others to manufacture a prototype. By the end of the discussion, saltpeter was a controlled commodity; all distribution was in the hands of the state of Lagash, controlled by the Council of Advisors, which in turn was controlled by Taiku. Cardate, the catalyst for the grenades wasn't widely used, and so was much simpler to regulate.

***

Large forests of stone cedar trees grew just to the south of the Mountain of Destruction. Named for the incredible strength of the wood, stone cedar was valued for the way it held its shape, not warping as it dried. It was the favored material for construction, arrow shafts, and many other things. Originally, the trees were floated all the way downriver in large booms, but too many were lost. As the population of lumberjacks grew, they decided to mill the wood closer to home and then sell the finished beams to merchants in Lagash. It was a common sight for barges loaded high with cedar to float into Lagash to await merchants and traders. The fresh cedar gave the docks a pleasant scent till it was carted off. The sailors who traveled on the barges also smelled like fresh cedar by the time they arrived in Lagash.

It was the smell that gave them away. Tamsyn was in the Academy courtyard drilling the students. Half of them held wooden swords, the other half were defending themselves, unarmed. There were many sore arms and legs, black eyes, swollen lips. The mood was upbeat.

"We're being attacked" came Baryon's yell. Tamsyn smiled, pleased that he was finally participating in a drill. Her smile disappeared when she saw the movement behind him. She caught a whiff of cedar wood as Baryon came charging out of the building, his arms loaded with macanas, which he threw towards the students. Tamsyn ran towards him, but wasn't fast enough as the bloody point of a sword emerged from his abdomen. She spat on the attacker; he was dead before Baryon hit the ground.

Heads fell to the ground; limbs flew through the air. A few bodies were practically sliced in half. Some of the corpses had no visible injury. It was a slaughter, and it was over quickly. Highly skilled soldiers armed with long, sharp swords against students who had devoted most of their lives to texts, who had only recently started learning to fight; people armed with sticks. But those sticks embedded with obsidian were quite effective at chopping through flesh, and the students had a deadly trainer. The eight attackers had expected to slaughter defenseless scholars. They had no chance against eighty fighters.

Tamsyn knelt over Baryon. He struggled to speak, blood leaking from his mouth.

"I smelled something, and went to the window. I saw them sneaking through the trees."

"Your warning saved us. We'd have all been killed." Tamsyn glanced quickly around. "I have to look after the injured, and interrogate any surviving attackers. I wish you a peaceful journey in the Abode of the Dead."

Baryon nodded, closed his eyes, and exhaled a last time.

The students were already looking after their wounded colleagues. Tamsyn went among the injured students, binding the wounds she could, comforting those whose injuries were beyond her help.

Ner, Taiku and Simon were beside her by the time she finished. They took in the carnage, and Tamsyn's treatment of the injured.

"Fire Snake, indeed." Taiku shook his head in wonder and turned to Simon. "Dinah saved many lives today."

Simon nodded silently, and went among the students, offering praise and encouragement. Tamsyn walked with Taiku over to a prisoner, only mildly wounded.

"I may look like a human, but in truth, I'm more than that," she addressed him. "I can kill you faster than you can blink. You're going to answer questions now."

The man didn't respond.

"First: do you want to die as a man or as a eunuch?"

He started to sweat.

She took a knife from her belt and reached towards his groin. "Man, or eunuch?"

"Man," came the whispered response.

"We were going to change our last prisoner into an ox and tie him to a plow, but he made things easier for himself by cooperating. We even lent him a woman. What's your name?"

The captive started to turn his head.

Simon poked him with a sword. "What's your name?"

"Omer," he said.

"How did you get into Lagash?"

He clamped his lips closed and stared up defiantly.

Tamsyn turned to Taiku for the signal to adjust Omer's gender. He motioned instead to Ner, standing nearby. "We'll give him to Zeresh."

"Tie him up," she ordered a couple of her fighters, who quickly obeyed, and then dragged Omer away.

Tamsyn surveyed the courtyard. Eight of the enemy had snuck into Lagash and targeted the Academy. Seven students had been killed. Another handful had been severely wounded. She walked around with Taiku, inspecting corpses and sniffing the air. There were no cedar trees nearby, but there was a cedar smell. It was coming from the attackers.

"Did they hide in a cedar grove?" Taiku asked.

"No, that wouldn't leave such a strong smell. It had to be freshly cut wood."

"The docks... A barge!"

Taiku whispered some instructions to one of his soldiers, who took a sword from a dead attacker and left. "Making room for the new captive," Taiku told Tamsyn.

An inspection showed that Taiku had assumed correctly. The lumber barge tied to the dock had a hollow area in the center. What looked like a pile of beams was actually a roof, which the attackers had hidden beneath. Abner walked with him as they examined the boat and its cargo. There were tracks leading into the woods.

"I can't tell how many were on the boat. There may be more in hiding around Lagash." Abner pointed to a couple of bloodstains on one of the gunwales. "They probably killed the original crew after interrogating them about docking procedures. Judging from the fading of the bloodstains I'd say they took over the barge a couple of days ago, which would have been at the Sumer River junction. Logically, these men were sent north from Samarra, then west along the Sumer. But how would they have known how to find their way?"

"Shor answered that: maps. Ja'ix's soldiers can find their way around places they've never been to." Taiku had first thought Ja'ix's map-making to be a foolish waste of resources, unnecessary for a real soldier. Now he realized those maps were invaluable. Who made the map of Lagash? How detailed was it? Sufficient for the attackers to know where to hide, and where to find the Academy.

The Academy. All the casualties so far had been Ebers. He was doing a lousy job protecting them, as he had promised Asenath. And now he was their leader: alone, without even his Councilor, a victim of the assault.

And the pomegranates? Had Baryon progressed far enough that the others could carry on without him? He was about to send someone to fetch Ruben, but then recalled that his son was among the handful of dead students.

This was too much. He was a tough warrior when it meant scaring a few people around the village. Most of Lagash treated him with deference, the refugees adored him, and the Tungus respected his abilities. But that wasn't enough; he needed his enemies to fear him. He didn't want respect; certainly not the peoples' love. He didn't want to be toyed with.

He had to strike back.

***

Zeresh winced as the man lowered his lacrosse stick and charged into Vlad's side. You don't do that to Huitzil, even in a game. Vlad slammed into the ground, the ball coming loose. His attacker scooped it up and ran towards the goal. He didn't get far before he joined Vlad in the dirt.

The crowd was starting to pay attention. Good. Many people had argued against the Games, saying they were too concerned about the coming war. Zaytea had insisted, saying the war was the reason the Games needed to go on. They were the best antidote to panic. From the excitement of the spectators, it seemed the medicine was starting to take effect. The sweating, shirtless men on the field were certainly having an effect on many of the women.

Zeresh pined for Shor, her young, gullible, virile captive. His commander was nowhere near as entertaining. Omer couldn't control himself under the wet cloth, and had practically neutered himself yanking on the ropes that bound him. She should have tried harder to prevent Shor's execution.

Zeresh gazed at the players, at the spectators, wondering how they would do under her towel. She listened for conversations that would give her an excuse to put someone there.

The crowd roared as a defender was shoved from behind in front of his own net, giving a clear throw to the Vulture Captain. The goalie had been crouching in anticipation of a low shot; a wild stab upwards with his stick couldn't stop the ball from arcing in over his shoulder.

Arms shot up as Vultures shouted with happiness at their team's drawing first blood. Nobody could give a good reason why the Games were important, but they were doing their job: everyone was caught up with them.

It was a match of three goals: whoever scored them first, won. Games could last minutes or hours; there were no breaks. If a game dragged on too long, by the end it was much more of a pushing and shoving contest than one of speed and skill. If the other goals today came as quickly as the first one, this would be a short contest.

They didn't. Players ran, players fell, balls were thrown, shots were blocked... The excitement of the first goal faded. The enthusiasm was still there, but the spectators' attention lagged. Some leaned on trees, others chatted with people beside them. At first all the discussions were about the game, about strategy, who were the strongest players... After some time, the discussions were about grain prices, the lack of rain, would they be better off surrendering to Ja'ix?

Zeresh's ears perked up as she caught the drift of the latter conversation. What would their fate be if they surrendered, someone asked? It would mean the death of all the Clay People, but at least they would live. Would they? And what kind of life would it be? Could the Ebers be trusted not to turn them over to the enemy?

Zeresh gave a quick glance over her shoulders, to see who was talking. A refugee- one of the newcomers to Lagash, and Jonah, a Madai dockworker. Zeresh walked over to tell Ner, who was on the Vulture soccer, rather than lacrosse team.

"Get your equipment and bring it to the Meeting House," Ner said. He signaled a few soldiers, who immediately grabbed the two men.

Abner was waiting for her at the door of the Meeting House. "Jonah was on duty when a barge loaded with stone cedar wood arrived, carrying the attackers. You have to find out if Jonah deliberately let them stay concealed."

"What about the refugee he was talking to?"

"He's tied up, and under guard."

When Qimiq had first captured Shor, Zeresh had offered to interrogate him for her own amusement, to see if her water trick was effective for more than a personal squabble. It was, and now she was Lagash's chief inquisitor. She walked into the Meeting House, seeing a familiar, nervous-looking man seated on a bench.

"Hi, Jonah." Zeresh sat down opposite him with a smile. "So, you think the Games should be played without any clothes. You offered Zaytea and me the opportunity to run around naked with you. I'm honored, but my sister is married to... you know, to the Chief. He's the jealous type, and probably won't like his wife being propositioned that way. What do you think his reaction will be when he finds out?"

Indignation and fear painted Jonah's face. Everybody knew that Taiku was in the room. Nobody except Zeresh and Jonah knew that she had fabricated the story.

Zeresh lifted her hand. "I don't want anybody to hurt him. He didn't mean any harm; he was just caught up in the spirit of the game. He pictured us running around naked and told us about it."

"Why am I here? I said no such thing! I was watching the game, chatting with my friend, when suddenly soldiers surrounded us and pulled me away."

Zeresh took a couple of steps forward, and slapped Jonah across the face with all her strength. It knocked him off the chair; the ring on her finger drew blood from his lip. "How dare you," she screamed. "I just saved your life, telling the Chief not to punish you for planning to molest his wife, and you call me an idiot. Worse, you call me a liar."

Zeresh kicked at his face, but he grabbed her ankle, blocking her. Blades were instantly pressing against his flesh. Jonah let go. Zeresh kicked again; this time he didn't try to protect himself.

"When a man puts his hand on my leg, it's because he plans to move it higher. You just proved that I was right about wanting to screw my sister and me." Zeresh stepped back, enjoying the consternation of everyone in the room.

"Your deception is going to stop. I'm going to get the truth out of you, and you're going to retract your accusation that my sister and I are liars and whores."

Jonah's hand was to his face, trying to staunch the blood running from his nose. "Tie him to a bench," she ordered.

Zeresh was friendly with Jonah's wife, a small, but hardheaded woman who traded with the Elam for rare medicinal plants. Samiya gathered them in caves along the river above Lagash. They had a few young children. No one ever had any trouble with Jonah; his probably innocent conversation could cost him his life. At the very least, it would bring him a great deal of pain.

"No, that's not necessary." Zeresh stopped the men who were about to truss his genitals. She didn't want Jonah to suffer any permanent injury if he hadn't done anything wrong. She walked over to the door, opened it, and motioned for everyone to leave. Zeresh grabbed Ner's arm and shook her head as he tried to follow. She needed her recorder.

She walked over to Jonah and stared at the bloody, confused face. He wasn't protesting anymore. Sitting down, she took his hand in hers, but didn't look at him.

"Ner."

He jumped. She had kept his presence quiet at other interrogations.

"Who won the game?"

"Vultures, three to one."

"Wonderful!" She looked down at Jonah. "We have something to celebrate."

Jonah opened his mouth, but Zeresh didn't give him the chance to respond.

"Unless your being a Vulture is also a deception. Are you really a Hummingbird?" She took her hand back and put it mockingly over her heart. "Protect me from the vicious Hummingbird."

Jonah was silent.

She looked down at her victim. The blood flow from his lip and nose had slowed. She took a cup of water, and without warning, dumped it on Jonah's face. He spluttered, he coughed, his eyes opened wide.

"Jonah, I'm going to ask you some questions. From your answers, I'm going to learn how to tell when you're speaking the truth and when you're lying. I don't want you looking at me when I speak, so I'm going to cover your face with a cloth. I don't want the cloth sticking to your injuries, so I'll occasionally pour water on it, to keep it damp.

Zeresh started the interrogation with his desire to see her and her sister naked. She listened to the tone of his voice, the inflection of his words, the patterns of his breath. She queried him about his wife, his children, about his work on the docks, about not being a Vulture. All questions she knew the answers to.

She asked about the Ebers, why he wanted to sacrifice them to Ja'ix. She listened as he described their witchcraft, their greed, how they thought themselves better than everyone else. How he feared they were turning the Chief away from the interests of his own people.

"Me against my brother. My brother and I against my cousin. My cousin and I against my far cousin. The Elam against the Madai. The Elam and Madai against the Marsh People. All the people of Lagash, Madai, Elam and Marsh against the Ebers."

His recitation stopped short. Destroying the Ebers was sufficient for Jonah.

Zeresh had barely used any water. After one cup, Jonah was too eager to speak. She grew sick of his ranting, but kept listening. She asked about the refugees, and the invaders on the boat. He told her which of the refugees were Ja'ix's people; how they had contacted him, promising the attackers would only slaughter Ebers, and then flee. To Jonah, it was a proposal in which everyone came out ahead. In exchange for his help, they promised that when Ja'ix's forces finally took Lagash, Jonah's extended family would be protected. He saw the betrayal as a way of saving lives.

When Jonah finally had run out of words, Zeresh explained to him that Taiku along with Zaytea were the ones making decisions. Not a dockworker. His family would be punished, not protected.

"Your wife and children will be impaled on stakes. They won't die quickly, but will linger in pain. Their bodies will be placed in the center of town, for everyone to see the consequences of treason."

Jonah begged for mercy, he cried, he pleaded. Not for himself, but for his innocent family. Zeresh took a spoon off a table and scooped out his eyes. She used her knife to slash him on the torso, on his legs, on his arms. Deep enough that he could not recover, shallow enough that he would die slowly. She had Ner place him in a wooden chest, so he would do so alone.

"I won't do it," Ner whispered. "No one will."

"Do what?"

"Impale his family."

"Are you sick? Of course not. I just want Jonah to die thinking we will. His wife doesn't even know he's a traitor. It will hurt her to find out, and she doesn't deserve that pain. She's the best goalie on our Lacrosse team."

The little prison became the interrogation room. One by one, the refugees Jonah named were brought in for questioning. The man Zeresh had overheard with Jonah at the Lacrosse game stood up to the water interrogation, refusing to talk except for declaring his loyalty to Ja'ix. Ner peeled some flesh away from his abdomen, poured a handful of ants over his guts and chained him outside the door. The rest of the refugees were cooperative.

A few agents had been sent to stir up people against the Chief and the Ebers. They were supposed to stay a few months, and then flee. A few more refugees liked Ja'ix's message about the Master of Spirits. They had run to Lagash out of fear for their safety, but other than getting killed, liked what Ja'ix had to offer.

The rest of Jonah's group had come as genuine refugees, wanting to avoid Ja'ix's murdering hordes as well as his doctrines. But they didn't like the backbreaking work they had been given in the obsidian mines. They didn't like the engineering works they were assigned to. They wanted Lagash to take care of them, and when it didn't, they listened to the words of its enemy.

Ja'ix's agents were impaled. They were carefully lowered onto sharpened stakes, the wooden points coming out their mouths. The stakes were planted on the road at the eastern entrance to Lagash. It wouldn't take long for the bodies would be torn apart by scavengers, but Taiku counted on enough remaining that no one would misunderstand the fate of spies and traitors.

The refugees that simply liked Ja'ix's message were executed. A knife to the heart brought them what they had come to Lagash to avoid. Those who wanted to be taken care of, who complained about hard work, were given a less physically demanding task, assembling pomegranates. The cardate had to be kept carefully apart from the other ingredients, or the "granates" would explode prematurely.

The membrane separating them was hard to get right. Dried animal skins were inconsistent. A thin ceramic divider was impermeable, but fragile; a bump could shatter it, causing a premature explosion. Ruben suggested using coarse-grained clay. Reinforced by slivers of wood, they were strong, yet easy to shatter when struck by a detonation pin.

As a master craftsman, Ruben had been working with Baryon on manufacturing the weapons. After the death of the latter, after the loss of his own son, he became obsessed by the need to return death to those who had drowned his heart in it. He was an old man, not a warrior, so the 'granates became his fists. He would make them deadlier; he would make them faster. One group of workers produced the casings, another the ceramic dividers, a third the metal shards. One person measured out the tar and chemicals for each granate, and the disloyal refugees put the parts together.

The pomegranates were thus round ceramic balls, designed to explode when thrown against a target. They would also explode if dropped, manhandled, or if there was a flaw in the divider.

The unhappy refugees now had a less physically strenuous job. A terrifying, potentially lethal job, but less physically strenuous. They all agreed that they had been better off digging obsidian.

They were still better off than the animals used for testing sample 'granates. One would be thrown against a goat or lamb. The resulting injuries were studied, to determine effectiveness of the design.

Weapons that failed to explode against animals were examined for defects. If an ingredient was missing, the person who assembled it would take the place of an animal for the next test. The workers became very meticulous in assembling the ingredients.

One of them, trying to make up for his earlier shortcomings, suggested dipping the metal shards in an extract of rotted clover. This extract was usually used to control rats, causing them to bleed to death from the inside. Much to his delight, the refugee's suggestion got him moved from assembly to producing the casings.

Zaytea asked for larger 'granates to use with catapults at the river defense. Ruben and Zeruiah soon discovered that simply enlarging the original design didn't work: the large dividers were too fragile. Rather, each of the bigger 'granates was two explosive devices sealed into one large casing. Production accelerated, limited only by the supply of cardate. Most were immediately sent to the fortifications on the road to the east, and the river pass to the north. Lagash was ready, and was getting more so with every passing sunset.

35 EARLY BRONZE AGE 14

The pigeon found what it was looking for. It flew gently down, and hovered next to Zakhor. He spotted the little case attached to its leg and extended his arm, allowing it to perch. He extracted the small parchment.

"Three days." What does that mean? Zakhor pondered the question.

"Who sent you?" he asked the bird. "How did you find me?"

The pigeon took off without answering, without even a reward of food. It headed east, flying high. Zakhor watched it go, an inexplicable tightness in his stomach. He beckoned to one of his men, showing him the parchment.

"This just arrived by pigeon. I don't know what it means."

The man examined it and then grinned. "I'm three days away from here."

Zakhor eyed him, puzzled.

"The rest of our warriors arrive in three days. This is wonderful."

"I don't know..." Zakhor shook his head.

"Can you think of anything else?"

Zakhor shook his head again.

"I'll ride over to Taiku and give him the message. He'll be pleased."

The Tungus were all one. Zakhor had no authority to stop the man. "I have another message for you to deliver as well."

Taiku was at home, conferring with Jared and Vlad. A variety of stones and twigs were on the table, marking out potential military strategies.

The Chief was thrilled. He sat the messenger down at the table and gave him a beer. The man was halfway out the door when he remembered. "Zakhor says not to depend on 'three days' meaning what you want it to mean."

Vlad, Taiku and Jared sipped their beer, contemplating the possibilities. Sounds from outside penetrated the walls, but not the intense concentration of the people inside them. Zakhor's message subdued the glee the pigeon had aroused.

The mugs were dry when Taiku stood up. "We'll send a large battalion of regular soldiers up the Klee-Dekel, and then along the Sumer river. I want weapons production intensified. We'll also make a battalion of refugees, which will stay in reserve, under Jared's command. When the Tungus reinforcements arrive, we move to Mattara to lift the siege. Together, we end the scourge."

"Who stays to guard Lagash?" Vlad asked.

"The other half of the Tungus fighters, and the rest of the refugees."

"Leave Lagash in the hands of outsiders?"

"We have to trust them. We are one."

***

As the Klee-Dekel River flowed past mountains, gorges, forests of cedar and pine, the hills became gentler. There was room in the broad valleys for small hamlets and villages. Occasional docks jutted from the shore, where roads led inland to transport lumber, saltpeter, furs or metal ores.

Small boats powered by the current were guided downstream by their crews. Others, powered mostly by burly muscles, moved upstream with goods traded in exchange: grain, cloth, tools... Further downstream the Sumer River flowed into the Klee-Dekel, together forming a wide, peaceful waterway.

The valley narrowed again between the cliffs of Sipress Pass, just before the river reached the woodlands above Lagash. Steep hills forced the rough road alongside to narrow as it hugged the side of a mountain. The river itself stayed calm, with only one set of mild rapids as it made its way to the plains. Further south, in the meadows, the river curled loosely towards itself like a rope gone slack. The river was shallow at the southern part of the bend, with rocky scree on the outer shore. The Elam had suspended a rope across the water there, and crossed back and forth using a small barge tilted into the current.

It was on the rocky scree that the cargo boat finally drifted to a halt. It was loaded with crates of furs, barrels of salted trout, and other odds and ends bound for Lagash. The handful of sailors that made up its crew were unarmed, but that didn't stop whoever it was from putting arrows through all of them. The Elam shepherd had found them sprawled on the deck; the boat run aground.

Taiku rolled the blood-coated arrow in his fingers. It was a short, thick wooden bolt with a metal point. The first time he saw one of these arrows in the box Qimiq had captured, it had fascinated Taiku. Now it terrified him. Two days had passed since Zakhor had received the cryptic message. There were no signs of approaching reinforcements, despite his having sent out riders to greet them. Now there was a sign of approaching invaders. Three days. Was it a warning, rather than a promise?

The Council was grim as the bolt was passed around.

"If the attack was at the Sumer River, it could mean one or two attackers. The current is slow there, and the shooter would have had time to release multiple bolts. If it was at Sipress Pass, it would have had to be a group of men shooting simultaneously; the boat would have moved through quickly. The person who found it thinks the sailors were all killed before they realized they were under attack."

The Council members sat in silence. They had been about to take the war to the enemy, but now it had suddenly landed next to them. A servant poured beer as they listened to the wood crackling in the fireplace. The smell of burning pine wafted through the room. Taiku paced, his boot heels sounding against the loose plank floor. The alcohol wasn't easing the tension.

Taiku spun around to face Tamsyn. "You must protect the Ebers. They're always Ja'ix's primary target."

He resumed his pacing.

Simon spoke up: "We've been training, and want to do our part."

Taiku ignored him and spoke again to Tamsyn. "If you have to fight, do so, but if Ja'ix gets near, get the Ebers out of here. Take them to the Tungus' home. The students can defend the rear."

Taiku looked over at Zakhor, who nodded.

Jared spoke. "We can't sit here waiting to find out. I'll take my refugee battalion north, as we were planning. Even if it was only one man who fired those bolts, it means others will come. We should position men on either side of the place where the cargo boat ran aground. We also need more people at the docks."

"Take enough composite bows; take enough granates." Taiku looked over at Zaytea. "Are the catapults ready?"

"Some."

"Bring tar bombs," he instructed Jared. "Hold the enemy there, and let us know if it's the attack that Shor told us was coming."

"What about the road to the east?" said Vlad. "Abner and Qimiq are defending the far entrance to Edrai Pass with just a few hundred men. Shor said there was going to be a diversionary attack along the road. If he was right about one, he's probably right about the other."

"But Jai'ix is laying on a siege of Mattara," Simon said, practically pleading.

"Maybe they've abandoned that?" Vlad said.

"Or maybe they've already taken Mattara. Maybe they have so many troops that they can attack many places at the same time."

Several Councilors nodded at Jared's somber explanation. There were signs of dampness in some eyes.

Zakhor rose. "I'll guard the road at Lagash. What about the reinforcements arriving tomorrow?"

"Zaytea will stay here to coordinate. Reports should go to her. As my queen, she'll decide where they're needed." Taiku gave his wife a grin. She squeezed his arm in fear and appreciation.

"It's already late afternoon; we only have a few hours till dark. But both moons will be full, so you can travel. Organize your men; get your supplies. Do as much as you can. Zakhor, Tamsyn, be ready to evacuate the Ebers. Vlad, you're in charge of our troops at Edrai Pass."

"Where will you be, my husband?"

"The prisoner said that the main attack will come along the river, from the north. Tomorrow morning, that's where I'll go.

"I don't intend to lose Lagash," he said. "The reports we've had are that Ja'ix's troops will go after Ebers, follow and slaughter them even when it means abandoning important military targets. That could be turned to our advantage."

Taiku climbed onto the table and looked around the room. He raised his dagger above his head. "Be it a handful of invaders or an army of thousands, we will prevail. We're ready for this. Our defenses aren't complete, but they're formidable. We have trained fighters; we have lethal weapons. We will stand our ground. We will protect our home."

A cheer went up, fists and daggers rose in the air in agreement. The Council adjourned, and the Councilors stood to leave. Taiku jumped down, grabbing Tamsyn and Simon's arms.

"Here's your assignment, Tamsyn. It comes before everything else. It comes before your life, it comes before my life; it comes before any one person or any group of people. Much more than the battle for Lagash is at stake here."

Taiku pointed his dagger at Simon. "He lives. No matter what, Simon lives."

Simon opened his mouth to object.

"Silence!" Taiku shouted. "As Chief; no, as King of Lagash, as Head of the Ebers of Lagash, with the authority vested in me by Tanayt Asenath, that is my order. There shall be no disobedience, no discussion."

He glared at each of them till they acknowledged his command. Tamsyn took Simon's arm, and walked out the door.

Zaytea sat at the Council table, waiting. After all the others left, Taiku explained to her some things that Asenath had told him long ago. The world was like a seething caldron of chemicals, and the Ebers were a buffering agent. As a people, they tempered the reactions, stabilized the world. Paradoxically, the Ebers were also a catalyst, stirring the chemicals, energizing people. It was one of the paradoxes, Taiku explained, which were the essence of life.

When Zaytea responded to her husband that Asenath was more than a chemical, that she was a bringer of wisdom and light, Taiku broke down and wept on her shoulder. He didn't believe that they could prevail without his friend.

The report from the north the next morning was terrible. There was a huge force, perhaps five thousand soldiers gathering above Sipress Pass. Even with their composite bows, with their granates, tar bombs and catapults, how could Taiku and his soldiers hold off so many?

He had ordered all the Elam into town for protection. Many had complied, but some of the Clan Mothers ordered their people to flee, to scatter themselves in the woodlands. Lagash was starting to panic, though the battle had not begun.

More news came from the east road, beyond Edrai Pass. A few of Ja'ix's men had been captured, but killed themselves before they could be interrogated. They were advance scouts for something. For what?

The worst news didn't come from the north, though. Nor did it come from the east. The worst news was the report from the riders sent out to greet the Tungus reinforcements. There was no one to greet.

Taiku had committed the balance of the regular Lagash forces to Sipress Pass and was moving quickly north. A few hundred soldiers remained in town, guarding the entrances.

A command center in the midst of a war should be a busy place. Leaders shouting orders, messengers bringing information, strategists making plans... This one was calm. One woman sat at a table, pipe in hand; a mug of tea, and a piece of flatbread in front of her.

Another woman, holding a knife, leaned on the wall next to the fireplace, staring at the flames, picturing her world as the red, smoldering embers. She idly dug the knifepoint into the wood frame, carving her name. Long ago, an Eber had taught Zeresh how to read and write. She expected to be dead soon; at least let there be this memorial to her. Zeresh looked over at her sister's back, and added "Queen Zaytea."

"We should leave this place."

"I'm not abandoning my husband or my people."

"No, Zaytea, that's not what I mean. We should all leave. Lagash will be destroyed. Everyone here will die."

"We can prevail. Why should Ja'ix have our home?"

"Let him die in our place."

"You're not making sense. We're not leaving."

"Maybe we should make a trade," Zeresh suggested as she walked over to her sister's chair.

Zaytea eyed her suspiciously. "Trade with whom?"

"With Ja'ix. Give him something he wants, in exchange for the lives of Lagash."

"What can we give him? Saltpeter or cardate, so he can conquer more lands? Grain, lumber? He doesn't need us to offer it to him. Ja'ix will just take whatever he needs: supplies, women to rape, or children to be his next fighters."

"You know what I'm talking about, Zaytea. You know what he wants. We lock them in the Academy, and then the rest of us are allowed to leave while he collects his payment. "

Zaytea shoved her chair backwards as she quickly stood, the top of it slamming into Zeresh's midriff. She whirled around, slamming her right fist into her sister's jaw. As Zeresh's head snapped to the side, her hand stuck a knife under Zaytea's chin. Both women froze, panting for breath.

"You could have just said no."

Zaytea stared at her sister. She lifted her chin off the knife, slowly turned, picked her chair off the floor and sat back down at the table, her face resting in her hands, her back once again to her sister.

"I am queen of Lagash. My husband is king, and leader of the Lagash Ebers. It's my duty to protect them, not trade their lives away."

Zeresh gently put her hands on her sister's shoulders. "There are difficult choices ahead. I wish you a long reign, but will be very surprised if that wish is realized."

"Do you have any better suggestions?"

"No. That and leaving are all I can think of."

***

A fast stream running west to the Klee Dekel had cut into the soil above Sipress Pass. Zeruiah had men dig out the road, widening the rift. East of the road the terrain tilted up wildly and unevenly; roughly forested at the start, barren as it soared upwards. The rift and the terrain around it wasn't impossible to cross, but impossible to do so quickly, in large numbers.

Zeruiah built a log wall blocking the road on the south side. Archers positioned behind it could prevent anyone from approaching from the north. To the east of the wall, going up the hill, more archers took cover behind trees.

One battery of catapults was aimed at the river. Another pointed across the road, where Ja'ix posted sentinels behind a little barricade. His army was not far behind.

Taiku had finished his examination of the defenses, satisfied that Ja'ix would not get through easily. That wasn't good enough though.

He had taken about twenty men, as well as Samiya, Jonah's wife, to an area a little south of Sipress Pass, where the cliffs begin to rise from the woodlands. Samiya had spent a lot of time here gathering plants, and demanded the right to atone for her husband.

There was a small trail running right along the river's edge, leading to a series of grottos. It was rumored that the combination of caves and trails led halfway from the Pass to the Sumer River. If that was so, it meant that Taiku could surprise Ja'ix from behind. The enemy would have Taiku in front of him and at his heels. The mountain would hem him in, and his back would be to a cliff.

Taiku had never been through these grottos; Zaytea told him the rumors of their existence. They had supposedly been used many hundreds of years earlier, when the Madai first came out of the mountains.

Each of Taiku's people carried a torch treated with lime, so it would stay lit in damp caves. They walked two abreast when possible, single file when not, edging sideways with their backs to the gray-white base of the cliff where the path narrowed. Though it wasn't a far drop from the trail to the river, the waters here were deep, and the current chaotic. Taiku watched his feet at the same time that he watched the men ahead of him. Could Zeruiah widen this trail? At this rate, it could take too long to get enough soldiers through to launch an effective attack.

He studied the terrain on the other side of the river. He was a little south of the fast stream that separated his army from Ja'ix's. The entrance to the grottos should be just ahead.

A rock pan extended into the river from the cliff wall. A scattering of stubborn shrubs had managed to root themselves in a small accumulation of soil, not tall or healthy enough to conceal a round opening, the height of a man's waist. Samiya grinned nervously in response to the others' compliments. The atonement for her husband was about to begin.

Ner's task was to remember their path: what turns they took, what trails they followed, what landmarks they passed. He was to lead the attack force along the route they plotted through the grottos. He bent his legs and hunched through the opening.

It was the entrance to a tunnel. He crawled on his knees and elbows, holding the torch with one of his hands, his staff with the other. The rock floor was dry, but the air clammy. The others followed, leather gloves protecting their palms as they shuffled through pebbles, dried animal droppings and other things they didn't want to think about. The torchlight reflected off the striated grey-white walls of the tunnel; a light breeze behind them kept the air clear. They heard the quick, scrabbling footsteps of small animals fleeing their approach. They heard the breath of the people around them, and the sound of their own hearts beating.

They unfolded their limbs in a dark cavern at the end of the tunnel. The smell of the dampness was strong, but there was space to flex their cramped muscles. There were three openings to this room: the one they had come in through, an egg-shaped opening near the floor that they would have to lie on their stomachs to enter, and a V-shaped cleft a step up from the ground.

Taiku weighed the options. "Try the lower hole, but don't go far."

He motioned to a soldier carrying a coil of rope, and tied one end around Ner's ankle. "Go as far as the end of the rope and then report back."

Ner looked down at his foot, up at Taiku, and went into the hole.

No one spoke as they listened to his receding sound. Some of them coughed as the quiet air mixed with smoke from the torches.

The rope came to an end. The man holding it gave a couple of gentle tugs, signaling Ner to return. There was no resistance as the rope came back to him.

"Ner!" Taiku called down the tunnel. Silence.

This was too soon to start losing people. Taiku looked over to Samiya. Her small size gave her an advantage.

He took a leather lace from one of the soldier's boots, and tied it into a double loop, which he fastened to her belt. He knotted the rope through the loop. "Don't let go of the rope," he instructed.

Samiya looked up at Taiku. She had been warned it was hazardous when she volunteered for this. Before it was an abstract danger; now it was imminent. If she died while atoning for her husband, her children would be orphaned in perilous times.

"You'll be fine. Go."

She wiped her arm across her eyes, and climbed in. They heard her moving away, and waited. Did sending a second person through mean a second loss? Maybe this plan for a pincer attack through the caverns was a bad idea. Even if they discovered a route, could they find their way back without Ner? The man holding the rope attached to Samiya gave it a tug and it came back, again without resistance.

A sound, like a shower of small rocks. Footsteps. The tunnel Ner and Samiya had gone through was too small to take steps in. The soldier who had given up his bootlace stood beside the V-shaped cleft, his dagger ready. Another soldier pulled out a 'granate, ready to throw it in the opening. Taiku motioned to put it away; an explosion in the confined space might kill them all.

Ner stepped through, followed by Samiya. "Both openings lead to a large, high cavern. The low passage bends around and is longer. Once I got through, I saw your torchlight through the other opening."

"And?"

"It's divided in two by a wide stream. It looks deep, but it's hard to say. There's another opening on the far side of the stream."

"Can we get across?"

"There's a very flimsy, old wooden bridge. We can cross, one at a time."

Taiku smiled. A bridge meant that this had to be the route they were looking for. It meant his strategy would work. They hurried through to the next cavern.

The bridge traversed two rock tables bisected by a gorge. A double set of logs ran to a truss resting on boulders submerged under the rushing, thundering water. From there another set of logs ran to a second truss, and from there to the far side. There were no rails to hold on to for balance, and the wood was slimy from the dampness.

"Give me the rope," Samiya shouted. The roar of the waters made normal conversation impossible. She wrapped one end a few times around her wrist, stood in front of the bridge, took a deep breath, and ran across. The ancient wood wobbled, but held. At the far side she stood a moment, her chest heaving. She tied the end of the rope around a large boulder, turned to the bridge, and waited.

The man who had been holding the rope also tied his end around a rock, making a grab-rail for balance. Ner gingerly put his foot on the log, and slowly made his way across, his gloved hand sliding along the rope.

Taiku was about halfway across, the bridge groaning under his weight when he noticed what seemed to be a light under the water at the truss. His mind was trying to digest this when blue flames shot out of the water, engulfing the truss he was approaching, engulfing the logs he was trying to cross. He turned quickly to go back, but the truss he had just crossed was also on fire. How? The bridge swayed; the trusses were giving way. He grabbed the rope tightly with both hands and jumped. He didn't like abandoning his torch or getting wet, but it was better than burning, or falling into the river without a lifeline.

Why did the rope let him sink so deep into the stream? It should be tighter. As he squeezed it to his chest, he realized that one end had come loose.

The current was powerful. He needed to get to the surface to take a breath. He wrapped his arm around the rope and pulled himself towards the side where it was still attached. The other end of the rope came right to him as the current ripped him away from his soldiers, away from his friends, away from any hope of catching his breath. The current whipped him into darkness.

36 MODERN AGE 10

The grey sky, the light drizzle didn't seem to disturb the feasting wildlife outside the Central Facilities. Saima had never seen so many animals congregated in one place. There were ravens, rats, dogs and more, all busy eating. Any gaps at the serving table were occupied by a variety of insects. Occasionally some of the banquet guests would turn from the main course and dine on the creatures beside them.

When some of the hanger doors of the Central Facilities had opened in anticipation of the wagons' arrival during the General Failure Alert, swarms of bats had taken to the air, blackening the sky.

As the first wagons had approached the building, some flew straight into the swirling creatures. The people in those wagons, if any, didn't hear anything through the shells, opaque to light and sound. Most bats bounced right off, leaving no sign other than their broken carcasses beneath. When some of the wagons crashed into hangar doors that had failed to open, the impact was more notable. The Central Facilities had been designed to be impermeable. Nothing, not a mountain falling from the sky, not a piece of dust drifting in the wind could penetrate unless it was supposed to. The wagons were supposed to fly into the hangars, but the doors were expected to open first, and not all of them did.

The wagons were designed to protect their occupants against radiation, crashes into other wagons, even crashes into mountains. Few people had any concerns about high-speed travel in crowded skies. The automated safety systems, the precision navigation protected them in all circumstances.

Except in the case of a General Failure Alert. The wagon shells were made of advanced alloys that reacted to different electrical charges. The bioelectrical brain in each wagon, linked to the primary processing unit at the Central Facilities, determined exactly what was required in a given situation.

With the General Failure, only one signal was being generated: home. With no charge, with no program, the wagons had all the strength and resilience of blown glass. The people in them had no inkling of what was about to happen, as they sped towards the closed hangar doors. The failsafe system had never been tested, and it proved deficient.

Saima and Detective Finer had circled the building several times before landing. The carnage appeared horrific from the air, more so on the ground. It was uneven; most areas covered with dead humans, broken wagons and scavengers; others a thin layer of dead bats. They had quickly realized they could do nothing about the bloody limbs, heads, torsos scattered around them. The scavengers were already days into cleaning up the mess: chewing on fingers, pecking on ribs. Soon the weather would turn cold again, and the leftovers would be laminated in ice.

The broad roadway that led to the Facilities stopped at a series of huge doors, three stories high and just as wide. There were no obvious seams; no buttons, scanners or controls of any kind. The overhanging dome sheltered Saima and Finer from the rain as they stood close to the polished ceramic wall. The dampness, the smell of the exposed flesh, the squeaks and growls of the scavengers was enough though, to keep them cold and uncomfortable.

"They're automatic," Tammy said. "The doors open when needed."

Saima was testy; agitated by the carnage and something else, he didn't know what. His fingertip stayed in his mouth as he gnawed bits of skin around his nails. "Then why aren't they opening? We need to get in."

Finer was calm. "The doors don't know that."

"How do we tell them?"

She took a deep breath and yelled. "Hey door! You need to open!" She waited a few seconds, turned to Saima and shrugged. "I didn't think it would work."

"I wouldn't let you in either if you yelled at me like that. It's probably a violation of the Codes. Maybe it will understand this." Saima kicked the wall with the side of his foot. "Maybe not."

"Do you think the Central Facility is upset?" Finer tried to smile but shivered instead. "It's very sophisticated, designed to work without human intervention. I don't know anyone who's ever been inside. Did I tell you the story that it's filled with demons, who were trapped there long ago?"

This caught Saima's attention. "Demons? You said 'people'"

"People who turned into demons. Like Sheyds. It's a scary children's story."

"Detective Finer, don't you see?"

"No."

"What are the walls of the Central Facilities made of?"

"Ultra-hard Ceramic. Forget about breaking in."

"When we approached the Central Facilities from above, what did it look like?"

"A giant mushroom."

"Ignore the pedestal. What's the shape?"

"An upside-down bowl..."

"Continue," he said.

"An upside-down ceramic... pottery bowl!"

"Which is rumored to be filled with trapped..."

"Sheyds!"

Finer fingered the door seam in front of her, her mind elsewhere. She abruptly grabbed his sleeve. "We're going back to the wagon." She started walking quickly, careful not to step on any major body parts or interfere with the feasting animals.

Saima followed, taking his seat.

"Put a restraining harness on." She tossed one over to him. "How's your stomach?" she asked.

"Okay. Why?"

"You know how you were twisting and turning the pieces of pottery in order to read them? We can't do that to the Central Facilities. We're the ones who are going to twist. At low altitude, the horizon compensators don't help. Expect to be sick."

Saima quickly scanned the area immediately beside his chair, looking for something.

"If you have to vomit, just go ahead. The scrubbers will pick it up."

"Is there a Sheyd-trapping inscription on the Central Facilities?"

"That's what I want to find out."

Saima had grown up traveling perilously: flimsy boats making their ways through rough, ice-strewn seas, dog sleds riding in blinding blizzards or over thin autumn ice. It wasn't danger that made him queasy. He assumed that if Finer was planning to fly upside down, she had the skills to do so. Nor was it the shattered bodies scattered around him. Saima was accustomed to the smell of death.

Rather, he was agitated because he was afraid of confronting his expectations. When he had left the northlands for this place, it was to recover something that belonged to his people. He still didn't know what it was, but the huge ceramic bowl above him, together with the small clay bowl Tammy had brought him from five thousand years ago, convinced him that whatever he was after was in the Central Facilities. He fastened the harness.

Finer startled Saima by making the shell transparent. He was used to traveling perilously, but floating through the air in what felt like a bubble of clear ice was beyond his ability to ignore.

It had been early morning when they arrived at the Central Facilities. It was early afternoon by the time they finished inspecting the massive ceramic bowl, unable to find any inscriptions. To Saima's relief, the twisting and curling in the air hadn't turned his stomach too badly. And the scrubbers did their job when needed.

"Markings would have had to be painted on. They would eventually fade, which could explain why we wouldn't see them." Tammy frowned, concentrating. "They never mentioned any in my training."

"We have to get in," Saima said.

She set the wagon motionless in the air, disconnected the harness, and put her elbows on a panel. She rested her face between her fingers, her chin on her thumbs, fingers over her eyes, as she considered Saima's obvious, but difficult observation.

They ate lunch from the wagon's storage reserve. Saima was surprised at how good the food tasted, given that it might be hundreds of years old.

"Okay, we're going in."

Saima looked at her in surprise. "What?"

"I'll go alone if you're not coming."

"Did you figure out how to open the doors?"

"No."

"Well then, how are we going in?"

"I think we just drive at the doors, and they open."

"What if they don't?"

"Look at the ground. There's either human flesh mixed with broken wagons, or bats. I suspect that the areas without corpses are under doors that opened when they were supposed to, letting the wagons in. Those would be the missing people I'm looking for."

"And the people below would have been from wagons that crashed into doors that didn't open. You said that we wouldn't be hurt if we crash into a closed door. Tell me, what happened to them?" Saima gestured towards the carnage below.

"General Failure Alert, caused by Sheyds. We're not in Failure Alert now, so the doors should work. "Listen," she said as she re-connected her harness. "I could simply declare that I need a stress leave and the job would be given to someone else, who would also refuse. Before I met you, it's probably what I would have done. Would you rather wait outside? I can try to fly in, and if it works I'll come get you."

Saima reached for the harness on the floor beside him, and buckled himself in. "Let's go."

Finer tapped a control. Except for the view screen, the wagon quickly became opaque as they accelerated towards the huge dome. A few birds fled their nests as a hangar door quickly opened, then snapped closed behind them. Saima exhaled, not realizing he had been holding his breath. He took Tammy's hand. She frowned and let go of the controls.

"The wagon's switched to automatic. I can't turn on the lights."

The building that was impenetrable to a piece of dust or a mountain falling on it was utterly dark. Saima and Finer were pushed back into their seats as the wagon accelerated. They squeezed each other's hands. It was all they could do as they sped forward through the darkness.

"Notification: arrived."

The cabin lights rose gently, till it was bright enough to see the thin sheen of perspiration on his face. Finer wasn't looking at him, though; she was peering through the now open wagon door. He wiped his forehead with his sleeve, unbuckled his restraints, and stood. Finer put her hand firmly behind his neck and pulled him into a quick kiss. "In celebration," she said.

A sign informed them they were on platform twenty-seven, sector six. Diffuse lights illuminated the dusty landing platform, which was covered by rows upon rows of bright yellow ellipses. Most were just large enough to contain a wagon like the one they had stepped out of; some were smaller, a few larger.

"This way," Finer said.

Saima glanced at the dusty floor. Faint scuffmarks indicated a lot of people going in the direction Finer had pointed.

The platform in the Central Facilities was vast. Its light beige finish was smooth and unvarying, except for the bright yellow landing marks. It wasn't a terrain he understood.

"I don't like this." Finer pointed at the floor next to a large ellipse. Whoever had come from the wagon last parked here took much smaller steps. Saima estimated that there were maybe thirty children, accompanied by two adults.

They continued in silence. The diffuse lighting illuminated only about ten spans up from the platform, a little more than a person's height. Saima wondered what was in the darkness above.

All the tracks ended at a wall, with a series of steel gates.

Tammy walked right up to it. A paper came out of a slot; she took it, a gate slid to the side and the wall opened. She continued through and disappeared.

Saima took a paper for himself and passed through. Finer examined at his ticket.

"Table seven, bed three fifty-nine. I'm also table seven, bed four hundred. We're not too far."

"I'm not sleeping here!"

"Let's go to our table."

Saima didn't like this place. He was confined; his actions were being directed by someone, by something. The automated landing, being told where to sit, where to sleep... It was too inhuman, and his companion was taking it too calmly. How did she know those doors would open? How did she know where to go?

No. He shouldn't let himself be suspicious just because she's not panicking like him. If they were up north, stranded in a blizzard rather than a ceramic dome, he'd calmly take charge. Saima chided himself; he should be grateful that she led. This was normal for her.

Table number seven had two place settings.

Finer picked up an empty plate. "I'm not hungry, but we're supposed to have hot meals waiting for us."

They scanned the rest of the vast dining hall. All the other tables were empty.

"Maybe they ran out of food."

Tammy laughed.

"Why is that funny?"

"The Codes say there's abundant food in the Central Facilities."

"Who replenishes it?"

"What do you mean?"

"Forget the Codes. If something gets used, it has to be replaced. Eventually you run out. It's simple mathematics."

Tammy rested her chin on her palm and considered this.

"How much food is kept here, and who replenishes it?

She lifted her head. "I studied the Central Facilities when I trained to join the police. There was nothing about replenishment."

"'Activate your mind, Detective. Did you learn anything useful when you studied the Central Facilities?"

Finer slid her chair back. "I know where the storage containers are. Let's go see."

There was no food there either. From the footprints on the floor, it was clear they weren't the first to check. The containers were each the size of a small room, with sliding doors either left ajar or pulled off their tracks. The containers weren't all empty, though. When they slid one of the doors open, they found a number of corpses. A young, neatly dressed woman lay on her back, a knife in her chest. There were five savagely broken small children in a corner, one thrown on top of the other. They were all bruised, beaten around the face. Two had dried blood around their mouths; a jagged bone poked through the flesh of another's arm. A man wearing a bloodstained olive-green jumpsuit lay beside them. He was police, but had no weapons on him.

Finer paled. "They must be from the children's wagon we saw. Brady," she pointed at the man, "was trying to protect them."

She rested her forehead on Saima's shoulder, sniffling. Saima stroked her hair. "He was my training partner. He was so looking forward to his daughter's class trip to the zoo."

A terrible thought lit in her eyes. "Nancy," she shrieked. "Look for Nancy; Brady's daughter." Her voice was desperate, as she reached to separate the pile of children's bodies. "She has long, curly brown hair, and wears a headband. She's the sweetest girl you'll ever meet. Brady told me he was escorting her class on a trip to the zoo."

Her desperate eyes met Saima's. "She has to be okay."

She wasn't among the corpses. Finer bent down to inspect a pool of blood under one boy's leg. She rolled up his pants to his knee: the flesh on the back of his calf had been sliced off. She staggered to the side and wailed.

Saima sank to his knees.

Finer tried to comfort him, comfort herself. "It's horrible, but at least he didn't suffer when they did it. They must have been desperately hungry to cannibalize the dead. He's at peace now."

"No, he's not! That's just a wish of yours. How can he be at peace after being eaten alive?" Saima pointed at the dried pool of blood. "If he had been dead when they cut him up, there wouldn't be so much blood under his leg. Look how uneven the cut is. He was struggling as they did it, trying to pull his leg away. This little boy felt all of it! He won't be at peace until he's avenged."

Finer didn't bother wiping the stream of tears down the sides of her face. "Brady was too gentle. He should have gone into re-harmonization. Please, Nancy, be okay," she whispered.

There was something sticking out of the dead woman's breast pocket. Saima bent over and pulled it out. He unfolded the paper, read it, and passed it to Finer. "We have to find Eric," he said.

She read the big, block letters on the paper: "Warning: your students are disrupting the harmony of the Central Facilities with their declarations of hunger. There will be severe consequences to them and to you unless you resolve this. Officially noted- Rand Eric, Harmonizer, 2nd Degree."

Saima glared at her. "This is what your so-called harmony leads to."

Linda nodded. "Eric was probably trying to keep everybody calm." She squeezed the boy's cold, stiff hand to her cheek.

"You don't believe that, Detective."

"No... I don't."

Saima bent down and took her other hand. "Good. I wouldn't marry you if you did."

She stood as she scanned the container, the blood, the corpses, the man who could marry her... "How can we avenge them?"

Saima was a little shocked. He had just effectively asked Tammy to marry him, and she ignored it. True, it wasn't the most romantic setting. "Let's find the rest of the missing people."

They went next to the Slumber Hall. A series of parallel walls each contained hundreds of ovoid sleep tubes stacked neatly one upon the other. Movable ramps provided access. Finer explained that all the people assigned to a level would line up across the top of the ramp. It would lift them to the height of their assigned tubes, give them a few seconds to climb off, and then drop down to take the next group.

Each tube had a narrow cot, a small toilet and sink. There were no doors, because otherwise ventilation would have been too complex. Each wall of tubes was about thirty spans from the next. There were no provisions for privacy, or variation in sleep schedule.

All the beds had been used recently. Finer found the controls for the ramp, and Saima inspected them quickly. None had any toilet paper left, and some of the bed-sheets were soiled. Fortunately, the constant air movement kept the smell down.

"Where to now?"

"The Central Facilities are divided into Regions: Access, Accommodation, Storage, Physical Processes, and Computation. Visitors are allowed into Access, which is the landing hall, and Accommodation; the sleep tubes and dining area."

"We found the bodies in the Storage Region, in the food containers."

"No. Those containers are considered part of Accommodation. Come, I'll show you a plan." Finer led him to where they had entered the Slumber Hall, and examined the wall around the door. She spoke into a little baffle: "Detective Superintendent Tammy Finer. Present Security Panel."

A display lit up, showing a plan of the Facilities. Saima expected it be like the one in the Old Post, but this one showed a static image, without much detail. Finer touched a part of the panel and said "enlarge." The plan zoomed in, displaying more.

"Can it play back, like the panel at the club?"

Finer shook her head, as she enlarged the image all the way. "It's an older model."

Saima looked at the plan, seeing the walls, the ramps, even a mark where a pillow lay on the floor. The panel showed two spots next to a wall.

"Is this the design of the Central Facilities, or is it a map of it now? Look where these dots are. This must be the wall we're next to."

She nodded.

"Now watch them carefully." Saima stepped back a few spans. "What do you see?"

"No difference."

"Why didn't it change?" He approached the wall again, to look for himself.

"Go back," she told him. He stepped backwards. "Further. I want it to be clear."

"Now?"

"Security Panel off." She took a deep breath and spoke again into the baffle. "Detective Superintendent Tammy Finer. Present Security Panel." She crooked a finger at Saima.

He stared at the panel, at the one dot now behind the other. "The Security Panel shows the Central Facilities at the moment it's activated. It shows us. That means it will show other people."

She nodded.

"That means we can check the whole place while standing right here! Think of how much faster it will be."

Finer shook her head. "I don't know. Will it be as effective as walking from hall to hall, inspecting for ourselves?"

Frustration creased Saima's face. "What about changes in sound? Thousands of people, if they're here, will make a lot of noise."

"It will take just as long to listen to the entire Central Facilities as to scan for visual signs."

"Something visual can be blocked. A wall would keep us from seeing the person. But a noise, even the sound of breathing, would go around the obstacle. Maybe we can listen to the whole building at once, and then narrow down any sounds."

"The rooms might be soundproof." She turned back to the panel. "Detective Superintendent Tammy Finer. Present all sounds in building."

A low rumble came from the wall. They put their ears closer.

"Detective Superintendent Tammy Finer. Increase volume."

A louder, low rumble.

They listened to the throb of the machinery somewhere in the distance, the whisper of air being pushed through ducts, the faint trickle of water in pipes. No human voices, no human sounds.

"I don't think there's anyone here," Finer shook her head. "Where did they go?"

Saima shrugged. "Ask the Central Facilities."

She gently squeezed his arm, and then turned back to the panel. "Detective Superintendent Tammy Finer. How many people in Central Facilities?"

"Two."

"How many people in Central Facilities yesterday?"

"Establish identity."

She frowned. "Detective Superintendent Tammy Finer. How many people in Central Facilities yesterday?"

"Zero."

"Detective Superintendent Tammy Finer. How many people in Central Facilities two days ago?"

"Specify parameters."

It took a few moments for Finer to understand what it was now asking.

"Detective Superintendent Tammy Finer. How many people in Central Facilities two days ago, eighteen hundred hours?"

"Zero."

"Detective Superintendent Tammy Finer. How many people in Central Facilities two days ago, twelve hundred hours?"

"Three thousand, two hundred thirty-one."

"Detective Superintendent Tammy Finer. How many people in Central Facilities two days ago, eight hundred hours?"

"Three thousand, two hundred thirty-eight."

"Detective Superintendent Tammy Finer. Where did the three thousand, two hundred thirty-eight people go?"

"Seven in food container one hundred seven. Three thousand, two hundred thirty-one, data unavailable."

"Detective Superintendent Tammy Finer. Where did the three thousand, two hundred thirty-one people exit Central Facilities?"

"Zero people exited Central Facilities."

Saima and Finer looked at each other.

"Detective Superintendent Tammy Finer. Are the three thousand, two hundred thirty-one people currently in the Central Facilities?"

"No."

"They were here, they didn't leave, but they aren't here now. Do you understand it?"

Saima shook his head.

"Detective Superintendent Tammy Finer. Present all sounds from building, two days ago, seven hundred hours."

A jumble of voices poured out of the wall. There was crying, yelling.

"Detective Superintendent Tammy Finer. Present all sounds from building, two days ago, ten hundred hours."

The same jumble of voices, this time with an overlay of fear.

"Detective Superintendent Tammy Finer. Present all sounds from building, two days ago, sixteen hundred hours."

Silence.

Finer pondered her next question.

"Detective Superintendent Tammy Finer. Where was the presence of the three thousand, two hundred thirty-one people last noted?"

"Storage Region, Section four, Level three."

"Detective Superintendent Tammy Finer. Show on Security Plan."

A series of cross sections lit up on the panel. One area was highlighted.

"Detective Superintendent Tammy Finer. Show access route."

"Hazard restriction; access denied."

Finer looked up at Saima.

"Ask for the route the others took, and we'll follow it. We've spent enough time talking to a wall."

"Wait." She turned back to the Panel. "Detective Superintendent Tammy Finer. Are there any Sheyds or Demons in the Central Facilities?"

"Query not understood."

"I hope that means no," she said to Saima.

"Detective Superintendent Tammy Finer. Highlight route to Storage section four, level three, taken by the three thousand, two hundred thirty-one people."

The panel showed a circuitous path, going through the upper reaches of the dome, then down a few levels, past a series of sealed portals. Saima and Finer were soon kneeling at a portal that had been cut open. There were burn marks around the edge of the frame.

"They used Brady's cutter." Finer showed him a black enamel instrument from her belt. "With patience, this can go through anything."

"Could they have cut their way out of the building? Maybe that way, the Central Facilities wouldn't have known."

"Let's find out."

37 MODERN AGE 11

It took them about an hour down steep, narrow stairs to get to Storage Level three, Section four. As expected, nobody was there. What they didn't expect was that it was far from the outer perimeter of the building. No one had left by cutting a hole in the wall.

There was another thing they hadn't anticipated. Section four was virtually empty. It was a huge room, the walls thicker than elsewhere. But the only things there were a few empty metal bins against a slate blue metal wall, and multiple footprints leading to six identical devices, each about two spans high, four spans wide and twenty spans in length. On top of each was a scuffed and frayed gray rubber mat. The far end of each of the devices had a series of luminous, dark blue ovoid hoops, tall enough for a person to pass through. Saima shivered as he walked around, inspecting. There were no footprints where people would have stepped off.

"Hey! It moves!" Finer climbed onto one, and the gray conveyor belt started carrying her towards the hoops.

"Get off," Saima screamed. He ran, and yanked her to the ground.

Saima pointed to the footprints. "These devices are how they left the building."

She sat herself up, rubbing the back of her head. "Well, shouldn't we follow them?"

"Where?"

"Wherever they are."

"If they'd used these devices and been able to return home, they would have done so. We wouldn't be investigating their disappearance." He reached out his hand and helped her up.

Finer walked slowly around the device, surveying the floor, eyeing the hoops. She opened her utility bag, dug out a small pad, and lobbed it the length of the device. It passed straight through the hoops, falling to the floor behind. She turned to Saima, who shrugged, and picked it up.

She went back into her bag. She took out a small black metal box, from which she withdrew a compact, glass-domed machine, about the size of her hand. Finer flicked a switch, placed the device on the conveyor belt, and stepped back. She then unclipped a miniature display panel from her belt. Saima nodded as he recognized the image: the room they were in, as viewed by the device.

"This will show us where they went. It has a broadcast range of two days' travel by wagon. The signal can go through anything."

Finer examined the conveyor belt, looking for a control to get it moving. She finally climbed on, and it started to roll forward. She jumped off when the belt had enough momentum to carry her little device through the hoops. It disappeared.

They looked at the blank screen, waiting.

There was no image, no sound. The panel wasn't receiving any signal.

"I'm glad you didn't go through the hoops, Detective."

"Maybe the display lost the signal, and it's sitting outside the Central Facilities."

"Two days travel... signal can go through anything..."

Tammy took a breath and wiped the sweat from her forehead. "The specifications are quite clear. The signal cannot be blocked."

Saima walked over to the wall and banged at it. He went to the doorway to section four and examined the thick cross section of wall. He peered at the ceiling and stomped on the floor.

"I'm not certain, but this part of the Central Facilities seems to be reinforced, compared to other areas."

"Why?"

"The only thing I can think of is that these devices are dangerous."

"If the wrong people use them?"

He didn't answer. His mind seemed somewhere else.

"Saima...?"

"I don't think so. The walls are very thick, but there's no extra security measures to keep people out. The devices must be dangerous. Maybe they're unstable... explosive. Think of all the power that's needed to transport people, or even that little device of yours."

Saima ran his fingers over the hoops, very careful not to let his fingers go inside them. He went from device to device, stroking, almost fondling the hoops. He breathed loudly, his chest rising and falling like a child who had just skinned his knee, and was trying to hold back his tears.

Finer walked over to the metal bins, examining them. There was a carefully printed sign in one: "DEPOSIT ALL PERSONAL BELONGINGS IN BIN PRIOR TO PASSAGE."

There was a faded but readable handwritten addition underneath it: "LIGHTERS PERMITTED." Curious. Why lighters? Tammy picked up the sign and walked over to Saima. He read it and stopped breathing.

At least that's how it looked to Finer. She put her hand to his cheek, and quickly pulled it away. His skin was cold and clammy; his breathing was quick and shallow. She took his wrist, feeling for his pulse; it felt feeble. She looked in his eyes for some assurance that he was alright. She recoiled at the huge, black pupils.

Saima was in shock. He had already been upset about something when she had shown him the sign. It pushed him over the edge.

Finer had to deal with his condition quickly; there was no way to call for help. She measured her thrust carefully as she smashed her fist into the side of his face. She grabbed him by the shoulders as he fell, alternately shaking and kissing him.

His eyes lost their faraway look. He peered into hers.

"Are you trying to kill me or make love to me?" Saima licked the blood trickling out of the corner of his mouth.

"If I wanted to kill you, I wouldn't use my fist." She caressed his cheek. "This isn't the place to make love."

He winced.

Tammy sat him down on the edge of one of the devices. "Explain."

He sighed. "When the Ebers were exiled across the Edge of the World they had to leave everything behind, except their lighters. These awful machines are what sent us."

Tammy reached a hand behind his neck, and leaned forward, gently bringing his head to her shoulder. She wrapped her arms around him as he wept.

He didn't cry for long.

"The thousands of people who were in this room a couple of days ago are now dead or dying, unless my people found them quickly. This is a treacherous season. Travel is difficult; game is scarce. And even if it wasn't scarce, the missing people don't know how to turn animals into food. If I could get word home, I could have them rescued."

Finer walked back to the bins and put back the signs. "What do you think?"

"The people scattered on the ground outside are better off than the ones who got into the Central Facilities."

"How could anything be worse?"

Saima flinched, and grabbed Tammy's shoulder for support. "No. They're all dead, your friend Nancy included."

"How—"

Saima pointed to his communicator. "I've seen these before, at our village. There's a collection of them in the Dance House by the escarpment. They're as old as the grain parchments, from when we were first exiled."

"Did your people bring their communicators?"

"I don't think there were any back then."

Saima walked over and put his hand on a hoop. "Not only did the people you've been looking for get sent to the same place as my ancestors, these things sent them back in time. I didn't recognize the communicators earlier, because a connection wasn't in the realm of possibility. Now it's a certainty."

Misery painted Tammy's face.

"It's not necessarily bad. Nancy might have arrived in the northlands, lived a long life and died of old age. For all I know, she's my great-great-grandmother. If the device sent the people to the same place it sent the Ebers, then there may have been help. There are the remains of a forest, and streams with lots of fish. It's a good place to hunt bears."

She made a sour face. "What about Eric?"

"He probably died the same as the others, suffering no special punishment. There's nothing we can do."

"I'll send a note through the device, instructing whoever finds it to make sure he's killed."

"Why would anyone do what it says?"

"I'm a Police Superintendent. It would be a violation of harmony not to listen. When I speak, people obey."

Saima shook his head. "These people are probably starving, definitely freezing. They're not going to care about harmony."

Finer sighed. She walked slowly around the devices, running her fingers over them. "Our society was built on good will, on peacefulness. You're tearing it apart, Saima, laying waste to the world. I understood what was going on before. I knew what I was supposed to do. Now it's chaos."

"I didn't destroy anything. I've simply pulled the plugs from your nostrils, so you can smell the rot."

Tammy grabbed one of the hoops with her hand, and gasped. Saima ran over as she folded forward, trembling. He was by her side in seconds, but she was already pulling herself back up, taking short, noisy breaths. She was covered in sweat.

"My stomach suddenly felt as if it was being ripped apart from the inside. I'm okay now." She took a long breath. "Let's send the note. We can't finish the job of dealing with Eric, but we can start."

Finer pulled Eric's paper from her bag, and wrote carefully, below Eric's note: "Rand Eric is extremely dangerous, and must be killed. By order of Police Superintendent Detective Tammy Finer."

She handed it to Saima, who added: "Eric is dangerous. Kill him. Saima, son of Jako, Leopard clan." He put it in the box that had contained

Finer's little device. Saima took out his knife, a beautiful turquoise-hafted weapon. He put it on top of the note and put the cover on.

Finer removed the lid and pulled out the knife. She turned it over in her hand, running her fingers over the handle. She took out the note from the box, and, placing the knife's business edge perpendicular to the page, cut off Eric's warning about the children.

"You're sending away your beautiful weapon?"

"It will be returned to me when we go home."

She tilted her head just a little to the side, smiled, and put the knife and note back in the box. "It was already returned to you."

"It's not mine anyways. It belongs to my Games League Alliance, Hummingbird." He paused. "How's your stomach?"

"I'm also Hummingbird. My stomach's okay. What do you mean 'when we go home'?"

"Are you going to come home with me?"

She wagged a finger in front of his face. "Even to the Dead Lands. Wherever you go, I go; wherever you live, I live. Your people are my people." She took his hands in hers. "Nothing but death can separate me and you. Besides which, I think the Ebers could use a Fire Snake."

Finer released his hand, closed the box, and put it on the conveyor belt. She took Saima's hand again as she stepped onto the machine to send the box on its mission. She held it as she fell off, doubled over in pain.

Before he could do anything to comfort her, she was already straightening out, gasping for breath.

"We have to find out what's wrong with you."

"I'm okay." She held on to his shoulder as she pulled herself upright. Her hand was on her stomach.

"That's twice. Something's wrong, and we have to find out what's wrong."

Her eyes opened wide. "I know what it is. We have to get to the bridge right away." She started to run, stumbling at first, but then catching herself. It was all Saima could do to keep up. He was running too hard to ask any questions.

She touched the button on her collar. "Wagon, stat." She raced up stairs, through corridors, pulling Saima along with her. As they passed through the gate into the Access Region, they saw the wagon flying towards them; Finer squeezed his hand in assurance. It hovered as Saima and Finer leapt in. The door sealed itself as it took off through the dark corridors.

"Opinaca River Bridge, blue tower, stat." The wagon became completely opaque as they were shoved back in their seats.

"The stomach pain was a message from a friend. I didn't understand it the first time. He needs my help. You wait here."

"Where are you going?"

The wagon touched down on the bridge, and the door slid quickly aside.

"Five thousand years ago. I'll be back in a few minutes." Finer was through the hatch before Saima could open his seat restraints; through the tower door before he climbed through the hatch.

She ran into the tower, out the other door, grabbed Aua's arm, and jumped off the bridge.

"Taiku ordered Tamsyn to get Simon away safely. She needs your help" was all he had time to explain.

She emerged in front of a horse paddock next to a road. From the position of the sun, it looked to be late afternoon. Behind her people were frantically climbing onto horses. Armed men in beige coveralls and gauze shirts were helping up frightened old men, children, women with babies... As each person mounted, they took off at a gallop, holding desperately to the reins. These people didn't look to be experienced riders, but whatever they were running from was more terrifying than a galloping horse.

Finer ran towards her grandmother, who was fighting a grey-shirted man holding what looked like a flat, wooden sword. She smiled as she saw the twin knives in her grandmother's hands. The man had no chance as he backed away. Finer screamed, and ran to intercept one of the men in beige charging her grandmother's back. She made it just on time, slicing off the man's arm. The taste of blood warmed her, and she raised her sword to finish off the grey-shirted man now on the ground in front of her.

"Tammy, no!" The voice came from behind, not from the woman she just saved. "Don't kill Simon; protect him."

Finer looked at his violet eyes and recoiled. The woman lunged at Simon, her knife piercing the ground to his side as he rolled over quickly. She hurriedly removed it, and turned to defend against another sword coming at her back.

"Anahita, my twin, fighting for Ja'ix," Tamsyn explained as she attacked her sister.

"Tamsyn, my twin, with the witches," answered the woman.

Another fighter came charging at the person Finer now believed to be Tamsyn. She turned to defend herself, but this gave Anahita an opening. Before she could use it Finer spat in her face. Anahita stopped, started to wipe her eye, then fell to the ground as Tamsyn broke the other attacker's neck.

"We have to get Simon out of here," Tamsyn yelled.

Tammy reached out her hand and yanked Simon up, smiling. "Sorry for the misunderstanding. I'm going to marry you in five thousand years, and give you the daughter you want." He looked surprised but didn't say anything.

More attackers were coming. A flat metal hoop, about a span in diameter, its edge razor sharp, headed straight for Simon's head; Finer knocked it out of the air with her sword. She turned to see a group of archers gathering, aiming at them. She wouldn't be able to cut down all their arrows.

Finer tried to understand what was going on. The Ebers wanted to get on horses and flee. The armed men in the beige coveralls were helping them do that. Another group of defenders, wearing leather vests, were engaging the attackers in battle. They were in defensive positions, trying to give the Ebers more time. From Anahita's words, Ja'ix's people considered the Ebers to be witches.

Foolishness. If they were witches, they would use their craft to defend themselves. Maybe it was time for Detective Tammy Finer to use some of the witchcraft she had received when she was promoted to Class 'L.' She hadn't yet received her Superintendent level magic.

A sharp metal hoop took off the head of a boy helping an Eber child onto a horse behind his mother. An attacker swung his sword as the mother pulled her son on. There was another child next to them on the ground, waiting to be lifted onto the horse. Finer quickly pulled out her gun, didn't bother to check the settings, and shot. A silent flash of brown light pulsed from the end of the barrel, and the attacker's head exploded in a rain of gore. The mother reached down, yanked her second child up by the arm, and took off.

Strong setting, but she dialed it down, so the capacitor could recharge more quickly.

Another woman kicked the flanks of the horse she had just mounted, her two children clutching her tightly, an infant strapped to her back. The horse started to run when a hoop sliced off half its leg. The riders pitched forward as the animal fell. A hoop flew in, separating the mother's head from her body as a pair of arrows brought down her children. Finer picked up the hoop that she had knocked out of the air and sent it back to the man who had thrown it, slicing his chest open.

More hoops, more arrows were coming in. Lots of them, from the same direction. Tamsyn was off to the side, fighting. Tammy grabbed Simon and pulled him close, one arm squeezing his shoulders. The other arm touched a control on her belt, and then wrapped around the small of his back. She twisted to the side so that her body was between the approaching missiles and Simon. Simon shivered as he saw death about to strike; flinched as it fell to the ground just in front of them.

"Did my mother teach you that?"

"Who's your mother?"

"Asenath."

"I haven't met her yet, but I will." She smiled at the frightened face in front of her.

Simon was too scared to ask. Finer touched her belt again, and released him.

More attackers were coming from the east. A group of seven archers on a hillock targeted the Ebers who had successfully gotten onto horses. Their long bows were astonishingly powerful. They were too successful for Finer's liking.

"Tamsyn! I'm going to take them out," she pointed. "Get him on a horse, now." She shoved Simon towards her.

Finer was too far. At that distance, she'd have to have to set the gun to full power. There wasn't much cover, so she'd have little protection while the capacitor re-charged. If she'd had the Superintendent level shield it would have protected her while she moved.

The archers hadn't noticed her. She ran towards an outcrop of rocks, and ducked behind as she spotted her next cover: a short, thick olive tree in full flower. Finer braced herself to sprint, putting her hands on a boulder to push herself off.

Her right foot was stuck. No, not stuck, but held down. Finer peered, and pulled at her leg. Her boot was immersed to her ankle in warm, black goop. Tar, from the smell of it. She used both arms to free herself, and wiped the bottom of her boot on the grass next to the dark puddle. She scanned the ground, spotting several more of the little seeps. She had to watch where she stepped.

She ran, and crouched behind the olive tree, enjoying the sweetness of the flowers. There was no more cover between her and the archers, and she was still too far to blast all their heads off. Could she disable them quickly enough to safely get closer? She could go for their eyes, one per person. But she would have to aim too precisely, and that took time. The technology she had with her now depended on capacitors that needed to recharge. Longbows and arrows were faster.

She squeezed off seven low-power shots and ran towards the archers.

Five of them dropped their bows, grabbing at their injuries. They all looked angry, as they tried to understand what had hit them, and from where. One pointed to Finer, shouting. Another man, who still had his bow to hand aimed and released. She adjusted her gun as she ran. The arrow came on, but was heading a few spans off to the side. She pulled the trigger, and blood spurted from the neck of the man who fired. Another arrow came towards her as she timed the recharge and fired. The arrow landed just short; had she been a little closer, it would have taken her out of the fight. A man bending down for his bow continued all the way down.

She ran forward towards a hail of arrows, firing again. At the last instant, she saw the arrow coming straight at her chest. She tried to twist out of the way but was too late to avoid it. She felt the arrowhead splitting her flesh as it made its way inside her. She stumbled, got off another shot and fell to the ground, rolling to her side. Her last thought before she lost awareness was that now the enemy would take her weapon and kill her grandmother, her future husband, and the rest of the Ebers.

The sudden cramp in her stomach told her she was still alive; thank you, Aua. The ground was strangely warm; a few scattered curls of smoke rose in the air around the battlefield. Tammy Finer had no strength to move, no strength to bend over in pain. That was good, she realized; the three archers running towards her would be careless, thinking she's dead.

Two of them had put aside their bows and drawn knives; not careless enough. Finer carefully checked the gun lying in her hand, her finger barely on the trigger.

The lead man raised his knife as he approached. She tilted her hand and fired at the one behind. His thigh exploded as he fell over with a scream. The man over her was already bending down to stab her, when he turned to look at his partner. Finer spat, hitting his face. He turned back, his eyes gaping at her, and then fell over. This time Tammy's weakness worked against her. His knife was still locked in his hand as he fell, the blade penetrating her thigh. Once again, she felt her flesh part.

"Die, witch!" It was the last archer, and he was behind her. She couldn't do anything, except what he had told her to. She took a last breath of air, the sweet scent of wild flowers filling her lungs. The roughness of the soil tickled her fingertips. A curl of smoke began to rise from a small ant-hill near her arm. Her eyes were filled with the green of the grasses in which she lay. Her ears were filled with the sound of something whistling through air, towards her neck. It was followed by a grunt; not hers. Something hit her back and bounced off.

Beautiful violet eyes peered into hers. "A few little injuries aren't getting you out of your promise. I'll be waiting for you in five thousand years." Simon was holding his strange wooden blade.

A tongue was on her thigh. Tamsyn rolled her onto her back, licked her leg again, and then cut open her sweater where the arrow was embedded. The something that had bounced off her back, the last archer's head, stared at Finer.

"It's barbed," Tamsyn said. "I'll break off the shaft. Take it out when you get home." She dabbed saliva all around it to stop the bleeding. "Don't delay."

"We've got to get out of here." Simon pulled Tammy to a sitting position, and pointed to the road, packed with Ja'ix's troops. They overflowed the sides, filling the surrounding hills and fields. A woman was walking at their head.

"Zeresh." Tamsyn spat at the ground.

"Who is she?"

"Elam. The Chief trusted her, but now she's with the enemy."

"Their prisoner?"

"A prisoner doesn't walk at the head of the troops. She betrayed us."

Finer grabbed Tamsyn's sleeve. "I'll deal with her. Help me up."

Most of the Ebers were gone from the paddock, having left either by death or on horseback.

"We have to get away now," Simon said.

Tamsyn pulled Finer to her feet. "Come with us."

"No. There are some things I have to do in five thousand years. First, I'll buy you time. Go now."

Tamsyn touched her arm affectionately.

Simon kissed Tammy hard but quick, on the cheek. "I'll get the rest of that later. Make sure you're there for me," he said as he climbed onto a horse that Tamsyn had waiting.

Finer turned back towards the battle. She pulled out the grenade from her utility belt, adjusting it to its strongest intensity. She set the targeting scanner to a few paces behind Zeresh and clicked 'engage.' The little device flew from her hand, hovered over its prey, and ignited. Zeresh and hundreds of soldiers around her collapsed to the ground, their bones shattered into crumbs. The troops continued forward, oblivious to the misery of their comrades.

Finer's injured leg could barely support her weight. The arrow in her chest throbbed, but she put it out of her mind. She had made a couple of conflicting promises. How could she buy them time without getting killed? And how could she marry Simon in five thousand years if she did get killed? She activated her shield to have a chance to regain some strength. The arrows, the hoops kept raining in on her, but her foes quickly turned to targets where they had a better chance of causing harm.

A series of catapults at the edge of the paddock were lobbing ceramic bombs towards Ja'ix's soldiers. They caused tremendous carnage where they exploded, taking down maybe ten or fifteen soldiers at a time. The shrieks of anguish were beautiful music to Finer. She turned off the shield and hobbled towards the catapults. A couple of Ja'ix's soldiers, ahead of the rest, charged her. She shot them before they could point their weapons.

Her progress towards the catapults was slow. She fell a couple of times, and had a difficult time getting up. She was too far from Ja'ix's archers to be targeted accurately. One arrow glanced off the ankle on her wounded leg, but it didn't make her slower than she already was.

The ground under her feet was moving more quickly. Finer realized that someone, no, two leather-vested men were dragging her to the line of catapults. She stood before a fierce-looking man with penetrating deep, blue eyes. He took her weight from the others and motioned them away.

He squeezed her in a tender hug. "My wife told me about you, grand-daughter. You saved her, and you saved Simon. You must go home now."

"No." She pushed Vlad's arm away. "I have to give them more time."

"We're doing that, with the granates."

"Do you have enough?"

"Not really. We're hoping to ignite the seeps. You just killed Mustafa, their General. Do you have any more of those weapons?"

"I only had one grenade." Finer raised her eyebrows, remembering the wisps of smoke, the air curdled with the smell of tar and fear. "Ignite the seeps?"

"The tar seeps. I see you stepped in one." He pointed at her foot. "If we can get a few burning, that will slow them down more."

"Is that what's in the granates?"

Vlad nodded.

Finer tried to concentrate. It wasn't so much the pain, but the lethargy that was creeping over her. She tried a focusing exercise from her training, staring at the explosions from the granates, seeing nothing but the flames rising in the gathering darkness. There was something in them, though, besides fire. Tammy thought of Linda's students dying a slow, tortuous death. She thought of Aua saying she decided to kill the Dead Lands. Finer shut down her other senses and stared, as awareness formed in her mind. She understood.

"How many seeps are there? How far apart are they?"

"It's all one actually; a huge underground lake of tar. Most seeps are connected to it. Ja'ix's soldiers are on a large one. Their feet are probably full of tar."

Police Detective Superintendent Tammy Finer knew what she had to do. It wasn't something she had been trained in, but it was within her authority to act. Brady had explained the technique to her, how the shield and gun, working in tandem, could be rigged to cause a feedback reaction. If she was right about what was in those flames, it would be more than a tight fission explosion. She made the decision Aua had told her about.

"I need to sit. I need a large empty granate shell and twine. I need five minutes."

Vlad nodded, and sent someone to get what she needed. He led her over to a tree stump.

"I am going to destroy the enemy. Once you launch this, I'm going home. You have to run away as fast as you can. What kills them will kill you too."

"What if it doesn't work?" another soldier asked.

She looked up at Vlad. "It worked, grandfather. I just don't know if you live through it."

Some of Ja'ix's soldiers had broken through the lines, gotten past the granates. Hand to hand combat, long sword against short sword, was coming closer. Some of his cavalry charged into the Academy students who had refused the order to abandon their posts. Macanas took off horses' legs, took off attackers' heads. But with each swing of the macana, more obsidian was dislodged from its edge, till soon the students were swinging wooden sticks at fully armed soldiers.

Finer tied the gun and shield together. She activated the latter to the diameter of the granate and set the gun to overload. She had about three minutes till the capacitor was fully charged. She engaged the auto-fire.

"Aim for that bubble of tar. Everything depends on this granate being there in three minutes." She adjusted the timing, dropped the weapons into the granate, took the twine, and tied it shut. She handed it to Vlad as she stood up.

"Goodbye, grandfather. I am pleased to see you, and will be pleased if you leave in health."

She was going to restore harmony to these lands by obliterating them. Finer hobbled off yelling 'AUA' and disappeared. She disappeared before she could witness her special granate launched towards the seeps, before she could see the metal crossbow bolt strike it in mid-air, shattering the ceramic case before bouncing off the shield. The gun and shield generator flew apart, falling separately to the ground about fifty spans from the seeps where they were aimed.

Saima was barely in his seat when he felt a rumbling in his stomach. Was it a signal from Finer's friend? He darted through the hatch and ran towards the tower door. He yanked at the padlock; it fell apart in his hand. He swung the door open and ran inside. Tammy was on the ground, being kicked by silver-skinned creatures with huge bird-like feet. She looked seriously hurt, not moving in response to their blows.

"Upended, overturned, quelled are all Sheyds, all those without merit, all rock-spirits, and Liliths, and Mekelats, and idols and goddesses, and barren ones, and pregnant ones..."

The Sheyds snarled and shrank back as he spoke. Saima didn't stop to wonder, or even finish. He scooped Finer up in his arms and ran back out the door, kicking it shut behind him.

He laid her carefully on the wagon floor. Fresh blood was dripping from a gash in her thigh. It looked like it had already dried and crusted over once, and been re-opened by the Sheyds. A broken arrow was embedded in her chest; Saima couldn't tell how deeply it was lodged. It looked also like she had been stabbed in her ankle. Finer's pallor contrasted harshly with the bright blood that was leaking out of her.

Saima dug into her bag, looking for something to use. Her knife was sharp, and looked clean. He rummaged in the cabinets under the wagon's view screen, pulling out a dark bottle marked 'disinfectant.' Next to it were envelopes of different sizes. From the illustrations on them, he understood that they were for covering injuries. He poured some of the liquid over the gash in her thigh, over the cut on her ankle, bandaging them as best he could.

Now the arrow. He tried to pull it out, but there was too much resistance. He had to cut it out of her.

He dripped water into her mouth. She coughed softly. A good sign. He gave her a little more.

He cut through her jacket, then sliced off a large section of her sweater. He poured liquid from the dark bottle onto the knife to clean it, and then poured it over her flesh around the broken arrow. With his left hand, he pulled lightly on the shaft; with his right, he cut into her. Finer flinched as the blade opened her flesh. He had been worried that she would thrash around, but she didn't. Weakness, or astonishing self-control?

He poured the cleaning liquid over his fingers, making sure that it got under his nails. He gently poked his finger into her flesh, feeling for the barbs, and pushing the meat off them. The arrowhead slipped out. He spread the wound open with his fingers and poured in more of the cleaning fluid. He jiggled the skin around the wound to make sure it penetrated, sat back on his heels, and gasped for breath.

Not for long. The arrow wound wasn't deep, but with all the shoving, poking and jiggling, the blood was a torrent. Saima pinched her flesh between his thumb and index finger, arranged himself into a comfortable position beside her, and tried to imagine what had happened to Tammy in the minute or so they had been apart.

It was still bleeding too fast. Saima was patient but concerned. He dripped more water in her mouth. She was breathing more regularly now, as if deep in sleep. He remembered when his cousin had been mauled by a bear. His uncle had stuffed all the injuries with ground-up lichen, stopping the bleeding. His cousin slept for a few days and then died; his body too weak to mend itself.

Tammy's injuries weren't as bad. Maybe if he could get some food into her... But he didn't dare let go of her wound. He looked around. The blood on her thigh was mostly dry. His eyes went to the jacket he had cut off her, the starched collar, the communicator button...

With a start, he reached up for his own collar. *Linda or Alex, please respond*, he begged. Why hadn't he thought of this earlier?

"Congratulations!" It was Alex.

"What do you mean?"

"You've used your communicator. You were always too fussy about allowing it to touch your mind. Congratulations: you're linked to us now, through the Central Facilities."

This wasn't the time to discuss technology or personal dignity. Saima briefly explained his predicament to Alex, who instructed him how to get the wagon back home. It was quite simple, actually: just tell it where you want to go. Within minutes, the wagon was setting down in front of Linda and Alex's. They were standing outside, with a table on casters.

"We have to lift her very evenly to get her on to the table. I'll support her back. Alex, you take her feet. Linda, you take over pinching. Are your hands clean?"

Tammy moaned.

Linda gave him a dirty look. She pulled a container from her pocket, ripped it open, and pulled out a bizarre looking plastic device with metal jaws, about the width of a hand.

"Pinch the sides of the cut to raise the flesh," Linda said. "Then we'll all carry her together."

"Hold me," Tammy moaned.

"Do it," Linda ordered.

He pinched the flesh. The jaws on the little device spread apart, Linda flicked a little lever and the metal jaws locked onto Finer, holding the wound closed. There was a slight odor of burning meat.

"Let's get her inside."

Tammy's mouth opened slightly. Saima bent towards her.

"The kisses you owe me, my future husband."

38 EARLY BRONZE AGE 15

The sight of salmon swimming upstream to spawn is wondrous indeed. The fish thrash against the current, throw themselves in the air, crash against rocks; all to make it home to give birth to the next generation. By the time they reach their destination, they're bruised, beaten, and ready to die.

Had anybody been watching, the human crashing into rocks, head mostly under water, would not have been as wondrous a sight. It was fortunate for him that the waters poked his head into the air once in a while, as they whipped him downstream. Darkness had overtaken Taiku, so any breaths were purely reflex. It would have been a horrific sight for a sympathetic spectator, but this was an underground stream, racing through dark caverns. There was no one to see it.

His eyes were raw, his stomach hurt. His chest felt as if someone was jumping on it. His right shoulder was on fire. He had leaped into the water to escape, so how could his shoulder be on fire? Then again, how did flames come from the rushing water in the first place? Taiku heard breathing, a person grunting with effort. Someone was indeed jumping; no, pressing rhythmically on his chest.

Taiku coughed.

"Good, good. Cough it out."

A woman's voice... Samiya?

He coughed some more, and then threw up the part of the river that had been inside him.

"He's going to be okay," the woman said.

"Who is he?" a man asked.

"Taiku," she said.

"The Chief?"

"That's who you have now."

"How very fortunate."

In the part of his mind that was slowly becoming aware of his surroundings, Taiku wasn't pleased. He dimly understood that a person who didn't recognize him wasn't from Lagash. That the person considered himself fortunate to 'have' Taiku implied that he wasn't a friend.

"It's amazing that his head wasn't split open," the woman said.

"Amazing for us. Not so good for him."

Taiku coughed again, a deep racking cough, which shook his whole body. His legs twitched as his lungs tried to clean themselves. He rolled onto his side as more river poured from his mouth.

Taiku rubbed his eyes with his knuckles as he lifted his eyelids. There were grey-brown rocks above him, but this place was too bright, the light too diffuse to be part of the grottos. He looked to the side. It was a shallow cave with a wide opening, and a stream running between large, flat rocks. The stream he had been swept under, apparently. There were two people inside: the man that had him, and a woman. Not Samiya; too tall. What happened to Ner and Samiya?

"Okay, Chief; you've had your rest. Time to go," the man said.

Taiku rolled onto his other side. He couldn't feel any of his weapons pressing against his leg.

"We were going to leave you naked, but Abijah was too distracted. We put a breechcloth and sandals on you. No weapons. Now get up."

Taiku's vision was returning. He focused on the woman's face. It was familiar, as was her name.

A kick to the side of his neck jolted his gaze. "Get up."

Taiku lifted his head and back off the flat rock, trying desperately to make sense of what was happening. One thing was evident to his still-clouded mind: he had not been rescued by a friend.

He sidled towards the rushing waters. He would throw himself on the mercy of the stream, hoping to land in a better place, such as the Abode of the Dead.

No. There was a rope around his ankle, tied to something. Taiku wasn't going anywhere on his own. He reached over to the water, dipped a hand in, and washed himself off, as if that had been his intent.

His captor had one of those impossibly long swords that Taiku had heard about. According to the refugees, it was as solid as any short sword. Taiku noticed that the toe end thickened slightly before coming to a point. That extra weight made it a slashing, as well as stabbing weapon. It could probably take off his head with a single blow. A thick, pointed bronze pommel meant both ends were threats. Taiku stood up as the man glared at him.

"Follow me," Abijah instructed as she led him out, pausing to unhook the other end of the rope from a post. She wrapped it around her wrist.

"Remember," the man told her. "You lose the arm holding the rope if you lose the man at the other end."

"I'm the guide, Aydan. You're the soldier. Getting him to Mustafa is your responsibility.

Aydan, Aydan... No, he hadn't heard the name. Abijah? His wife could probably identify her. Mustafa? That was the name of a General the refugees had mentioned. He couldn't recall any details; he vaguely remembered the trepidation it evoked.

Taiku recognized the scent of the Klee-Dekel. He stuck fingers in his ears to clear out the water, and recognized the sounds of Sipress Pass. He looked up to see a rock ledge overhead, hiding the flat area they stood on from anyone above. The occasional debris falling past them from above meant there were people there; soldiers... His?

His lungs were still sore from almost drowning, so when he weakly yelled "look below" as loud as he could, Aydan walked over to the edge, and peered at the river a few feet beneath them, thinking that Taiku was talking to him.

"What did you want me to see?"

"Your burial place," Taiku said, "along with all your soldiers."

Aydan leaned his arm against a boulder. "No, I don't think so."

"These are our mountains, trees and trails. This place is the beginning of your end."

"That's not what I was talking about. I don't think the water here is deep enough to hold the twenty thousand soldiers we have with us. Ja'ix is going along the coastal road with our main force."

Taiku tried to keep himself from flinching. Twenty thousand? And that's the secondary force? He struggled not to gag. This information was painful, much more than his time in the water.

"And another thing," Aydan said. "You know the terrain above the river. Thanks to Abijah, we know the trees and trails above, the caves and pathways below. She's been working with our mapmaker, and we have it all charted out. The cliffs here are honeycombed. Maybe Mustafa will show you our chart when you meet him. You're no threat."

"I'll tell you what a threat is." Abijah gave an angry tug on his rope.

Taiku looked at her again, knowing they'd met before.

"It's when someone says they're going to destroy your life and your reputation unless you give them all your possessions and abandon your home. A threat is someone who tortures your father and then falsely accuses him of molesting children and animals.

"We had large flocks, beautiful grazing lands, we had happiness. Till my so-called 'friend' Zeresh stole everything we had and drove us out of our home. Tell me Taiku, how is my friend?"

Taiku stammered, struggling for the appropriate words. "She's well," he finally said.

"When we take over Lagash, I am going to make Zeresh suffer for what she did. I'm going to make her family suffer for what she did to mine. My father was never the same afterwards."

Taiku tried to conceal his panic. *When we take over Lagash...?* What did that mean? "I remember you now, Abijah. Your father used to trade with my grandfather, Muuad. They were friends. He wondered why your family disappeared."

Abijah tugged at his ankle again, and led him into a rock cleft. Aydan and another couple of soldiers followed. They had to slither sideways, backs to the wall along the narrow passageway. The light from outside was blocked by the soldiers behind them; nobody carried a torch. The gash on Taiku's shoulder was smoldering, igniting in pain every time he brushed the wall. He didn't bother looking where he was going any more. He just followed the pull of the rope.

"The ground gets uneven here. Watch your footing," she said.

Taiku sensed that they were moving uphill. There was a faint, yellow light ahead.

He was relieved to be able to move forward by putting one foot in front of the other. Taiku was stunned to walk into a huge underground chamber, long stalactites decorating the ceiling. Torches, looking like they were permanently attached, decorated the walls. He hurried to keep up as Abijah led him through an opening on the other side of the room. The corridor it led to was wide enough for three people at a time, tall enough for a horse and rider. This was not a just-discovered path.

"Watch where you put your feet."

Taiku looked down, and managed to just avoid the horse droppings. His panic rose as he wondered how many people had gone through this tunnel. Where was it taking him?

The trail went generally uphill. He had no idea of direction because of the way it twisted and turned. Everywhere, there were torches affixed to the walls. Occasionally he saw a cleft off to the side, with riders waiting for his procession to pass. Occasional shallow streams afforded the opportunity to rinse his feet from the manure he inevitably stepped in.

Taiku was tired and thirsty; it was a long walk. His shoulder was burning; his head was pounding, and he was still coughing up water. He wasn't looking forward to arriving to wherever they were going. He knew it would only be more painful there.

***

Although surrounded by hot plains and deserts, Lagash was pleasant most of the year. In winter, enough moisture came in off the sea to provide rain. The snow that accumulated in the higher elevations watered the rivers throughout the summer, as cool winds blew down from the mountains.

In recent days though, the breezes had stopped. A haze, a heat hung over the coastal lands from the edge of the desert in the west, to east of Edrai Pass. The cool mountain air refused to descend. The haze obscured the sun, not allowing it to witness the events below.

Simon was furious. He wanted to scream, he wanted to kick, he especially wanted to kill, but he could do none of these. Taiku had assigned Tamsyn the task of keeping Simon alive, acting within the authority accorded by his mother. For Simon to object to Tamsyn's keeping him from the fight would be disrespectful to Asenath. Tamsyn knew how great the temptation was, so as a kindness she didn't give him the opportunity, keeping him away until the squad of Academy students went to join the other fighters at Edrai pass.

The former were equipped with macanas, the latter with poison darts, javelins and granates. There was a high ledge over the Pass, from which Qimiq and his troops planned to rain death onto those funneled into the narrow canyon. The Ebers were to stand at the western end to cut the legs off horses, and the heads off any people who made it through.

All Simon could do was listen to Tamsyn and Zaytea organizing, giving orders. He wanted to go after the enemy, but his assignment was to live. Fighting others could get him killed, and that would be shirking his responsibility.

"I want to do my share, Tamsyn."

"Much of the work of war is behind the lines. We'll do our part."

There was a lot to do. A line of refugees handed out weapons to the mounted fighters, led by Vlad. First javelins, which they strapped to one side of their horses, followed by a padded sac with small granates, carefully fastened to the other side. The Tungus riders were given the powerful, but hard-to-draw composite bows. Some soldiers carried long spears; all had swords in case they ended up in hand-to-hand combat.

Refugee women carefully loaded tall, rectangular wood-leather shields onto the wagons. The infantry that would carry the shields had left on foot for the pass in the middle of the night, expecting their equipment to catch up.

***

When Abner and Qimiq had set up the interim defenses east of Edrai Pass days earlier, it was not with the expectation of an imminent war. They had used granates to blast away parts of the road, and then piled rocks in front of the sections that remained intact. Just west of the barrier, they dammed an icy mountain creek, diverting it onto the road. It caused just enough flooding to hide randomly dug potholes. There was no room for a troop of soldiers to charge, but space enough for a single wagon to maneuver through. Any travelers, any merchandise that came through would be interrogated, examined, and if harmless, allowed to pass.

Qimiq had been in fights before: he'd mutilated animals, burnt a few houses... Tricking the Far Marsh people with poison berries had been an unprecedented escalation; violence at a level never experienced before. When he arrived at Edrai Pass to set up the defenses, that was the scale of warfare he contemplated.

When the first panicked travelers from the west showed up at his barrier, they told him of a huge army on their heels. Qimiq comforted them, that they'd be safe behind his fortification. Some of them laughed at this joke. More of them cried. "You're all dead," they advised him. Qimiq chuckled, trying to cover his growing sense of panic.

By the time Ja'ix's army arrived, Qimiq had managed to calm himself enough to focus on what he had to do. As he pulled back west of the barrier, he wondered how many of his people would die before reinforcements came. True, his archers were picking off the attackers coming slowly through, but the same obstacles that slowed the enemy also provided them cover. They were shooting back with the nasty metal-tipped wooden bolts, which were more powerful than anything his fighters had. Qimiq surmised that whatever was used to launch them took a long time to reload, because his fighters could get off quite a few arrows for every bolt the enemy sent in return. A handful of people were, for now, holding back Ja'ix's hordes.

Qimiq's casualties were light: two of his cousins, five Madai. They were all his people now, including the Dry-landers. He recited the ancient mantra to himself: "...The Marsh people against the Dry-landers. The Marsh people and Dry-landers against the Elam. Our horizon against the far side of the horizon. Our world against the next..."

No one could remember it ever going beyond the level of the Marsh People against the Dry-landers. What would follow? Fighting another world?

The late afternoon arrival of reinforcements did little to ease Qimiq's taut nerves. He was focused but frightened as he and Vlad deployed everyone, gave them their orders. After that, all he could do was listen, watch, and dread. Every unexpected sound, every unfamiliar voice made him flinch.

The sun was going down. On a clear night, with both moons in the sky, there would easily be enough light to spot enemy soldiers trying to slip through the barriers. This night the yellow moon was in its place, a thin crescent in the western sky, but the red moon was nowhere to be seen. The dusk had instead painted the air with a blood red haze, which might provide enough camouflage for Ja'ix's army to simply walk past. Vlad had assigned soldiers to picket duty, but if they couldn't see, how would it help? Pinpointing a stealthy foe through sound was not something you wanted to rely on. Extra archers were stationed behind outcrops of rocks, to keep watch on the barriers through the night.

The after-effects of the carnage of battle had arrived beforehand, in anticipation. The smell of freshly slaughtered meat hung over the soldiers, as if they were camped between the ribs of a huge, festering beast. Flies and mosquitoes filled the air, a moveable feast for countless blue-black dragonflies. Vultures and ravens waited on branches in hungry anticipation; a banquet greater than insects was coming.

Abner startled awake on the moonless dawn to the sound of pebbles hitting the boulder in front of him: three pebbles, a pause, then another three. He had expected this signal from the lookout, but wasn't happy it had come. It meant Ja'ix's men were making their way up the rocky slope to the south of the pass, between the road and the sea. There was a crest line about fifty spans below them. Abner's unit had the job of keeping the enemy from passing it. The Lagash archers shifted their weapons to protect them as they made their way to their position.

The cover fire was successful. Abner led his fighters onto the southern slope, untouched by enemy arrows. They scrambled to their places above the crest line and lay silently on the bare rock. The plan was to wait until the heads of the enemy became visible as they clambered up, and then chop through the ropes holding logs they had prepared. The timing had to be just right: if they were released while the enemy was too low, the angle of the slope could send the logs flying over the attackers' heads.

The whispers of an incoming rain of arrows from below broke the silence, followed by the screams of injured soldiers. It was a blind rain, sent by archers who could not see their targets, but guessed at the location. The high overhead shots had arced down and penetrated a few limbs and a couple of torsos. Abner's squad had three men for each of his fifteen logs, plus some extra. Only two were needed for each. The Lagash fighters pulled in their arms and legs to present a smaller target.

Another volley caught a few more of them. They still had enough men for the task, but how many volleys could they take? If they sat passively through another downpour of arrows, there might not be enough people to send their logs flying down the slope.

Abner whispered to a man near him, who crawled forward to a lonely tree protruding sideways from the rock face. He stood slowly, and holding onto a low branch for support, leaned out to peer over the edge. An arrow hit his shoulder as he stared. Startled, he let go of his support and tumbled downwards. Abner and the others listened to his body crashing towards their foe. They chilled at the sound of the cheer below them as he landed. They listened to the screams of their fallen comrade.

Abner knew the man. He was not physically large, but he was quietly tough. He wouldn't cry out like that unless he had a reason.

"Aim for the screams," Abner ordered the men. He pointed his arrow skyward, hoping that it would arc and land in the right place. He was not accustomed to aiming at targets he couldn't see.

"Now!"

They all released their arrows, which rained down towards the screams of their fallen friend, who had used his last breath to mark the location of the enemy.

"Remember his courage, and avenge him," was the sum of his eulogy.

The next upwards volley was weaker, not striking anyone. Abner motioned his men to hold their fire. They sat hunched up, their axes and bows ready, offering as little of themselves as possible to anything that might come down from the sky.

It came from below, this time. Not arrows, but small hands, followed by foreheads and furtive eyes. A line of them, climbing the dark slope.

"They're children!"

The faces coming over the rise were small and smooth-skinned. They looked to be mostly just about the age of puberty, and they looked terrified. They each had a knife in one hand. The soldiers turned to Abner.

"Fire at will."

They had been warned about this by the refugees; how Ja'ix put children on the front lines, using the moment's hesitation of his foes to his advantage. Abner didn't waver, as one by one his men picked off the little enemies coming up the slope.

Abner estimated that his archers killed over a hundred children before they stopped. He wondered if he should tell his men not to feel guilt over slaughtering them, but to feel hatred instead for the ones who sent them to die.

But Abner was not a talkative person. He signaled everyone to remain in place, waiting for more deadly rain, or more climbers. The men were nervous. They'd lost friends; they'd killed children. What would be next?

The sun was considerably higher into the sky, burning into the haze, beating down upon the rocks where the soldiers watched, tense, ready to attack, ready to duck. The air shimmered from the rising heat; the men shivered in anticipation. Abner forbade any movement, never mind any conversation, as they lay in wait.

The sound of falling rocks pierced the tension like an arrow. Whatever was next, it was climbing up. More hands, followed by faces with furtive eyes. Abner stared. It wasn't children this time, it was grown men. He swung his arm in a chopping motion, and within seconds, ropes were cut apart, and entire trees trimmed of branches went crashing down the slope onto the climbers. There were curses, there were screams, there was dust rising in the air from below, then there was silence. They waited, but there was only silence.

Abner took a drink from his water bladder, signaled his men to resume their positions. He scanned the area, concern on his face. His men were exchanging smiles. The plan had worked, the flanking attack pushed back. There was an itch at the back of Abner's mind: a couple of the climbing faces he glimpsed looked familiar. None of the adult climbers seemed to be carrying weapons.

The reports from all fronts were good; their preparations were holding. Obstacles had been placed inside Edrai Pass and to the east. Compound granates had blasted away parts of the road, with rocks piled in front of the small sections that remained intact. The few trees that had managed to grow on the barren rock above the pass were tumbled down as additional obstacles. Now that the battle was upon them, there was no need to leave the road passable. The Marsh People were in position on the ledge above the Pass; the Eber students were stationed at its western end. A deep line of infantry closed the east entrance.

Ja'ix's troops were busy as well. The icy creek that had been flooding the road now ran elsewhere, no longer camouflaging potholes. A group of women, girls maybe, went out with buckets of rocks to fill them in. They had no shields, no weapons to protect them from Lagash arrows. They had no clothes on either; a message to Lagash that they were prisoners, stripped of everything.

Vlad signaled the archers with the composite bows. He wanted each arrow to be precise, a kill shot. He didn't want these women to suffer. He lifted his arm, and they all went down.

Another group of naked women came out from Vlad's lines, grabbing the buckets from the first, and running to the holes. They managed to get a few rocks into potholes before they died, and another group was sent out.

Vlad told his archers not to shoot the women when they were near corpses. If bodies piled up, they would provide protective cover.

This couldn't go on. His arrows should be used against the enemy. Ja'ix's supply of naked road-workers was endless, as if he had all the women of Mattara with him. Vlad shuddered, realizing it probably wasn't *as if*. If Ja'ix was using captive women this way, it confirmed that the entire population of Lagash was in danger, not just the Ebers. He had to move the battle forward.

He signaled, and the Lagash archers disappeared behind the infantry, allowing the women to complete their tasks. Vlad hoped that Ja'ix's soldiers would pull the corpses of the earlier road-workers out of the way, but that was not to be. As the last girl ran back to Ja'ix's position, a double line of wood and leather chariots came racing out, trampling her. Each chariot was drawn by two horses and ridden by a driver, with a second man carrying a bow. The horses were draped in leather covers, which, Vlad realized, would protect them from the Marsh poison if they made it into the Pass.

The Lagash soldiers appeared confused by the approaching chariots. They looked at each other, picking up spears, drawing swords, and then putting them away. They shouted, they gestured at each other. There were even a few shoves exchanged. One side of their line moved tentatively forward as if to counter-attack, and then stopped, seeing others staying put.

Some of the Lagash fighters pointed fearfully at the oncoming onslaught. Perhaps they had noticed the whirling knives protruding from the chariots' wheels, and were hoping to avoid having their legs chopped up.

Ja'ix's soldiers were professionals. Most of Vlad's troops were an amateur militia. It seemed apparent that soon Jaix's chariots would be decorated with Lagash body parts. The horsemen cracked their whips in the air, urging their animals forward while their archers readied their first barrage.

The volley from the amateur militia came too abruptly, and at too short a range to be avoided. The charioteers' armor was ineffective against the power of the Lagash composite bows. The milling, frightened soldiers at the front line had actually been cover for skilled archers. The feigned confusion had ensured their targets would come close enough to ensure that each arrow loosed was a kill.

The chariots didn't stop for so trifling a thing as the death of their riders; many lifeless hands still held tightly to reins. The surviving archers on the chariots loosed their arrows, but it was a much weaker attack, and it was at a line of men who were suddenly holding full, body-sized shields in front of them. The surviving horsemen didn't have time to know how many of their colleagues had just died, so they continued forward, aiming for gaps in the line.

The gaps disappeared as the chariots came near, and the galloping horses found themselves facing a solid, angled wall. The animals didn't know that it was a wall of simple wood and leather they could destroy by racing forward. To them it was an impenetrable barrier. The horses ignored the demands of their riders and veered sharply to the left, throwing many of the remaining charioteers off, where they were trampled by the animals behind them. As the horses were forced onto the rock shoulder at the south edge of the entrance to the Pass, Abner's men picked off the startled riders one by one. The chariots lost their momentum, and other Lagash soldiers quieted the surviving horses. The harnesses were disconnected, the vehicles thrown over the side, and the animals brought behind the Lagash lines. Another successful skirmish, with barely any casualties.

"How many horses?" Most of Vlad's men weren't skilled riders, but each horse they gained would be one less for the enemy, and the Tungus could put them to good use.

"At least a hundred. A few were injured as they came up the shoulder, so we sent them over the edge." Abner's expression darkened as he spoke. "There were screams from below as the chariots were thrown over."

This meant there were more soldiers trying to flank them. It meant Abner had to get back to his position above the crest line of the southern slope. "You've done well. Hold your position above the ridge, and we'll deliver you more trash to throw at the enemy below."

Abner clasped Vlad's forearms. "The ravens will have a magnificent feast."

A noise rose from the soldiers behind them. Vlad turned to see a storm cloud of bolts crash into the center of his infantry line, going through his men's shields as if they were leaves, opening a wide hole. Two streams of chariots raced towards his men, one on either side of the road.

The two streams came together, punching their way into the Pass through the breach in his line. One set of their archers looked to the left, another to the right. They pulled their bowstrings as one; they released their arrows as one, clearing a way through. Deadly darts poured down off the ledge in response, bouncing off the leather blankets on horses, bouncing off metal helmets on soldiers' heads. A few found their mark, but not enough to slow the procession. Javelins targeted the horses, but once thrown, they were spent.

Arrow positioned, bowstring pulled back, arrow released... It was a well-rehearsed dance, perfectly synchronized. Jaix's attack angled forward.

The Marsh People near the western end of the Pass had more than poison darts with them. They heard the approaching chaos and picked up granates. A few men carefully lifted compound granates, and with their eyes said goodbye to their friends. A little beyond them, the Eber students gripped their macanas. They had spent most of their lives bent over books, struggling with ideas. Now they crouched, ready to struggle with those who would take their lives.

The yells were coming closer: screams of rage, war cries from the attackers. There were also screams of terror from the few whose horses were felled by obstacles, men who were suddenly thrown under the relentless stream of their own knife-hubbed chariots.

The rain of arrows prefaced the chariots' arrival by a few seconds. It was just the right delay to force the Marsh defenders into a crouch, out of position when the chariots were in range of their darts. Ja'ix's forces expected resistance, and weren't slowed down by casualties.

Qimiq stood up. "Now!" he shouted.

Bits of horseflesh, bits of human flesh rose into the air like a fountain. Harness poles, leather sheathing, hub knives and wheels blasted outwards in every direction. Every chariot hit by a granate had been stopped. The ones hit by the compound granates had been obliterated. The few horses that had made it all the way through had their legs mutilated by macanas.

There were holes in the road from the explosions. There was debris from wagons, from limbs and torsos of soldiers, pieces of horses. No more chariots could pass, yet there was still a thundering coming from the east. Cavalry riders picked their way over the carnage, holding their reins with one hand, brandishing long swords in the other.

These riders and their mounts didn't have the same armor as the chariots, and many fell to Fire Snake poison. Others were simply knocked down by Taiku's soldiers wielding javelins as staffs. Some horses were maimed by javelins wielded as javelins, the riders losing their balance and dying beneath those weapons, or more often under their own horse's frightened hooves.

Qimiq sat on the ledge above the road, an arrow jutting through the center of his chest, wondering about the missing red moon, and thinking of his dead son. He watched riders as they were cut down by darts or granates, but was too weak to be concerned about the ones getting through.

The Ebers at the far end of Edrai Pass swung their macanas at the horses coming at them. Metal weapons, though, are much more effective at killing than wood embedded with stone. Those Ebers who came at a rider's sword-hand side died quickly. Those who were fortunate enough to come at the other side were mostly able to dismount the rider and then fight sword-to-stick. A few riders were injured enough by their falls that the students could finish them off and take their swords. Those swords were useful, because the macanas were useless after being used a few times.

For every ten cavalry riders that charged into the Pass, one or two made it out the other end. For every two that made it out the other end, at least one student died. Forty students were stationed at the Pass, the rest were kept in reserve. Ja'ix's cavalry had thousands of men and horses.

Another shower of arrows from below descended on Abner's position. His men returned fire, guessing where their enemy might be. Swarms of arrows were soon raining in both directions, like two competing thunderstorms. Abner had the help of gravity; his enemy-- quantity.

It was a drenching rain. Abner's position was soaked with the blood of his soldiers. They must have weakened their enemy, but the storm of arrows kept up its onslaught. One of the storms petered out, and shortly afterwards hands, followed by heads with furtive eyes moved up towards the crest line. Once they saw that their opponents had been taken out, they signaled below, and a swarm moved up past the crest line, no longer furtive. They charged into the side of Vlad's infantry, from a position where he thought he was protected.

Vlad turned his forces to defend against this unexpected assault. Seeing this, Ja'ix's main force started up the road towards the entrance to the Pass.

39 EARLY BRONZE AGE 16

The night was dark and dank, filled with mosquitoes and black flies. A sliver of yellow moon hung over the treetops, casting weak shadows below.

Stars were missing. Usually they covered the sky, a huge bright net whose nodes formed a shifting mural of constellations. Tonight the mural was torn, the net ragged, the stars gathered into seven clusters; intense, like mountains blazing in the sky. Balthan wondered if it was the brightness of the seven concealing the rest of the stars. Or could the burning mountains have actually swallowed the others?

It wasn't the missing stars or the seven fiery mountains that made the sky so fascinating that night. All the travelers, both captives and Cannibal Society soldiers gazed upwards at ten columns of white fire and smoke slowly pushing something dark, something ominous ahead of them. They were pushing southward through the heavens, making their way down. Down towards Lagash, Balthan surmised.

But not even the fiery columns held Balthan's attention. What puzzled him were his captors. Not the soldiers, but the Sheyds. They were panicking. Over what, he didn't know. Something to do with the strange sky, he assumed.

Some of them tried to hide inside people, darting into the throat of anyone who sneezed. But all it took was a little cough, and the Sheyd would be expelled, sent running for some other form of shelter.

Other Sheyds sprayed fire over themselves, as if that would protect them from whatever had made them so frantic. A few went around touching people, giving them such violent diarrhea that they collapsed.

This caused some panic among the humans, who couldn't see the frenzied creatures. Except for Balthan, all they saw was green dust swirling and twisting around, as if moved by a windstorm. But the air was still.

Mekelat ran up to Balthan, his eyes filled with tears, his hands trembling. He took a deep breath through clenched teeth as he grabbed Balthan's sleeves. "This isn't over. You still belong to us. We'll be the prison for everyone here."

Balthan didn't understand. Mekelat was thinning rapidly. Not becoming leaner, but more insubstantial. With every breath, the air he took in replaced the flesh, such as it was, of his body. The Sheyd pulled back an arm, and punched Balthan in the mouth. It was a solid blow, cracking Balthan's lip, breaking a couple of teeth. Mekelat turned and ran as Balthan spat blood.

***

Taiku stood before Mustafa in the shade of a canvas canopy. The General was tall and thin, with bright blond hair, a round face and gentle eyes. He grinned and raised his hands, palms turned to the side. Taiku was confused by the gesture of submission.

"I'm honored that you accepted the invitation to visit us. We're happy to offer our hospitality."

Taiku didn't know what to say.

"Abijah was invited to return to Lagash. She offered to take us along. When we were finally ready, we sent a message to get your attention. Everything is right on schedule."

Taiku remembered the faces of the dead sailors who had been bringing furs and fish down to Lagash. They hadn't expected to carry messages on their boat, especially not at that price.

"Aydan will show you around our camp. After that, we'll have a discussion." Mustafa turned to Abijah, as she passed the rope holding Taiku's ankle to Aydan. He wrapped it around his wrist.

"You've done well, Abijah. I thought many soldiers would die before I could have this discussion with Taiku. But you've delivered him into my hands. You'll have a rich revenge on Zeresh, as promised."

Mustafa nodded to Aydan, who tugged at the rope.

The camp was huge. Taiku marveled at the number of tents arranged on the steep hillside. He felt a grudging respect for Mustafa, but his admiration was tempered by dread, as he saw what he was up against, and why Mustafa wanted him to tour the camp.

Taiku staggered, and had to lean against a tree when he recognized a particular rocky slope. Aydan walked up close to him and peered into his eyes.

"Now you understand." Aydan's arms were crossed over his chest, a nasty grin on his face.

Taiku did understand. He was south of his troop's position. To his army's north was Ja'ix's army, commanded by Mustafa. To its west were cliffs, with the Klee-Dekel River below. To the south was more of Ja'ix's army, and to the east was virtually impassable terrain. If Taiku's soldiers could flee before Mustafa moved into position to block the road... No, there was no way to get word to them.

"We've built a rough road that makes it easy for us to move quickly into place, cutting off your troops." It was as if Aydan had read Taiku's mind. Then again, his thoughts upon realizing his men were surrounded were predictable.

The tug on his ankle told him to walk. They were circling back towards Mustafa's tent, giving Taiku a wider view of what he was facing, giving him a deeper sense of the futility of resistance. Had it been hopeless all along? Were all the months of preparation like a children's game? He had been playing at being a warrior, compared to what Mustafa, under Ja'ix, had accomplished. What about all the refugees who had pledged their allegiance to him, expecting he would redeem their suffering?

It was like Asenath all over again. She had trusted him, and he failed her. He caused her rape; he caused her death. He even caused her daughter's death by demanding the creation of Fire Snakes. Everything he tried to fix, he made worse. Why couldn't he understand the problems he was creating? Why did everything he did go so wrong?

Aydan tugged on the rope. "Time for you and Mustafa to make some arrangements."

They passed an armory as they walked back, where men with grindstones sharpened swords, attached metal points to wooden bolts.

They passed storehouses, corrals for animals, repair shops... It was a small city, devoted entirely to bringing death to his people.

Samiya sat on the ground at Mustafa's feet. Her clothes were torn and wet; there was a bloody gash on the top of her head, which leaked down over her forehead. She did nothing to wipe the blood away. She looked up at Taiku with numb eyes as he approached. Her mouth remained closed; her hands remained fixed on the ground beside her.

"Ah, you're back. I trust you found your tour enlightening." Mustafa rose cheerfully, grasping Taiku's arms, and giving them a friendly shake. "You're pleased no doubt to see that we rescued your friend. Unfortunately, the man with her didn't make it. His head was smashed against the rocks by the current."

Ner.

"Samiya is going help prepare for our discussion. I've explained how to her, and though she's not eager, she'll help us avoid disagreements. She's going to clarify an important issue. Don't interfere. It won't help."

Mustafa stepped back, and one of his soldiers bent down to Samiya's hand. He pulled at a dark spot with his fingers until it came up: the head of a long, thin metal spike, which had fastened her hand to the ground. The soldier repeated the action on her other hand. Tossing the spikes to the side, he put his arms under hers, and hauled Samiya up.

Blood was dripping from her hands; blood was dripping from her head. Taiku moved over to her side, jerking at the rope when Aydan resisted.

"Let go of the rope. He's not going to run away," Mustafa said. "Follow me."

Taiku put his arm around Samiya to help her walk. She barely acknowledged his presence. "We'll get through this somehow," he tried to assure her. She silently turned her eyes to him. They still looked numb, but tears now poured down her face, mixing with the blood from her wound.

Mustafa stopped between two trees, whose heavy branches had been lashed and pulled agonizingly towards each other with thick ropes. A soldier pushed Taiku away as Samiya collapsed to the ground, vomiting. Another couple of soldiers walked over to her, one with a coil of ropes over his shoulder.

Taiku shivered as his stomach started to roil. His mind didn't grasp what was taking place, but his heart understood.

Thick ropes were wrapped tightly around Samiya's chest and under her arms, which were then attached to one of the tree's limbs. The soldier then tightly wrapped other ropes around her waist and thighs, which were attached to the other tree. Taiku watched, fascinated, nauseated, his mind still refusing to acknowledge what was in front of him.

Samiya hung suspended sideways between two trees. She looked at Taiku. The tears, the vomit had stopped. The soldiers holding Taiku pulled him over between the trees, facing Samiya from a few paces away. They latched tightly onto his arms, while they faced backwards.

Taiku's mind could no longer deny what his eyes were seeing, especially as another soldier took a machete, and started chopping at the ropes binding the branches to each other.

One, two, three swings... The rope let go, the heavy leafy branches returned to their natural positions. A thick stream of meat and blood, Samiya's innards, splattered Taiku's face, coated his body. Taiku couldn't see through the blood in his eyes. He could only watch through the blood, through the horror in his heart.

A bucket of water struck his face, clearing his vision. Mustafa stood between the two halves of Samiya's carcass, ripped in half at the waist, hanging from separate trees.

"We made it easy for her. Sometimes we tie each leg to a different tree. The pain is much more severe. I hope it goes as well for the next one."

Taiku sighed, raised his arms, and walked over to the tree, standing between the pieces of the woman who wanted to atone for her husband. The woman who could have avoided any part of this by running away with her family, like so many others. Taiku raised his arms for the soldier to bind them.

"No, no... We would never do that to an esteemed guest like you. If you're torn in half, you can't talk." Mustafa pointed to the side, where Aydan's legs were being bound to separate trees.

Aydan was saying when the ropes were positioned properly, when they were tight enough. He was cooperating, but he was pale.

"I want you to appreciate our sincerity. My youngest son will be a martyr, just to help you understand."

"Samiya made it clear enough." Taiku pointed to Aydan. "Don't."

Mustafa signaled, and the soldiers untied Aydan. He sagged, grabbing a shoulder for support.

"I think you're ready for our discussion." Mustafa's eyes were no longer gentle.

The soldiers dragged Taiku to the shelter where he had first been introduced to Mustafa, pulling him down onto a comfortable pillow. Another soldier placed a cup of water and a bowl of fruit beside him.

"Eat something," Mustafa ordered. "You need your strength."

Taiku drank some water.

"We'll keep this short." Mustafa raised his hands in front of his face, palms turned sideways. "I'm going to make you an offer. If you accept it, raise your hands as I have done twice. You only have to do it once.

"Tell your troops to lay down their arms and leave. Not back to Lagash, but away. Each one of them will be branded and then allowed to escape through the forest. Any of them found in the region will be treed. The people of Lagash will be allowed to live as before, provided they submit to Ja'ix's teachings. Any who wish to leave can do so, provided it's before I get there.

"If you refuse my offer, your troops will die. I don't have the rope or time to repeat what I did for your lady friend. But I assure you, I have other ways that are just as pleasant. Also, if you refuse, I will tie every one of the Lagash Ebers between trees. Understand?"

Taiku understood. Lagash was lost. Was he wrong to have tried? Was there something he could have done differently that would have led to a better outcome? There was no way to know. It had been his obligation to try. Organizing the soldiers, the refugees, uniting the Marsh, Madai and Elam... He could not know the results of his actions before he carried them out. One thing did not necessarily lead to another. Every event, every day, was discrete, separate. No action led to a definite result. He was not wrong to try.

Would Tamsyn be more successful in saving Simon?

"You said all the people would be allowed to accept Ja'ix or leave. Does that include the Ebers?"

"I said the people of Lagash would be allowed to accept Ja'ix or leave. What's your decision?"

Taiku closed his eyes, covering them with his fingers. His mind was soaked with tears. He grieved for Samiya, for Asenath, for everyone soon to be oppressed or exiled. He felt as if the heavens had collided inside his heart, the fragments exploding into columns of fire. He opened his eyes, but the vision Aleku had related to him remained.

"Well? Your decision?"

Taiku looked down to where little pieces of Samiya still clung to his leg. He took a small chunk of flesh and put it in his mouth, chewing slowly, wanting to be nauseated as he raised his hands, palms turned to the side.

Taiku walked back to his soldiers, approaching them from the south. Some of the men who had seen him swept under the water were overjoyed at his approach as he appeared out of the haze that had settled over the hills. Only when they noticed the others behind him did they understand this wasn't a moment for happiness.

"Ja'ix's army has surrounded us. Our only opening is to go over the cliffs into the river," he announced.

"I've agreed to lay down our weapons. We'll be branded, and then allowed to leave, provided we never return to this area. The people of Lagash can remain if they accept Ja'ix's teachings, or leave, provided they do so immediately."

An angry wave of objections poured from his men. Taiku held up his arm for silence.

"Ja'ix has more soldiers here than we have people in Lagash. He has even more attacking Edrai Pass. We did all we could, but it wasn't enough. Put down your weapons. It's Lagash's only chance."

By now, the immensity of Mustafa's force was becoming visible to Taiku's troops. They began to remove their weapons, throwing down swords, quivers, daggers... Mustafa's soldiers moved silently, gathering them.

Most of Taiku's men were angry. They muttered amongst themselves, angry at having been neutralized so easily. Many were refugees; men who had given up on the idea of a stable life, who had thought they had found it again. Now they were back on the run, unable to even rejoin their families before fleeing.

Taiku had expected that once his men had disarmed, Mustafa would resume a pleasant demeanor. But his eyes were ablaze now, his lips locked in a sneer.

"I love Aydan. He's my youngest son. You're going to suffer for what happened to him."

"I did everything you asked," Taiku said. "I did nothing to Aydan."

"He was going to be a martyr, have a glorious reward. You stole that."

Mustafa's men had withdrawn from amongst Taiku's soldiers, and now formed a line around them. They had their swords out.

"It was you who needed the lesson he wanted to give. You're going to pay for your theft."

A group of soldiers immobilized Taiku's limbs and hoisted him onto a little platform they had brought with them. A powerful hand latched onto his head. Mustafa grabbed Taiku's ear with one hand, pulling hard. He sliced it off with a knife in the other hand. A soldier pressed on his wound with a cloth that had been soaked in some strange liquid. It hurt horribly: the cut, the liquid.

"That will keep the wound from killing you," Mustafa said. "This won't kill you either." He grabbed the other ear and sliced it off.

"Not even this will." Mustafa slashed down with his blade, removing much of Taiku's nose.

Taiku was reeling from the pain. His soldiers reeled with shock from what was happening to their leader, and what it implied for them. Some started to rise, but were immediately shot by archers. The others remained on the ground, in their places.

A man came over to Taiku, and locked an ox-collar around his neck. This was even worse than when Tamsyn held a knife to his neck. Why hadn't she killed him, and saved him from this suffering? No, he was the Chief, he was in charge. He had to get control.

Of what? Not the enemy who captured him. Of his soldiers? They were disarmed, waiting to die.

Himself. He had to reach through his pain to get control of himself.

The man cracked a whip in the air, and ordered Taiku to get down on all fours, like a beast of burden. Why? What was the purpose of getting control of himself?

The man cracked the whip cracked across Taiku's back, ripping skin and flesh. It re-kindled the agony of his other injuries, tearing at his mind.

His men. That's why.

"Run now! Save yourselves as best you—" Taiku put all his heart into shouting this order, one he expected to be his last.

Another crack of the whip pulled him face first onto the platform. Taiku couldn't see if he had been obeyed. He couldn't hear anything over the angry shouts of the men surrounding and kicking him in the chest, in the groin, in the face, the ears...

"Enough." Prodding with his boot, Mustafa rolled Taiku onto his back.

"A lot of people are going to suffer because you rudely opened your mouth."

"You were going to kill my soldiers anyways." Taiku barely eked out the words.

"Yes, but now we have to torture them."

"If a few get away, the suffering of the rest will have been worthwhile."

The pain was still ripping at Taiku's mind, trying to tear him to pieces, a slower version of what the tree had done to Samiya. His resistance though, was holding him together.

"None will get away. I'm rescinding my promise about the Ebers. Each one of them will be treed. You can't imagine what I'm going to do to Asenath once I get hold of her."

No one understood Taiku's tears. They were from joy, because he knew now that Mustafa was bluffing. Not about everything, but his control was not as complete as he pretended. For the moment, Taiku felt stronger.

Mustafa took a horn trumpet, and blew nine short blasts. His soldiers looked up.

"I spoke words of peace to Taiku. I made him a generous offer, to benefit from Ja'ix's wisdom. His people may have respected Taiku, but we know he's a fraud. His body houses a corrupt spirit, which I will reveal to you by removing the shell which conceals it."

Mustafa's soldiers cheered, hacking at prisoners in celebration. Taiku looked at his slain and bleeding soldiers, at the carnage that reached as far as he could see. A few of Mustafa's men were bleeding, and there were gaps between his men. Some had apparently gotten away. Maybe they would be able to warn Lagash.

A couple of men pushed Taiku up against a thick spruce tree. The resin stung the open wounds on his back; the rough bark opened them more as his wrists were tied above his head.

More rope bound his feet to the base of the tree. A cord below his hips held his torso firmly in place. A tall man standing nearby held a small, thin knife, the sharp blade about the size of a man's thumb. He approached, stood on a stool, and very carefully put the blade to Taiku's wrist.

If the tall man was an executioner, he could simply slit Taiku's wrist. The small knife was for something else.

The blade described a shallow circle around Taiku's wrist, followed by a line leading down to his armpit. It was so precise that it hardly drew any blood. This was an experienced craftsman.

He then placed the knife-edge along the line, lying almost flat, and began working it underneath. He loosened the skin around Taiku's wrist, and started peeling it back, keeping it intact.

This wasn't pain. Pain was something he had experienced before when shot by an arrow or stabbed by a blade. Having the skin carefully removed from his arm was not the same category of experience.

Taiku could see Mustafa in front of him. He could see Mustafa's grinning soldiers watch him being peeled like a ripe fruit. He saw his soldiers who weren't able to get away. He would have wondered if they would be sharing his fate, but that kind of thought required a coherent mind. Peeling his skin had removed whatever it was that held his mind together.

One arm was finished, the skin hanging loosely behind his shoulder. The craftsman moved his stool over to the other arm, and began his careful work again.

Taiku was thirsty. He would do anything for a sip of water. He tried to speak, but his mind couldn't assemble the necessary words. He was Mustafa's guest. Surely his host would give him a drink. Where was Ner? Mustafa said he was in water. Why wasn't Ner bringing him any?

Taiku's lips were pushed open. Something wet in his mouth was dripping down his throat. He heard the craftsman speaking, but couldn't understand the strange words.

A raging anguish grew inside him. Taiku felt like he was being torn apart. He was. The water brought him back to awareness, to the beyond-pain that he was suffering. Every point of his exposed flesh was a pillar of white fire, a burning, tearing agony that was ripping the sky apart, the displaced stars searing his heart. The man resumed his work.

Taiku screamed wordlessly, he prayed thoughtlessly, he searched blindly for an escape. The wet rag had been removed from his mouth, and he was again dying of thirst. He stumbled through the forest, pulled by he didn't know what as his flesh was uncovered.

There were sounds in the woods: birds chirping, water rushing. Taiku ran towards the light that was coming through the trees. It was Asenath; he knew it. She must be pulling him towards the glade. What was he going to say to her? His soldiers, pretending to be Far Marsh people, had stolen and maimed a few Low Marsh animals. He had expected the Marsh people to ask him to settle things, which he would do by making them part of Lagash, under his control. He didn't expect his stunt to kill his friend. Somewhere in the tangled roots of his mind, he remembered that he was still alive, and she wasn't.

The craftsman walked off, resting his arm. In a few minutes, soldiers would turn Taiku around, so he could remove the skin from his back.

Taiku came to an open area in the woods. He saw a brook pouring from a Rock made of pure light, its waters pleasant and soothing. He listened to it gurgling. The wind rustled lightly, the air smelled clean and whole. Birds chirped; even little frogs sang sweet hymns. All were praising the Source of the water: the Rock, the Light. Taiku bent down, cupped his hands together, and drank the sweet pureness of the brook. A small, blue hummingbird hovered at the side his head, singing, revealing, to the remains of his ear. Taiku listened carefully to Huitzil as his senses coalesced into a formless understanding that could not be put into words. He knew how to destroy Mustafa's army at Sipress Pass. He knew how to destroy the army that had forced its way through Edrai Pass.

Taiku gathered his will into a point of profound intent, and drew a breath from deep in the bowels of existence, where time boiled in an icy broth seething with desire, with causality, with meaning. He focused the power of the brook, its purity and its strength.

A woman was standing in front of him. Not Asenath. Not anyone he knew. She had shoulder-length brown hair and deep blue eyes. She was dressed in many layers of clothes, too many...

"I'm a Fire-Snake. I'll release you."

She puckered and licked her lips. Screaming soldiers brandishing swords were almost upon her. She put her mouth to his in a gentle kiss, and disappeared.

Taiku leaned against the Rock, gazed at the brook, re-focused his intent, and released his will, sending forth the annihilation of his foes.

"It won't work now."

He looked up at Asenath's tear-filled eyes.

"You had to do it while you were alive. You're not, anymore."

Taiku's pain was gone, his thoughts were clear. She extended her hand to him.

"Come, my friend."

***

A person might be a strong swimmer. He might know how to row a small boat, or how to sail a craft capable of holding ten or twenty people.

But if such a person thought this knowledge enabled him to stand against a tidal wave, he would be a fool, a dead fool.

Vlad was not such a person. As Ja'ix's forces poured towards him, he understood that Lagash was lost. He could hold on, he could delay the enemy, but he could not keep them out. Even if he unleashed all his granates in Edrai Pass while the enemy was riding through, it would only slow them down.

And that was his best hope. He ordered his soldiers back; he ordered the Tungus back to Lagash. Their task was now to warn everyone, to get as many people away as possible. He also instructed a group of riders to head up the Klee-Dekel, to advise his brother of the danger. It would be the worst possible outcome for Taiku to be fighting Ja'ix's army to the north, and then be surprised by them coming up from the south.

He would let Ja'ix into the pass, destroy it as best he could, and then go back with the rest of his soldiers. If they had the time, they would burn their homes. The less they left for Ja'ix, the better.

More importantly, he would get his wife. He wasn't sure how he ended up in love with Tamsyn. Maybe it was her mysterious talents, which she had used to enchant him the first night she had climbed into his bed. He was certain though that it was his own heart that tied him to her now. Her ferocity, her beauty were more captivating than any mysterious power she had.

She was no doubt deadlier than him, but Vlad still wanted to protect her. He wanted to be with her, to have children with her. That meant getting away. It meant getting away and making sure that Simon was safe. Taiku's orders were that Tamsyn had to protect Simon above all else. She would not ignore that responsibility, no matter the cost.

The Elam would be able to blend into the hills, moving to higher pastures. The Madai would have to move to new lands. They were mostly farmers, craftsmen and merchants. The Marsh People, well... The Marsh People had started the killing amongst themselves, and then assassinated Asenath. Perhaps some Madai families would take them along as servants, or maybe slaves. Not many of their men were surviving the battle. They were exposed, their deaths made inevitable by the protective coverings on the enemy horses, the helmets on the enemy soldiers.

The Ebers would have to flee to the home of the Tungus. They were always on the run, one tidal wave after another.

His brother knew that it wasn't merely bad luck that chased them around the surface of the world. Taiku loved Asenath. There was something more to her life, something more about the Clay People. Taiku could never explain it to him clearly, but Vlad believed in his brother. Vlad and Tamsyn would protect Simon.

40 EARLY BRONZE AGE 17

"**Y**ou have to run!"

The man barged through the door of the Meeting House, clothes torn, blood oozing from a gash across his chest. Zeresh and Zaytea rose in alarm.

"We were surrounded on all sides." The man spoke quickly, trying to get his words out before something could stop him. "Taiku was captured, mutilated. He screamed at us to run. I jumped into the river."

"My husband..."

"Dead, if he's lucky. I don't know..." Sucking deep gulps of air, the man sat down on the floor, his back leaning heavily against the wall.

"Do you know what happened? How did they get south of our troops?"

"They were waiting for us the whole time."

Zeresh and Zaytea looked at each other in shock.

"Are they on their way here now?" Zaytea asked. "Are you the only one who survived?"

He pointed at Zeresh. "There's a woman asking for you."

"For me? What does she want?"

"She walked among us after we put down our weapons, asking about you, your family. She asked a lot of questions about your flocks. She greeted a few people by name. She says she wants to put a towel on your face."

The man broke out in a bout of coughing. Zaytea put a comforting hand on his shoulder.

"Rest," she said. "Thank you for bringing us the information."

"There is no resting," the man replied between coughs. "They're coming."

Zeresh leaned against the table, her face ashen, her body trembling. She knew how Ja'ix had managed to get his forces around Taiku's: Abijah had received her unsigned note. Ja'ix was arriving right on schedule- the red moon's schedule.

"Let's go." Zaytea grabbed her arm.

Zeresh steadied herself. "No. There is something this man must do, and there is something I must do. You have to flee." She turned to the wounded, winded soldier.

"Get pitchers of tar from the storage areas outside. Pour them over every parchment in the Eber Academy. Burn the building to the ground. You must do this now. Then you are released from service." She bent down, grabbed his arm and forcefully yanked the man to his feet. "Go! You must not fail. Too much depends on it."

The soldier looked at Zaytea, who nodded. He stumbled out.

"Why do you hate the Ebers so much?" Zaytea asked. "We're in danger, but before saving ourselves you want to destroy even the memory of them."

"Do you remember why Shor's gang came to Lagash? He wanted to find Asenath to translate the document on how to make a Fire-Snake woman. What other documents do the Ebers have? What secrets?"

"I don't know."

"Neither do I, but I don't want Ja'ix to get his hands on them, whatever they are. We can't stop him, but we can limit Lagash's usefulness to him."

Zaytea took her sister's hand. "I understand. Now let's save ourselves."

"No. You go. Make sure everyone is out of Lagash. Get to Tamsyn. There are some things I have to do."

"Are you crazy? They'll kill you. And that woman...?"

"Abijah. If I hadn't tortured her father, they wouldn't have given our family their flocks. They wouldn't have left the community. She wouldn't be seeking revenge, and she wouldn't have shown Ja'ix how to get through the caves of Sipress Pass. I'm responsible for what happened, Zaytea. It's up to me to slow them down, to give everyone time to get away."

Zaytea was beside herself. "How can you, one woman, slow down an army? Are you out of your mind?"

"I'm not out of my mind. Besides which, our cousin gave me a task to carry out."

"Our cousin? Who? What are you talking about, Zeresh?"

Zeresh took her sister's face gently between her palms. "Life is too precious to throw away. I'm unable to give you any reason why life is as it is. I can explain nothing. Go now, my sister... my Queen."

Zeresh kissed Zaytea's forehead, turned her around, and pushed her towards the door. Zaytea took a last look at her sister, and ran.

Zeresh waited till she heard the outer door closing before walking over to the fireplace. She rubbed her hands together, feeling the warmth as she concentrated on remembering the instructions. Her cousin had long ago said she would find what she needed, so she would know when it was going to happen. One glimpse at the parchment from Shor's chest of treasures told her it was the sky chart she needed; she had accepted Qimiq's price immediately. It had taken all of her knowledge, all of her experience to understand it; to be terrified by it. Looking at the chart, Zeresh also understood why astronomy was considered a form of witchcraft.

She took a handful of ashes from the edge of the hearth and rubbed them into her long black hair, streaking it grey. She took more, and rubbed them into the skin of her face, onto her teeth. With her knife she drew a line in the palm of each hand, and then rubbed blood into the ashes on her cheeks and forehead. Zeresh stared at the flames that floundered weakly at the back of the fireplace. Using tongs, she lifted a glowing ember from the back of the fire, which she placed in her bare, bleeding palm.

She was ready now to greet them: the enemy soldiers, the red moon... She pulled the strange, small fire-emitting device from her pocket. "Fusion cell," it said in tiny letters, whatever that meant. Someone had tried to take it apart, but only managed to crack the casing. The device must have been left in the Eber Academy for a reason, and that reason must be now.

There were shouts outside. Whoops, cheers... The rumble of approaching riders. Zeresh stood up, looked at her name carved in the wood frame of the fireplace. What more would remain of her? Of her sister? She went through the door.

The approaching soldiers were heading straight for her. Zeresh looked at the thick, hazy sky. She stretched her charred, bloodstained fists upwards, and then folded them over her heart. "Come to me red moon," she whispered. "It's time for your freedom." If her calculations were right, if the chart was right, the collision of celestial bodies was taking place at the same time as the collision of armies around Lagash.

The riders slowed as they approached the Meeting House. Zeresh lifted her eyes to them as they dismounted, casting her gaze right and left. They stepped forward and then stopped unexpectedly, as if they had walked into an invisible wall. They twisted, they turned; they could do anything but move from where they stood. More riders approached.

"Take her," an officer shouted as he stalked forward, wondering why his men were holding back. Tens of soldiers were struggling with the invisible ropes that bound them. Soon it was a hundred, and soon it was more. Zeresh struggled to keep the knots tight, knowing they would give way soon enough, knowing the men would fall upon her. In the distance, she heard the whoosh of flames, smelled the tar from the burning Academy.

As she glanced at her charred palm, she recalled the many hours she spent preparing, studying with her cousin. "Help me, Asenath," she pleaded silently, as she threw the glowing ember, as she ignited and threw the lighter at the legs of the attackers. Zeresh watched the tar catch fire under the men's feet. Hundreds of men were behind the ones she had tied with invisible ropes; they could not get through because of the ones anchored in front of them. All of them were burning now, flaming tar bubbling up from the ground, hissing, splattering.

She knew they would make her pay for this. It didn't matter. The "fusion" thing from the Academy would be her price. The red moon would be her price. The death of Mustafa, of his troops, of the lands would be her reward.

Would the rivers of tar beneath the ground carry the flames any distance? Would they burn fiercely enough to release the poison that radiated from the seeps?

Two sets of powerful arms grabbed her from behind, hoisting her off the ground.

"Let's see you do your magic now, witch!" A man pulled out his sword.

"No," the other raised his blade to stop him. "Keep her alive. She's Taiku's wife, the Queen. Ja'ix promised her as a gift to Mustafa, who will rule Lagash. That will make him into a King."

Good. They didn't recognize her. It meant that Zaytea, the real queen, had a better chance to escape. Mustafa would only be a pretend king, and that for a brief time.

"Maybe Ja'ix would want her," the first soldier said. "He can be king."

"He's already got a gorgeous wife. She doesn't let him have other women." He laughed, and pointed his sword at Zeresh. "This one is for Mustafa."

The first soldier smiled, sheathed his sword, and bowed scornfully to her. "Lead us, my Queen. March at the head of your troops."

***

The smoke, the ashes were chasing Balthan. The columns of heavenly fire and the red moon they were pushing had landed, making the planet tremble. Had they cracked the world apart? The head-splitting boom that had slammed through the air terrified everyone. Some of the soldiers, including most of the officers, jumped into a freezing river to get away. Others simply ran. Prisoners cowered on the ground, too fearful to flee.

Mekelat had warned Balthan this was no opportunity for him to escape, though the Sheyds had all disappeared. Balthan stood on a hillock facing southwest, facing his former home.

The place he was on was particularly exposed to the smoky winds. Balthan took off his clothes, letting the snow and ashes swirl on to him, attach to his body. He felt numbness creep into his toes, then his limbs. Some of the soldiers, some of the prisoners gathered around, watching him. Frost started to sear into his skin, into his flesh.

No. He wasn't going to escape Mekelat by freezing himself to death. He reached down, pulled his clothes on, put a coat on, and started giving orders, organizing the frightened band of Cannibal soldiers and captives. Balthan knew that none of them would ever return home. He would bring them north, to their new one.

41 THE EDGE OF THE WORLD 13

"**H**e seems comfortable and he's eating well. There are no signs he's developing any problems. He smiles, which is amazing considering his condition."

Every time Norma brought Osnat the scouts' reports, it was good news again. Falun had been carried to the bottom of the gorge two days earlier and placed in a tent. Twice daily someone climbed down to feed him, give him water and clean him up. Except as an infant, he had never in his life been so diligently served. The biggest risk for Falun, besides the aftereffects of Death in a Box, was being attacked by predators. But those had all been eliminated, and had yet to return.

They only brought him down there three days after Death in a Box had been detonated, erring on the side of safety. The inconvenience caused by waiting was not worth the risk of a slow, agonizing death.

Osnat was especially pleased with the reports that Falun had no lesions on his skin, no blood in his urine. His teeth were firmly in place, and his stool was regular. If it wasn't safe below the escarpment, there would already have been some indication from his body. The killing power of Death in a Box had been designed to be short-lived: the instant annihilation of every living thing in range.

Osnat wanted to build a new world below the escarpment, and the first step was to clean away the old; the Tunniq were too brutal.

The bleak mood of the people on top of the escarpment matched the grey clouds in the skies overhead. A couple of men, imagining themselves to be explorers, had ignored warnings not to climb onto the glacier. One of them slipped into a deep hole that drained melt-water. Osnat refused to consider a rescue, instead lecturing the survivor and everyone else that if they want to thrive in these lands, they had better learn from the Tunniq how to behave.

Some people resented that; they considered the Tunniq to be savages. But Zimri, Ijiq and Haran were the ones who caught and distributed all the food, so resentment was for the most part stowed beneath the surface.

Osnat decided it was time to descend.

Norma arranged everyone for the trip down the gorge. They took the rougher route, closer to the village. Osnat and Dina carried their babies in the backs of their jackets, stopping occasionally to rest, or to let the babies relieve themselves on the ground. Each of the two women were surrounded by men, whose job it was to take their arms, to ensure they stayed on their feet where walking was difficult.

They passed the remains of a bear. A little to the side was a red blotch and some cracked skull bones; what was left of the new Eric's head.

If Death in a Box had worked properly, they were heading towards a lot of corpses. If it hadn't, they were heading to a lot of people who wanted to kill them. And if it worked, but not as expected, Death in a Box might still poison them.

At the bottom was the same terrain that they had seen before climbing, but with no esker. Other than the lifeless stands of dead trees, the only outstanding feature on the snow and mush-covered scree was the tent with Falun, which Osnat was now walking towards. Ijiq and Wendy trailed behind; she wanted to see him alone first.

The tent reminded Osnat of her husband lying battered and helpless, unable to clean himself. Falun, the man responsible for that, was now lying paralyzed, able to wiggle a couple of fingertips at most. Rather than remove his head, Osnat had been sending people to care for him. Someone had already run ahead to clean him up, to make him presentable. Clean and naked, lying between some furs. Smiling. She remembered Falun's smile from when he had softly pushed the tip of a spear into her husband's throat.

"Thank you for the food and water, and all the visitors. You're very kind to me."

Osnat felt her stomach rising along with terrifying memories. She pushed them both down; the life of her son and her people wouldn't be served by dwelling on the past. She pulled the blanket off Falun, looking closely at his skin for any lesions, any unusual marks. Clinically, methodically, she examined his eyes and ears for traces of blood. Plastoquinone came to mind again. Replicating its action in animals rather than vegetation was a key element of one of her research projects. If she could bring him to her lab, maybe she could undo his paralysis.

"Open your mouth." There wasn't really enough light, but she wanted to make sure his gums weren't bleeding. She held her face over his, which she pushed slightly to this side and that, to get a better look.

Osnat was concentrating on his gums; she didn't see his fist coming. The punch to the side of her head was sudden and overwhelming. Before she could recover enough to understand what was happening, there was a filthy gag in her mouth, her wrists were pinned behind her back, and a naked Falun was on top of her, his vicious smile obstructing the rest of existence. He wrapped a hand around her throat and began to squeeze. She struggled to pull in a breath.

"Simon wanted to have sex with you. As his wife, you should have opened your legs, but you killed him instead."

Osnat was too focused on getting a breath past the hand constricting her throat to understand what he was saying. Her senses were fading. She tried to scream, but had no strength. Besides which, there was the gag.

He waved a small piece of bloody flesh in her face. "My wife promised that Simon or I would rip open your belly and remove your baby. Your baby's out, my Simon's gone, so all that's left is to give you this part of him, and then open your belly. As you die, you're going to fulfill your responsibility as his wife, so Simon so can have what is rightfully his."

He yanked down her pants. Osnat felt him groping, pushing something inside her... then slashing at her abdomen with a knife. She felt her skin tearing, flesh coming apart. Her pain faded as her mind dissolved into darkness.

Osnat found herself at the brook with the Rock of pure light. The other times she was here, she had been alone. Now there was another woman standing beside the brook, looking dismayed. Tall, with a full figure, her violet eyes and straight black hair gave her a commanding demeanor. Her dress rustled lightly in the breeze as she spoke. Osnat didn't understand how, but knew she was very close to her.

"It's not time," the woman said, tears in her eyes.

"What can I do? I have to live," Osnat said.

The woman stepped closer. "It's not in our hands."

Osnat turned and addressed the Rock of pure light. "What can I do?"

There was no response; water continued to pour into the brook.

"Many people's lives depend on me."

"Many depended on us when I was killed," the woman said, wrapping her arm around Osnat's shoulder. She looked deeply unhappy.

Osnat pulled back. "I want a solution, not commiseration."

"That's all I can offer."

"I'll do anything necessary to get back. Anything." Osnat took a menacing step forward, and then stopped. "Huitzil! I need you, now!" she screamed.

He came up behind her. A leather engraving hung from a thong around his neck. It depicted a hummingbird hovering over a man's chest, picking at the flesh of his heart.

"Tanayt. I am here." He bowed to Osnat.

She flinched.

"Tanayt." He bowed to Asenath.

"I'm not the one to whom you should bow," the tall woman answered. "I am not the Source." She closed her eyes in concentration.

Osnat stared at the man she had summoned, stared at the leather engraving before speaking. "I need to get back to the Abode of Life. You're a Master of War; death is in your hands. Undo mine."

"Death, yes. Life comes only from the Source of Blessing."

"Bring me to it."

He pointed at the Rock. "It's where you are."

"I spoke to the Rock, and got no response, just water," Asenath said. "You must bring me closer. We must get back."

Osnat flinched on hearing the woman's words. She extended an accusing finger: "You're me?"

Huitzil's hand was over his eyes in concentration, squeezing his temples. He let go, and cupped Asenath's face with his hand.

She pointed to Osnat. "Her."

Huitzil looked at Osnat, hesitating.

Asenath grabbed Osnat's arm. "If you're asked a riddle, try to solve it." She let go.

"Do it," Osnat said to Huitzil, wondering what she had just insisted on, wondering what she had just been told by her other self.

Huitzil pulled out a knife, Wendy's beautiful knife, grabbed Osnat's face, and carved out her eyes. Before the pain could even register in her mind, he pushed her under the water of the brook. It filled her nose and mouth as she thrashed desperately; his powerful arm kept her under. She couldn't escape by climbing out. She swam towards the light of the Rock.

There was an opening, a crevasse. Osnat glided in, realizing that the rules, the paradigms through which she understood anything were meaningless here.

Her vision was clear. With eyes, she had only been able to see three dimensions; that was blindness compared to what she now beheld.

She looked out from an ancient stone tower to a beautiful seacoast. The warm air had a gentle scent of salt. The sand was a shimmering turquoise, the waters beyond it a bright magenta. Swarms of great eagles soared towards the clouds, and then swooped down over the beach, over the water, stirring up clouds of sand, sprays of crystalline liquid with the beat of their wings.

Men's voices came from an adjacent room. One was complaining.

"An old donkey driver kept pestering me with riddles. What is a snake that flies in the air with an ant between its teeth? What is an eagle that builds its nest in a tree that never was? What is the beautiful lady without eyes, and a body hidden and revealed?"

Osnat could help them with the last one. She stepped into the room. "I am the lady. Why were my eyes removed?"

They jumped in surprise. The eldest answered. "I am Simon, my Lady. You stand in the Sphere of Understanding, very close to the Sphere of the Singularity. Its light would burn you up, had you eyes to receive it. We're in the Sphere of Judgment, far beneath. Why did you come here?"

Osnat's heart jumped. Her Simon? "I have to return; I want my death undone."

"Do you deserve it?"

"Send me back in the merit of any good I've ever done. If that's insufficient, do it in the merit of the many thousands of innocent people sent across the Edge of the World to die. But ultimately, send me back in the merit of the few that survive."

Simon frowned, stood up, and stared deep into her heart. "We would both be happy if you stayed here with me." He kissed her hand.

Osnat couldn't cry; one needed eyes to do that. And anyways, the feeling that coursed through her was much more profound than tears could express. It tore at every particle of her being with something deeper than love, much hotter than anguish.

"I cannot."

Simon sat back down. The men nodded at each other. "Three Taanas demand that the Source undoes your death. Do you make it four?"

Osnat added her assent. "Is my death undone?"

"The donkey driver outside is waiting for you."

"Will I—"

"You must leave now. Take what you need."

Osnat looked around the room. "Thank you, my Teachers." She lifted her hands sideways in front of her face, and left.

She had a massive headache, a pounding just below her left temple. Osnat winced, feeling a warm wetness on her chest. She opened her eyelids, and saw Wendy applying something to her belly. She reached down, but Wendy intercepted her hand.

"I cut you when I took Falun's heart from the back. The lichen will stop the bleeding." Wendy looked frightened.

Osnat sucked air into her lungs. She touched her fingers to her eyes. "What did you do?"

"I knew something was wrong, so I came in. I'm glad I didn't wait too long."

"I'm glad, too." Osnat shuddered as she felt something inside her. "Wendy, I think Falun stuck his son's penis in me. Please, take it out!"

Wendy's hand shot down between Osnat's legs, and ever so gently removed the alien object.

"Osnat, I'm so sorry." She held the severed organ in her fist and sniffled. A tear started to roll down the cheek of the Master of War. It stopped. Wendy took Osnat's hand and put on her fiercest scowl. "Get over it."

Osnat looked at Wendy's menacing expression as she remembered her own harsh directive when they first met. Osnat squeezed Wendy's fingers, and laughed.

"This belongs to you." Huitzil offered Falun's still-beating heart to Osnat. "Eat."

She had chewed on Balthan's beating heart, and this occasion was certainly as deserving of a ceremonial meal. But why was she getting the chance to gnaw on Falun's heart? Why were her guts still inside her skin? She had felt herself leave the Abode of Life. Or did Wendy kill Falun before he could kill her?

Special relativity taught that there is no such thing absolute time. As a war deity, Huitzil could surely rearrange chronological reference points. "It's not time," Osnat had heard. Or did she merely dream what the tall woman said? Why wasn't it time? There was no order to life, so there could be no appropriate time. Osnat had been in these wild lands long enough to know that one day wasn't connected to the next; there was only chaos. She had been a dutiful Tunniq daughter, had learned her lessons well.

The law of the conservation of angular momentum taught her differently though. Quantum entanglement taught her differently- the smallest particles of existence were inextricably tied to other such particles at the far end of the universe. It was something she had learned on the other side of the Edge of the World. As a Quantum Biologist, she knew that everything was intimately bound; beyond space, above time. 'It's not time,' the woman had said. Was there a schedule, an order? Osnat sat up. "Thank you, but no. It's not the way."

Huitzil frowned. "Death is necessary."

"Yes, we've certainly done a lot of that. I'm very pleased that you killed Falun."

"How could he have hurt you?" Wendy asked. "A moment later, and you'd have been gone."

"It may have been a moment later. I don't understand."

Osnat brushed the gore off her chest as best she could, then rubbed her hands against the now-ruined furs.

"When you cut my eyes out, I thought I was lost. Why am I'm still alive? Did you use your power?"

"Cut your eyes out?" Huitzil closed her eyes momentarily, and then put her hand affectionately on Osnat's cheek. "You have to understand something, Osnat, my darling: I don't have any power of my own. You're way stronger than me."

Ijiq's voice broke in from just outside the tent. "I smell blood."

"We're fine," Osnat said. She looked back at Wendy.

"I'm merely a messenger whose task is to forcefully decrease entropy."

Osnat knew what entropy was, and that it didn't decrease in a closed system. Huitzil's explanation didn't help.

"The Rock made of light; you know..." Huitzil said. "Did you notice where the brook ran over some rocks, splashing, getting stirred with air?"

Osnat nodded, as she pictured the brook from underneath and above.

"Those rocks, that's me, the Master of War. The turbulence, the troubles I stir up make life possible."

Wendy tamped some more lichen into the wound on Osnat's belly. "Many thousands of years ago I told a tortured, dying warrior how he could use the power of the Source to destroy his enemies. It would have changed the path of the world had he succeeded. A woman took pity on him and killed him seconds before he could do it. That incident reminded me that I'm just a messenger, with an assigned role."

"Osnat, our baby is hungry." Ijiq's voice broke in again.

"Bring him to me, please."

Osnat pulled up her top. She put the baby to her breast, as Ijiq affectionately rubbed her back. There was genuine relief in his eyes; he had heard horrible noises from inside Falun's tent. Osnat leaned against him, closed her eyes, and drifted away in thoughts of Aua, Simon, and the black-haired woman.

42 THE EDGE OF THE WORLD 14

There was nobody in the village. There were no corpses in tents, no dog carcasses outside them... The sleds were lying around, their traces empty.

Osnat ordered everyone to wait near the cluster of empty homes. She and the other Tunniq, along with Huitzil, silently followed the footprints leading towards the escarpment. The winter Dance House had been replaced by a tent. A rough fur-covered wooden frame stood against the cliff, which formed one of the walls. A smaller structure marked the entry vestibule. They could see a pile of boulders in the distance against the escarpment, where Death in a Box had been detonated. The explosion had left what looked like an angry visage on the cliff.

Ijiq pulled the pelt door aside and stopped. The vestibule was filled with dogs. "Where are the flies, the rats?"

"You know the answer," Huitzil said.

Ijiq thought for a moment. His eyes widened, as he understood the scope of the destruction they had unleashed. He picked up the dogs, throwing them outside. Some legs detached as he pulled at them; pieces of meat remained on the floor. Osnat put her hand on his shoulder once a path was cleared through the carcasses.

"I want to be the first to face what I've done."

The Dance House was filled with corpses. Osnat walked to the center of the room, the others following her in. She stared down at the faces of the people she had lived amongst through the harsh Tunniq winter. She looked at the two boys that had been playing with a dead puppy when Aarluk killed the storm. She saw the little girl that had been happily trying to snatch it from them.

Osnat shuffled around the Dance House, looking into the face of each of her former neighbors, remembering what they were like when they were alive: their smiles, their scowls...

Puah, whose arrogance towards Aarluk had provoked the fight that led to all these deaths... No, not really. It was before that; the killing of Osnat's husband had started her down this path. She looked around at the bodies and fought off a moan.

"Osnat, what do we do with Nisuin?" Ijiq interrupted her rumination. He was holding a swaddled tot in his hands, the one whose droppings Falun and Puah had playfully attacked each other with. Osnat looked into her eyes. Many of the villagers had died with their eyes frozen open.

She jumped when the baby blinked. Two thoughts hit her simultaneously. She rushed over to Ijiq and took the baby from him. It was too weak to cry, but there was life on her face.

"Cut every neck, quickly," she said. She pointed to the children. "If they're alive, don't hurt them. Don't get blood on the clothes."

Osnat lifted up her jacket and put the baby to her breast. Its face was against her, but it had no strength to suck. "Wendy, hold the baby, keep its mouth open."

Osnat stood over the baby, and kneaded her breast, getting a few drops of milk into its mouth while the men went around making sure everyone else was dead.

Ijiq paused as he sliced throats. The necks leaked, rather than poured blood, indicating the dying had taken place a while ago. "What do you want to do with the child?"

That was a good question. Osnat hadn't thought beyond feeding it.

"You're saving the Tunniq." Wendy smiled as she rubbed the baby's legs.

"Let's adopt it," Osnat said.

"Who? A child can't have two mothers."

"Um... Ijiq and me."

Ijiq smiled. "That's fine, but I want you to carry my baby as well."

"Let the two babies we have now grow a little, then we'll have more." Osnat was absolutely stunned by what she had just proposed to Ijiq.

"I can wait."

"But one more condition: while you're waiting; in fact, for our entire lives together, I'm the only one you have sex with. No other women, no men, dogs... I'll make the same commitment to you."

Ijiq nodded.

"Another thing: we won't remove names from the living. We'll agree on a name, and then pronounce it. The baby I just gave birth to is Simon. Okay?"

Ijiq let out a breath and smiled. "Fine. How long are you going to keep adding rules?" He pulled Osnat's hands off her breast and started kneading it himself. A little stream started dripping from her nipple. He eased off to make sure it didn't make the child gag.

Osnat looked at him in surprise. First, for his presumptuousness in putting his hands on her breast, but more so how he was able to get milk flowing so easily.

"Ijiq, it's not appropriate for a woman to have her breasts touched by a man who isn't her husband." She waited until the baby had a little more to drink, removed Ijiq's hand, and kissed his fingers.

The others in the Dance House had finished ensuring that everyone else was dead. Zimri approached, took Osnat's hand in one of his, and Ijiq's in the other. "I remember how you married Wendy and me. I'll do it for you."

Osnat looked around at the people on the floor. "Not now. I want more lively witnesses at my wedding."

"Our baby is still thirsty," Ijiq said. "It's not good to keep it waiting."

Zimri, Haran, and Wendy were all peering at the child, and at Osnat's breast.

"Go ahead," Osnat said. Ijiq's hands went back to her breast. The tot drank thirstily, and then quickly fell asleep.

Osnat put her jacket back on, and took a last look at her former neighbors lying on the ground, holes in their necks. She recognized her adopted child's birth mother, remembered her joy in the Dance House. She recognized Tuli, the father of the boy who for a very short time was named Eric.

She handed the baby to Wendy, bent down over Puah, whispered in her ear "we kept our promises to each other," and went outside. She walked over to Norma, who was waiting with the others.

"It's time to get what we came for. We need to remove the clothes from all the bodies. Send in people with strong stomachs. Gather up pelts, weapons, anything useful from the tents. Pack it carefully on the sleds. We have more to carry, but we don't have more dogs."

Osnat turned away, wandering back and forth between the forlorn homes. She sniffed, she measured, looked at the ground. She ignored the misery of the people assigned to undressing corpses in the Dance House. She ignored the people climbing into tents to gather sleeping furs. She was searching.

Ijiq watched her carefully. He walked over to a small, clear area between tents, and beckoned. Osnat kneeled at his feet, digging with her hands at the little mound in front of him. The snow was frozen solid below the surface, so Ijiq passed her a stone axe to chop at the ice. She hacked away till she finally exposed a pair of feet frozen to the ground, raggedly severed just above the ankle.

Osnat stared at the feet, at the chipped bones. "I free you," she whispered.

A light snow started to drift down as Osnat looked at the remains of the person who stole her husband's name. She killed the boy solely for revenge.

Ijiq put his hand under her arm, pulling her up. "Simon needs you."

She grabbed the feet and beckoned to one of the people taking down the encampment. "Bring these into the Dance House."

The man recoiled, wanting nothing to do with the grizzly trophies.

Osnat put the feet on the ground in front of him and spoke loudly. "Ijiq, I'm going to take care of my babies now. If the feet aren't in the

Dance House before I reach our tent, put this man's feet in the Dance House, but leave the rest of him over here."

The man raced to the Dance House, the detached feet tucked tightly under his arm as Osnat made her way to the tent. Good to be civilized, she told herself.

"Osnat." Norma spoke her name like a desperate plea.

Osnat turned to her. "If anyone argues about their assignment, their alternative is to join the villagers."

She took a step forward and stumbled, catching herself on Norma's arm. She took a deep breath, trying to straighten her legs. Did her recent death weaken her? She pulled herself erect.

"Osnat, what happened?" Norma nodded towards the Dance House.

From the faces of the people around her, it was clear this wasn't just her question. Osnat looked around, gazing into the many eyes clustered close by. She tried to form words. She was nauseated.

"I ki—bru—"

"She killed them." Kenny came forward, pointing an accusing arm. "She executed Eric because he wanted peace. She murdered these people. All of them. We mustn't be led by a genocidal maniac. Who will she—"

Kenny's words ended in a clipped gurgle. His eyes widened as he collapsed to his knees, and then all the way down. Norma wrenched her stone knife from his back.

"You did what you had to do, Osnat," Norma said. "One Eric was enough."

"I... you killed..." Osnat tried again to speak.

"I'll not have anyone breaking their oath to you. Asking questions is one thing; I'll not have anyone challenge you."

Osnat gave up trying to answer. She swooned instead. Kenny's twitching eyes were the last thing she saw as she fell into darkness, as her own eyes fell away.

She sat by the brook, fighting the urge to spit into the water as it crashed into boulders, tore into fierce eddies, roared over jagged ledges. She leaned her back against the Rock of pure light, her face damp from the cold, sweet spray. Osnat drew her knees up, hands squeezing her temples as a powerful breeze blew small holes through her flesh. The wind whistled through the openings as if she was a sieve, caressing, purifying each cell, each elementary particle of her existence. Slowly, one shard at a time, it wafted her fury, wafted her agony away.

Osnat knew that every physical thing consists mostly of empty space. She was no longer material. She was the void, the space between matter held together by scattered dots of being, flashing back and forth in time. A void now filled with the light of the Rock, and nourished by the sweet, bubbling brook that flowed from it.

She stood up, gathered her will into a barbed point of seething intent, and pulled rage back into her heart. "What did you make me into?" she screamed. Her eyes darted around till she spotted what she wanted. She picked up a stone, heaving it with all her strength at the Source. The light flickered slightly and then came back. No, the light didn't flicker; her sense of it had. She fell on her knees in front of the Rock, in front of the Source, and wrapped her arms around it. She wasn't one for prayer; argument came more naturally. She sang, her words pouring into the brook, bubbling and frothing as they flowed into the Rock.

"Answer with strength, untie the bound people

Receive the song of those who seek you

Untangle us, guide us, bless us, purify your congregation

Accept our return, and hear our cries, Knower of Mystery."

The ice in Osnat's heart melted. The world, the stars, all existence faded away. The tall woman with violet eyes sat down beside her, leaning her head on Osnat's shoulder.

Osnat rested, gazing quietly at her earlier self. Without eyes, she could see across the timescape, feel everything she had lived over thousands of years. It was clear to her. She shivered, kissed Asenath's cheek, and pulled herself back to consciousness.

She was lying between furs in their tent. Ijiq sat beside her head, stroking her hair with one hand, while bouncing a hungry-looking Simon.

"Our son is hungry."

Osnat sat up, threw her arms around Ijiq's neck, put her head on his shoulder, and cried.

"Our son is still hungry. Our daughter is outside, waiting to come in."

She lifted herself off Ijiq's shoulder and took the baby into her arms. Ijiq scrambled outside and came right back in with Nisuin.

Osnat nursed Simon while Ijiq played with the girl. The baby's laughter didn't erase Osnat's misery over what she had beheld in the Dance House.

"You're the most dangerous of all the Tunniq."

Was Ijiq mocking her unhappiness?

"Your mother knew you were dangerous, but loved you too much to kill you."

"She loved me too much...?"

"Ever since she raped you, Aarluk wanted to keep you close to her, to take care of you. The only way to do it was to adopt you."

Osnat gazed at her baby as she recalled her 'mother.' She switched Simon to the other breast, trying to distract herself from brooding thoughts.

"Why didn't you rape me when you had the chance?"

"I was terrified of you being unhappy."

"You're terrified?"

"You threaten people for not following your orders quickly. You kill them for questioning you. You tie people up with invisible ropes and cut parts off them while they're still alive."

"We'll be married, Ijiq. A husband and wife are supposed to care for each other."

"What if I don't do what you expect of me? I don't know how Eber husbands are supposed to act."

"I'll try to be a good Tunniq wife, you a good Eber husband. We'll do our best."

"What if I ask the wrong question?"

"Ijiq, I would never hurt you. You're the only person here I'm not afraid of, and that's including me. You can ask me, tell me anything. In a few days we'll get married, unless you're too frightened of me killing you."

"I'm not worried about that. My fear is you being unhappy."

Simon had fallen asleep at Osnat's breast. She gently tugged him away and pulled her jacket back down. Nisuin was blissfully resting her head on Ijiq's lap as he gently ran his fingers through her hair.

"You could have abandoned all these people and lived without the burden. Instead, you went looking for them. Your brutality is for their sake. It's kindness."

"Sometimes I'm brutal for my own amusement."

"You may think so, but I know your heart."

"Really? How do you know I won't cut out and eat yours?"

Ijiq pulled out his knife and tossed it to Osnat. He put his hand on his chest, and bowed his head.

"I bind my heart to you, Osnat. Will you trust me with yours?"

Osnat sighed. She looked at Ijiq, and then slid over to him, careful not to wake Simon. She leaned her head on Ijiq's shoulder, put her hand on his lap, and cried. "Don't fear me. Love me."

"I do. Very much, I do."

She sat next to him, her mind empty of all thoughts, except a vague sense of astonishment that she could feel so close to someone again. "Where is paradise," her father had long ago asked her. "Here," she silently answered him now.

43 MODERN AGE 12

Saima finally brought Finer her jacket. He had locked it in a closet when its communicator started flashing and making an irritating noise. He surmised it was a message for her, possibly something urgent for her to do. She wasn't strong enough yet.

But by the third day, Saima concluded that it was really her decision as to what she could or could not do. She had barely moved from her bed the first couple of days, but in the brief periods when she was awake, she was clear-headed. The clamp that Linda applied to her injury had done its job; it was hard to even find a mark where Saima had dug out the arrowhead. Now, on the third day, she was up and about, doing whatever work she could.

Saima walked into the room with the noisy jacket, wondering how to explain his keeping it from her.

Her eyes sparkled as soon as she heard it. "Thanks for not bringing that to me sooner. I wasn't ready."

"Any idea what it's buzzing about?"

"I hope it's something silly, like Wendy threatening to cut my heart out for missing lacrosse practice." She took the jacket; Saima sat down next to her.

"But it might be something more serious. Would you mind waiting outside?"

That was a peculiar request. He rose and went to the kitchen, where Simon was peering into cabinets, and Linda had the table covered in arrowheads. Most were like the one he had pulled out of Tammy; there were also a few nasty metal-tipped wooden bolts. At least Saima presumed they had been wooden bolts, because all that remained were charred stubs.

"How come they're like that?" Saima asked.

"I can't explain it. The arrowheads come from different places in the Dead Lands. The lab analysis shows that they were all burned at the same time, in the same fire. It's as if the Dead Lands suddenly burst into flames."

"How can that be?"

"There are anomalous minerals in the dust. A geologist I consulted speculated that something broke up in the sky and scattered over the Dead Lands. The pieces would have been white-hot, igniting everything when they landed."

"That must have been terrifying to live through."

"I doubt if anyone did." Linda picked up an arrowhead, fingering the point. "His hypothesis doesn't account for the radiation that permeates the Dead Lands. Those people were in the bronze age, using spears and arrows. No fusion-powered weapons."

Saima nodded and sat down beside Linda. He put on a glove and picked up an arrowhead, looking carefully at the charred remains of the haft. Linda put a hand on his thigh, which Saima gently removed with his ungloved hand.

Linda touched his cheek. "Tammy?"

Saima nodded.

"You know she's a Fire Snake?"

Saima nodded again.

"She's enticing, but deadly."

Saima wasn't sure whether Linda was teasing him. "Are you—"

"The Collective Council has summoned me to an urgent meeting." Finer walked into the kitchen and sat down opposite Linda. She gave a shiver. "They want me to come up with a plan to deal with the descending chaos, and restore harmony."

"Descending? It's already landed." Alex paused his inspection of the kitchen's food supply.

"Is that your official poetic declaration, dear?"

"Yes. Please tell me we have more groceries in the storage containers, or I'll have to write a sonnet about hunger. It's been too long since the last delivery."

"We first have to deal with the Sheyds," Saima said to Finer. "They can't put this all on your shoulders. You can't end the chaos yourself."

"You've been making a fuss about responsibility ever since I met you. Now you're trying to keep me from it. If you do your sealing acts, the rest should be easy."

Saima reached for her hand. "I lost a wife to her responsibilities. Not another. Don't forget the daughter you promised me." He squeezed her fingers and let go. "Think of yourself as an eagle, fiercely guarding her own nest. Not the whole forest."

"Don't be ridiculous. I'm a snake, not an eagle. And if I was a bird, you're asking me now to look after a nest in a tree that doesn't exist. Saima, I respect my obligations. There are too many people depending on me." She pulled her jacket more tightly around herself.

"I thought you had three sons," Linda said, looking at Saima.

"So far."

Linda turned to Finer. "Your animal allegories remind me: when you brought Saima the bowl, you said you fought a woman, and killed a goat by spitting on it. I sent the leash and the glove with your saliva to my lab. The stain on the leash was also your saliva. Did you fight the same woman again? First time she split your lip. This time she shot you with an arrow?"

Finer shook her head. "I killed her sister." She rubbed her eyes with her fingertips. "I almost killed you, Simon. We have a long history together."

Linda opened a box, and passed it around the table. It was full of bone fragments.

"A skull that's been blown to pieces. I couldn't explain it before; the Dead Lands didn't have the technology." Linda looked at Finer. "But you did."

She shrugged, and then shivered. "I'm cold."

"I'll get your..." Saima realized she already had her jacket on.

"The Dead Lands radiation... it's all from your weapons?" Linda said.

"I don't know. I'm freezing."

"Do you have a fever?" Saima immediately put his cheek to Tammy's forehead, worried about infection. "No. Why are you shivering? You have to go back to bed."

"It's kind of cold, actually." Alex folded his arms across his chest. "Linda, can you get her a blanket? Saima, please fix the heat."

Alex still considered him a handyman.

"Come with me." He wanted Alex to stop being so dependent; he wanted Alex to stop giving him orders. They walked into the dark furnace room together and stopped, waiting for the lights to turn on.

"Seal doors."

Neither Alex nor Saima had spoken.

"Lights on," the raspy voice said.

Mekelat, the creature from the Old Post, from the ancient bowl.

The Sheyd sprayed fire from the blowtorch in his hand. Alex's clothes, his hair ignited instantly as Mekelat turned towards Saima. His distended, rubbery lips stretched into a wicked grin, exposing a set of perfectly aligned snow-white teeth. "Everyone you know will suffer, trapper. We're free now. Your daughter helped Balthan get away, but she's not here to help you. It's my daughter's turn."

Saima looked desperately for something to use to put out the fire... It took him a moment to realize that water was coming from valves in the ceiling, soaking everything. But the flames continue to envelope Alex.

"Upended, overturned, quelled are all Sheyds, all no-good-ones..." Saima recited from memory.

The flames were out. Alex lay on the floor, his clothes burned off. Mekelat was gone.

"Help!" Saima screamed at his communicator.

No answer. He ran to the kitchen, cursing. Sheyds were supposed to be afraid of this house.

Mekelat was lying on Linda, drool dripping onto her face from his now-chipped yellow teeth as he rose up and down. They were both naked.

Bone arrowheads were sticking out of Linda's mouth. Her eyes were wide and round, the air was thick with the terror of her stifled screams.

Where was Tammy?

Never mind. "Upended, overturned, quelled—."

The Sheyd cupped his hands around his mouth and yelled. "Don't worry Alex; I'll be right back to play, now that I got you hot. I'll get Saima ready for you also." Mekelat grinned.

Saima stopped his recitation. Rape was rarely fatal, burns often were.

"Why don't you try me, you silver bag of slime?" Tammy stood at the door to the kitchen. Her blouse was partly open; she lifted the edge of her skirt with one hand as she leered at Mekelat.

The Sheyd must have done something to her, to make her act that way. Mekelat had his hands all over Tammy before Saima could even blink. Free of the weight of the Sheyd, Linda rolled on to her side and moaned in pain. Finer pulled a hand from behind her back, and started reading.

"Upended, overturned, quelled are all Sheyds, all those without merit, all rock-spirits, and Liliths, and Mekelats ..."

The Sheyd backed away. Its face twisted as it tried to shake itself loose.

"...I, Detective Class S, Tammy Finer... performed a sealing act by the name of me and in the merit of the names of those before me..."

The kitchen filled with a foul-smelling steam, which was quickly dispersed by the ventilation system, now blowing warm air. Mekelat was gone, trapped under the bowl.

Finer winked at Saima. "It works." She bent over Linda.

Saima was astounded. "Leave her for now. The creature set Alex on fire. We've got to help him."

The utility room smelled of wet ash. Alex was sitting on the floor looking confused. His clothes, his hair, even his eyebrows were burned away. Saima was shocked to find him intact, never mind conscious. Tammy touched his arms; Saima put his hand to Alex's chin, and peered at his face. His skin appeared undamaged. They inspected him closely, both stopping when they saw that Alex was enjoying the attention.

"Now I know what I have to do to get you interested in me."

Saima turned red.

"Your wife was raped by a Sheyd. Get dressed and come to the kitchen," Finer instructed.

When Finer and Saima got back to the kitchen, tears were streaming from Linda's eyes. A pile of arrowheads lay on the floor, some with saliva on them, some with blood.

Tammy put her arm around her. "He's gone now. You're safe."

"He hurt me," she bawled. "He was ripping me apart."

"May I check?"

Linda nodded feebly, and lay back on the floor.

Tammy did a quick examination. "I don't understand. There's no sign of it."

"He raped me. I'm didn't imagine it," Linda protested.

"We saw," Finer said. "Alex wasn't harmed by a fire. You weren't injured by the rape. What's going on? You should both need medical treatment."

Finer sat on the floor next to Linda, who pressed her face into the comfort of Finer's shoulder.

A newly bald, but fully dressed Alex came into the room, saw the women on the floor, saw the Sheyd trap upside down on the counter. He hesitated, before walking over to a cabinet. "I'll make everyone a hot supper."

"We have to go," Saima said.

"Where? You're going to need your strength, wherever it is. It won't take long to eat something."

There was little conversation, because the only possible topics were the ones they didn't want to think about. By tea, Linda was a little better.

"How is it that I'm okay? I felt myself being ripped open."

"Why wasn't I damaged by the fire?"

All eyes turned to Saima.

"Sheyds are real, but they're not completely there. That could explain why the results of their deeds aren't completely there."

"They can still do a lot of damage," Finer said.

"The carnage at the Central Facilities, the thousands stranded in the northlands... The Sheyds have ended your community's pretense of harmony. Life has come to avenge itself."

"What does that mean?"

"Where there's life, there's conflict. You refused to recognize that. Now the Sheyds aren't giving you any choice. You have to rebuild your society, but on a different basis." Saima glanced at the arrowheads on the floor. "And soon."

"You have to come with me to the Collective Council, Saima. I don't know what to tell them."

"You want me there?"

Tammy nodded. "You said 'we' have to go."

"Jackson?" Alex asked her.

"I hope so. He rarely sees anyone except other Council members and his personal staff."

"This is important. Our future depends on you."

"Who is Jackson?" Each time Saima heard the name, it stirred a vague sense of unease at the back of his mind. He'd heard it before, in some story.

Linda took his arm. "He's the source of our harmony, and our leader."

"He's ancient; nobody knows how old, Finer said. "People say that he shaped our way of life through fairness and sharing. He's like a prophet, who can foretell events."

"Really? What did he foretell?"

"Well..." Tammy paused, concentrating. "He said unless everyone shared, the community would be divided into different classes of people: those who had everything, and people who suffered. People who couldn't afford food, medicine, or even proper housing!"

"And his prediction came true?"

"No. Many years ago, way before my great-grandparents were born, he expelled the people who refused to share, so we never had the problem. He saved us from their greed; from their witchcraft."

"He expelled them," Saima repeated flatly. He knew which story it was.

"Yes."

"I really want to meet him." Saima understood now what he had left home to do.

"What do I say to the Council?"

"We'll work it out on the way. Can you get Jackson to see us? The situation is serious enough."

"I don't know… I'll put in a top-level request for an audience. It should get processed quickly." She straightened her skirt. "We'll go back to my place. I have to wear my best uniform in case he agrees. Maybe you can change into something fancier?"

Saima didn't want her excitement to wane. "I'll go pick something nice."

He put his caribou skins on, the first time he'd worn them since arriving. He examined himself, removed them, and put on a white button-down shirt with pinstriped pants. Saima slipped his small, stone knife into his pants pocket, patting himself to make sure it wasn't obtrusive. He splashed his face with water and dabbed himself with perfume; Linda said it was a sign of elegance.

Linda, Alex and Finer were waiting in the front hallway.

"This will make an epic poem: the noble savage rushing to tell the most civilized man how to maintain harmony and order. Such sublime irony." Alex was standing as far from Finer as possible.

Saima was thinking of another irony as Linda handed him his jacket: an Eber would come with the head of the police to stand before the man who had ordered the police to exile them. If indeed, he was the same person. It shouldn't be possible.

His ponderings were interrupted by Finer's communicator. When she looked up a minute later, her skin was pale.

"Rape reports are pouring in to the police. Men, women, children are being assaulted. Swarms of rats are attacking homes, biting people. Fires are breaking out all over."

Linda turned to Saima. "It's getting worse. You have to do something,"

"What do you expect me to do?"

Finer's eyes were fierce. "Saima, we have to go. Now."

"Will Jackson see us?"

"He has to." Her expression was grim.

"Are we going straight there?"

"No. I told you I want to put on my nicest uniform."

Rats, rapes, fires, and she still wanted to change her uniform first? It didn't sit well with Saima.

"We have to stop," Finer said as their wagon lifted off. She pointed to a nearby cluster of homes, red and green flames rising high into the air.

"No." Saima indicated other glows in the distance. "It's futile. We have to deal the cause."

A 'tree' building near Finer's home was metal and ashes. "Grab anything important," Saima said as they landed at hers.

She packed a couple of bags, changed quickly into a deep V-neck red blouse, an olive-green jacket and knee-length skirt, with two slits reaching almost all the way up her thighs. "It shows respect," she explained.

"It shows more than that."

Finer took an assortment of weapons from a drawer, clipping them to her utility belt, stuffing them in her pockets, in her cleavage. A sword went over her shoulder.

"Why are you equipped like that?"

"Jackson likes his police well-armed."

Saima's idea of Finer was rapidly changing. He had initially thought her a foolish dilettante. Now he understood she could be quite lethal. The police from his childhood stories were deadly. That they were foolish in so many ways made them even more dangerous. Linda's warning came to mind.

"How many people have you killed?"

She tossed him a curious look. "Eight, not including five thousand years ago. Why?"

"Did you kiss them all goodbye?"

"No. I've kissed three, shot two, and stabbed another. One I threw off a building. I crushed a policeman with my wagon."

"With your wagon?"

"My boyfriend refused to carry out his orders, so I crushed him."

His next question was *How are you planning to kill me?* Instead, he said "You look striking."

She put a hand behind his neck, and pulled him into a quick kiss.

His goodbye kiss? Saima closed his eyes.

Saima calmed himself down as they flew over the fire-dappled landscape. In the gathering dark the blue tower of the Opinaca River Bridge was glowing menacingly, a pillar of incandescent flame flecked with green.

There was no blaze around Police Central; just ash and burnt flesh. The fireproof facility had burned down to its foundation. Trails of smoke rose from the charred walls, from the charred corpses packed inside.

Finer wanted to land. Saima wouldn't let; there was nothing she could do for them. They compromised, and she set the wagon down at the adjacent armory, which was unscathed.

She spoke into the little baffle at the side of the entrance: "Detective Class S Tammy Finer. Open." The door silently slid aside and the two of them stepped down through the entrance. A series of arched, white-tiled corridors branched off from the vestibule, and Finer marched down the one on the far left.

She moved too quickly for Saima to be able to gawk at the vast array of weapons displayed along the wall: swords, knives; but mostly things he couldn't identify. Finer identified herself to another baffle, and a door popped open, revealing the Superintendent supply area. She tossed her old weapons into a chute before re-arming. She showed the replacement gun to Saima: "The capacitor on this one recycles instantly. I wouldn't have been exposed to those archers."

She also took a Superintendent rank shield, and a couple of striped cloth patches which she attached to the shoulders of her jacket. A long, menacing sword with a pointed bronze pommel and thickened toe went into a scabbard over her shoulder.

She also picked up a message: "Jackson is waiting for you." It was written by hand on a neatly folded paper in an envelope marked "Tammy Finer," which was sitting on a table. Saima frowned. Why it was delivered like this? Finer didn't stop to wonder. Jackson was expecting her.

44 MODERN AGE 13

The Collective Council's headquarters looked very much like all the other spiral communities Saima had seen. It looked peaceful with its verdant symmetry and thatched roofs, but there was still a knot in his stomach as they approached.

"Where are the guards?" Saima asked.

"Guards? Why?"

"If this is where all the important decisions are made, shouldn't there be protection?"

"Saima, come on. You've been here long enough to know that we live in harmony. Everybody gets along. If people disturb the harmony, we send them to a camp. If there's a lot, we exile them, like Jackson did."

Saima nodded, disappointed that his future wife hadn't figured out whom Jackson had exiled. Either that, or she didn't care.

They landed beside a building at the center of the spiral. Almost half-buried, it was much bigger than anything he'd seen, except for the Central Facilities. A couple of tiny machines, each about three spans long, hovered as they walked towards the entrance.

"What are these?"

Finer blushed. "Security drones, to make sure there's no disharmony."

"And if there was?"

"The robots would activate a shield over the entrance and dissolve the problem with acid sprays. But don't you worry, love," Finer said. "I'm the highest-ranking police officer. They won't attack us. Everybody takes orders from me now."

"Even Jackson? The Collective Council?"

"No, no," she said, laughing. "Not the Collective Council; certainly not Jackson. Everyone else, who wants to stay healthy."

The security robots flew away as Saima and Finer were identified. Finer instructed Saima to put his hand into a ceramic slot. He winced as he felt a little scrape at the tip of one finger.

"Gene sample," Finer said. "They check visitor DNA against the database to identify their closest family."

"What? Why their family?"

"They need someone to hold accountable in case of trouble."

"But if the visitor is causing problems—"

"It's a very effective way of preserving harmony." Finer frowned at the readout. "You have no family."

Saima frowned as he realized how mistaken he had been. He had considered harmony to mean everyone getting along peacefully. It really stood for something else: blind obedience. He squeezed her hand. "You're going to be my family. Remember?"

She nodded, continuing to frown at the readout. "We'll have to collect samples from everyone across the Edge of the World." She held up a finger for silence. "Security over-ride, Superintendent Tammy Finer, authority level Jackson two." Now smiling, she squeezed Saima's hand in return.

What did "authority level Jackson two" mean?

"Come." She tugged his hand. They entered the Council Chamber, a huge circular hall with polished ebony-wood walls and thick purple carpets. The ceiling was a high dome, painted with an elaborate, colorful image of what could have been any of the spiral communities: the houses, trees, birds... Security panels, like he had seen at the Old Post and the Central Facilities, were everywhere.

Police lined the perimeter of the Council Chamber, all dressed in olive-green jumpsuits. Their eyes followed Finer, their new commander, as she walked briskly across the room. The people Saima presumed to be

Councilors were all standing, also watching Finer and him. They were dressed in all kinds of different outfits. The thing that set them apart was the abundance of jewelry that they all wore around their necks, pinned to their cheeks, or stuck through their eyebrows.

Finer didn't acknowledge anyone's greetings as she strode across the room to a gilded, guarded doorway; Jackson's quarters. She and Saima marched right through.

"Please, come in. Sit down."

The old man stood at the far end of a long, narrow table. He had a primordial aura, an ashen complexion, a frailty that said he should have returned to dust long ago. Small raised red dots on his face looked like mosquito bites. He smelled of dampness, he smelled of heat and rot. He reeked of cologne.

He waved at two chairs at the other end. Finer pulled one out for Saima to sit on, and took the other.

"How can I help you?" He beckoned to a hooded, veiled assistant, wearing a grey, floor-length robe. Gloved hands poured water for everyone, and the assistant retreated to a wall, holding on to a small, bronze pitcher.

Saima looked at Finer, deferring. This was her meeting.

"No, Saima, you go ahead. What's on your mind?" Jackson asked as he sat down opposite them.

Finer must have advised Jackson he was coming with her. "Sheyds are going to destroy your society."

"Yes, it seems that way. What do you suggest?"

"They have to be trapped, sealed away."

Finer pressed her hand over Saima's on the table; she smiled warmly with her eyes.

"Yes..." Jackson sipped from his drink. "You mean like I sealed and trapped you and the rest of your selfish people?"

Saima started to rise.

"Sit," Finer hissed.

He sat. Finer was still smiling, her hand was still on his, but there was something unsettling in her gaze.

"You were married to that avaricious bitch, Osnat," Jackson said. He turned towards Finer. "She wouldn't renew my nephew's manufacturing license. The Ebers have no concept of harmony, only greed."

He leaned forward in his chair, pointing. "His wife came up with all kinds of inventions which could benefit everybody. She did it for personal profit, not to make the world better." He shook his head in disgust.

Saima bent his head towards Finer. "We have to get out of here," he mouthed.

She licked her lips. "No."

"What about the dog, Superintendent? Did you get an answer?"

"Saima viciously broke its leg, cut it open and ate its flesh."

Jackson shuddered.

Saima shuddered too, but for a different reason.

"It fits. One of Osnat's lab assistants was secretly working for my nephew. I won't tell you the extent of her cruelty, but it's why we're so careful about not hurting animals." Jackson leaned back in his chair. "That's why we have the Codes, to protect against such brutality. Something Saima's ilk are incapable of understanding."

Finer rose and stood behind Saima. She rested her hands on his shoulders, her touch at once warm and terrifying.

"What do you want from me?" Saima would have stood also, but Finer held his shoulders firmly, fingers resting against the sides of his neck.

"I've been trying to get rid of Simon, his mother, his family, for five thousand years. You've done a great service by bringing him in, Detective."

"Yes. And our arrangement?"

Jackson eyes narrowed slightly. "Yes, that... Are you sure you want the job?"

Finer nodded.

He hesitated, then tapped a switch. The tabletop lit up with a display of the Collective Council Chamber. The Councilors were standing, looking confused.

"Attention, Council. Police Superintendent Tammy Finer has accomplished much in the performance of her duties. I want her to accomplish even more, so as Prime Minister, I officially declare her Second Minister, next in command. Only I have greater authority than her. The Collective Council will follow the directives of Tammy Finer, Superintendent of Police, Fire-Snake and Second Minister. Swear to it."

There was some confused muttering from the Council Chambers.

"Harmony will be maintained," Jackson said. "Swear to it now."

They all swore; some mumbling, some declaring loudly.

The table went dark. "Done. They always follow my suggestions."

Finer's finger's pressed again on Saima's neck. "Thank you."

Saima was frantic. He had trusted her, put himself in her hands. Wrongly. "What do you want from me?" he asked again.

"The grain."

The sound of water hitting the floor turned everyone's eyes to the assistant, who, at those two words had crushed the bronze pitcher in his hands into a little ball. He tossed it onto the table. Jackson wore a sly smile as the robed figure approached him.

"What?" Saima said.

"Your wife's grain. Do you know how much money she would have made if I hadn't sent her off? Her greed made us all suffer. You can make up for it, by giving it to me. She took the secret with her."

Simon's thoughts turned to the ancient grain parchments, filled with arcane texts and formulas. What could be so important?

"And then you'll leave us be?"

"No. Then I send you back to the northlands, and figure out how to make sure that the only way to leave there is by dying."

"I'll consider giving you the grain, on condition our exile ends, and we get back what was taken from us. Besides which, the Sheyds are your biggest problem now, not grain."

"Such arrogance..." Jackson stood up and paced. "I'm not offering you a choice. If you don't give me what I want, I will bring all the Ebers down here, as you want. You'll watch as we tie them between trees, or peel their skins from their flesh."

Jackson put his arm around his assistant's waist, before turning back towards Finer. "Now that you're second in command, you have to understand what I've been trying to accomplish for the last five thousand years." A wide grin split his face. "I'm spreading harmony throughout the world." He pointed at Saima, and the smile disappeared. "I was about to destroy Simon along with all the Ebers in Lagash. We were skinning their Chief alive, but some bitch killed him before we could finish."

Finer's fingers dug painfully into Saima's shoulders at the word "bitch." "What happened?" she asked.

"A witch somehow ignited the tar seeps, and pulled the red moon to crash down on Lagash. It wiped out most of my army and turned the place into the Dead Lands. My wife was able to keep me alive though, so I could rebuild. Now, with money from the grain and your venomous lips, we'll be able to fix everything."

He turned to his assistant. "Your devices worked perfectly, my darling. Allow me to introduce you."

The assistant gently rested a hand on Jackson's shoulder as she unhooked her veil and slipped off her robe, revealing a cascade of luxurious blond hair, full red lips, green eyes, and high cheekbones covered by flawless, silver skin. Her voluptuous figure squeezed against the linen of a cobalt-blue dress. "Of course the hoops worked perfectly." Her voice had a dulcet, seductive tone. Her milk-white teeth pulled attention to her every word.

"My wife, Lilly. She's sustained me through the years."

Lilly smiled, but didn't look happy.

Saima felt Finer's hands press harder on him. What could he do? "Upended—"

"It won't help, my friend." Lilly's voice was enchanting, pulling Saima's thoughts into a dense fog of bewilderment. "My marriage protects me."

Was the Sheyd his friend? She was beautiful beyond thought. Was Finer his friend? She was holding him down. Saima tried to rise. Finer's hands held him down.

"You're not getting up till I want you to," Jackson said.

Saima was the one who was trapped, who was going to be sealed away. Maybe worse: Jackson could send the Ebers through the hoops again, and this time scatter them into nothingness. Finer's fingers still pressed against the side of his neck, thumbs massaging his shoulder blades. Did she have to mock him with that comforting gesture?

Lilly grabbed Jackson's arm. "You want... grain?" She sounded puzzled. "Our marriage contract has come due. The five-thousand-year term is over. You don't need her fancy grain."

"I'm extending the contract."

She raised an eyebrow.

"I love you too much to divorce you. We'll both be supremely wealthy when Simon gives me what I want."

"Oh, please. That's enough." She went over to a drawer, pulled out a scroll, and handed Jackson a pen. "It's time to sign the divorce. There are your witnesses." She turned to the side and waved an arm at Finer and Saima. The back of her dress had dark red blotches, like old bloodstains.

"You need to be married to a human, or he'll trap you." Jackson pointed at Saima.

"I'd rather be stuck under a clay bowl then be in this marriage any longer. The Edge of the World is gone; I don't need you anymore."

Jackson picked up the little bronze ball from the table, turning it over in his hand. "I really liked this pitcher. It was five thousand years old, like the scroll." Jackson ripped the scroll, crumbled it, and placed both balls on the table together. "I'll have to write a new bill of divorce and get a new pitcher. It will take time."

Saima's mind was clouded. Why were they arguing about a divorce now? Why didn't Lilly care about the grain? Finer continued to rub his shoulder blades. Was that also part of her arrangement with Jackson?

Jackson pointed to Saima but spoke to Lilly. "He has to give me the grain. And Finer... well, we'll make a terrific threesome. You can teach her some of your tricks. Maybe she can teach you hers."

Finer stopped massaging, though her hands still rested firmly on Saima's shoulders.

"I can kill without her venom. And besides, since you won't be around it doesn't matter to you." Lilly's skin was pockmarked, her hair the texture of straw. She radiated heat, like bottled fire. She went to her robe and pulled another scroll from the sleeve. She gently took Jackson's hand in hers, and with a sneer raised it to her lips. He immediately doubled over, vomiting. From the smell, it seemed he soiled himself as well.

Lilly had her hands on her hips. There were flames in her eyes, smoke coming from her skin. "Well?"

Jackson forced himself slowly up. He scowled at Lilly. "You're my wife forever."

He turned to Finer. "We're going to be spending a lot of time together."

Lilly picked up the former bronze pitcher and squeezed. It dripped, molten, to the floor, igniting the carpet. She put her hand on the table, and it too, burst into flames. She reached for Jackson.

"No, my darling. We promised to protect each other when we got married."

"We're getting divorced!"

"Only the man can institute a divorce. You knew the rules when we made our arrangements."

Sprinklers tried vainly to douse the flames as Lilly stomped towards Finer and Saima. "If we're still married, then I have the right to keep you from this woman." She extended an arm towards Finer.

"I'm disappointed in you, Lilly. You should be more up to date." Saima struggled against the fog in his mind, keeping his voice calm.

"What are you talking about?"

"Many things have changed in the last five thousand years."

Lilly stopped. "Oh?"

"It's easy to divorce someone. Either party just has to say it three times, in front of two witnesses. That's it."

"Why did I not hear about that?"

"Maybe your husband didn't want you to know."

Lilly stood absolutely still, looking at him.

Saima shivered. The flames disappeared; the room was suddenly cold, as if she had taken back all the heat she had exuded, and more.

"You two are my witnesses." She turned to Jackson. "I divorce you; I divorce you; I divorce you."

Jackson's arms flailed wildly. "You can't! The man has to divorce the woman. I'll die if I'm not married to—" He twitched, and then fell to the floor, his limbs trembling.

Lilly bent down over him. "That was five thousand years ago, lover. The rules have changed."

He gave a final twitch, and exhaled. The room smelled horribly of rot.

She straightened, looked up from Jackson's shriveled body, and wiped her eyes.

Finer let go of Saima's shoulders.

"Upended—" Finer started.

Saima sprang upwards, knocking Tammy to the floor, interrupting her recitation.

Lilly smiled at him. "Thanks. I owe you my freedom, in more ways than one." She blew him a kiss, and faded.

Finer was furious. "What did—"

Saima had to run. It was his only chance. He dashed into the Council Chambers, stopping short when he saw police blocking the exit. Two men seized his arms.

A gasp came from the other side of the room as Finer stormed in, her long sword pointing straight at Saima.

"We caught him for you."

"Hold him," she said.

Saima glanced back towards Jackson's quarters. Where was Lilly? Could she help him now?

Finer stepped onto a little dais, and stood behind the lectern. "I am Tammy Finer, Superintendent of Police, and Second Minister. You are all sworn to obey me, and I hold you to your oaths. Our beloved leader, Jackson, has died—"

The immediate bedlam cut her off.

One of the Councilors jumped up on the dais, wagging a finger. "Then you're no longer Second Minister. We'll elect a new Prime Minister, who will choose his own Second."

"Okay." Her voice was fiercer than the sword in her hand. She glared at the room. "Whoever feels he should be Prime Minister, come join me on the dais."

Her one opponent folded his arms across his chest. "It's you or me."

"Anyone else?" Finer asked. No one moved.

A woman at the back of the room shouted. "Put your sword away. You're scaring people."

Finer put it away. "Fine. Anyone else?" She rubbed the corner of an eye with her finger.

"This man..." she kissed her fingertips, then took his hand in hers, "...opposes me." He started to gasp for breath. "Does anyone else?"

He put his hand to his throat, and then sank to his knees.

"I am Tammy Finer, Superintendent of Police, and recently appointed Second Minister." The man fell to the ground.

"I am also a Fire Snake. With Jackson's death, I am now Prime Minister and head of the Collective Council. You will obey me." She pointed to Saima. "Release him."

The men let go and jumped back.

"I am appointing this man, my fiancé, as second in command. Saima, son of Jako, you are now Second Minister."

This couldn't be part of her arrangement with Jackson. What was she doing? The fog in Saima's head was being pushed away by simple confusion. Her fiancé? Did that mean he wasn't trapped?

"We face an invasion by Sheyds. The Second Minister's people, the northern savages, have expertise we need. But the Sheyds are only a symptom of a bigger problem. The Codes are hereby abolished. We have to develop a new code of life that respects people's accomplishments, as well as their failures." She licked her lips. "A code that respects conflict as much as it respects harmony."

"Excuse me, um... Prime Minister. May I speak?" One of the Councilors stood nervously.

Finer licked her lips again. "Is there a problem?" she asked.

"Our world is in chaos. Buildings are burning; people are hungry. How will you take care of us?"

"People will have to learn how to take care of themselves. The chaos is caused by Sheyds. I'm going up north to get married, and I'll be back in a couple of days with more northern savages. They know how to deal with the problem."

"We do?" Saima whispered.

Another Councilor found the nerve to speak. "How many northern savages are going to come?"

"Maybe a handful, maybe all of them."

"That's too many! What if they try to take over?"

Saima flinched. The Ebers weren't even back, and people were already resenting them.

Finer swept her sword slowly in an arc in front of her, pausing at the eyes of each Councilor. "Then you'll exile us again. At least, you may try."

She pointed the weapon at a sergeant. "Assign a crew to prepare Jackson's quarters for me. Leave a couple of police here; send everyone else out on patrol. I don't want them gathered in one place."

The Lieutenant paled. "Patrol? But the wagons..."

"Learn how to walk."

She shoved her sword back into its scabbard. "Get to work."

Finer stepped from the platform.

"'Exile us'?" Saima asked, as they walked out towards her wagon.

"I told you before: Your people are my people. Speaking of which, will our people want to move here? What about your sons? Will they come?"

"I just have to tell them it's easier to keep fingers warm here. They'll come."

Lilly was waiting for them beside the wagon.

Saima raised his hands in front of his face, palms to the side. "My condolences on the loss of your ex-husband."

"That's very nice of you. Thank you for saving me from Jackson's marriage trap." Lilly stepped up to them and grabbed Saima's arm. "I'm going to protect you and your daughter for the next five thousand years, to show my appreciation." She inclined her head and let go. "You need to get to work, making her."

"Sheyds won't harm humans anymore?" Tammy asked.

Lilly shook her head. "I didn't say that. We each do what we want. We're not slaves to a code." A wicked grin etched itself onto her face. "I'll put him in the mood, Prime Minister. Your wedding present." She pulled off her dress, standing utterly naked as she handed it to Saima. "I cleaned your daughter's blood off. I'm returning her dress."

Saima averted his eyes.

"I want a goodbye hug." She wrapped her arms around him, her flawless body pressing against his.

Tammy covered her face with her hand.

"Get going." Lilly released him and stepped back. She turned and disappeared as Tammy and Saima stepped through the hatch and sealed the door.

"What do you make of that?" Tammy asked.

"I don't want to have her angry at us." He took a step towards Finer. "We better do what she said."

"You're going to explain something before we do anything." Hands on her hips, she also took a step closer. "There's no law that anybody can divorce by repeating it three times in front of witnesses."

"I made it up. They both believed me, so they felt divorced. Without the protection of being married to a Sheyd, he died of old age."

Tammy stared at him before laughing. "The Sheyds are going to be much easier to deal with than you."

"Well, Prime Minister, make a retroactive decree, so it will have been true." He grinned, and took her hand as they sat down.

Saima spoke into a baffle. "Northlands, village at southeast edge of escarpment." He reclined his chair, and closed his eyes.

Finer turned a knob, and the wagon became transparent.

"No, opaque. We have to get started on our daughter, before Lilly gets mad."

Finer shook her head. "Let's work out what we're going to do when we return from the northlands."

Saima looked around the wagon. "Where's Lilly when I need her?"

Tammy scowled "You seem to want to jump to her orders."

"If she's as persistent as Mekelat, we have a useful ally."

"I better not catch her naked with you again."

"Don't worry, I..." Saima pointed. "Look!"

"At what?"

"It's gone. When I left there were just a few holes in it."

"What's gone?"

"The Edge of the World. That's what Lilly was talking about. Our prison has disappeared." Tears streamed from Saima's eyes. "We're free."

"Are you going to trap the Sheyds for us?"

Saima wiped his eyes with his sleeve. "I'll bring our most experienced Sheyd trapper south after we're married."

"Good. We'll need the best. Who is he?"

"The Sheyd trapper I'm bringing north with me now."

"Come on, Saima, we need your people."

"'We? Your people?' Detective, you're an Eber now. Remember? 'My people are yours.' I am yours." Saima took her hand in his. "You, Prime Minister, are mine."

Tammy Finer pressed his palm to her face. "I am yours, Saima. Truly, I am."